TO GRACE
SURRENDERED

CROSSWAY BOOKS BY
DEANNA JULIE DODSON

IN HONOR BOUND
BY LOVE REDEEMED
TO GRACE SURRENDERED

TO GRACE SURRENDERED

DeAnna Julie Dodson

CROSSWAY BOOKS • WHEATON, ILLINOIS
A DIVISION OF GOOD NEWS PUBLISHERS

Cover design: Cindy Kiple

Cover illustration: Laura Lakey

First printing, 1998

Printed in the United States of America

Library of Congress Cataloging-in-Publication Data
Dodson, DeAnna Julie, 1961-
    To grace surrendered   /   DeAnna Julie Dodson.
      p.   cm.
    ISBN 1-58134-018-4
    I. Title.
PS3554.03414T6   1998
813'.54—dc21   98-21417

11	10	09	08	07	06	05	04	03	02	01	00	99	98
15	14	13	12	11	10	9	8	7	6	5	4	3	2	1

DEDICATION

*To the Giver of gifts
and the Opener of doors—*

Non nobis, Domine . . .

ACKNOWLEDGMENTS

To Jacky Chappell and Shawnita Lusk,
for continuing excellence in editing, proofreading,
constructive criticism, and putting up with me—

To my sister, Linda Katherine Horn,
for knowing the inestimable value of speaking the truth
in love... and the value of a well-turned phrase—

To Jill Carter for everything—

To everyone who wanted to know
what happened next—

What can I say but thanks and ever thanks?

PROLOGUE

THE FIRST DAY OF THE NEW YEAR DAWNED BRIGHT AND CRISP, THE night's fresh-fallen snow touching all of Winton with its dazzling purity, capping the spires of the cathedral and the castle towers with white and lying in thick drifts against the city walls. Inside the castle, only the servants had begun stirring. The rich tapestries that hung over the windows in the king's chamber shut out the sparkling winter light and held in the night's still peace for the two nestled together in the luxuriant bed.

Philip Chastelayne, king of Lynaleigh, stretched his sleekly muscled shoulders and pressed closer to his wife's warm body, making a scarcely conscious decision to go back to sleep. A solid thump from inside her rounded abdomen changed his mind.

"The baby is awake," Rosalynde said, sleepy amusement in her emerald eyes.

Smiling with one side of his mouth, he stretched the whole lithe length of his body. He laughed softly to feel another sturdy kick.

"Are you certain he is coming in two months and not two weeks?" he asked, caressing her stomach through the fine linen of her shift.

"Joan is of the firm belief that this one is a girl."

"What? With such a kick?" He laughed again. "Surely not."

"It would not displease you, my lord? I mean, were it to be a girl?"

"Faith, love, not a bit of it." He kissed her forehead. "God has given us two fine sons. Surely He best knows whether we need another." He turned toward her, looking into her sweet face, caressing the smooth, blooming curve of her cheek with the back of his hand. "Who am I to deny the world a copy of the fairest thing in it?"

She feathered her fingers through his dark tousled hair and nuzzled his cheek. "Sweet."

He pulled her into an awkward, tender embrace, and her arms went around his neck.

"Sweet," she murmured again, pressing nearer, closing her eyes as she surrendered to his kiss.

There was a discreet knock at the door, and with a rueful grin he sat up.

"Come in, Rafe."

"They've begun to arrive already, my lord," the stockily-built, brown-bearded old man said as he began setting out the bread and fruit he had brought for their breakfast. "Good morning, my lady."

"Good morning, Master Bonnechamp."

"And there are two young gentlemen who demand an immediate audience with your majesties."

"They demand, do they?" Philip asked, and Rosalynde smiled at his feigned displeasure. "Well, I suppose such boldness commands our attention, does it not, my lady? By all means, Rafe, admit them."

A moment later Rafe returned, bringing two dark-haired little boys with him.

"Good morning, my angels," Rosalynde said, holding out her arms, and the children scampered across the room and began struggling to crawl into the high bed beside her.

"Take care, John," Philip said, lifting the younger boy over her, setting him between them with a kiss. "And you, Robin."

He pulled the three-year-old up into the bed, too, and was rewarded with a tight hug and a smacking kiss. Then Robin threw his arms around Rosalynde's neck and kissed her, too.

"Good morning, Mama," he piped. Then he leaned over and pressed a careful kiss against the bulge in her middle. "Good morning, baby."

"Mornin', baby!" John crowed, patting her vigorously. Rosalynde laughed and Philip grabbed his hand.

"Shh, John, the baby is sleeping."

"Mornin', baby," John whispered as he nestled against his mother's stomach and patted it very softly.

"There's my sweet boy," Rosalynde said, putting her arm around him. He put his thumb in his mouth and looked up at her, his big eyes as green as her own, and she cuddled him closer. "My pretty baby."

He flashed her his father's bright smile and patted her again. "Pitty baby."

Philip smiled, too. Then he picked Robin up and sat him astride his chest.

"You and John are to come to court today, remember?"

"Because the people are coming?"

"Yes, and all of them will want to see you both."

Robin leaned down and propped his chin against his father's. "Why?"

"Because you are their princes, and one day they will come to you for justice."

Robin considered this for a moment. "I need to ride my pony," he confided finally, his dark eyes solemn.

Philip laughed and sat up, letting him slide down into his lap. "No pony for you today, Robin."

"Ride the pony," John gurgled and Philip tugged his ear.

"Nor you, mite. Come now, both of you, let Mama and Papa have breakfast." He hugged both boys once more and set them on the floor. "See that Joan has them properly dressed, Rafe."

"I will, my lord."

Once Rafe had led the boys away, Philip pulled on his dressing gown and went to the window, not surprised by the sight he saw below him. Despite the early hour, people of all ranks and conditions were making their way toward the castle, well bundled against the cold that had not dampened their holiday humor.

"Rafe is right, Rose. They've come already. More of them than ever, by the look of it. Are you certain you feel well enough—"

"You spoil me terribly, love," she said, taking a pear from the breakfast tray. He got back into bed beside her and stole a bite out of it.

"Thief," she accused, pulling back from him. With a playful light in his blue crystal eyes, he stole a kiss instead.

It was the fifth New Year of King Philip's reign, and in keeping with tradition, people had come from throughout the city bringing their homage, their good wishes, their petitions before their young sovereign. It was tradition, too, to have all the royal family present for the occasion. So in the great hall under the banner of the white saint's rose that was the emblem of all the sovereign Chastelaynes, alongside the king and queen and the two little princes were the king's younger brother Thomas, Duke of Brenden, and his wife, Elizabeth.

Tom and Elizabeth were also expecting a child, this one their first. Because her time was so near, Elizabeth was allowed to sit in the king's presence at the formal audience, a privilege usually granted only to the queen herself. By late afternoon she was shifting uncomfortably in her chair.

"Let me take you upstairs, sweetheart," Tom told her quietly while his brother settled a dispute between two merchants. "You ought to rest now."

She smiled at the concern on his face and at the little boy asleep against his shoulder. "We'd not want to wake Robin, my lord."

"He'll scarcely notice, Bess. Come, let me help you up."

"Oh, not yet. Please, my lord. I want to see this mysterious king of Reghed when he arrives."

"If he arrives. Surely, were he truly coming, his servants, some of his lords, his steward at the least, would have preceded him to see all was in readiness. We should have had some word of him beyond the one message he sent."

"Perhaps not, my lord," Rosalynde put in, shifting John to a more comfortable position in her lap, careful not to wake him either. "We know little of Reghed's ways, and from what I hear of their king, even they think him peculiar."

"Do you think the stories true, my lord?" Elizabeth asked.

Tom shook his head, suppressing a smile. "You ought not to heed such macabre tales, Bess—much less take such delight in them."

There was a repulsed fascination in her dark eyes. "But do you think it true? That when he became king, he truly dressed his dead mistress's bones in the royal robes and crown and forced his nobles to swear loyalty to her? Even to kiss her hand, though there was no more flesh left on it? Ooh, it chills my blood!"

"There's been nothing but such fables come from Reghed these twenty years and more since he became king and shut up all his kingdom's borders."

"Then why has he decided he must come to Winton now?"

Tom shrugged. "He's not said. Perhaps trade, perhaps defense, perhaps—"

"Perhaps we shall learn why now," Philip interrupted, with a nod toward the rear of the great hall.

"His Imperial Majesty, Sarto, King of Reghed," the herald announced. The attention of the entire court fixed on the hooded figure that swept toward the throne, attended not with the pomp and splendor of his courtiers but with a grimly armed guard, all marked with his emblem—the hissing red-eyed dragon of Reghed.

"Your majesty," Sarto said, his voice a low rumble in the silence of the great hall.

Philip returned a slight nod. "Your majesty. You are welcome to Lynaleigh and to Winton."

For a long moment, Sarto said nothing more, did not move, did not lower the hood that concealed his face.

"Is there something Lynaleigh might grant your majesty?" Philip asked finally, exchanging an uneasy glance with his brother.

"Merely allow me a moment more to look upon heaven."

Rosalynde's eyes widened in surprise as Sarto seized her hand and pressed it fervently to his lips. Then he lifted his head, and the hood fell away from his face.

She took her hand from his and shrank back a little at what she saw. It was not that Sarto's features were particularly unhandsome. He had the corpulence of a once-comely man who through drink and dissipation had grown fat. Now, as the last remnant of youth was waning into old age, his flesh had begun to sag on him, but there was nothing unsettling about that. It was more his eyes, the dead gray-green of something cold-blooded, that unnerved her.

"Your majesty is too kind," she murmured, pulling John instinctively closer. Philip put one hand on her arm.

"It has been many years, my lord, since the king of Reghed has ventured beyond his own borders," Philip said. "We are honored."

Sarto spared him only a brief glance and then fixed his eyes again on Rosalynde. "It is time our two lands benefited one another, my lord king. Reghed has prospered, and I have heard much of your own kingdom's bounty." His piercing gaze moved from Rosalynde's face, down her body, and again to her emerald eyes. "And beauty."

"Lynaleigh has many treasures," Philip agreed, his expression cool and wary, "though not all of them for trade."

Their eyes met, and Sarto's intensity faded into an amiable smile. "Of course not."

"So you come to open trade with us, my lord?" Tom asked.

Sarto bowed negligibly, favoring him, too, with a glance. "Perhaps, my lord of Brenden. For now I merely wish to become acquainted with my neighbors to the south."

Just then Robin awoke and blinked his dark eyes in sleepy bewilderment at the stranger that stood before him.

"Your child, my lord?" Sarto asked.

Tom held the boy a little more snugly. "Prince Robert is my nephew, sir."

"You must forgive the error, but your lordship and his majesty resemble so strongly."

That was true enough. Except for the fine scar on Philip's left cheek and Tom's eyes being brown rather than blue, the brothers might at a careless glance have been mistaken one for the other. The children, too, had the same look—fair-skinned, dark-haired, handsome far beyond the ordinary—the look of the royal Chastelaynes.

Sarto's heavy lips curved again into a smile. "But I see, my lord, you are at any moment to have a child of your own." He looked amused at Elizabeth's obvious awe of him. Then once more he set his eyes on Rosalynde, and his mild humor turned intense. "And his majesty is yet again to be favored as well. It must please you, my lord king, to know that, should any mischance befall you, fortune forfend, your house shall not be lacking in heirs."

"I thank God," Philip said gravely.

"And to know that your lady is as fruitful as she is wondrous fair."

"Again I thank God," Philip replied. "My lord, is there something you wished?"

"Death to the tyrant!"

The cry rang through the hall, and a gasp rose from the court as a man sprang upon the king of Reghed out of the crowd. They struggled, a dagger flashed. Then men from Philip's guard and Sarto's seized the assailant and dragged him to his feet.

"Are you hurt, my lord?" Philip asked urgently, waving away the soldiers who had moved to protect him, helping his guest to stand. Sarto merely smiled again and pressed his silken handkerchief to his side, quickly staining it with blood.

"Slightly, my lord. Only slightly."

"Take the children to the nursery, Rafe," Philip commanded, seeing that Robin had taken in every detail of the incident and that it had awakened John as well.

"Why do they fight, Papa?" Robin asked, owl-eyed, as Tom handed him to Rafe.

"You go with Master Bonnechamp now, son," Philip said. "We will speak of this later. Come, John."

The two-year-old huddled closer to his mother. "Stay."

Philip gave him a stern look, and Rafe scooped him up, keeping his voice cheerful to ward off the tears that threatened. "Come, my princeling. We will see if Mistress Joan has something nice for your supper."

"Some of you go with him," Philip ordered his guard. Then he turned to the silver-haired courtier standing to his far left. "My lord of Darlington, take three or four of my men and see the queen and Princess Elizabeth to their chambers as well."

"Surely the danger is past, your majesty," Elizabeth protested, pleading with her eyes against Tom's insistent expression.

"Yes, surely, my lord," Sarto agreed. "I would not be the cause of these ladies' departure for all my kingdom. Take my assurance, my lord—there will be no risk to them."

Philip looked uncertainly at his wife. "Rose?"

She smiled faintly, and he turned again to his guest. "Very well, your majesty. You must accept my apology that such an incident has been allowed in my court, perpetrated by one of my own people."

"No, my lord," the would-be assassin said, a proud lift to his head. "I am from Alderness . . . in Reghed."

"I have long dealt with such rebels," Sarto said. "I ask your pardon, my lord, that the ruffian chose such a place for his treachery." He picked up the dagger and turned to his attacker, a tall, very thin man with fiery, reckless defiance in his eyes. "Well, knave, you've hit more chain mail than flesh. Trust me, my executioners shall not be so inept, nor shall their dealing with you prove so short-lived."

"I would take such torture a thousand times over, butcher, for even the hope of ending your life."

"This is your king, man," Philip reproved. "Dare you speak so? After such treason?"

"I will not call him my king, your majesty, nor would your lordship call him so if you knew what we suffer at his hands."

"There are always malcontents, my lord," Sarto told Philip blandly. "Surely even in your own kingdom."

"True enough."

"But none, I think, would step so far in hate," Tom observed, studying the prisoner. "It takes a grievous wrong to fuel such passion, does it not, man?"

The man stared fiercely back at him. Then he swallowed hard and took an uneven breath. "I have been a loyal man, my lord, but there is only so much loyalty will bear."

"Tell me."

"Ask him if he does not remember Alderness, my lord," the prisoner said, jerking his head toward the king of Reghed.

"The law was broken," Sarto said calmly. "I was bound to punish the guilty."

"All Alderness was burned, my lord of Brenden! With the people shut up in the church to burn with it! Were they all guilty? The children as well?"

"The punishment is set down in the law," Sarto replied, unmoved.

"The law you made?"

"What wrong was done, my lord?" Philip asked tautly.

"Tell them," the tall man insisted when Sarto made no answer. "No? It was a heinous crime, my lords, truly. One of the milkmaids dared laugh on the Day of Mourning."

Philip and Tom looked at each other, baffled.

"The Day of Mourning?" Rosalynde asked.

Sarto turned to her, surprise on his face as if she should not have had to ask. Then he smiled slightly. "This is a matter for Reghed alone, my lord king. I will see that this man never again causes such a disturbance in your court." He signaled his guard. "Take him."

Rosalynde looked beseechingly at her husband. "My lord—"

"It is beyond my sovereignty, my lady," Philip told her. "He says true. This is a matter for Reghed alone."

"Please, your majesty." Rosalynde came to stand before Sarto, making an eloquent plea with her eyes. "Please."

"What would you have, gracious lady?"

"Mercy for this man, my lord, I beg you. Banish him to Lynaleigh if you will. I will stand surety for him."

"He is a traitor, my lady."

"Spare him the torture at the very least, my lord, for mercy."

"Reghed law is quite specific." He looked at the dagger he still held and then again at Rosalynde, that odd intensity rekindling in his eyes. "But if you would have him shown mercy—"

With one swift stroke, he cut his prisoner's throat.

Gasps of horror rose from the onlookers, and Rosalynde hid her face against Philip's shoulder. He held her there, his eyes blazing.

"Dare you, sir? In my court? Before my lady?"

Once more Sarto looked surprised. "I did not think—" Instantly, he was on his knee. "Please, gracious lady, forgive me. I would not by the merest thought offend you."

"By your leave, my lord," Philip said, his face taut with anger. "I will thank your majesty to withdraw from my court until such time as we are prepared to discuss terms of trade."

Sarto stood and bowed coolly. Then he took Rosalynde's hand from Philip's arm, not seeming to mind that she did not lift her head. "Until such time."

She caught a trembling breath when his lips touched her skin, and Philip held her more tightly. With another curt bow, Sarto swept from the great hall.

"Dismiss the court, my lord of Darlington," Philip commanded over the murmuring of the people. Then he turned to his brother. "Tom, I—"

He stopped short, and now Rosalynde did look up. Tom was kneeling at his wife's side, supporting her in her chair as she stared at the blood-drenched corpse Sarto's men had left behind them.

"Bess?"

She was clutching her stomach, sobbing and gasping, her eyes wide with sudden fear.

"Is it the child, Bess love?"

"Tom—oh, Tom."

"Shh, sweetheart," he soothed, managing a shaky smile. He lifted her into his arms and gave Philip a worried look when she cried out in pain.

Rosalynde patted Elizabeth's hand, her gentleness calming the other girl some. "Do not fear. This will be nothing to you once your little one is born."

"You remember when John came," Philip told his sister-in-law, a forced lightness in his tone. "They sent messengers to bring me back from the hunt when my lady had her first pains. When they found me and brought me home not three hours later, she and John both were fast asleep."

Elizabeth smiled wanly, then gasped as another pang hit her. "Tom," she breathed, twisting her fingers into his shirt, clinging desperately to him. "Stay with me, Tom. Stay with me; do not leave me."

"Shh, Bess love. I will stay as long as I am allowed."

Philip watched him carry her up the stairs, and then he pulled

Rosalynde into his arms, holding her just as desperately. "Are you all right, Rose? Sweet heavens, Sarto is mad!"

"I am fine, my love," she murmured, kissing his shoulder. "The baby is fine. But that poor man—"

They both looked at the lifeless form sprawled at their feet.

"Mercy and grace," Philip said, feeling some unnamed dread inside himself, "what a place this Reghed must be."

Rosalynde stooped down and whispered a prayer over the man. Then she squeezed Philip's hand. "Now you must let me go see to Lady Elizabeth. She is frightened enough without all this other, and your brother will need you."

He said something quietly to one of the soldiers. Then he took her arm and helped her up the stairs. A short while later, only a dark stain on the stone floor of the great hall bore witness to that day.

CHAPTER

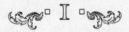

I

HE STOOD WATCHING THE FLAMES CLIMB HIGHER. IT WAS ONLY A small village church, and he knew it would catch quickly. He could hear the pop and crackle of the wood and see the smoke that billowed thick and black out of it, but as close as he was, the heat did not scorch his skin, the smoke did not stifle him, the ashes did not sting his eyes.

He realized it was always that way, though he had never thought it strange before. Then he heard the pounding, desperate thuds against the flimsy wood of the church doors, and wondered why the ones inside did not simply break through them. *They must not want out very badly*, he thought. Then he noticed the iron bar across the doors. It occurred to him that he could move the bar, but he saw the flames licking at the metal and thought perhaps he might burn his hands if he touched it.

He turned his back, and the pounding grew louder. He knew too well what came next. Still it grew louder and louder and louder, and then—

Philip forced himself awake and exhaled wearily. It had been almost three months since Sarto's would-be assassin had told his tragic tale, and Philip had dreamed the same dream over and over in that time. Truly it was a terrible thing, but he had heard of worse. He had seen worse. Why should this come to him again and again? He had not mentioned the dreams to Rosalynde. The story of Alderness was an ugly thing he did not want her to remember.

The pressed anxiousness of the vision faded as he looked at her nestled there against him, her satin cheek pressed to his shoulder, one soft hand spread over his heart and the dark rills of her hair spilling over them both like a shared cloak. He whispered a prayer of thanks for her as he did almost every time he saw her, every time he touched her, every time he thought of what he might have become without her.

She was so small and dainty, barely up to his chin, and even after three children, still just the span of his hands around the waist. He could not fathom yet how such a delicate creature could hold such an inexhaustible wellspring of love through everything that came.

He touched his lips to her forehead, but she did not stir until the baby made the first hint of a cry.

"Mmm, yes, shh," she murmured without opening her eyes.

Feeling her moving to get up, he held her there. "It's all right, love," he whispered. "I will go."

He slipped out of bed and took the tiny whimpering bundle from the cradle, cuddling it to his bare chest.

"Shh, my honey-love," he soothed as he crawled back under the warmth of the coverlet.

Rosalynde smiled sleepily at the two of them, and Philip shifted her once more against his shoulder, putting one arm around her and using the other to cradle the baby against her breast. Soon he heard the little one's soft suckling sounds and Rosalynde's slow, contented breathing. She had fallen asleep again, trusting him to watch over them both.

After a while he peeped under the coverlet. The baby was asleep, too, her rosebud mouth a perfect miniature of the one touching his shoulder, her baby skin hardly fairer or softer than what lay sheltered in his other arm.

He cuddled both of them closer, remembering how afraid he had been when this little one was born. The midwife and the physicians, too, had not expected the child for another two weeks, but she had come anyway, just at the dawning of St. Valentine's Day. Rosalynde had been all night in labor, and he remembered her lying there scarcely conscious, her delicate features almost ethereal, as if she were already no longer of this world. Then the weeping midwife had laid the baby in Philip's hands, blue and still, a tiny, perfect little girl without even a breath to make up her life.

"Oh, Jesus, God," he had murmured, too staggered to pray anything more than that. Then Joan, the woman who had brought him and his three brothers into the world along with countless others before and since, had bustled into the room, snatched the child from him, and scolded the midwife for her incompetence. Without hesitation, Joan dunked the baby into a basin of warm water. Then she breathed into the tiny mouth and nose and dunked the baby again. After a third time, she turned the child upside down and gave her a smart swat on the bottom.

That was followed by a tiny gasp and the sturdiest baby cry Philip had ever heard. Gathering her up against his chest, dripping still, he had cried, too, and laughed. "Faith, sweetheart, both your brothers together never made such a row."

That had been more than a month ago, six weeks after Elizabeth had lost her child, a baby boy, stillborn on that New Year's Day Sarto had come to court. She and Tom had been married more than five years now, and the loss after so long a wait seemed that much more cruel.

Joan had tried to save that child, too. She had been with the mother throughout her labor, knowing it was bound to be difficult after the shock the girl had been through that day. But that had made no difference. Elizabeth had yet to recover from her grief, and it had cast a shadow over the joy the birth of the new little princess had brought.

Philip had been almost afraid to show the baby to his brother, afraid of the new sorrow it might bring him, but Tom had come, eager to see his first niece. He had cradled her in his arms, looking into her face with moist-eyed longing.

"What do you call her?"

"Alyssa."

Tom had nodded. "It is lovely."

"A boy would have been called Thomas."

Philip had regretted the words the instant they left his mouth. Tom's little one had been buried under that name. Tom had closed his eyes, cuddling the new baby close, and was silent for a while.

"What a miracle it is," he had said finally, looking up with a tight smile. "I am happy for you, Philip. I am."

"Tom—" Philip had faltered there, recalling his own fear for this child, too easily imagining his brother's pain. He had put one arm around Tom's shoulders. "I wish I knew what to say to you."

Tom had shifted the baby back into his arms. "Just be thankful. Be very thankful."

Tom had walked away then, and Philip had heard Robin out in the corridor. "Uncle! Uncle!"

Philip had looked out of the door to see Tom scoop the boy into his arms.

"Are you sad, Uncle?" Robin had asked, a look of puzzlement on his little face.

"Faith, no," Tom had told him heartily. "How could I be sad on such a day? You are not sad to have a fine new sister, I'll wager."

Robin had made a face. "I had rather God gave Mama a brother for me."

"You have John already," Tom had said, managing a laugh.

Robin had considered that for a moment. "I know, Uncle. You should take the new baby to Aunt 'Liz'beth so she will have one, and then God will give Mama another, this time a boy."

"I think He knows when to give us what's best for us to have," Tom had answered him lightly. Then Tom had carried him off to play, and Philip had stood there with the baby, watching them. He had hurt for Tom, and then he had grown angry. He felt that anger again now, anger that Tom who had never wronged anyone should have such grief to bear. And Sarto was to blame.

Rosalynde shivered against him, and he held her and the baby closer. It angered him, too, remembering the old tyrant's covetous eyes upon her and how he had, in the name of mercy, slit a man's throat before her face. Dare the barbarian come so to his court and expect to make alliance with him after that? The effrontery was not to be borne.

Deciding he was perfectly justified in sending Sarto's most recent ambassadors back to Reghed unheard, he closed his eyes and hoped the dream would not return.

After he had spent most of the afternoon in court, standing at his brother's side as he dismissed the ambassadors from Reghed, Tom went to see Elizabeth. An hour later he closed her door softly behind him and stood in the spring sunlight that flooded from the open doorway of the chamber opposite him, a welcome change from the dimness he had just left. He had tried to coax Elizabeth into leaving, too, into walking with him as she used to do in the forest or by the river or at least sitting for a moment or two in the garden. But she had told him as she did every day that she could not yet. Perhaps tomorrow.

He had begun to fear that that tomorrow would never come. When she lost the baby, she had taken an intense fever, and he had feared he would lose her as well. For almost three weeks he had stayed beside her, listening to her call for him and for their child, realizing she did not know him when he was there, that she did not understand that the child was gone.

When the fever broke, she had asked again for the baby, and the physicians attending her had told her as gently as they were able what had happened. It was the next day before they would allow Tom in again to see her, and then only with strict instructions that he was not to upset her with talk of the baby or with mourning or with anything but gentle cheerfulness.

He had agreed and had obeyed, even when it was almost beyond him to hold her as she wept and not weep with her, when his own heart was breaking, and he could not share his grief with the one closest to him. Soon after that she no longer wept, no longer clung to him, no longer took much notice of his comings and goings, and he felt more helpless than ever. She had taken notice of him today, but what she had told him had done nothing to bolster his hope that they would one day regain the happiness they had once had.

"Oh, God," he whispered, leaning his head back against the door, closing his eyes against the sun that seemed suddenly too bright. "Can You not make it right again? Can You not bring her back to me?"

From the very beginning, there had been little of the commonplace to their marriage. They had come to the altar as strangers, their fathers having agreed to give them only one brief week together until the war then being waged came to an end. It was more than two years after that that she had come back to him and their marriage had truly begun. Even then it had been turbulent, for she had been unable to believe upon such brief acquaintance that he could love her as deeply and as truly as he did. Her mistrust had left her vulnerable to seduction and adultery, and he had almost died in a duel to win back her honor. He still carried the scars of that day, in his side and across both palms, but they were well worth it to him. They were irrefutable proof of his love and forgiveness and had won her to him, heart and soul.

Even now he did not doubt her love for him, but he feared that it was so drowned in grief that it would be too weak to ever again struggle free. If only she—

He looked up, realizing he was no longer alone. A thin, dark-haired girl dressed in the plain, neat garments of one of the castle servants stood a few feet away, watching him, looking as if she were trying to summon up the courage to speak to him. He rubbed his eyes and tried to make his expression more pleasant.

"Did you want something of me, Molly?"

"Pardon me, my lord, I did not wish to disturb you." She hesitated. Then she came closer to him, pity in her eyes. "Forgive my boldness, my lord. I know it is hardly my place to speak of it, but I could not help seeing—I thought perhaps I might—My lord, I am sorry about your lady and about the child."

He nodded in acknowledgment, fearing that if he said anything, he might break down here before her.

She reached out her hand as if she wanted to comfort him, and then she drew back. "Is there nothing I might do, my lord?"

"Pray," he said thickly. Before she could say more, he walked swiftly to the end of the corridor and disappeared down the stairs. His step did not slow until he had left the palace and was in the courtyard.

As he passed the forge and neared the stables, he decided that perhaps a ride would clear his head and settle his nerves. In these past weeks he had faced many days such as this, days when his grief seemed to take on a will of its own, and he was helpless against it. But those days had passed, and he had survived them, and each one had less of a hold on him than the one before. He reminded himself of that now, reminded himself that no pain was forever. But he could not help thinking, too, that he could have faced the pain better had he not faced it alone.

No, he was not alone. There was a deep knowing inside him that would not let him believe he was alone. It gave him comfort—that knowing, but it was comfort for his spirit, for his soul. It was nothing he could cling to in the night, nothing that could take him in its arms and hold him close, nothing that could lie beside him in the darkness and keep the pain at bay.

"Oh, Bess, I need you," he whispered. But after what she had told him today, he feared that his marriage was buried in Winterbrooke Cathedral along with his son.

For a moment he stood unmoving, listening to the mourning-bell clang of the blacksmith's hammer. *Dead. Dead. Dead.* The black word pounded again and again inside him like the dull pain in his heart. *Dead. Dead. Dead.*

The clanging stopped when the smith saw him there. "You honor me, your highness," the big man said with a lumbering bow. He wiped the glistening sweat from his face and waited for Tom to speak. When he did not, the smith went back to his work, his muscles bunching, then stretching as he pounded the heavy hammer against a red-glowing horseshoe.

"Might I do that?" Tom asked abruptly. Again the clanging stopped.

"So please you, my lord," the man said quizzically, handing him the hammer. The weight of it felt good in Tom's hand, and he brought it down again and again against the anvil, harder and harder, until he, too, was drenched in sweat.

"Whatever enemy you have laid out on that anvil, I'd not take his place for all the world."

Tom looked up. "Philip. I did not see you there."

Philip took the blacksmith's tongs and picked up the horseshoe, looking at it with a critical eye. "I should like to see the horse that was made for."

It was pounded almost flat, completely useless. Philip laughed, and Tom smiled tightly and gave the hammer back to the smith. "Sorry, friend."

The big man bowed and went back to his work.

"Were you seeking me, Philip?" Tom asked as they left the forge. "I did not think the council met until Thursday."

"True. Can I not speak to my own brother except on a matter of state?"

Tom smiled once more, a little more genuinely. "Of course."

"How is your lady these days, Tom?"

Tom's smile tightened again. "No better, I fear."

"I want you to think on something. I know it would please the queen if we went to Westered for a time, to her father. Robin's grown so, and Lord James has not even seen John or Alyssa yet. They're children such a short while." He faltered there, seeing the effort Tom was making. "I thought we might spend the summer there, and perhaps you both would come along. It might help your lady to come away from her sorrow awhile, where she will not always be reminded."

"She will never agree," Tom said, resignation in his voice.

"Why?"

Tom merely shook his head.

"Why, Tom?"

"She is afraid," Tom said tautly. "She is afraid it will happen again."

"Nonsense," Philip insisted. "Your next child—"

"There will not be another child."

"Of course there will be. Then you shall—"

"She's sent me away from her, Philip. She told me today she cannot bear to lose another child, and there can be nothing more between us."

Anger flashed into Philip's eyes. "After all you've suffered for her sake, she dares to—"

"You do not understand," Tom said wearily. "There were two others as well. Three summers ago and then the fall before last."

Philip was silent for a while. "Tom, I am so very sorry."

"She was not far along enough for it to really show those times. She did not want the court to know. But we thought this last time, since she carried him so long, we thought sure . . ."

"Why did you never tell me?" Philip asked after a silent moment. "What is a brother for?"

Tom looked up at him, his dark eyes filled with a pleading pain. "To help pick up the pieces?"

Philip squeezed his arm around his shoulders. "Come with us to Westered. Rosalynde always says there's healing in the sea air, perhaps for hearts as well."

Tom exhaled heavily, then nodded. "I will ask my lady."

It took Tom until after supper to summon courage enough to go back to Elizabeth. Even then he turned back twice on his way to her chamber, telling himself that it was too soon to speak to her yet, that she would be already asleep, that she would not want to hear what he had to say. But he knew he had to try. He could not lose her altogether.

He had almost reached her door when he saw Molly there at the end of the corridor, her arms full of towels and her dark eyes humbly downcast. He knew from the tinge of red in her cheeks that she had been watching him again.

"Where are you off to then, Molly?" he asked kindly, hoping as he walked over to her that a touch of the everyday world would steady him a little before he faced the task he had set himself.

"The nursery, my lord." She smiled shyly, and the color in her cheeks intensified. "Mistress Joan was bathing the boys, and Prince John pulled most of the towels we had right into the tub. Then Prince Robin thought he'd best see to dousing the rest."

He smiled, too. "And you thought my brother was rewarding you by moving you from the laundry to the nursery. Perhaps you'd as soon go back."

"Oh, no, my lord." She clutched the towels more tightly against her, a look of genuine alarm on her thin face. "Please, my lord, do not send me away unless—" She ducked her head once more. "Unless the king has thought again and decided it is not fitting that I should help tend his children. Or—or if you think it so."

"Now no fear of that, Molly. You know he would never have given you such a charge if he did not think you fit for it. It is little enough payment for all you've done for us and for the kingdom."

"I could never do enough to repay all the kindness you've shown me, my lord," she said, not lifting her head.

He was well aware that it was not the desire for less rigorous work that made her so averse to returning to the laundry, but he did not have the heart to scold her for it. Despite the roughness and ill treatment she had known before coming to Winton, she had a gentle nature, and he knew she would most likely wilt before his mildest reproof. Besides, even with the awkwardness he felt, there was something flattering in this girlish infatuation that had never sought more from him than a kind word, something that seemed to soothe his weary spirit a little.

It pleases her, he told himself, *and there is no harm in it.*

"Well, perhaps you'd best take those on then," he said, "before the little rogues make some other mischief."

"My lord, I asked you this morning if there were something I might—"

"Keep us in your prayers, Molly," he said, the sadness coming back into his eyes. "There is nothing you could do that would give me more comfort."

"I will, my lord," she promised. "Always."

When she was gone, he went back to Elizabeth's door and knocked tentatively. Nan, the tall, sturdy redhead who attended his wife, gave him a quick, hopeful little smile when she saw he had come. Immediately she shooed the other servants from the room, leaving him and Elizabeth alone.

"Have you a moment for me, Bess?" he asked. She looked up at him listlessly and then turned again to the window.

"You should have come to supper, love," he said cheerfully, sitting beside her. "We had a venison pasty from that buck Philip took yesterday and those cinnamon cakes you favor so much. Shall I have some brought for you?"

"I've eaten, my lord."

There was a plate on the table near the hearth, piled high still with meat and fresh bread and even some of the cakes, showing signs of no more than a slight rearrangement of its contents. He sighed and slipped his arm around her shoulders, noticing not for the first time how thin she had become. She seemed to notice nothing but the darkness outside her window.

"You should have seen the gown Lady Clarissa wore tonight at supper," he told her airily, remembering the interest she had always shown in the fashions the other ladies of the court wore. "Faith, it was cut so low in front I think Philip would have dismissed her from the hall except, she being a woman of more than three-score years, he did not wish to—"

He broke off, realizing he was heard by no one but himself.

"Bess?" He slipped his hand from her shoulder to stroke her arm. "Bess love?"

She finally looked up at him with her dark, hollow eyes. "You were saying, my lord?"

"What is it that holds you there, love?" he asked. He could make out only a few shadowy shapes in the night—the guild hall, the armory, the cathedral—little more.

"It looks different in the mornings," she said. "And in the spring."

"Morning will come again," he assured her, "and spring is already upon us."

"Is it?"

"It will be summer before long." He slipped his hand further down her arm, linking his fingers with hers. "Philip and his lady are going to Westered soon, Bess, to visit her father, and I thought perhaps we might—"

Her body tensed. "I must stay here."

"Think on it, love," he coaxed. "The sea and the mountains and—"

Again she stared out the window, not hearing, and sudden realization put a hot, strangling tightness in his throat. The cathedral was down there, the cathedral with its marble saints, with its relics, with its tombs.

"Bess, please."

"I must stay here," she repeated. "With the baby."

He squeezed his eyes shut, fighting the quick stabbing pain. "It stops, Bess." His voice was low and stiff. "It stops now. I have let this carry on too long. Now there must be an end of it."

"I cannot leave him."

"He is dead!" Tom cried, shaking her by the shoulders and then crushing her against him. "He's dead, he's dead, he's dead." A tearing sob warped his words, choked them down inside him, and she began to cry, too, inconsolable, brokenhearted mourning that cut him through with remorse.

"Shh, love, shh." He held her closer, rocking her against him. "Forgive me, forgive me."

"Let me stay," she begged, lifting her tearstained face, clasping her hands in entreaty, pleading as if for her life. "Do not take me away from him."

"Shh, you shall not go. You shall not." He kissed her forehead, her eyelids, her face. "Please, Bess, I love you. Do not cry anymore. Please, love."

He brought her clasped hands to his lips, and a single tear fell on her wrist. She stared at the place, quieting with a sudden, shuddering sob, and then she brushed her fingers across it.

"You never wept," she whispered, brushing her fingers across his wet cheek, too.

He closed his eyes. "I am sorry, love," he said, struggling to draw steadier breaths. "It is only that sometimes—"

"You never wept," she said again, a look of bewildered realization on her thin face. "Never all this while."

"I meant to be strong for you, Bess. I did not want to grieve you more."

She put her arms around his neck, clinging to him, crying again. "I thought you did not care, that it meant nothing to you, my losing him."

"Oh, Bess," he murmured. Then he held her closer and told her how very much it did mean.

In the shelter of his arms, she had finally fallen asleep. Now long past dawn she woke to find herself still there, still sitting with him in the window, with the morning sun pouring its warmth over them both. There had been something clean and healing in the tears they had shared, and here in the light the darkness of the night before seemed very far away.

"You should have slept," she said, hesitantly touching his cheek, wondering if, in all this while, sleep had been as rare a visitor to him as to her.

"I wanted just to hold you," he said softly. "It has been so very long."

Last night for the first time she had seen past her own grief into his. It had been written there all along, she realized, in his tired face and in the loneliness he could not always hide. She laid her head again on his shoulder.

"Will you forgive me, my lord?"

"For what, sweet? You know I understand."

"For all those times you held me and would not cry, all those times you grieved alone and had no one to comfort you, for all those times—"

"Shh," he whispered, stroking her hair. "It does not matter now."

He kissed her forehead and then, very gently, her lips. She pressed closer, hardly realizing it when she slipped her arms around his neck, barely aware of the way she was nuzzling his cheek. It seemed only natural, kissing him as she had countless times before, holding him closer, feeling the quickening beat of her heart.

He responded hesitantly at first and then, when she did not object, with growing passion.

"Tom," she murmured, melting against him. Then without warning she stiffened and pulled away. He shook his head, bewildered at the fearful pleading in her expression.

"Bess?"

"I cannot."

"Please, Bess, we must go on now. We've lost our child. Let's not lose each other as well. If we both grieved together all the rest of our lives, it would not bring him back to us." He took her hand in his. "He is dead, sweetheart, but you are not. I am not. Remember him. Love him. I will. But I will go on living, too."

"Tom, I do love you. You know how I want you. I would never wish to hurt you again, but you must understand. As I told you before—" She pressed his hand to her face, fresh tears in her eyes. "You do not know how I've longed for you to come to me, to hold me as you used to do, to kiss me until I could forget the pain even just a little, to make it the way it was before, but it can never be. It can never be again."

She was crying in earnest now, and he took her back into his arms to soothe her.

"You needn't decide such a thing now, sweetheart," he told her. "In time we will speak of this again and perhaps—"

"No," she sobbed, "I cannot. If we had another child, it would be the same all over again, and I could never bear it."

He was silent for a moment.

"And this is truly what you want?" he said finally.

"No. It is not what I want."

"Then—"

"But it must be so, my lord. It must be so." She reached up to caress his cheek, brokenhearted determination on her face. "But I'll not play dog in the manger. I'll make no complaint if you wish to seek solace elsewhere."

Stunned, he said nothing for a moment. She dropped her hand, but he caught it up in both of his, cradling it against his heart. "You could never mean that, Bess. Please tell me you would never want that."

"No," she breathed, "but it is hardly fair for me to expect—"

He drew her to him again, pain-tinged understanding in his dark eyes. "Do you love me, Bess?"

That was all he asked, all he had ever asked. She was scarcely able to answer him for the sharp pain in her heart. "Yes."

Tears brimming in his own eyes, he pressed a kiss into the auburn curls piled on top of her head. "Then we will be all right, sweetheart. We will be all right."

She knew he meant it as comfort, but it only made her cry.

CHAPTER

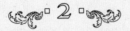 2

SEVERAL NIGHTS LATER A QUIET STIRRING IN TOM'S CHAMBER brought him out of his sleep.

"Who is there?"

The hearth fire had died down, and he could see only a vague shadow near him in the darkness, a shadow with a woman's shape.

"Bess? Is that you?"

One finger laid upon his lips silenced him, and then there was a gentle shift in the bedding. He felt the hesitant touch of a kiss on his cheek and another, tender and sweet, pressed into the palm of his hand. Recognizing the sign and the scent of her rose water, he smiled.

"Bess."

The kiss was repeated, this time lingering longer, and he felt a soft hand caress his face.

"I am so glad you've changed your mind, sweetheart," he murmured, closing his eyes as he pulled the silken warmth beside him into his arms. "You will see, love. There is nothing to fear in trying again and so very much to gain." His lips sought hers in the darkness. "Bess," he whispered, beginning a kiss that held just a hint of all the passion pent up inside him. He slipped his hand to her throat, and then with a lightning flash of realization, he was fighting free of the arms riveted around him, of the soft, seductive flesh that sought to ensnare him.

"Molly!"

The girl tried to hold him yet, tried to wrap herself around him, to cling to him until he had no choice but to succumb, but he would not allow it.

"Please, my lord," she begged, still reaching for him.

He broke away. "Stop! Stop it in heaven's name!"

He rolled off the bed and threw on his dressing gown. Then he lit a candle, his hands shaking with deep anger. Molly sat huddled in the bedclothes, hiding her face from him.

"How dare you!" he spat. "Dare you so overstep your place to come here like this?"

He snatched up the plainly made dress she had left on the chair and threw it at her. "Get dressed. Then get out and never try such a trick again!"

He turned his back, to give her a moment's privacy, but when he turned again, she was still sitting as she had been, her eyes lowered and the dress clutched in her hands.

"Get up! Sweet heavens, would you have my lady find you here? She would never—"

"She sent me to you, my lord," Molly said, her voice almost inaudible.

"She would—"

"She sent me to you."

"She—" He sat down heavily at the edge of the bed. "Oh, Bess."

For a moment he was motionless, and then he ran both hands through his hair. "Molly—Molly, I—" He shook his head. "I hardly know what to say but to ask your forgiveness. She should never have demanded such a thing of you."

"My lord, I love you."

"She should never—"

"I love you."

She looked up at him then, and he could see the raised whip scar that went from under her chin down the side of her neck to join the others on her back. She had taken those lashes on his account, a great part of the reason he had always felt it his special charge to look after her since.

"Molly—" Again he shook his head, hardly able to bear the

young, pleading earnestness he saw on her face. Then he let his breath out in a rush. "Molly, you haven't any idea what you are saying."

"Yes, I do. Surely you know what I feel for you. I love you." She put her hand over his. Then she leaned over and touched her lips almost reverently to his wrist. "I've wanted for so very long to say so."

"You know this can never be."

He slipped his hand out of hers and stood up. She dropped her head again.

"I should have known you would never want me. I knew you could never love me, but I thought maybe as your mistress—" She managed a faint laugh. "I suppose even you cannot forget what I was."

"That has nothing to do with this."

"You mean you do not care that I was a harlot?"

"I care." He turned her face up to him, his touch so gentle. "I care that you were used so when you should have been left your innocence and your childhood. I care that your father showed you no better love than to force you into such a trade. I care that you feel you are somehow to blame. I care, little Molly, I care."

"Oh, my dear lord."

She held his hand there against her cheek and pressed it with another kiss.

Again he pulled away from her. "But I do not love you," he said firmly. "And you do not love me."

"I do."

"No. If you loved me, you would not urge me to something that I would hate us both for afterwards." There was a sudden insistence in his tone. "I love Elizabeth, and, even did I not, she is my wife. You know I belong to her."

"She does not want you anymore, my lord."

"She hardly knows what she wants."

There was an awkward silence.

"You must pardon me, Molly," he said finally. "I should never have allowed you to go on thinking such things of me all this while. I've hardly played the part of a gentleman."

"Of course, my lord, if you wish it, I do pardon you, but that does not make anything I have said untrue."

His expression tightened with exasperation. "Did you mark nothing I have just told you? I do not love you, and you do not love me." Seeing the pain in her eyes, his tone softened. "Molly, surely there is a good man among the soldiers or the servants or among the tradesmen in the town who would be proud to call you wife, someone who could love you with all his heart and offer you more than mere kindness."

"None," she said with bleak certainty. "None who would find it easy to forgive and forget what I have been, none like you."

"Only because you blind yourself to those who would, clinging to what can never be."

"Only because I know them, my lord. Do you think I did not see it often enough when I lived in Breebonne? The men who would come to my father's with a coin or two at night were the same ones who spat at me if they saw me in the town by day. No good man would want to take a common strumpet to wife."

"I'll not have you call yourself that still, Molly," he told her sternly. "You never chose that life, and you quit it as soon as you were able. Would the king have a common strumpet to look after his children? You've shown yourself better than that, and it is time you no longer saw yourself in that light."

"It is what I am, my lord, no matter how I might cover it over."

"It is what you were. What you are is nothing but gentle constancy, all a man could ask of a woman. You are worth a great deal if only you would believe it."

She dropped her head again, hiding her tears. "Can you speak to me so, my lord, and yet expect me not to love you?"

"You cannot say I have ever once led you to believe I want that of you."

"No, my lord," she admitted with a sigh. "Not once."

"Molly, you cannot, you *must* not love me. You must not speak such things to me any longer, nor even think them."

"As you wish it, my lord," she said in a small, tight voice. "I will say no more. And you need not fear I will try to deceive you ever again."

Again there was a long silence.

"Do not squander all your life and love on me, Molly. There is something better meant for you than that—if you would only see it."

He left her there huddled under his coverlet, still with her eyes downcast and her dress clutched against her and her shoulders drooping in resignation.

Tom went from his own chamber into Elizabeth's, the heavy door making no sound as he opened it and closed it again after him. She was sitting in her window, a blanket draped around her against the still-chilly spring night. She had her knees drawn up to her chest, her arms wrapped around them and her cheek resting on top of them as she stared unseeing into the darkness. Her thick hair hung down beside her, almost touching the floor with its tumbled waves. He came up to her and laid his hand on it.

"Bess?"

She hugged herself more tightly. Then she looked up at him, her dark eyes filled with tears and unflinching resolution. "It was the only way for both of us, my lord. Surely you can see that now." There was a forced steadiness in her voice. "The girl will be discreet, and you need not fear I will be hurt by your association with her. Having refused you myself, I cannot rightly deny you someone else."

"How could you send her to me like that? In the night when I was asleep and vulnerable? I felt her there in bed with me—God help me, Bess, I thought she was you, that you had changed your mind."

The tears fell down her cheeks. "I know you, my lord. I know you for a man of honor. I knew you would not have taken her, not at first. Now it is done, and you can see it is the only way for us."

"Have I said I want this?" he asked. "Have I made demands on you that you could not bear? I told you before, this is not how I would have it be between us, but I do understand. Even did I not, that makes no change in what is right and what is wrong. I pledged before God that you would have my faithfulness. Always. Now you send someone to me, to deceive me in the darkness and make me false to you and to Him against my will?"

"My lord—"

"You cannot expect me to use that girl, not after all she's done for your sake and for mine."

"It is an honor for her," she told him. "She went willingly."

"An honor? To be used for a harlot again? Just for my ease and for the ease of your conscience? An honor, Bess?"

"You know she loves you. You would be blind not to see it."

"All the more then. She thinks she loves me. She told me so herself tonight. Can I hurt her the more by using that love selfishly?"

"Then choose another," she said stubbornly. "I've seen more than one here at court who would sell her covetous soul to have that place in your arms."

"Bess, you know I could not. Even if there were such a woman, even if it were her will and yours, and even if God allowed such a thing, I could not do it."

"Then Molly—you did not—"

"No."

"Oh, Tom."

She leaned her head against him, and he stroked her hair again.

"Would you have me false to you, Bess? Would you have me false to myself? I cannot be but what I am, and loving you is woven through every part of me."

She slipped her hand up to his, holding it tightly as she began to cry. "You should never have loved me," she sobbed. "Not this way. I deserve a selfish, faithless love—not yours. And you deserve someone who can truly be a wife to you."

"Shh." He shifted her into his arms and sat down with her cuddled in his lap. "You are my wife, sweetheart, my best beloved. There is no one else. There can be no one else. I've waited for you before, and I will wait for you again, as long as need be. Just do not take your heart from me. And do not ask me to give mine to another."

She sat silently for a very long time, clinging to him, trying to understand why he should offer her such love undeserved. Finally she lifted her head.

"I will go with you to Westered."

Over the next several days, there was a steady stream of wagons traveling from Winton to Westered carrying all the "little necessities" Rosalynde had selected for the summer-long visit.

"You might think we were sending an army west, with all this gear," Philip grumbled, watching her supervising the packing of the large tapestry she was working and the loom that held it.

"Put the broches there, Julia, with the rest," she told her maid as more bundles were brought out to her. "And put Lady Marian's baggage there."

Philip turned her to face him. "Lady Marian is going along with us now, I see."

"I can hardly go without her, my lord," she said with a pert smile. "She is helping with the tapestry."

"I thought all your ladies were working that with you."

"They are, but without Lady Marian I shall never finish in time."

"In time for what?"

"You shall see."

"What is the thing meant to be anyway? You've yet to show me."

"You shall see," she said again.

He scowled. "Your father shall have to put us in the stables when we finally get to Westered. After all this, there shall be no room for us in the castle."

Smiling, she patted his cheek. Then they noticed John carrying a well-fed gray and white cat toward the wagon. His arms were clutched firmly around her, leaving her lower two-thirds hanging down limply and her striped tail dragging the ground. There was only patience in her gold-green eyes as he struggled to put her up with the other baggage bound for Westered. With a helpful push from her hind legs, he succeeded.

"What's this, son?" Philip asked laughing.

"Grace go, too."

"Oh, no. Grace must stay here this time. She will look after things for us while we are away. All right, John?"

"Grace go, too," John repeated firmly. He bit his lip, and his eyes grew guiltily round as another voice came from behind them.

"There you are, rascal!"

Philip recognized the voice before he turned, having himself been stopped short by the no-nonsense tone more times than he could count. With a determined speed that refused to be hindered by her ample size, Joan shot across the courtyard. John tried to hide himself in his mother's skirts, knowing his father was no match for his nursemaid when she had that particular look on her face, but Rosalynde merely turned him back toward her.

"John, have you run away from Mistress Joan?" she asked. He nodded solemnly, looking from her to Joan to his father.

Philip got down on his haunches to have his eyes level with the boy's. "Have I not told you that you must not do so, son?"

Again John nodded. Then he grabbed his father's hand with both of his little ones. "I want Grace go, Papa. She will cry."

Philip's stern expression softened at the earnest concern on his face. "She'll not cry."

"She will be afraid at night," John insisted, "and cannot find us."

Philip was suddenly reminded of the tender-hearted boy this child had been named for. His youngest brother John had raised Grace from a tiny kitten just hours old, feeding her with a milk-soaked rag, sleeping with her cupped in his hands, until she was old enough to look after herself. He had always had a gentle way with animals, especially this one, and it seemed that his namesake took after him.

"Please, Papa."

Philip looked up at his wife and saw by her expression that as always she knew what he had been thinking.

"It would do no harm, my lord," she said, and he stood to stroke the cat still sitting on the bundles in the wagon. She stretched up against him, purring in contentment when he scratched between her ears.

"It seems everyone else is to come with us, Grace. You may as well come along, too."

John hugged his father around the legs, but Philip made his

expression stern once more. "Now, John, you must never run away from Mistress Joan again. Are we agreed?"

"Yes, Papa."

"And what must happen if you disobey me?"

"I must have a punishmit."

"That is right." Philip stroked back the boy's dark hair. "Now what about Mistress Joan? You've made her very sad."

John turned back to Joan. "I did not want Grace to be afraid," he explained, patting her hand to comfort her. "I'll not run away again."

She picked him up, and he hugged her tightly around the neck. "Are you sad now?"

"Not now, my honey-love," she assured him, "but I should be very sad to have to switch those princely little breeches."

"I am certain that will not be necessary, will it, John?" Philip asked. John shook his head cheerfully, looking very virtuous.

"And what were you saying, my lord, about sending an army west?" Rosalynde asked once Joan had taken their son back inside.

Philip shrugged. "I suppose it makes little difference if we add one more. Still I hope you've found room in all this for a fresh shirt or two for me."

She laughed. "Your things went days ago, and it was a good bit more than a shirt or two, as you well know, peacock."

"Peacock?" he sputtered.

She hugged him around the waist and kissed him under the chin. "Precious, softhearted, honey-sweet peacock."

"Hussy," he muttered with a glance at the grinning servants. Seeing she had embarrassed a touch of color into his face, she laughed again. He shook his head. "I'd no idea I had married such a saucy wench."

"Sometimes, my lord, sauce makes an otherwise dull dish irresistible."

"Never dull," he assured her, "but a trifle more impudent today than usual, I must say. Never tell me you haven't some mischief in hand when you take that tone to me. Why is it truly you want Lady Marian along?"

"Pardon me, my lord king."

Philip turned to see that his squire, a lanky, sharp-featured boy of nineteen, had come into the courtyard.

"What news, Jerome?"

"The ambassador from Reghed has again requested audience with your majesty. Lord Darlington wishes to know what answer you would have him given."

Philip frowned. "I will go speak to Lord Darlington. Go on with your weaving, my little Arachne," he said to Rosalynde, "whatever you've knotted your web to catch. I must see to more trifling matters."

With a secretive smile, she curtseyed, and he went into the castle. The boy made as if he would follow, but she stopped him. "Are you prepared to go to Westered, Jerome?"

"My duty is to see to the king wherever he goes, my lady," he said stoically. "He's taken me from stable boy to page to squire for little more reason than his own bounty, and I'll not likely shirk any task he asks of me now."

"His majesty and I both owe you much, Jerome, for your faithfulness. It pleases him to give you what favor he can. And Westered is not such a dreadful place. Some even find it rather pleasant."

"I am certain it is, my lady. I meant no disrespect."

"But you had rather stay here in Winton?"

"That must be as pleases the king."

"It is very odd though, for I think Lady Marian is rather reluctant to go as well, though she has consented to it."

There was a sudden infusion of color to his face. "She is—Lady Marian is going to Westered?"

"She is. But if you wish me to speak to the king on your behalf, Jerome, I am certain I can convince him he need not take you along, too. As I said, he pleases to give you what favor he can."

"No, no, my lady, you, uh, you need not trouble yourself. I shall, of course, do as my lord bade me do. I am certain Westered is a beautiful place. A glorious place!" He dashed back toward the castle. Then, remembering himself, he made a hasty bow. "Pardon me, my lady."

He turned to sprint away again and stumbled into a slight, fair-complected girl with moonlight-pale hair and a suddenly flustered expression.

"Jerome!"

"Forgive me, Lady Marian," he gasped. "I am a clumsy fool. Have I hurt you?"

"No, no, of course not," she managed to answer him. "I merely came to bring her majesty—"

"Allow me, my lady," he said, snatching her bundle from her and spilling its bright contents at their feet.

"My thread!" Rosalynde cried.

Jerome scrambled to gather it all up. "I am so sorry, my lady."

Seeing him drop more than he picked up with each attempt, Rosalynde laughed and knelt down with Lady Marian to help. "When we are in Westered, Lady Marian, you must promise me you'll not let Jerome help with my things again."

"In Westered?" Marian's pale face was tinged with sudden pink. "I shall be certain he does not, my lady."

She kept her eyes on the threads she was collecting, almost but not quite brushing his hand with hers as she did. Even so, it took only a moment to put things right. Rosalynde herself placed the bundle in the wagon.

"Now, Lady Marian, if you would be so good as to fetch the combs for the tapestry." She smiled. "You may have Jerome help you with those if you like. He cannot tangle them."

"At once, my lady," Marian replied. Then she lifted her eyes hesitantly to Jerome's. "Will you come, boy?"

He nodded, tongue-tied, and followed her across the courtyard. When he reached the doorway, he bowed to the queen once more, flashing his lopsided grin. "Thank you, your majesty."

She waited until they were both out of sight. Then, because it seemed to be a day for it, she laughed again.

In her chamber high above them, Elizabeth stood watching the loading of the wagons, trying not to look beyond them to the cathedral.

"You will be glad of this later, sweet," Tom told her, seeing the uncertainty in her eyes. "Will you trust me for that much?"

She smiled a little to please him. "Truly, my lord, I will."

She looked back into the courtyard, leaning against him just slightly. Then he felt her stiffen.

"Is she to go to Westered with us, my lord?"

He, too, looked down and saw Molly near one of the wagons, packing several bundles of clothing into a chest.

"Bess, you know she helps Joan mind the children. We can hardly go without her."

"Any of the serving wenches would do as well. Could you not have one of them take her place?"

"And tell the king what? That you are ill at ease in Molly's presence because of what you bade her do? And then shall I tell him what that bidding was?"

"I suppose I should not marvel that you are still angry with me," she said shamefaced.

He pulled her close to him. "Not angry truly, but even forgiveness does not exempt us from facing the consequences of what we have done."

"Consequences?"

"Sweetheart, I cannot make her suffer for this nor turn her from the place her loyalty has earned her, not for your ease nor for mine. Do you think I do not feel some awkwardness with her now?"

"But I cannot bear to have her along, after—after—"

"I have spoken with her already. She will have a care to stay out of your sight as much as she is able."

"And out of yours?"

"You need not be jealous. You know I care nothing for her, not the way you mean it."

"But she cares for you, my lord, in just that way. Do you think I've not seen her eyes on you?"

"She would never have dared put words to those looks, Bess, but that you sent her to me. I've told her she must not think such things ever again."

"The knowing one must not think a thing and the not thinking it are two very separate matters, my lord."

"If you truly wish it, Bess, I will ask Philip to command that she stay here in Winton, but he will ask me why, and I cannot lie to him. Or if you had rather, I could say nothing and let the whole matter die."

She laid her head on his shoulder. "It seems everything I mean to do to make things better only makes them worse."

"Because you do not yet trust me to look after you."

"I try, Tom, truly I do."

"Then try again now. Please, love, let's not carry this with us to Westered. Leave it behind here to fade out of remembrance. It will, sooner than you know."

"You need say nothing to the king, my lord," she said. Then, her lips trembling, she smiled. "And I will trust you that it will be as you have said it will be."

He gave her a sweet kiss, and she smiled again.

CHAPTER

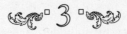 3

A FEW DAYS LATER, WITH THE CITY SAFELY ENTRUSTED TO LORD Darlington's capable hands, the king's party set out for Westered. They traveled toward the sea in pleasant uneventfulness, the sky bright and cloudless, the roads excellent. With spring turning to summer all around them, it was impossible for winter's sorrow to keep its hold. As Tom had hoped, Elizabeth began to smile once more. Her appetite gradually returned, and she even began to take interest in her nephews again and in her new niece as well.

She frequently held the baby as they rode along, cooing and caressing, sometimes with a wistful tear in her eye. Sitting in the carriage beside her, Rosalynde was content to talk or keep silent as Elizabeth chose. The two women had grown close in three years of friendship, and Tom was pleased to again hear them chatting as they used to, giggling with the serving girls and Lady Marian over their husbands and sweethearts, talking of clothes and court gossip.

Philip, too, brought to bear his considerable charm in coaxing his sister-in-law out of her mourning, competing with his brother to see which of them could win the most smiles from her over supper or who could first make her laugh aloud. It was all done with such light spontaneity that she felt little awkwardness in being in company once more.

She sat among them now on the blanket the servants had spread for their noonday repast in a wide grassy clearing alongside the road.

Robin and John were on either side of her, almost swallowed up in the napkins Joan had tied on them in a sure-to-be-futile attempt to keep them clean through an entire meal.

"One at a time, John," Rosalynde said, seeing him with both hands in the heavily laden bunch of grapes that draped the fruit basket. Sitting cross-legged beside them, Tom pulled off a tangy half dozen and gave them to John. Then he picked up a boiled egg.

"Have care, my lord," Rafe said as he set down a platter of roast pheasant. "They've just come from the pot."

Tom tossed the egg from hand to hand to cool it. Aware of two pairs of curious little eyes on him, he gave Elizabeth a sly look and picked up another egg and then another.

"Ow! Ow!" he said, juggling them, and Robin cackled.

"Ow, John, they are too hot to hold!" Tom said wide-eyed. "What shall I do?"

John bounced anxiously. "Put them down! Put them down."

Seeing Elizabeth trying not to smile, Tom winked at her, still juggling. "There's but one thing for it now, John."

He tossed one egg high in the air and caught it neatly in his mouth, swallowing it down in one quick gulp.

"Do it again!" Robin demanded, but John merely looked at him, his green eyes round and solemn. Suddenly he giggled and kicked his heels.

"Silly Uncle Lord Tom."

Rosalynde laughed. Then she grabbed Robin's hand, seeing him trying to imitate Tom's performance with his own dinner. "Such manners you teach them, my lord of Brenden."

"They learn best by example, my lady," Philip observed. "I like to have Tom near them so they may see how not to behave."

"Always pleased to be of service, my liege," Tom replied with a grin. Then he handed Robin and John each one of the eggs he had left. "For eating, not juggling. Agreed?"

The boys giggled again, promising nothing. Elizabeth smiled, and Tom was content.

An hour later the servants had cleared away the empty dishes and were busied with preparing to travel again. Joan had taken the sleeping children back to the carriage for their naps, and Tom and Elizabeth had wandered into the forest for a walk. Philip sat on the blanket still, his long legs stretched out in front of him and his back comfortably against a tree. Rosalynde was curled up against him.

"Perhaps we should have gone walking, too," he said drowsily.

"Let us give your brother and his lady this little while alone," she replied, holding a plump, fresh strawberry under his nose until he opened his eyes enough to see what it was and ate it.

"I am so pleased you asked them to come along with us, my lord," she added. "I'd've worried over them all the while we were away had they not. I believe this will do them both much good."

"It seems to have done them good already."

She fed him another strawberry, ripened to perfection, and he closed his eyes again, savoring the juice that ran sweetly in his mouth.

"Almost," he said with kingly profundity, "*almost* as sweet as your lips."

"You've not kissed me for full half an hour," she told him, as though she were greatly offended. "How could you remember, to make comparison?"

He sat up and looked at her as if he were pondering some deep question of state, and then he kissed her. Apparently undecided, he ate another strawberry, considered for a moment more, and then kissed her again—this kiss slow and passionate.

"You are right," he said softly in her ear. "The strawberry's the sweeter."

"Black-hearted scoundrel!" she cried, pushing him away. "You are no fit judge in this—confess it."

He pulled her back into his arms and kissed her again.

"I confess, my little shrew, that you have the sweetest lips and the sharpest tongue in all Christendom."

"Well, now I know for certain that your judgment is of slight value, but I can say no better of my own."

"When have you been anything but wise?"

"Wise in all things but one perhaps," she conceded.

He grinned. "And that one thing was in loving me, I suppose."

She gave him a sweet smile. "Foolish, I know, but I could not help myself. I am the same way with new lambs and mongrel puppies."

"Very flattering, my lady. I thank you."

She put her hand up to his cheek, a teasing light of love in her eyes. "Truly, I never did like you much, but for charity I thought I should marry you."

"For charity."

She nodded matter-of-factly and brought her lips close to his. "I knew no one else would have such an ill-favored wretch."

"Saint and martyr all at once," he said, his expression full of awed admiration. Then he shook his head and kissed her, grinning again. "You are a wicked girl," he murmured as he drew her closer. "Very, very wicked."

She kissed him this time, satisfying and tantalizing all at once, until he finally pulled away from her. "Wicked," he breathed. "You know we must leave here soon, and it's hours until we stop for the night."

"Perhaps the waiting will make my lord more appreciative," she replied saucily.

He caught her by the wrist and pulled her close once more, a sudden intensity in his eyes. "Does it please you then?"

She smiled, puzzled. "What, my lord?"

"To call your slave 'lord'?"

She pushed his hair back at the temple with a caressing touch of her hand. "Then I am slave to a slave who makes me a queen," she said, and she put her arms around his neck. "What am I to call you in the face of that?"

He looked deeply into her eyes. "Nothing but 'love.'"

Drawn by the vulnerable tenderness in his expression, she leaned down to kiss him once more, and in another moment she was again pressed tightly to him, savoring the faint taste of strawberry that was still on his mouth.

"Mama?"

Hearing John's sleepy voice, she sat up and saw him toddling toward her, one little fist pressed to his eye and his clothes rumpled from his nap. Philip reached out his hand and pulled the boy into a huddle with them.

"Are we at the sea yet, Papa?"

"Not yet, baby," Philip soothed, laying the little curly head on his shoulder. "Soon now."

"Not a baby," John murmured in protest.

Rosalynde stroked John's cheek. "I suppose we ought to go on now, truly, my lord."

"As pleases my lady," Philip replied standing up. "Are you ready, son?"

John was already fast asleep again.

⁂

Out in the forest, Tom and Elizabeth had stopped alongside a smooth-running stream. On impulse she had kicked off her velvet shoes, shed her stockings, and stuck her toes into the water. Tom stood on the bank with her, watching a pair of swans drift by on the lazy current. She smiled up at him and drew a languid circle in the water with her bare foot. He smiled, too.

"A pretty place, is it not, Bess?"

"It smells all of spring still," she replied.

He sat down beside her, admiring the fresh tinge of color in her cheeks and the pretty turn of her ankle under the lace of her petticoats.

"It's the beginning of summer already," he observed. "It always puts me to wonder seeing how spring comes back new each year. After the winter seems certain to have killed everything, spring always comes back." He looked up at the cherry trees that grew there, already ornamented with newly ripened fruit. "And spring brings the summer quickly after."

Smiling, she pushed back a long tendril of dark auburn hair that had escaped her combs, and he noticed the golden bracelet that cir-cled her wrist, engraved with linked violets and their initials T and E. It had been his very first gift to her, one that had taken on special meaning for them both in those days after the war when she had first learned to love him. Seeing it now gave him a spark of hope that, despite her insistence that there be no more intimacy between them, she still held him dear. Even in the deepest, most desperate days of grief, she had never taken it off.

"So much pheasant has made me sleepy," he said, stretching out next to her.

"It was delicious. Why do they never prepare it so at home? I have never tasted any that pleased me better."

He smiled, knowing everything they had been served had been prepared just as it always was back in Winton.

"Now if I only had some of those ripe cherries and a long nap in this sweet grass, Bess, I should ask no more of my life."

"You are easily pleased, my lord," she said.

Again he smiled. "I have all I need right here, love, so long as you stay alongside me."

"It would be sweet to stay just so," she agreed, leaning back with him. Then she looked up at the bountifully weighted branches above her. "Those cherries do look tempting, my lord. Might we have some?"

"My lady needs only ask," he said, jumping to his feet and pulling her up with him. He scrambled up into the tree and began tossing cherries to her, laughing at her attempts to catch them all.

"You will bruise them, my lord, flinging them down like that."

Dropping the last few he had picked, he hung upside down from one of the branches so his eyes would be level with hers. "Should you think you would make a better job of it, my lady, I would be most pleased to allow you to."

She looked surprised for a moment, and then she gave him a challenging grin. "So please you, my lord, I think I will."

In another moment, with his help, she was seated securely in the sturdy fork of the tree, surrounded by leaves and ripe cherries.

"Take your work elsewhere," Tom said, shooing away the pair of startled honeybees she had displaced. "And where is this great harvest of cherries you promised, my lady?"

She pulled a few from above her head and popped them into her mouth. "Ooh, they're wondrous sweet."

"You're to pick them, not eat them," he chided.

She took a few more, making a great show of her enjoyment of it. "Pity you haven't any, my lord," she said.

He laughed. "I've a whole tree of them."

"But none as sweet as these I have."

"Then I'll have those."

He lunged toward her. Giggling, she jerked her hand back to keep the fruit from him and found herself tangled, wrist, sleeve, and bracelet, in the branches and leaves above her head.

"I am caught fast," she said, tugging hard. She stopped abruptly, hearing the tear of delicate lace. "Oh, now I've spoilt my sleeve."

"Do not fret, love," he told her, shifting position so he could assist her. "We'll have it mended or have you a new frock the moment we reach Westered. Stop pulling now."

"But I've twisted my bracelet somehow." She tugged again. "Ow."

"Stop pulling, Bess—you make it worse. I can see where it is caught, and you cannot. Let me do it."

It took him only a few seconds to work her sleeve loose. He soothed the scratched places the ragged branches had left behind. "Poor scraped wrist," he murmured, touching his lips to it. "When will you learn to be still, Bess, and let me watch after you?"

She nestled against his shoulder. "You always take such care of me, Tom."

"Because I love you."

She looked up at him, caught by the tenderness in his voice, and tears sprang to her eyes. "My lord?"

"Now, never cry, love," he said swiftly, fondling the bracelet as he pressed her wrist with another kiss, praying he had not undone with those few longing words all the progress she had made since they had left Winton. "You do not know how it's pleased me to see you as you've been these past few days. I could not bear to think I had made you unhappy. Will you not smile for me again? Nothing would please me better."

"You are easily pleased, my lord," she said, but she smiled, and he gave her cheek a cheerful, smacking kiss.

"Now, my lady, we were to have picked a whole tree full of cherries before we had to be underway again, and here's Jerome come to fetch us back. Be still; he does not see us."

"My lord?" Jerome called as he walked into the empty clearing. "Lady Elizabeth?"

"Look lively there, boy!" Tom said, tossing down a handful of fruit, which Jerome was too startled to catch.

"My lord?"

"Be ready this time, Jerome. You must not drop what I am sending you now. If you will, my lady."

He took Elizabeth firmly by the wrists and lowered her down to Jerome, who caught her around the waist and set her, laughing, on her feet.

"Tom!" they heard Philip roar from the camp, and Tom did a quick somersault to land at Elizabeth's side.

"Swiftly now, love," he said, snatching up her shoes and stockings from the riverbank, "or I daresay we'll be walking to Westered."

They ran back to the wagons, not noticing that the golden bracelet, its delicate clasp worked open with much tugging, was lying in the grass at the foot of the cherry tree.

❧

From his perch in a thick-leafed oak, Hugh Smithson watched as a lone rider mounted on a long-legged black horse came at an easy canter down the forest road. The rider was in his middle twenties, tall and well built, sitting his fine horse with the ease of one born to it, a perfect match to the description he had been given.

"I earn my pay easy today," Hugh told himself, "and before true sunrise."

Just as his prey passed under him, he sprang down, knocking the rider to the hard-packed road. The terrified horse bolted into the trees.

The rider sprang to his feet and backed warily away, sizing up his formidable attacker. Hugh was tall and burly, with a long diagonal scar from his brow to his right cheekbone. The blade that had left that mark had taken his eye as well, and the surgeon had simply stitched the lid over the empty socket. It was not a very tidy job.

"You've just run off all I have worth the taking, friend," the rider said.

Hugh's laugh put a nasty twist into his thick lips. "They say you're a commodity just of yourself."

The rider smiled a dazzling smile and shook his head. "Not for sale."

Hugh drew his sword. "I never offered to buy, your majesty."

With a small show of surprise at the title, the rider shrugged in resignation and began walking toward him. "Of course, you realize—"

In another instant the sword was lying twenty feet away in the underbrush, and the two men were scuffling in the dusty road. Hugh was powerfully built, but his lumbering might was no match for the younger man's wiry agility. After a few minutes' struggle, he found himself facedown in the grass.

With a roar, he snatched up a heavy branch and struck the rider across the back of the head, leaving him in a crumpled heap at the foot of a tree. Once he had paused to regain his breath and wipe the sweat from his red face, he reached down and seized a handful of his captive's dark hair.

"So this is the king," he said, wrenching the young man's head backwards and looking into his still, bloodied face. "Are you certain, Owen?"

Another man, smaller and craftier than his confederate, came out of the trees. "Yes, yes, of course." He examined the ruby ring on the captive's hand and then turned the unconscious man's head to one side. "Did you notice a scar there?"

He touched his fingers to the rider's left cheek where the tree's rough bark had scraped it raw.

Hugh shrugged. "May have. You're the one who has seen him before. Is it or is it not the king?"

"Of course it is," Owen said after an uneasy hesitation. "Bring him."

"Where did you say he went, Palmer?"

"Back to that stream where we stopped at midday yesterday, your majesty. He meant to be back before we left Lord Eastbrook's house this morning."

Philip looked at his brother's serving man in disgust. "For a bracelet?"

"Lady Elizabeth wept over it so, my lord, certain she must have left it behind there, and he's tried so to cheer her."

"That place is miles back."

"That was why he took your lordship's horse. It's faster than any of the others, and with his own mount throwing a shoe last night, Lord Tom saw no harm—"

Just then one of the soldiers came up the walk leading Alethia, riderless, behind him.

"Your majesty's horse was found wandering down at the edge of the forest. So please you, I've brought him back."

"You did not see my brother nearby?"

"No, my lord."

Philip shot Palmer a hard look. "And you let him ride out alone."

"Please, my lord," Palmer stammered. "He commanded me—"

"Give me my horse, soldier," Philip ordered. "Then go to your captain and tell him to assemble his men."

"At once, your majesty," the soldier said, and he darted back into the trees.

"Perhaps he was merely thrown, my lord, and is returning afoot," Palmer suggested, following Philip to the door.

"Not Tom," Philip snapped. Then he handed Palmer his horse's reins. "I must tell the queen what has happened. Then I will be leading the men in search of him."

"I will saddle my horse, my lord."

"I think you've done enough for one day, Palmer. You'd do as well to stay here with the women."

Palmer's usually stoic expression tightened at the caustic words, but he said nothing. Philip stalked into the house.

"What has happened, Palmer? Where is my lord?"

Palmer looked up to the open window above him. "Lady Elizabeth. Pardon me, my lady, but we do not know where he is. His horse has come back without him, and the king is taking out men to search. Pray God he's not met with some harm."

Elizabeth glanced at her bare wrist, and tears sprang to her eyes. "Oh, Tom."

"Have courage, my lady. He has his quick wits and God's holy angels to keep him safe."

"I want to go with the soldiers," she said, lifting her head. "Get me a horse."

"You cannot, my lady. The king would never allow it."

"Get me a horse, Palmer. You shall take me."

"My lady, you scarcely ride, and Lord Tom will have my ears if I allow—"

"And I shall have them if you do not! Get me a horse, and when the king has gone, you shall take me after him."

⁊⳺

Tom came to, gasping and sputtering, half-choked by the bucket of water that had been thrown into his face.

"What—"

"Good afternoon, your majesty."

Tom stopped struggling against the tight bindings on his wrists and scanned the two faces looking down on him.

"We are pleased to have you with us, my lord king," Owen said. Then puzzlement crossed his face, and he walked slowly around his captive, studying him, looking into his dark eyes. Finally he swore. "This is the other one, curse the luck."

"This is not the king?" the one-eyed man asked.

Owen glared at him. "Allow me to introduce you, Hugh. This is his royal highness, Thomas Chastelayne, Duke of Brenden and Prince of Lynaleigh. Not King Philip."

"What now?" Tom asked warily, tossing his dripping hair out of his face. "Since, as you say, I am not the king."

"I'll bury him deep in the forest," Hugh said. He took firm hold of Tom's upper arm and pulled him to his feet. "He'll not be found."

"There's a waste of ransom," Tom said quickly, and Owen looked briefly uncertain.

"No," Hugh told his partner, warning in his one eye. "Our master would be furious if any word of this got about."

Owen looked Tom over again, contempt, even hatred in his eyes. "Pity, my lord. You cannot always rely upon your wealth and noble blood to protect you. Sometimes those of us who have not been so favored still win out."

"What could you hope to gain by this?" Tom asked grimly.

Hugh jerked him a step forward. "I'll not be long."

"Wait, Hugh," Owen said, a sudden evil smile on his face. "It would be pity to waste such a choice find as this. We ought to save the throat cuttings for such worthless fellows as ourselves. What, man, a prince here, and you would leave him for the wolves to carry off?"

"We cannot ransom him, Owen, and we cannot merely set him free."

"Of course we must free him." Owen drew his dagger and held it to his prisoner's throat. "Your dukedom, your royalty, your fine blood, my lord prince, what's that to you now?"

"What it was before," Tom replied. "God's bounty and His to give or take. What of it?"

"It looks as if I am your equal now, my lord—perhaps your better. Shall we try that?" He spun Tom around and slipped the dagger between his wrists. "I hear you've been graced with speed along with all your other gifts, my lord. They say you're fleet as a deer."

The ropes made a popping sound as Owen cut them loose, and Tom stepped back, rubbing the marks they had left. "What of it?" he asked again.

Owen took a crossbow from his saddle. "A wager between us, what say you? Shall we see if the tale is true?"

Tom glanced toward the trees, making a swift assessment of the terrain, quickly choosing a path that would afford him the best cover and the best chance of escape.

"Well?" Owen asked. "Are you game?"

Tom lifted one eyebrow. "I suppose you have made me just that."

"Wait," Hugh insisted as Tom started toward the trees. "No use wasting this."

He yanked the pouch from Tom's belt, and Tom made a futile attempt to hold on to it. "That is my lady's!"

Hugh pulled the bracelet out of the pouch, looking disappointed to find nothing more, but Owen snatched it from him. "Your lady's, is it?" He looked at the linked initials. "But she'll have no use of it now . . . unless her next husband should be called Thomas." He grinned. "If he is, I swear I shall send it to her."

"I'll have it back," Tom told him. "Know that now."

Owen stuffed the bracelet into his saddlebag and then leveled his crossbow at Tom. "You may stay here and be buried with it if you choose. You have till my count of twenty to decide. One."

"I'll have it back," Tom warned again.

"Two."

Tom turned and sprinted into the forest, out of his captors' sight by the count of eight. The ground was damp and soft, leaving his every footstep a plain sign to his pursuers. There were the trees, of course, but they were set too far apart to be of much use. Tom searched the unfamiliar ground as he ran, trying to decide on the best strategy. If he could somehow muddle his trail and then double back, perhaps he could escape. If not—

He heard hoofbeats, and his heart raced in time with them.

Lord God, give me Your wisdom in this.

He looked again at the trees. It was early summer, and they were already thick-leafed. Perhaps there was a way after all.

He darted under an old oak and jumped to catch a low limb, pulling himself up. There was no cover this close to the ground, and the print of his boots, stopping abruptly under the tree, told a simple story that Owen could not miss.

The hoofbeats came nearer, and Tom climbed higher, into the denser branches and thicker leaves. Still it would not do. Owen would know he was here. He looked around, praying again for wisdom. There were two trees nearby.

The one to his left was not as tall as the one he was in, but it was easily within his range and shaded by other taller trees, making it difficult to see what, if anything, was concealed in its branches. The other tree directly in front of him was very tall, its heavy branches well able to hold his weight, even toward the top, but it had only clumps of foliage here and there thick enough to conceal him from the hunter below.

He climbed higher still, thinking he should choose the smaller tree, then wondering if the choice was not so obvious that Owen would make it, too.

Choose, he urged himself as the hoofbeats came even nearer. *Choose!*

Hand over hand, he moved along a thick branch toward the taller tree. The limb he had chosen to swing to looked large enough to take his weight. He hoped it was only the hammering in his heart that made it look too far away.

Was it his imagination, or were the hoofbeats slowing?

He kicked his legs for momentum and began to swing, once, twice. The third time he released the branch and went hurtling toward the other limb. An instant later the rough bark was digging into his palms, and a wave of relief rushed over him. As he scrambled for a better hold, he felt a searing pain in his right arm. He made a frantic effort to keep his grip and then fell the long distance down to the forest floor.

Lying on his back, gasping for breath, he was hardly able to focus enough to see Owen standing over him, fitting another bolt into his crossbow.

"Well run, my lord," Owen said, taking slow, deliberate aim, "but you see I am the better man after all. You will find your fine blood little use to you now."

Tom closed his eyes, still panting. "God, forgive him and me."

"Owen! Owen!"

Owen turned with an oath. "Devil take you, man, what is it?"

"Soldiers!" Hugh cried, almost falling from his saddle.

Tom's eyes snapped open. "Philip?"

He sat up, clutching his arm, the shaft of the bolt sticking from between his bloody fingers. Owen stalked over to him and snapped it off in the wound, leaving the point buried in Tom's flesh. Tom jerked and bit back a gasp.

Owen yanked him to his feet. "Take him, Hugh. We may have a chance at the king yet."

Palmer and Elizabeth followed at a discreet distance behind Philip and his men, keeping out of sight as the soldiers came to a halt before the half-finished ruins of an old castle. A man with a look of haughty satisfaction that did not match the meanness of his peasant garments stood triumphant on the high turret above them, with Tom bound and gagged at his side.

"Release your prisoner!" Philip demanded.

Owen draped his arm companionably around Tom's shoulders. "Take away your men, my lord, or I shall have no prisoner—and you no brother."

"What is it you want then?" Philip asked, his mouth set in a hard, taut line.

"Leave a bag of gold at the foot of that tree there, send your men away, and when I see they are gone, I will leave your brother here in your sight. By the time you have come for him, I will be gone."

"Agreed."

Tom shook his head, desperate warning in his eyes.

"I cannot merely let him kill you, Tom," Philip said.

Again Tom shook his head, and Owen seized his wounded arm and dragged him closer to the edge, letting him look down on the mossed-over stones half sunk in the soft earth below, stones that had been quarried when the castle was abandoned, unfinished, over a century before. A fall onto them could be nothing but fatal.

"Choose, your majesty."

"Hold, man!" Philip commanded. Owen leaned his helpless captive farther out over the wall. Tom squirmed in his grasp and shook his head again, the rag stuffed in his mouth forcing him to draw his breath hard.

"What choice does he leave me, Tom?" Philip asked. "What else is to be done?"

Tom looked at his brother, fiercely determined. Then he slammed his elbow into his captor's stomach and leapt from the tower.

Philip's face went white. "Tom!"

With a scarcely audible moan, Elizabeth slumped against Palmer and then slipped to the ground.

"Forward!" Philip commanded his soldiers, his face flint as he dug his spurs into his horse's flanks. "I want that man alive!"

His heart slamming into his breastbone, he drove his way toward where Tom must have fallen, but the trees had blocked his view, sparing him almost mercifully from the sight of Tom's body dashed against the unpitying stones littered at the base of the wall. He could be sure of nothing. Finally he reached the tower.

"Philip."

Philip stared in disbelief at the mud-covered figure slumped against the wall, his wrists still bound. He had managed to pull the gag away from his mouth.

"Tom!" Philip jumped from his saddle and threw his arms around him. "I should have you whipped for such a trick."

Tom grinned and then winced as Philip cut his bonds.

"Are you hurt?" Philip asked.

Looking up at the turret, Tom let out his breath in a sudden rush. "Not much." He managed another smile. "Not so much as I had feared."

He tried to flex the fingers of his right hand, but he could barely move them.

"You've broken it," Philip said, seeing the swelling in his wrist. "And your arm is bleeding. I marvel you did not break your fool neck as well."

"I knew if I jumped I could choose this low boggy place to land in rather than those stones. It was better than being killed."

"He asked only a bag of gold, Tom. I'd not have let him kill you over that."

"He did not want the money. He wanted you."

"Me?"

"There was a great one-eyed brute waiting to take you when you came for me. They would not have bothered at all with me, but that they mistook me for you."

"Why, Tom? What could they possibly hope to gain from killing you or me if not ransom?"

"They never said."

"There is no trace of anyone, your majesty," the captain of the guard announced as he dropped to one knee before the king. "Shall we make a search?"

"Take a few men and see if you can hunt them down. Tell the rest they will come back with us to keep guard."

"They have my lady's bracelet as well," Tom told the soldier. "I'll have a reward for the man who brings it back to me."

"Gladly, my lord."

"Come on, Tom," Philip said when the soldier had ridden away. "We'll have Livrette see to you."

Philip took Alethia's reins, and Tom swung up into the saddle.

"You have him back. I am glad."

"It was he who led us here to you." Philip stroked the black's nose, and Alethia nudged his chest affectionately.

"He knows the sound of praise," Tom said, patting the horse's neck with his left hand, "and thanks, too, I hope."

Just as Philip mounted one of the soldiers' horses, Palmer rode up to them, a look of wonder on his face.

"I scarce believed the soldier's tale, my lord, but I thank God you are alive."

"No more than do I," Tom replied.

"But you must come to your lady, sir," Palmer urged. "She is back among those trees over there."

"She is here?"

"She is, my lord. She swooned to see you fall."

"May God forgive me," Tom murmured. "I'd not for all my dukedom have had her witness that. Come, Palmer, show me where."

Elizabeth was lying on the ground still, watched over by a pair of young soldiers who snapped to attention when Tom and Philip rode into the clearing.

"Bring some water, man," Philip told one of them as Tom knelt at Elizabeth's side. "Be quick."

Elizabeth stirred a little when Tom cuddled her against him.

"Open your eyes, sweet," he said low in her ear. "Come, love, wake up."

Her lashes fluttered. Then her eyes did open, and she looked at him uncomprehendingly.

"Tom?"

"Forgive me, love, I—"

Whatever else he might have said was lost in her kisses and the tight squeeze of her arms around him. His bleeding arm and overwrung muscles vehemently protested the contact, but his heart reveled in it.

"Bess," he said on a breathless laugh when she finally gave him a chance. "I would have found a tower myself to jump from had I known it would earn me such a welcome."

"I do not see how you can tease now after frightening me to death," she sobbed. Then the sunniest of smiles broke through her tears, and she threw her arms around his neck. "Oh, you are alive."

He hugged her again, giving his brother a delighted, half-bewildered smile over her head, and Philip smiled, too.

"Next time you set out to impress your lady, Tom, let me know of it ahead of time."

"Let us have no more of these 'impressings,' my lords," the royal physician said as he came into the clearing. "As it is, I seem to be forever patching up one or the other of you."

He knelt down and took Elizabeth's pulse.

"You seem right enough, my lady. Now if you would loose my lord of Brenden, I will see to him."

"A word with you, Palmer," Philip said as Livrette began wrapping Tom's broken wrist.

"My lord?"

"For what I said to you this morning, Palmer—"

"Far gentler than the words I had for myself, my lord," Palmer assured him, "but I'll not allow such a thing to happen again."

"I know it is no easy task keeping up with one of us," Philip said, clasping his shoulder. "Rafe tells me so most every day. I often wonder how either of you manages it."

There was a touch of a smile on Palmer's stolid face.

Philip turned back to the physician. "Well?"

"He will mend, my lord," Livrette told him, finished with cutting the arrow point out of Tom's arm and bandaging the minor wound. "But he'd do better for a good rest before we go on to Westered. Is there somewhere close, your majesty, where we might go for the night?"

❧

Philip decided they would turn north and spend the night in Lord Darlington's home in Briarpark. It was very late when they reached the place, and the flustered servants were unprepared for their arrival.

"We have nothing provided fit for your majesty to eat," the steward said anxiously. "When my lord is at court, we have only plain fare here. We were not expecting—"

"What's that cooking?" Philip asked. "Whatever it is, it smells tempting."

The steward's smile was hopeful. "It is merely stew, your majesty, but we've plenty of it."

"Any objections, my love?" Philip asked Rosalynde.

She, too, smiled. "No. I know Robin will like it, and John has been long asleep."

"Tom?"

Tom nodded wearily. "So long as a bed comes after."

"The maids are even now making chambers ready for you all, my lord," the steward assured him.

"Pardon me, your majesty," Elizabeth said to Philip, "but my lord is very tired. Might we be excused?"

"Do you need Livrette again, Tom?"

"This is nothing," Tom replied, rubbing his arm, "but I think I will do as my lady suggests. Do you think, steward, I might have a plate of that stew in my chamber?"

"Immediately, my lord."

"I will go see everything is properly done, sir," Palmer said to Tom. Then he bowed to the king and queen. "Your majesties."

It was not long before he returned. "If you will follow me, my lord."

"Good night then, my lady," Philip said to his sister-in-law. Then he tugged the bandage on his brother's arm. "Try to stay out of mischief for once, Tom."

"I will try."

Palmer led his master and his lady to the chamber they had been given. "Let me help you, sir," he said once they were inside. He knelt down to take Tom's boots.

"Go and see if they've prepared my lord's supper, would you?" Elizabeth asked.

Looking up for Tom's approval, Palmer stood again. "At once, my lady."

Once he was gone, Tom sat down on the bed, grimacing as he flexed his wounded arm. He reached down to remove his boots himself, but his right hand was clumsy and uncooperative.

"Let me," Elizabeth said, kneeling before him. He smiled at her and leaned sleepily against the bedpost.

"If you like, Bess."

His boots were laced from thigh to ankle, and it took her unaccustomed fingers a long while to undo them. By the time she slipped them off, he was breathing in slow, peaceful rhythm, sound asleep.

"Leave it," she whispered when Palmer brought their supper back a moment later.

"I will see to him then, my lady."

"I will," she replied.

With a questioning look at her, he bowed. "As you say, madam. Good night."

When they were again alone, Elizabeth cradled Tom against her shoulder and unlaced his torn, soiled shirt. He stirred just a little when she slipped it over his head, winced a little when she eased his arm out of the bloodied sleeve, and then sighed in contentment when she leaned him back against the pillows. He was still deeply asleep. She slid the belt from around his waist and pulled the coverlet over him. Everything else could wait.

"Tom," she murmured, looking into his handsome, tired face, and tears came into her eyes. This strong, gentle man God had given her to show her His love—he was not lost to her, not now, but he might have been. So easily he might have been. "Dear, sweet Tom."

She struggled out of her dress and got into the bed, taking him into her arms, settling his head against her, remembering how many nights they had lain so, remembering his ardent tenderness. Sometimes his lovemaking was light and deft and playful; sometimes it had such deep intensity that she was lost to anything but his love and his touch, and there were nights when he held her so tightly she thought she would die if he did not release her and knew she would die if he did. It was all love, she was certain of it, a love that was worth any risk. And it had been made clear to her in one harrowing moment that she did not want to live to be irrevocably without that love, without that touch.

She cuddled him closer, glad to hold him once more, glad it was not too late to make amends.

Tom awoke late the next morning, groggy and sore, but he sat up quickly, the smell of porridge reminding him that he had never even tasted the stew from the night before. Elizabeth was immediately at his side with a tray.

"Are you hungry, my lord?"

"Famished," he replied, smiling into her eyes, thinking how

sweetly pretty she looked standing there, still in just her shift and with her hair tumbling over her shoulders. "Good morning, sweetheart."

She returned his smile a trifle shyly and leaned down to kiss his cheek. Then she set the tray on the table near him.

"Palmer brought this for you, but I sent him away again. I thought perhaps I might see to whatever you need."

"I thank you, love," he said, squeezing her hand, "but you needn't trouble with that." He slipped his arm around her waist and sat her down on the bed next to him. "I am perfectly well this morning."

With a wrinkle of concern in her brow, she pressed her hand to his cheek and then to his forehead and then to his arm, just above the wound. He was still slightly warm, but he was rested, and his long sleep had put the color back into his face.

He squeezed her hand again. "I promise."

For a moment she merely looked at him, and then she put the tray in his lap. "It is no more than porridge, my lord, but it is hot."

"I could eat crocodile this morning, love," he said with a grin. "Raw."

As he ate, she busied herself about the room, setting out fresh clothes for him, brushing off his muddied boots. When his bowl was empty, she took the tray away and brought back his wash basin and his razor.

"Now I will shave you, my lord."

He laughed and sat her beside him again. "Palmer will grow fat within the month with you to do all his work."

"I want to do it," she said, looking down.

"Bess, you need not—"

"Please, my lord."

She looked at him again, and he was surprised to see tears in her eyes.

"Bess?"

"I merely wish to care for you, my lord. Does that not please you?"

He pulled her closer. "I thought I was meant to do that for you."

"We're to care for one another," she replied, putting her hand up to his cheek. Then she drew an unsteady breath. "Or so I've been taught."

"You must have had a very wise teacher," he said lightly, trying to make her smile again, and she hid her face against him.

"Do not give up on me yet, Tom," she whispered, holding him tightly. "I do not always understand, I do not always choose rightly, but I love you. I do love you."

"I'll not give up on you, sweetheart," he promised gently, touching his lips to her forehead. Then, too aware of the warm nearness of her, he set her back from him and picked up the razor.

"I never did this well," he said, smiling unsteadily.

"Would you trust me to do it, my lord?"

He looked into her eyes. She had asked him that once before, the morning after their first night together, their first true night as man and wife. That night and that morning after, too, were sweet in his memory still. Were they in hers as well?

"If you like," he said, handing her the blade, but she merely put it back on the table, keeping her eyes locked on his. He swallowed hard, reading the intensity in her expression.

"I, uh—I do not have the bracelet for you, Bess." He could not look away. "I found it, but they, uh—"

She turned his hand over and traced one finger across the razor-straight scar in his palm. Then she touched her lips to it, softly, infinitely tender.

"Tom," she breathed, and she traced the scar again, this time extending the line around to the back of his hand until her palm was pressed to his. Of its own accord, his hand enfolded hers.

"Bess." He held their clasped hands against his cheek, suddenly breathless as she moved closer. "Bess, I know you have told me—"

"Do not give up on me yet," she murmured against his lips. Then she kissed him, and he pulled her into his arms in a passionate, fathomless embrace.

⁂

"I will have it back for you, sweetheart," he said softly just as the morning bells chimed ten. She nestled closer to him, drugged with his lovemaking, feeling a tenderness for him that seemed to flood through every part of her, no longer trying to reason why he loved her, only profoundly grateful that he did.

He kissed her hair. "I pledge it to you, love."

"What?" she asked languidly.

He lifted her wrist to his lips. "The bracelet. I promised you would have it back, and you shall."

"I do not want the bracelet," she said, tracing one finger over his mouth and across his cheek. "Not anymore."

"No?"

"It means nothing if you are not here to give it meaning." She cupped his face in her hands. "I want you, Tom. I want us."

He kissed her again, sweet and tender, and she slipped her arms around his neck, holding him close.

"Never leave me, Tom. I can live without anything but you."

"I will never leave you, love," he pledged. "Never by my choice."

It was midafternoon several days later when Westered finally came into sight.

"Look there, Robin," Philip said, pointing out the airy-spired castle that overlooked the sea. Robin squirmed in the saddle in front of him, straining for a better look.

"That was where Mama was borned?"

"Where she was born, yes, and where your grandpapa lives. Look, love," Philip said as the carriage slowed beside them, and Rosalynde looked up to the top of the cliff.

"It seems a whole lifetime since I was here, since I've seen my father."

He reached down and took her hand. "I should have brought you back long ago."

"Winton is home now," she assured him, "but it is good to visit."

"Ride, too, Papa," John said, reaching his arms out the carriage window. Philip caught him around the middle and pulled him to his side.

"No," Robin insisted, frowning. "Just me, Papa."

"John can ride Halcyon with me," Tom said, urging his golden-hued mount forward so he could take the younger boy. Then with a challenging grin, he gave his horse a nudge. "And we shall be at the castle before you both."

"Shall we let the traitors best us, Robin?" Philip asked.

Robin kicked his heels furiously against Alethia's withers. "Catch them, Papa."

Philip pulled up close to Tom, and both of them went up the hill-side at a careful canter, the boys squealing as one and then the other took the lead.

"Go, horse!" John shouted, yanking Halcyon's bright mane.

Robin kicked harder. "Faster! Faster!"

The castle gates stood expectantly open, and Tom and Philip made certain that both horses reached it at the same instant.

"We cannot deny we were fairly matched, Robin," Philip said, slowing Alethia to a walk. Then he noticed a brawny brown-eyed man of fifty coming down the castle steps into the courtyard. "My lord of Westered."

With a flash of a smile, Philip swung out of the saddle, and Westered dropped to one knee.

"You are welcome to Westered, your majesty."

"I'll not have you kneel to me, sir," Philip said, pulling him at once to his feet. "Surely not here at your own doorstep."

"You wear it still," Westered observed, noticing the scarred golden ring Philip wore on his right hand, in sharp contrast to the magnificent royal ruby he wore on his left.

"I wear it always, my lord," Philip replied, "a reminder of my Lord's faithfulness and yours."

Westered smiled and clasped his shoulders. "I am most pleased to have you, son, and you, my lord of Brenden."

"I thank you, my lord," Tom said, dismounting, too, and setting John on his feet. "Westered is as beautiful as I remember it."

"And who are these fine cavaliers you've brought for my army?" Westered asked, smiling at the boys.

Philip scooped Robin out of the saddle and then led him and John to their grandfather. "You'll scarce believe it, my lord," he confided, "but they are not from my elite horse guard."

"Then who might they be?" Westered bent down to study the boys more closely. "Are they perhaps Grenaven spies?"

John clung to his father's leg, suddenly shy, but Robin giggled. "No, Grandpapa. We are just Robin and John."

"No, faith, that cannot be!" Westered exclaimed. "Are you quite certain?"

Robin nodded vigorously. "And we are going to play in your sea."

"So you shall," Westered promised with another laugh.

Then the carriage pulled into the courtyard.

"Father!" Rosalynde cried, flinging open the door before the horses had even come to a full stop. She threw her arms around his neck, and he grabbed her up and spun her around.

"It has been much too long, sweetheart. Faith, I'd half forgotten what a beautiful thing you are."

Her eyes were moist, but she smiled. "But you've not seen the most beautiful thing." She leaned into the carriage and took the baby from Joan. "Your granddaughter Alyssa."

"Well, now," Westered said softly, looking at the baby's pink cheeks and the long dark lashes that rested on them. He pressed a tender kiss to his daughter's forehead. "It takes me back, sweetheart, it takes me back." Suddenly self-conscious, he cleared his throat. "Did you have a pleasant journey?"

"I feared we might never arrive."

"Trouble along the way?" he asked, his expression sobering as he studied Tom's bandaged wrist and scraped cheek.

"We had almost to turn back outside Briarpark," Philip told him, "but nothing came of it."

"Highwaymen?"

"A mere mishap, my lord," Tom said as he handed Elizabeth down from the carriage. "A pair of ruffians who I'll wager haven't spine enough to ever show their faces again. We're none of us the worse for it."

Elizabeth looked up at him, a shadow of uncertainty on her face, and he squeezed his arm around her.

"You've not met my lady," he told Westered.

The older man bowed deeply and kissed her hand. "Princess Elizabeth, you are most welcome." There was a warmth in his eyes that gave him a sudden resemblance to his daughter. "I trust you'll not be a stranger here long."

"You are kind, my lord, and her majesty has told me truly. Westered is a lovely place."

"You must see all of it, my lady," Westered told her. "Shall we go in?"

Robin quickly grabbed his grandfather's hand, but John was still clinging to Philip's leg, trying to hide behind him.

"Now, John—" Rosalynde began.

Westered winked at her. "Would you like to see what we have for you inside, John?" he asked.

John shook his head solemnly.

"Perhaps Robin would like to see."

"Is it a whale?" Robin asked, and Tom choked back a laugh, remembering both boys listening wide-eyed to his descriptions of the creatures that lived under the water.

"Not a whale," Westered replied. "We must keep those in the sea until we have a much larger castle. No, this is a little town with a cathedral and a castle and a fine house for the lord mayor all made of marchpane. Shall we go see it?"

Robin nodded eagerly, and Westered offered his other hand to John. "Will you come along, too?"

John looked at him uncertainly, still keeping hold of his father. "Might we eat it?"

"After you have had your supper, John, you may have the very first piece."

John looked up at his father and then at his mother. Then he took the hand Westered was holding out to him, and they all went into the castle.

The servants they had sent ahead had already arranged their things in the apartments they were to occupy for the summer, but Rosalynde only gave hers a quick glance before insisting that her husband accompany her elsewhere.

"This was mine," she said, showing him an airy tower chamber that viewed the sea on one side and the courtyard on the other. It was still as she had left it five years before.

"Come," she said, tugging his hand. "I must show you."

She pulled him to the window that overlooked the courtyard. "Do you remember?"

"Do I remember what?"

"Down there."

He looked down and then back at her, puzzlement on his face. "What, my lady?"

She stared into the courtyard with a disappointed sigh. "It has been almost ten years. I suppose it was such a slight thing . . ."

"You mean such a slight thing as a pair of fair green eyes and a sweet, innocent mouth and a glory of long dark hair bound in pink ribbon?"

She looked up at him, her pleasure putting sudden color in her cheeks. "You do remember."

"I remember thinking it a pity that the gentle sweetness I saw would not likely last till you reached sixteen." He smiled and slipped his arm around her waist. "But what would a boy of seventeen know of the ways of earthly angels?"

She pulled his other arm around her, too, and leaned back against him, looking once more into the courtyard. "I loved you from that very first moment when you and your brothers rode through the gates, when you looked up here just by chance and saw me watching you. Ankarette, my old nurse, said I was a foolish child to take such fancy from a mere glance, and I daresay I thought so, too, but it made no difference. I never did get over it."

He kissed the top of her head. "Would I had been so wise then, too, to know I would one day love you like this, but then perhaps I would never have realized just how truly you love me."

She turned to face him, still encircled in his arms. "But I would have loved you all the same."

"Would you? Or would you rather have had another?"

"You were ever my only choice, my lord. Ask my father if he did not have suits for my hand that I begged him not to hear."

He smiled. "Perhaps you would have me seventeen again before I was marked with war and my own foolishness. When I was truly the nonpareil you've always imagined me to be."

She touched the fine scar on his cheek and then kissed it. "You are just as I would have you, love." Suddenly uncertain, she toyed with a lock of his hair. "But you would have chosen differently had the choice been yours."

He held her tightly against him. "Sweet Rose, the past is dead. Who would bear with my arrogance and my temper and my stubbornness and love me still but you?"

"If you have the pride and the spirit and the tenacity of the royal blood of all the great kings of Lynaleigh that floods your veins, that is what goes into the making of Philip Chastelayne. I'd not recognize him without them, and, with or without them, I could not love him more."

"Oh, Rose," he said thickly, touching his finger to one delicately arched brow, "how did you come by those wondrous eyes that read the whole catalogue of my vices and see them all as virtues?"

"I merely invested a small quantity of love in the purchase of them, and I have been repaid it a hundredfold."

"Not enough," he replied. "Not enough."

"What would you do for me, my lord?"

"Anything," he swore immediately. "Everything."

She smiled. "More than enough."

They kissed again with growing passion. He pulled her up against him tighter and tighter, and then there was a thunder of little feet on the steps.

"Papa! Papa!"

The door flew open, and John and Robin threw themselves against his legs.

"Grandpapa showed us where the sea is!" Robin cried, and John tugged insistently at his father's hand.

"What?" Philip asked, still a little breathless.

"Grace catched a calipitter."

"A caterpillar?"

John nodded matter-of-factly. "And Mistress Joan made one of the soldiers take it away because it was nasty."

"I see," Philip said, feeling Rosalynde's silent laughter against him, trying not to laugh, too.

"We want to swim," Robin begged. "Please, Papa."

"Please, Papa," John repeated, hugging his arms around Philip's leg, looking up with his wide innocent eyes until Philip had to smile.

"Well, have Mistress Joan dress you for it, and I will come for you in a moment."

"Hurray!" the boys cheered, and they tore out of the room once more. From the corridor, Molly curtseyed and hurried after them.

"I suppose you must go now," Rosalynde said, laughing at his helpless expression.

He gave her a rueful kiss. "With those two about, it's a wonder we had opportunity to have a third."

"We will have more opportunity, my lord," she said with a subtle smile, and he kissed her one last time.

"I will take that as a promise."

HER DELICATE SKIN CAREFULLY SHADED FROM THE SUN, ROSALYNDE
sat on the beach with her sister-in-law watching their husbands and the two little boys play in the water and on the sand. She
noticed how the children were already beginning to show the sleek
litheness that marked them as Chastelaynes. Early June had brought
Robin's fourth birthday, and late July had brought John's third. It
amazed her how quickly they had ceased being babies, how rapidly
they had become little boys, and how soon they would be young
men.

They both had always shown definite signs of their father's daring, especially Robin, but she had been afraid when they had first
come down to the shore that they would be frightened by the wide
roar of the sea. Instead, they had both rushed eagerly into the surf
only to come up gasping with surprise to find it full of salt. That had
made Philip and Tom howl with laughter, but then they had both
gone into the water to watch after them. Now in these trailing days
of August, swimming was an almost-daily ritual, and the sun had
baked them all into bronze and left its golden traces in their dark
hair.

They made a handsome sight, all four of them sleek and spirited
young thoroughbreds playing on the beach with only their breeches
to distinguish them from the other wild things in the sky and in the
sea. Rosalynde's father had given the children a leather ball, and

today what had begun as a gentle game of catch had quickly turned into something a little more competitive.

"Here, John!" Tom shouted as he threw the ball, and Philip had to leap up to catch it.

"He's not yet seven feet tall, Tom," Philip replied, shooting it back.

"Me, Papa! Me!" Robin protested as it sailed over his head and hit Tom's bare chest with a resounding thud.

Tom drew back as if he would return the favor. Then he leaned down to his nephew and handed him the ball. "Throw it to John now, Robin, just as we showed you."

Robin hurled it with both hands and all his might, and it bounced to a stop a few feet away from his little brother.

"That's the way, son!" Philip cheered. "Get it, John."

"I can do it."

John scooped up the ball and tossed it along with a flurry of sand toward Tom and Robin. It stopped almost exactly between the two sides. There was an instant of hesitation. Then Tom and Philip both scrambled for it, with the boys scampering behind them. Tom reached it first.

"I was always fleeter than you."

Rosalynde laughed, watching him run into the surf with Philip lunging after him. Once it was past his waist, Tom dove into the water, and Philip tackled him and went under, too.

Elizabeth shook her head. "Do they never cease being boys?"

"I pray never," Rosalynde said, returning her smile. Seeing the children run into the water, too, she stood up. "Come back now, Robin. Come along, John. It is time for your supper."

"Please, Mama," Robin begged, glancing wistfully toward where his father and uncle were playfully trying to drown each other.

"Come along," she repeated. "The sea will be there tomorrow still."

Philip and Tom resurfaced, laughing and gasping, and noticed the children trudging back toward their mother.

"Must they, my lady?" Philip asked, still waist deep. "We've not finished our game."

"It seems to me that the children have been out of the game for the past half hour, my lord, but you and my lord of Brenden may play awhile longer if you like."

"My lady is most gracious," he said with a grin and a formal bow. Tom casually toppled him back into the water, starting the scuffle all over again.

Rosalynde smiled once more and took her two little boys by the hand to lead them away, but when Tom and Philip came up again for air, John broke away from her and ran back to his father.

"Help, Papa!" he cried, ignoring Rosalynde's calls. "Save me! Save me!"

Philip scooped him up. "Save you from what, mite?"

"Mistress Joan."

Tom grinned. "There was a time or two we wished that very thing, was there not, Philip?"

"Let me see, John," Philip considered, carrying the boy back to where his mother was waiting. "It cannot be you do not want your supper. Is it perhaps you know a bath comes after?"

John frowned mightily. "She will scrub my ears."

"Will she?" Philip commiserated. "Well, I shall speak to her, John. She'll not scrub your ears anymore, and when they've gathered enough dirt to sprout potatoes, we shall plant some."

"I do not want to sprout potatoes," John protested, clapping his hands to either side of his head.

"Then you had best let Mistress Joan do her scrubbing, and you had best tell your mama you are sorry you did not come when she called."

John looked up at her with the tiniest hint of a stubborn pout. Seeing that, Philip turned him upside down and held him securely by the ankles, making him shriek with laughter.

"Tell her, John."

"Sorry, Mama," he giggled, and Philip flipped him right side up again and dumped him on the sand.

"Much better."

"Let me, Papa," Robin insisted, trying to climb into his arms, and Philip obliged him.

"Look at the two of you," Rosalynde observed when both boys scrambled to their feet, "brown and naked as heathens."

"We're not naked, Mama," John insisted, tugging at his little wet breeches.

Robin looked up at her earnestly. "Papa is brown. Is he a heathen?"

Philip laughed.

"Your papa is one of our Lord's bravest and best knights, Robin," Rosalynde said, suppressing a smile. "You must try every day to be like him."

"Me, too, Mama?" John asked.

She squeezed his hand. "You, too, John. And when you are both grown into men, people will say, 'He is a fine king to have such fine sons,' and that will please him better than if they remember he has won great wars or built grand castles or even slain monstrous fire-breathing dragons."

The boys grinned and walked a little taller.

Smiling at her behind them, Philip shook his head. "You should not fill their heads with such nonsense, my love."

"It is not nonsense, my lord. It is meet that all boys should believe their fathers to be invincible and unparalleled."

"And when they are old enough to know that is not true?"

"So long as their fathers love them, they will carry the idea of it in their hearts anyway."

They climbed the steep, narrow path that led back up to the castle. Tom watched them for a moment, and then he reached down for Elizabeth's hand. "Shall we go in with them, Bess?"

"Will you not spend a moment with me alone?"

He stretched out on the sand beside her. "You should have come into the sea with us, love. It was beautiful today."

"It pleased me just to watch you all playing, my lord." She smiled wistfully. "Your brother must be well pleased with his lady for having given him such promise as she has in those children. Little wonder he loves her so."

"I trust he loves her for more than just that," Tom replied. "It would be unlike him to give his love in exchange for anything but love, no matter how dear the prize."

There was a touch of color in her cheeks as she looked up at him. "Unlike him or any true Chastelayne."

He kissed her hand, and she smiled again. Then she looked up toward the castle and saw that the others had almost reached the top of the path.

"Those two are like their father, sure. I see there's no hiding the Chastelayne blood."

"I suppose not," Tom agreed, watching her face.

"Are you ever sad because of them, my lord?" she asked.

He laughed softly. "No, love. Should I be?"

"Does it never put you in mind of the children we've lost?"

Again there was that wistfulness in her tone, in her dark, searching eyes.

"Sometimes," he admitted, stroking her cheek. "But it puts me more in mind of the ones we shall have."

She clung tightly to him, not caring that he was still dripping wet. "I will give you a child, Tom. I will."

He held her there, close and silent, until the sun sank into the sea. Bathed in moonlight, they climbed the path home together.

Philip spent the next morning hunting with his squire, and it was near noon when they rode back to Westered.

"Walk him awhile," Philip said, swinging from his saddle and tossing Jerome the reins. "Then see he's well curried."

"At once, my lord."

Philip started back into the castle. He noticed the pink roses that spilled over the top of the garden wall and decided he would take some to Rosalynde, certain they would win him a smile and a loving kiss. But he was certain, too, that even had he gone to her empty-handed, the smile and the kiss would have still been his.

Reaching the wall, he stretched up to pluck some of the fragrant blossoms. Then he paused, hearing the sweet, soft sound of singing from the other side. With the help of a nearby tree, he pulled himself up to look into the garden. Lady Marian was there cutting flowers, and he noticed Jerome leading Alethia toward the stable across the way.

The black horse whickered softly when the boy made an abrupt stop. Obviously Jerome heard the singing now, and obviously he knew the voice, too. The young man tightened his hold on the reins, looking determined to carry on with his task, but then she came into his sight, and he froze where he stood.

Her arms were laden with flowers, pink and white and red, violet and pale blue, accented with lush greenery, making a soft frame for her face. And still she was singing, sweetly unaware that she was being observed. Philip could not make out the words, not really, but he knew them from the tune. "'Gentle and silent, steadfast and true, love unspoken but with the eyes, untold but in the heart—'"

She broke off suddenly, realizing Jerome was there.

"My lady," he said, ducking his head so she could not see his flushed face. He jerked the reins and headed again toward the stables. "Come on, Alethia."

"Jerome?"

He stopped and did not turn to face her. "My lady?"

"I, uh—"

Finally he looked at her. "May I serve you, my lady?"

"The, uh, the flowers, Jerome. Will you help me take them to my lady's chamber?"

"Of course, my lady. I will." He looked around and saw one of the stable boys idling at the other end of the garden. "Here, Ned, come take his majesty's horse back to the stable."

The other boy obeyed him, grudgingly at first, and then, seeing Jerome's discomfort, with exasperating leisureliness. From his sheltered perch at the top of the wall, Philip laughed silently, seeing the second boy's fiendish delight in prolonging Jerome's agony.

"Now, Ned," Jerome growled. "My lady is waiting."

"Hardly your lady," Ned said half under his breath as he took the reins and sauntered off, chuckling to himself.

Jerome waited until he was gone, and then he went to Marian and took the flowers from her.

"They are very pretty, my lady," he said as she piled more blooms into his arms. "Her majesty should be pleased."

"The king has commanded that she be surrounded with flowers, at least while we have them here."

"Fair ladies should have such beauty always about them," he replied gallantly, and Philip grinned, hearing his own words repeated.

The young couple's eyes met briefly, and then Marian reached up to cut a heavily laden branch of wisteria.

"I have always favored these," she told Jerome. "They have such a fragrance."

She struggled with the branch, and he reached up abruptly to help her. Startled, she turned, and he jerked back with a yelp.

"Oh, Jerome, you are cut?"

"It is nothing, my lady."

"Let me see."

She took the flowers from him and laid them on the ground and cradled his hand in hers. It looked to Philip as if there was only a shallow cut across his fingers, but it was bleeding rapidly, filling Jerome's hand with blood.

"Here," she said, and she took her handkerchief from her sleeve and pressed it into his palm. He tried to pull away.

"My lady, you mustn't."

"It is merely a handkerchief, Jerome."

"But, my lady, it is something you have worked yourself."

"After I have caused you hurt, Jerome, is it not little enough?"

"But it will be ruined."

"You may throw it out, Jerome." She looked again into his eyes. "If it pains you so much to have something of mine."

He put his free hand under the soft one that still cradled his throbbing fingers.

"I thank you, my lady."

For a moment they were caught there in each other's eyes, and then she looked down and busied herself tying the cloth around his hand.

"You must forgive me this, Jerome, but I think you will soon be . . ."
She stopped there, caught again.

"My lady," he whispered.

She moved closer to him, lifting her face, not quite touching her lips to his. "Jerome."

He drew a quick breath and stepped back from her, scooping up the forgotten flowers.

"We mustn't let these wilt, my lady."

She blinked back tears. "Would it pain you so much, Jerome?"

"My lady, you know I must not."

She looked down at her hands, brushing away the dirt from the garden, lingering over a tiny smear of blood from his hand.

"It is because of my father, is it not, Jerome?"

"Yes, my lady, it is."

"Because he was a traitor to the king and had his lands taken from him."

"No, my lady. Rather because he was a baron, because your mother had a duke for her uncle, and because I do not even know who my parents were. That is why."

"Does that make you any more or less than who you are? Jerome, have we not known each other four years now? In all that time, I have yet to meet any man with a kinder heart or a gentler hand. Must you make me shame myself to say it first? I know it is hardly modest, but I will if you force me to it."

"Please, my lady, you must not. There can be nothing between us."

"The queen will be waiting for these," she said thickly, looking away again. "We had best go inside."

He followed her back into the castle, looking as if he were suddenly sickened by the fulsome, choking aroma of wisteria. Philip watched after them, saddened by the bleak turn the sweet innocence of their meeting had taken. He knew he should have at the very first slipped quietly away and left them alone, but there was something that had held him there, a remembrance that had caught at his heart and made him stay.

Before, he had scarcely noticed Jerome's attraction toward the girl, but now he saw that it was more than a boy's infatuation for a young lady hopelessly out of his sphere. This was something deep and meaningful, and it was not unrequited. It seemed a pity that only social convention kept them apart.

He sat there atop the wall for several minutes, considering what he had just overheard, remembering the sweet, rushing pangs of his own first love, remembering the opposition he had faced, understanding better than these two would have believed just how they felt.

He saw Jerome come from the castle and head toward the stables again. With sudden decision, he gathered an armful of roses and swung down from the wall. In another moment he was in the stable, too.

"Mind you do not take the hide off him, Jerome," he said, seeing the brusque strokes his squire was making with the brush he was using on Alethia.

"I must do what is expected of me," Jerome said in tight-lipped frustration. "I beg your pardon, my lord."

"I fear it is I who must beg yours," Philip replied.

The currying stopped. "My pardon, my lord?"

"Beautiful, are they not?" Philip commented, showing the roses. "You can see them from outside the west wall of the garden, and there is a little tree there that a man might climb if he wished to gather some for his lady."

"Yes, my lord?"

"From atop that wall, you have plain view of the whole garden, Jerome, and can hear most everything that's said beneath the large wisteria that grows alongside the rosebush."

Jerome's eyes widened. Then he looked down. "Your majesty heard what was said between the Lady Marian and myself."

"I do truly ask your pardon, Jerome. I should have made my presence there known, but by the time I realized the turn the conversation was taking, it was too late. It seems the lady cares for you a great deal."

"Perhaps so, my lord, but that is foolishness in her. She deserves better than to throw herself away on the likes of me."

"So you do not return her affection?"

Jerome turned back to his task, beginning again the taut, rigorous strokes, making Alethia shift restlessly.

"It is no matter what I feel for her, my lord," he muttered. "I have nothing to offer a lady of her quality by way of marriage. I've no wealth, no title, not even a fine appearance to commend me."

"Those things are of little importance, Jerome, weighed against true love."

"Pardon my bluntness, my lord, but I should think it easy for your majesty to say so, yourself having always had all that and in abundance."

"A mixed blessing at best," Philip assured him, "and brief as the flash of a firefly."

"If it were I who was of the nobility and she no more than a peasant, I could marry her and hang the gossips."

Philip smiled. "But you are too proud for her, is it?"

"Not too proud, my lord, but too humble."

"If she does not believe it so, should you? Ask her."

Jerome laughed, startled. "My lord?"

"Ask her, Jerome. If she loves you, she'll not refuse you."

"She is a lady, my lord, descended of the Chastelaynes. I could never presume—"

"Not everyone of noble blood has so mercenary a heart as you might think. Were you to ask her, you might find how little she values such things." He smiled, remembering a fragile sweetness long past. "Ask her."

"I could not, my lord. It would only mean condemning her to a life of lowliness, far below what she was born to know."

"So you would rather have her shamed to believe it was her father's treason that makes you deny her?"

"No, my lord, and I told her so."

"It seems strange to think it now, but had her father and my father had their way about it, she would be queen."

"You were to marry her?" Jerome asked, surprised.

"It was urged, but I refused." Philip smiled at his squire's indignation. "She was but fourteen at the time, Jerome, and I was already in love with another, but truly of all those my father gave me to choose from, had I been forced to it, I would have chosen her. Even then I saw what a sweet-spirited lady she was and how easily hurt.

Go to her, Jerome. Comfort her. We must learn to be gentle with the tender hearts that love us."

"But your majesty's horse—"

"I will see to him," Philip insisted. Taking the brush from him, he pressed the flowers into the boy's arms. "Give her these."

"But those are her majesty's."

"You've helped gather her an entire room full just now. She'll not miss these."

"But, my lord—"

"Must I make it a command, boy?" Philip asked, and with an uncertain, grateful smile, Jerome obeyed.

⁂

"You've known all along," Philip accused when Rosalynde lay cuddled against him that night. "That was why you insisted Lady Marian come along—not this nonsense about your tapestry."

"You must be the only one in all the court who did not know it ages ago," she replied laughing. "They are sweet, are they not?"

"They are both fools, both to let their pride be master over their love. I had to come near to ordering him to take her some flowers this afternoon."

"I saw him bring them," Rosalynde said, "and she wept over them once he'd gone. Poor girl—she is such a meek thing anyway, and it does not help that she still feels shamed for what her father did."

"I never held her to fault for that, Rose—you know I did not."

"I know."

"Faith, neither of them has anything to call his own save love, and that is all either of them wants from the other. With both of them living at court, he need not worry how he'll provide for her. I see no bar to this at all save pride, and love is too rare a thing in this world to be wasted on that."

"That is a lesson some learn with more ease than others, my lord," she said coyly.

Laughing, he put out the candle. "I may be slow to learn, sweetheart," he admitted, holding her close again, "but once I've conned a lesson, I do not easily forget."

"I am so very glad," she whispered.

As she and her ladies worked at the tapestry the next day, weaving the vivid threads into intricate patterns, Rosalynde considered what might be done to bring the young lovers together. Marian talked less and less and sighed more and more as the day went on, and Rosalynde hurt for her. But then a thought came to Rosalynde, and she could not feel sad any longer.

When the sun began to set, she stopped her work and went to tell her husband her idea. Told he had gone to walk alone at the shore, she decided she would go swim with him as she often did once the evening had come and the sun could no longer burn her fair skin. She shed her clothing down to her shift and, donning her cloak, went down to the beach.

She found him there, eyes closed, head thrown back, lying beneath the water that fell, white and rushing, down the sheer cliff. It bounced in a rainbow spray off the smooth rocks and off his bronzed flesh, bubbling into the deep pool at his feet only to be lost in the whirling flow of the sea. This reminded her of when she had first come to his father's court, when they were near strangers to be married the very next day, when she was half afraid to feel what she had felt at the unexpected sight of him standing there only carelessly dressed, with water running down his bare chest and slicked through his dark hair. Now the quickening in her breath had nothing to do with fear.

"My lord?"

He opened his eyes, and she was suddenly aware of the startling blueness of them against his tanned skin, as startling as the flashing whiteness of his smile. He held out his hand.

"Come sit with me, Rose."

Without a word, she stepped out of her cloak and walked into the pool, her eyes fixed on him until the water closed over her. There was a moment of rippleless stillness, and she rose up on the other side, her dark hair falling in long wet ringlets over her shoulders, down her back, clinging like her shift to her delicate rose and cream flesh.

"Daughter of the ocean," he said, the sinking sun behind her dazzling his eyes as she stood, dripping, over him. He got up on his knees there in the sand and reached out to brush the droplets of seawater from her cheek.

"I think there was a glimmer of moonlight once kissed the crest of a wave, and you were born of that union. Surely no common mingling of man and woman could have brought about such perfection."

Her lips curved into a soft smile. "Uncommon indeed when my plain-soldier Philip waxes poetical."

He put his hands around her waist, drawing her just the tiniest bit closer. "Such beauty breeds poetry, fair lady."

"Flatterer," she accused, and he drew her even closer.

"Why have you come here then, if not to be flattered?"

"To ask a boon of you, my lord."

He smiled indulgently. "What could the queen of all the seas ask of me that I'd not grant?"

"Give Lady Marian back her father's lands."

"Just that?" he asked. "Shall I not give her a dram of poison for her wine as well?"

"My lord?"

"Now do not have that vexed look, sweeting. Do you think I've not considered this before? She is long due those lands back, and I do not begrudge them to her, but if Jerome feels unworthy of her when she has nothing, what might he feel if she were suddenly to have all the holdings that belong to her nobility?" He touched his lips to hers. "Surely so tender a heart as yours can see that she had a thousand times rather have him than any quantity of land."

"Perhaps you are right," she said, threading her fingers through his wet hair. "Though I never saw so unlikely a matchmaker."

"Nor I so fair a water sprite."

Cupping his face in her hands, she bent down to kiss his mouth, and he drew her yet closer, his lips moving slowly to her throat. She arched her neck and wrapped her slender bare arms around him, holding him there.

"Sweet love," she breathed. Her sigh turned into a gasp as she felt a clammy, wet hand grip her bare ankle. Immediately Philip pulled her free of that hand, and its owner seized his wrists instead.

"Help us," the half-drowned man wheezed. Rosalynde noticed the frayed rope knotted around his waist. Looking out to sea, she saw the other end of it was tied to a small boat. As best she could tell, the boat was empty.

Philip tried for a moment to undo the sodden knot, and then leaving enough slack for the man, he hauled the boat in, wading out to it when it was close enough to drag onto the shore. She saw his face change when he looked into it, but he merely looped the rope around a heavy piece of driftwood and came back to them.

"What is it, my lord?" she asked.

He shook his head. "Nothing."

The man looked pleadingly into his eyes, and with a touch of pity, Philip again shook his head. The man turned his face to the sand with one desolate sob and breathed no more.

"Go back inside," Philip said after a moment, his voice unaccountably stern.

"But who is he? Where has he come from?"

"We will likely never know that," he told her, turning her away from the sea. "Go in now. Send back some of your father's men to see to him. I will stay until they come." He squeezed her arm, his expression softening. "Please, love."

She climbed the path back up to the castle, but when she glanced again toward the beach, she saw him there on his knees beside the man, his head bowed and his fists helplessly clenched.

ROSALYNDE WATCHED HER HUSBAND THAT NIGHT AT SUPPER, expecting him to be in a somber mood after the sorrowful events of the afternoon. However, he seemed in high spirits, giving her father an eager description of the new broadsword he was having made, feigning fierce contention with his brother over the last of the quail, and, with Tom's help, flirting outrageously with a pair of elderly dowagers, widows of two of Westered's knights. For Rosalynde herself, he smiled frequently, calling her his turtledove, urging her to be merry, insisting after the meal was over that she dance with him to every light tune the minstrels played. He had forbidden them anything in a minor key.

When they finally retired for the evening, she was exhausted, wishing she had gone to bed long before midnight rather than now, long after, but he had coaxed her again and again to dance one more, and then one more. It was unlike him to be the last to leave the great hall.

She was not surprised to find that her ladies had already gone to their beds, but he would not allow her to wake them to ready her for hers.

"Let me, sweet," he told her, sitting her before her glass so he could take down her hair. This was something he had done often in the past five years, and she leaned back against him now, content to have him do it yet again.

"It could never have come about by common chance," he said as he brushed the thick coils into a dark, shimmering cascade.

She picked up her silver-backed mirror, delicately enameled with white saint's rose and her initial, and he bent down to kiss her temple.

"Such beauty, my lady. It had to have been extraordinarily engineered."

"So you said," she replied, watching his reflection. "This afternoon."

Abruptly he turned his attention to the laces down the back of her pearl-trimmed burgundy gown. "Then I must have meant it."

She laid the small mirror down again. "Will you not tell me, my lord?"

He did not look up. "What, sweeting?"

"About that man on the beach. What was in that boat? Or perhaps I should ask who."

"Come, my lady, why should you think—"

"He said, 'help us,' my lord, not 'help me.' There was someone else in that boat. Someone who also did not survive."

He nodded, sobering. "You mustn't let it grieve you, love. After such exposure and starvation, there was nothing to be done for them. She had been dead at least since morning."

"She? Was it his wife, do you think?"

"I fear so," he replied.

She read something else in his eyes. "Was she the only one, my lord?"

"Have we not had enough of this, Rose? It is past helping now."

She pressed her hands to her heart. "There were children as well. Oh, I am glad I did not see."

"Would I had not," he said softly, and she reached back to take his hand. He smiled and brought her fingers to his lips. "But it has been seen to, and there is no more to be done. We must let it pass now."

He slipped her dress down off her shoulders, and she leaned back against him once more.

"Did they come from Reghed, my lord?"

"Why do you say that?" he asked, stopping again.

"Because there is no place north of Westered where they might have stopped save Reghed, and they would have stopped there had that not been the place from which they had fled."

He stood silent for a moment, absently fingering the lace that edged her shift. "I expect that's so," he said finally. "I know of few places more afflicted."

"Is there nothing we might do for them, my lord? Not for those poor souls today, but for all those left behind them?"

"But there are wretched people everywhere, Rose. Did not our Lord Himself say we would always have the poor with us? Even were I to give all I had to ease their suffering, would there not be still more left in misery?"

"We cannot help them all, my lord, but we can help some. Reghed is our neighbor. Surely—"

"Are there not enough of our own people in need? Should we not first see them cared for?"

"We are doing what can be done," she said, surprised by the brief harshness in his tone, "and they are learning to care for one another. Should not someone give such hope to the people of Reghed?"

His expression lightening, he pushed her hair to one side and kissed the back of her neck. "Come, love," he coaxed. "Can we not let matters of state rest for this one night?"

"Not a matter of state, my lord, but of Christian charity. Surely—"

"I will think on it, sweet," he said, pulling her close so he could nibble her ear. "But not just now."

She did not resist him, but there was still worry in her expression and more that she could not hide—disappointment. Their eyes met again in the glass.

He took a step back from her. "If you are angry with me, my lady, you need only tell me so. I have never been one to press an unwelcome attention."

She turned in her chair and crushed herself into his arms. "No, love, no. You are never unwelcome. It is only that I can see this troubles you more than you admit."

He hugged her tightly and then turned her face up to him. "You are a sweet thing, love, truly, but I think I've kept you up far too late talking here. In the morning you will see such worries have no more substance than the night mists."

He kissed her nose and lifted her into his arms, letting her dress sink into a billowing wine-colored drift around her chair. Once he had settled her in the bed, he bent down to kiss her once more.

"Go to sleep, sweetheart. I forbid you to fret over anything more momentous than which gown you shall wear to supper tomorrow."

"But, my lord—"

"I shall write it into law, my lady, if need be. 'The queen shall not be allowed under any circumstances to fret, bother, worry, or trouble herself over any matter so inconsequential as the king.' Now go to sleep. I will be back soon."

She sat up. "You are not coming to bed?"

He smiled again, but she could see that he was somehow uncomfortable with the idea of sleep, something she had noticed in him from time to time for several months now.

"I must see to the sentries, love," he said, "and some other trivialities I should have attended to earlier. I'll not be long."

She felt him get into bed beside her much later that night, but he did not answer when she whispered his name. She could not tell if he was already asleep or merely wanting her to believe he was.

Summer cooled into autumn, and no more tragedy marred the long, drowsy days by the sea. Philip seemed to have put the incident on the beach quickly behind him, and if upon occasion Rosalynde woke in the middle of the night to find him lying awake beside her, she had no way to disprove his claims that it was her restlessness that had broken his sleep. And if that was frequently followed by a playful bout of tickling or a passionate embrace, perhaps both, she had no complaint.

More often than not, though, after hunting and swimming and riding, after playing with the children and seeing to the court matters that were brought to him from Winton, sleep took him the moment he closed his eyes, and only Rafe's arrival with breakfast each morning woke him again. Sometimes she wondered if he purposed to do just that, to exhaust each day's energies so there would be no room for anything but oblivion at night, but perhaps that was taking her misgivings too far. Prayer was a far more productive practice than worry in any event, so she prayed for his peace and, remembering still, prayed that God would send relief to the people of Reghed. Perhaps when they returned home, she would be able to convince her husband to at least consider taking part in that relief.

She knew they would be returning soon. The last day of September would mark her twenty-fifth birthday. Philip had told her they would have to leave for Winton shortly after, to have the children safely home when winter arrived, but before that he meant to spare neither time nor effort nor expense in preparing a magnificent celebration in her honor. Among the festivities he had ordered, besides the musicians and the actors and the trained bears, was a great tournament, a test of arms for the nobility and a grand spectacle for all the people. She looked forward to it despite the touch of sadness she felt at the prospect of leaving this place and her father, both dearly loved.

The dawning of the great day was a celebration all its own. The sky was clear, and the golden autumn sun shone warm and bright on the lists, filling the air with the smell of sweat and sawdust. The people milled about restlessly, bored with watching the squires practicing with the quintains, eager to see the jousting. Soon a brassy fanfare split the air, and the hum of the crowd grew louder.

Dressed in the royal white, Philip and Rosalynde rode in procession across the field with Elizabeth and Westered and all of the brightly dressed courtiers strung like beads behind them. An exultant swell of cheering engulfing them all. The people quieted as the king and queen took their seats on the platform and the warder held up one hand.

"His majesty, King Philip, is pleased to announce that in archery, fencing, and jousting, he and his royal brother, Lord Thomas of Brenden, will take on those deemed best at each of these, to try their strength and prove the honor of Chastelayne, and in tribute to our fair Queen Rosalynde upon the anniversary of her birth."

The silence erupted again into cheers at the news and at the appearance of the combatants at the far side of the field. Tom was at their head, dressed also in white, riding proudly toward the king, smiling at Elizabeth as she sat beside the queen, showered with rose petals and kisses from the ladies. When they halted before the platform, Philip stood and raised Rosalynde to her feet beside him.

"Knights of Westered," she said, "I charge you in the name of our Lord to fight with all honor and true chivalry." A smile touched her lips. "And for the sake of your ladies, bear in mind you do but fight today in sport."

The people laughed, and Philip kissed her hand.

"In sport then, my people," he shouted eagerly. "Let the tournament begin!"

The first event was archery, and none of the contestants could touch the royal brothers save one wizened old knight who seemed not to even look at the target before he let fly, but who hit true every time. He bested Philip and only very narrowly lost to Tom on the final shot.

"Soundly done, Sir Harold," Tom said, offering the man his hand. "Your years serve you well."

Philip nodded. "Should you ever come to Winton, man, I could use you in the training of my soldiers."

The old knight displayed an almost-toothless grin. "Merely give them all seventy years' practice, your majesty, and they will be just as able."

Tom laughed and went to stand before the queen, surprised and pleased to see that she had passed to his wife the privilege of awarding the prize.

Elizabeth declared him the champion archer of the day and hung the victor's ribbon around his neck. Then she leaned down to give him the traditional kiss on the cheek.

"I am so pleased you won, my lord," she whispered. "Sir Harold smells awfully of fish."

Smiling, he shook his head, and the warder announced the beginning of the fencing.

"Wish me well, love," he said. Taking another quick kiss, he went back into the field. It was not long before he and Philip had defeated all of their challengers and stood facing each other.

"I daresay you'll better me today, my liege," Tom said, the mischief in his eyes making it obvious that he did not believe it.

Philip grinned. "I daresay I'll try."

They began slowly but soon picked up the pace, their hours of practice together giving their swift strokes a fluid grace. They talked and laughed as they fought, their words coming in time to the rhythmed clang of their blades. They were skillful and well matched, but the people were never content with a simple test of swordsmanship.

"They fight like children," someone called from the crowd.

Tom gave his brother a knowing look, and Philip raised one cautioning eyebrow. Tom returned an almost-imperceptible sly smile and began driving him back with a series of quick, aggressive strokes. Looking surprised, Philip countered awkwardly and then took a wild swing, missing Tom's ear by a hair. Tom laughed.

"You're lost, Philip. You were ever a poor match at best."

"You forget your place, my lord of Brenden," Philip replied with a cold, dangerous smile and a savage flurry of blows.

Again Tom laughed. "Is that your best then, my liege?"

He slashed at his brother's arm, ripping through his sleeve, and a look of towering rage crossed Philip's face.

"Dare you?" Philip shouted, redoubling his strokes. "If you wish to fight in earnest, I'm for you."

"If you think yourself man enough, come on."

After that, the only sound was the swift ringing of their swords and their labored breathing over the silence of the wide-eyed crowd. Back and forth they fought, first Philip, then Tom, then Philip again on the defense. Finally, Philip made a desperate, sweeping slash at his brother. Tom clutched his middle, his gasp echoed by the crowd as they leapt to their feet.

"Tom?"

Philip looked on in shock as Tom fell headlong to the ground, his sword still grasped in his outstretched hand. Rosalynde and

Elizabeth sat with their eyes fixed on the the their husbands. Stunned, Westered watched, too, as the warders began running onto the field.

Philip knelt at his brother's side. "Tom?"

He started to roll him over, but like lightning Tom jumped up and put his sword to Philip's throat. Immediately, Philip dropped his own weapon and held up both hands.

"I yield."

Tom handed his blade back to him, and the two of them traded wicked smiles. The people laughed in relief and then cheered, thinking it grand sport. The warders went sheepishly back to their posts, and Westered looked down on the brothers, an uncertain mixture of reproof, relief, and amusement on his face. Philip and Tom grinned at the crowd, bowed to their host, and took their seats on the platform, still engulfed in cheers.

"You're a fine pair," Westered observed, "but you brought them to their feet with that and, I daresay, stopped a few hearts as well."

Rosalynde shook her head. "They nearly frightened us all to death with that trick at the tournament in Winton last year."

"You loved it," Philip said, snatching a quick kiss from her.

Westered laughed. "As did they, son, truly, but you've spoiled the wagering now. No one won."

"They can win their money on the jousting, my lord," Tom told him. Then he elbowed his brother's ribs. "When one of your squires unhorses the king."

"That will be never," Philip returned. "And it's for certain you'll not be doing it."

"What say you, Bess?" Tom asked lightly. "Can I not—"

He stopped at the stricken look on her face.

"Bess?"

Covering her mouth with both hands, she bolted from the platform, and he sprinted after her. She did not stop until she reached the back of one of the armorer's tents. Then she almost collapsed against it, weeping hysterically, still with her hands pressed to her mouth, looking as if she might be sick.

"What is it, love?" he asked, trying to take her into his arms, but she would not allow it.

"How could you play at such a thing, my lord," she sobbed, refusing to look at him, "when you knew I was watching?"

"Forgive me, sweetheart. I thought surely you would know it was only sport. After the tournament last year. Play for play, it was the same. Surely you knew."

"Last year you told me of it beforehand! I thought perhaps this was the same; then I feared it was not. You do it far too well, and after I almost lost you—"

She was seized with a fit of rapid hiccoughs, and he held her tightly against him until they passed.

"It is all right, love," he soothed, relieved to feel her calming. He turned her face up to him and kissed her wet cheek. "Forgive me?"

She nodded and then giggled when one last hiccough escaped her. With a grin, he kissed her other cheek.

"Will it please you, sweet, if I do not enter the jousting today? I know you've always worried—"

She threw her arms around his neck. "Oh, Tom, would you? Just today."

He hugged her close. "Very well, my lady, today I watch."

Philip was disappointed to hear that his brother would not be entering the lists that day. Tom was always his best opponent at anything and kept his skills honed razor-sharp. Still he found a good match in a red-clad knight from the north of Westered, a local champion.

"At your pleasure, sir knight" Philip called to his opponent, the last remaining.

A moment later the red knight was on the ground, and Philip felt the exultant rush of triumph as he galloped past. He turned his horse and rode back to the gallery, oblivious to the praises and the roses the people showered on him, seeking the favor of only one. Rosalynde stood holding to the railing in front of her, her anxiety almost overshadowed now by proud, breathless admiration.

Their eyes met. Then, satisfied, he dismounted and gathered the flowers into his arms, acknowledging the people with a brilliant smile.

"I thank you. I thank you all. I see you people of Westered follow your lord in gracious kindness and hospitality. I am much bounden to you all for that, but I did not fight today for my own glory, nor for the honor of Lynaleigh, nor for any such petty cause. This day's victory, together with my heart, belongs to another."

Rosalynde smiled down on him as he approached the platform and presented the flowers to her, his voice growing soft and tender. "To my sweet queen, my lady, my love." He reached up and took her hand and brought it to his lips. "My Rose."

A glow of love in her eyes, she leaned over the railing. He stretched up to her, and their lips met over the fragrant armful of roses she held. The people shouted their approval once more. Still holding her hand, he turned again to the crowd.

"This is truly Westered's greatest treasure, and I thank all Westered for the gift of her. I thank most especially—" He paused and looked up at Rosalynde. "Where is your father, love?"

"Will you take one last challenger, your majesty?"

There across the field was Lord James mounted on a sturdy dappled gray, fully armed, lance at the ready. Philip took a step toward him, eager to meet the challenge until he saw the disapproval in Rosalynde's expression.

"I beg you, pardon me, my lord," he said lightly. "It would scarce be an even match."

"You think me too old for you, boy?"

"Not so, my lord." Philip held up his hands in smiling surrender. "I merely had rather not be put to shame before my subjects, opposite a man of such great experience in the tournament and in battle."

Westered grinned at him. "You've played politics too long, boy, when such flattery comes so easy."

Rosalynde shaded her eyes against the low afternoon sun. "Father, truly, you ought not—"

"You may be my queen, sweetheart," he interrupted, "but I am still your father and not yet in my grave."

With a murmur of impatience, she leaned down again to Philip. "Please, my lord, he ought to have given this up years ago."

"But if it pleases him, love—"

"Humor an old man, your majesty," Westered called to him.

"And I will show you how it was done when I was young, when there were still true warriors in the world."

"I will be easy with him," Philip told Rosalynde softly, and he smiled again at her father. "Come then, my lord."

Westered lowered his visor and leveled his lance. "At your pleasure, your majesty."

Philip winked at his wife, then mounted his horse, and nodded to the warder.

"Upon my signal, your majesty, my lord," the warder said. Then he dropped his hand, and the two combatants thundered toward each other. An instant later Philip's riderless horse was slowing to a walk at the far side of the field.

"Well hit, my lord!" Tom shouted, clapping his hands as Westered pulled up in front of him.

"Truly," Philip agreed, smiling ruefully as he struggled, breathless, to his feet. "And that was how it was done when you were young?"

"It was, your majesty," Westered said with a sly grin. "Would you have it shown you again?"

Tom laughed and Philip nodded, a gleam of competitive determination suddenly in his eyes. "I would."

"I expect you'll still be wanting to do such things thirty years from now, my lord," Elizabeth said anxiously.

Tom put his arm around her waist. "You must be a speedy worrier, Bess, to have already used up everything else that might possibly trouble you from this time till that and have nothing left but something so far off to fret over."

That teased a slight smile from her, but she pressed closer to his side as they watched one of the grooms lead the king's horse back to him.

"Once more, my lord," Philip called to Westered, mounting again.

"Yes, show him once more, my lord," Tom said, "and just that way."

"Rattle on, Tom," Philip replied as he moved back into position, "and you shall have the next lesson."

"Each of the three of you is worse than the other two," Rosalynde said, shaking her head, and Tom laughed again.

"Upon my signal, my lords," the warder said, holding up his

hand. Philip gripped his lance more tightly, tensing, waiting. Then the warder gave the sign.

Philip spurred his horse, hurtling toward his opponent, stiffening his back in anticipation of the impact. His lance caught Westered's shield dead center, hurling the older man to the ground before it splintered. Philip lifted his hand in triumph, acknowledging the cheers of the people as he rode to the end of the field. It was not until he turned to ride back that he saw that Westered was still on the ground, struggling unsuccessfully to get up.

"My lord?"

Philip cantered up to him and swung off his horse just as Rosalynde reached Westered's side, pushing through the crowd that was already surrounding him.

"Oh, Father," she scolded worriedly. "What have you done now?"

Philip knelt down beside them and eased off her father's helmet. Rosalynde pulled off his gauntlets so she could hold his hands.

"Are you hurt, sir?" Philip asked.

Westered laughed, then grimaced. "I've taken that fall a thousand times since my first tournament, and every time I've walked away."

He tried once more to stand and then fell back with a groan, clutching his thigh. Philip looked guiltily at Rosalynde and again at her father. "Believe me, sir, I would not for all the world have had you hurt opposite me."

"Pure mischance, son," Westered said lightly, "nothing that ought to grieve you. Any man who takes up a lance, even in sport, runs that risk, and this surely is nothing that will not mend."

A few minutes later, the physician arrived. Under his direction, Westered's serving men lifted their master onto a stretcher and carried him off the field.

"I am sorry, sweet," Philip said when he was gone. Rosalynde looked up at him, her mouth tight with annoyance.

"Truly I am," he said.

She could not resist a smile at his contrite expression. "I know, love." She wiped away a trickle of sweat from his temple, then caressed his cheek. "And he is right. It might as easily have been you or anyone."

"It was my wretched pride again," he said, a flash of anger in his eyes. "I simply had to prove I could take him."

"I think there was more than a little pride on both sides of that match, my lord."

"And you the only sensible one in the lot." He closed his eyes and pushed his fingers through his damp hair. "Thank God I did not kill him."

"Now it is not nearly so bad as that," she said, squeezing his hand. "He will mend and be none the wiser the next time."

He laughed and led her off to see to her father.

"You should have let me go down and see how badly he is hurt, Bess," Tom said, watching them walk away.

Elizabeth held his arm more tightly. "No. It is bad luck. If you come near it, it will only light upon you."

"Nonsense. Love, you cannot stop living for fear of what might be. It is a terrible waste."

"I know, my lord, truly I do, but were I to lose you now—"

"Little chance of that, sweeting," he said, holding her close.

She stiffened against him. "My lord, let me go."

"Come now, sweet, you know there is no need to—"

"Let me go, Tom!"

She wrenched away from him and disappeared again behind the tents. When he found her, she one hand on her stomach and the other covering her mouth, and he realized she had been sick.

"Oh, Bess, you should have told me you were ill. I would have taken you back to your chamber and had Livrette see to you. Why did you not let me know of it?"

She was too ashamed to look up at him. "It is nothing, my lord. Sometimes the excitement and the heat take me unawares."

"You cannot blame the heat, Bess. It is near October, and in any case—"

Without warning, she wilted against him, and he caught her up in his arms.

"Bess, what is it?"

"Do not be angry with me, my lord," she pled, dropping her head weakly to his shoulder. "I've been so afraid to tell you."

⁂

Philip and Rosalynde were sitting alone in the garden that evening, enjoying the twilight, when Tom interrupted the silence. "May I have a word with you both for a moment?"

"Always," Philip replied. "Come, sit."

"My lady," Tom said, bowing briefly before the queen. Then he sat beside her. "How is your father, my lady?"

"He will be well again soon, the physicians tell me. Pity they cannot cure foolhardiness."

"I need to ask his favor in something, my lady, but him being hurt just today, I did not think now a fitting time. Do you think he would object if my lady and I stayed on here until spring?"

"Until spring?" Philip laughed. "Faith, Tom, whatever for? You cannot mean to leave me to face the court alone all the winter long."

"I fear I must," Tom said. "Livrette said it would be best, and Joan claims so, too."

"Joan? You mean . . ."

Tom nodded, and a uncertain smile softened his anxious expression. "My lady is with child again."

Rosalynde squeezed his hand. "Oh, my lord, I am so happy for you both. When shall it be?"

"They think sometime in February, likely early in the month. But because of what has happened before, they think it best she should not take the journey back to Winton, and even staying here, she should keep to her bed."

"She is well now?" Rosalynde asked.

Tom nodded, smiling slightly more. "Only a trifle indisposed from time to time."

"Of course you are welcome to stay here," she said. "I am certain I can speak for my father in that, or, if you had rather, you may speak to him yourself in the morning. I am only sorry I must leave him now he's hurt."

"Would it please you, love, if we were to let the court keep itself until spring and stay ourselves?" Philip asked.

She threw her arms around his neck in delighted surprise. "Oh, my lord, might we? Of all the lovely gifts you've given me for my birthday, that would be the very best."

"I could be convinced," he replied. "With the right persuasion."

She kissed him happily, and he smiled, too.

"I will send word to Winton."

"Do you think you ought, Philip?" Tom asked. "You've been gone a great while already, and to add so many months to that—"

"Lord Darlington has managed the court famously without me thus far. I daresay he can a while longer. Besides, we still have messengers. It is not as if we were at war or had some great question of law to ponder, and I do owe my lady's father to look after his affairs for him while he is mending." Philip put one arm around his brother's shoulders. "You've been with me when my children were born, Tom. I'd not leave you alone for yours for all the world."

Tom drew a deep breath. "I must confess it worries me some, but, pray God, if I can keep my lady from believing everything she sees is an omen of ill-fortune, we shall have a child to present to the court come spring."

Rosalynde squeezed his hand again. "We shall pray it be so."

AS HIS FATHER-IN-LAW'S LEG HEALED, PHILIP TURNED HIS energies to the administering of the dukedom.

"You hardly even speak to me these days, my lord," Rosalynde told him when the last of Westered's clerks had bowed out of the library and Philip was left to review their accounts.

"As I remember," he said, not looking up from the figures he was checking, "I gave you my full attention just last night."

He jotted down the correct total and then gave her a significant glance.

She responded with a blush and a smile. "But you said very little."

He laughed and turned to the next page of the ledger.

"We may as well be in Winton again, my lord, if you're to work so hard every day."

"I've spoilt you with all this leisure, have I, Rose? You know it's not taken so very much of my time here." He pulled her down onto his lap. "I've not complained when you're at your everlasting tapestry, have I?"

"The everlasting tapestry is practically finished."

"When am I to see it then?"

"In time, my lord."

"Will you not at the least tell me what the thing's to be?"

"Of course, my lord."

"Well?"

She brought her mouth close to his ear and dropped her voice to a whisper. "What it is to be, my lord, is a surprise."

"Away with you, minx," he said, dumping her off his lap. With a giggle she ran to the door and threw it open just in time to have John fling himself against her skirts.

"Mama!" he cried.

She picked him up. "What are you doing here, John? I thought you and Robin were having your naps."

Rafe came into the room holding Robin firmly by the hand.

"Mistress Joan sent me to look for them, my lady," Rafe explained. "She'd set one of my lord of Westered's girls to watch them while she bathed the baby, and the silly creature fell asleep. I found the boys out in the stables trying to climb up on his majesty's horse."

Philip laid down his quill. "Is that so, Robin?"

"I took John to see the pony," Robin answered nonchalantly.

"Alethia is not a pony, Robin. He is a horse, very big and strong, which must be handled by men and not by children. I've told you this before, have I not?"

"I know how to make him be good," Robin assured him. "He likes carrots."

Philip did not smile. "You've both disobeyed me today. Bring John to me, my lady."

"No, Mama," John pled, but Rosalynde set him down at Philip's feet, her face as unyielding as his.

"Not this time, John," she said. "You must be taught to obey."

"I am sorry, Papa," he said penitently, but his father's expression did not soften either.

"Your mother is right. You both must be taught to obey. You know you're not to leave Mistress Joan. I thought we had an agreement, John."

John nodded, looking ashamed.

"And what was it?"

"That I was to have a punishmit if I runned away from Mistress Joan again."

"And, Robin, you pledged me you'd not go to the stables alone."

Philip saw himself in the stubborn tightness in his eldest son's mouth, in the flash of defiance in his eyes.

"I wanted to see the pony."

"And I said you must wait until I could take you, did I not?"

Robin sullenly answered nothing.

"Robin?"

"Yes."

"You both are princes, with all the honor of the Chastelayne blood, and a Chastelayne prince must never be false to his word. You shall not find me false to mine. Come here, John."

Philip turned the boy over his knee and gave him two quick swats, just enough to be felt through his sturdy breeches, and then stood him up again.

"I'm s-sorry, Papa," John sobbed.

Philip gently brushed a tear from his cheek. "So am I, mite, and I should be sorrier to have to punish you again or to know you had been hurt because you disobeyed me."

Rosalynde took John by the hand, and he leaned up tightly against her, wiping his nose with the back of his hand as he watched Robin step into his place.

"Now, Robin, you have not only disobeyed me, but you put John into danger as well," Philip said. "I will not have that again."

He gave Robin the same two swift licks he had given John, but this time there were no repentant tears. Nothing but scorn filled the dark eyes.

"Am I understood, Robin?"

"Yes."

"Then I will expect you to obey me."

Robin was silent for a moment. Then he thrust out his chin and looked up into his father's face.

"I can see the pony if I want."

"And if you go without my say, I shall punish you."

Robin shrugged. "Shan't care."

Feeling his temper heat, Philip bit back a sharp reply, well aware of the two young pairs of eyes on him, the defiant brown ones and the inquisitive green ones. Philip knew he would be judged by his response.

"Because you have disobeyed me, Robin, you shall not ride your pony for a full week," he said evenly. "Because you have defied me, you shall not be allowed into the great hall when the bears come."

Robin said nothing except with the rebellious toss of his head, and Rosalynde took him, too, by the hand.

"Come along, Robin. We must let Mistress Joan know you've been found. Then it's time you both were in bed."

"Shan't care," Robin muttered as she led him and John away.

Philip watched after them, too angry to trust his tongue.

"At least he comes fairly by it," Tom said as he came into the room, knowing from the little he had overheard and from Philip's exasperated expression what had just taken place. "Ask Rafe if you were any different."

"Indeed, he was much different, my lord," Rafe said.

"He was?"

"The young prince is not so stubborn by half."

Tom laughed, and Philip scowled.

"Can you say it is not so, my lord?" Rafe asked. "I seem to mind a time when you were a boy, not so young as your little one there, of course, when all the four of you boys were playing at soldiering. Your elder brother Richard, God rest him, took your castle, and you challenged him to single combat for it. At that age three years is a world of difference. You were still just a strip of a boy, and he had begun to flesh out into a man, but you gave him a solid fight for it, I must say. Then when he had you down, you'd not yield, no matter how fierce he twisted your arm. By the time old Nathaniel and I pulled the two of you apart, your arm was broken, but you never made a sound. For all his rough ways, I know it grieved him to have truly hurt you, but you never would make answer when he asked your pardon—just gave him that same hard look your boy had just now."

Philip shook his head. "Sweet heavens, Rafe, he's hardly more than a baby, and yet he as much as dared me to challenge him."

"My lord, you were a terror at four and worse at five, and you seem to have turned out well enough."

"But he's always been such a good boy."

"He was testing you, my lord, as any of them will. They learn early whose word is to be trusted and who cares for them enough to show them right from wrong."

"I daresay I am his dearest enemy at this moment."

"I daresay," Rafe agreed, "but that will quickly pass. Tell me, my lord, did your lady mother, our late queen, ever correct you when you were a child?"

"Hardly," Philip said with a cynical laugh. "You and Joan and Nathaniel saw to it I minded my ways, but never my mother. She never seemed to notice much what I did."

"And, looking on it now, who would you say loved you best?"

Philip put his hand on the old man's shoulder. "I suppose I've never thought on it much, Rafe, but I owe you three a great deal for all the effort my taming must have cost you. This training up of children takes a trifle more stamina than I had thought."

"And you've only just begun," Tom reminded him.

Philip smiled ruefully. "I suppose we've both a long task ahead of us, Tom. Just wait till your own child comes."

❧

That evening Elizabeth coaxed Tom into taking her for a walk in the garden.

"I feel very well tonight, my lord, and it is so lovely out. Surely it would do no harm."

"Do, my lord," Nan advised. "I would like to put fresh sheeting on the bed, and I can hardly do that with her ladyship always in it. Gran says it would do her good to go out some if she is careful."

"Well, if Joan says it would do her good, I'll not argue against it, especially since I would myself like nothing better."

It took Nan only a moment to have her mistress dressed and ready. Tom led her carefully down the stairs and into the garden. It had shed most of its verdant beauty, but it was still a pretty place, especially when colored by the setting sun.

"Shouldn't we have brought your cloak, sweeting?" he asked her.

She smiled. "You've not got yours, my lord."

"I've not been so long a while in bed either. Let me fetch it for you."

"Perhaps in a moment. Please, love, I swear I am not chilled. Let us just have a little time here alone without thinking on such things. I've missed our times alone."

"So have I," he admitted, slipping his arm around her. "But we shall have them again and not so very long from now."

She cuddled against him. Then she laughed and put his hand on her stomach. "Did you feel him? That was the first one. Oh, Tom, we shall have our own baby."

"Of course we shall, sweetheart."

The baby kicked again, and they both laughed.

"He knows his father," she said. There was a sudden gust of wind, and she shivered against him.

"You are cold, love. Come, we ought to have you back to bed."

"No, please, Tom, not yet."

"Bess—"

"Please, love."

"Well, you must let me fetch your cloak then. I'll not have you out here any longer without it."

Giving her no opportunity to disagree, he sprinted back into the castle and up the stairs that led to her chamber. He met his brother coming the opposite way.

"Where are you off to, Philip, with such a black-weather face?"

"Robin's crept out of his bed and disappeared again. I daresay I know where he's to be found."

"I'll go along with you. Let me just send someone to bring Elizabeth inside."

"As I told Joan and my lady, Tom, I can see to this myself."

"Best cool that temper first, brother. Firm and gentle will win him quickest."

Philip closed his eyes and took a deep breath. Then he shook his head. "How is it you always have such patience in everything, Tom?"

"I could not choose but learn patience. You forget, brother," Tom said with a grin, "I was raised with you."

Philip smiled slightly. "Come on."

❧

Waiting in the garden still, Elizabeth wished she had let Tom bring out her cloak in the first place, but surely he would return soon. She was not quite ready to go back to the room she had scarcely left for so many days, and the stables were not far from this part of the garden. Perhaps she could shelter there for a moment.

"Here, horse," she heard a little voice say as she entered the stable. "Robin?"

The boy was standing in front of Alethia's stall, holding out a carrot for the black to nibble. Hearing her, he lifted his head with a rebellious jerk.

"I am certain you ought not to be out here alone, Robin," she said. "You'd best come with me to your father."

"Shan't," he said coolly.

"Come here now. You mustn't get too close."

"I can if I want."

He sauntered into the stall, knowing fearful Aunt 'Liz'beth was unlikely to get so close herself, paying no mind to the empty bucket he upset. It rolled into the corner, and something rustled in the straw. Without warning, the horse began to rear and plunge, whinnying and flinging his hooves everywhere.

"Robin!" she cried, but Robin only stood there against the back wall, frozen with fear, eyes and mouth open wide.

"Robin!" she repeated helplessly, unable to force herself to brave the terrified animal that suddenly seemed so huge. "Someone help!"

The next she knew, Philip bounded into the stable with Tom only a step or two after him.

"Keep still, Robin," Philip warned as he grabbed the horse's halter. "Steady, Alethia, steady."

Showing the whites of his eyes, Alethia reared again, almost pulling Philip off his feet. Then an emerald-skinned snake slithered between the horse's front hooves and was immediately pounded into the hard dirt floor by the snorting beast.

"Easy now, boy," Tom said, taking hold of his halter on the opposite side, but the horse shied from him, shoving Philip hard against the wall, knocking the air out of him with a woosh.

"Easy!" Philip commanded, shoving back. He snatched Robin up and hurried him out of the stall, leaving Tom to quiet the still-skittish animal.

Robin clung to his father's neck, gasping painfully until his breath came back and he was able to cry. "I'm sorry, Papa. I'm sorry."

"Shh, little Robin," Philip soothed, his own voice none too steady. "You are all right."

"Wh-why did 'Lethia get so angry? I didn't hurt him. He never gets angry with you."

"That snake frightened him and made him forget to stand still."

Robin looked up at his father, wiping one eye with his fist. "You came and got me."

"Did you think I'd not have, son?" Philip asked, holding him close.

"I thought you was angry with me because I was bad."

"But I would never let you be hurt, Robin, not if I could stop it."

Robin's breathing grew a little more regular. "Did he hurt you, Papa?"

"Only a little. Mostly he just made me afraid."

Robin stared at him as if he had just spoken blasphemy. "You are never afraid, Papa."

"But I was. I did not want him to hurt you, and that was why I told you that you must never come out here alone."

Robin clung to him once more. "I'm sorry, Papa. I'll not do it again."

"You've worried Mistress Joan and your mama as well. Come on, Rob, let's see what's to be done with you."

"Are you hurt, Philip?" Tom asked as they passed by him and Elizabeth.

"No, thank God, we're both sound."

"You must listen to your father, Robin," Tom said sternly, and then he ruffled the boy's hair. "You'll save yourself a great lot of trouble if you do."

Robin nodded, his brown eyes round and solemn, and Philip carried him out of the stable.

"I am so glad you both were nearby," Elizabeth said with a relieved sigh.

Tom turned her to face him. "We heard you cry out. What happened, Bess?"

"I am not certain, my lord. I heard him in here, talking to the horse and feeding it, and I told him he must come away, but he told me he would do as he pleased. Then I told him again, and he went into the stall and—"

"You did not stop him at the very first?"

"I told him he must not. He would not obey me."

"He's but four, Bess, small enough to be carried away from whatever he's not to get into."

"But the horse, my lord—"

"He was quiet then."

"Yes, but—"

"Why did you not simply take Robin out?"

"I—I could not, my lord."

"Why?"

She looked reproachfully at him. "Have you forgotten our own child, Tom?"

"Of course not, but if you'd done something at once, neither child would have been endangered."

"You are not usually wont to take such a tone with me, my lord," she said with a catch in her voice.

He immediately put his arms around her. "I am sorry, love. I know you want to keep our little one safe, and so do I, but you do not know what a terrible thing it is to be trampled. I've seen it before. Pray God, I shall never see it again."

"Your mother was lost so," she whispered, only just then remembering. "Oh, my lord, I am so very sorry."

"Never mind, sweet, that was a long time back, but you mustn't allow everything to frighten you this way. Surely you could not have stood by and let Robin be hurt."

"But the baby—"

"Bess love, there are dangers every day, little things that might lose us that child—a stumble on the step, a winter's chill—any of a hundred things you might fret over without doing a bit of good. Or you could trust that God watches over us and believe He will care for us."

"I am trying, Tom, but after we have already lost three children, I cannot help being a little afraid."

"I know. I am a little afraid myself, but I'll not let that keep me from doing what I must."

"I am sorry," she said meekly.

He squeezed her tightly. "No harm done, love. Look. Alethia's gentle as a lamb now."

The black pricked up his ears at the sound of his name but continued munching oats, and Tom brought Elizabeth closer to him.

"See, he's not such a brute. He was merely afraid. You could pet him now."

Tentatively, she reached out to stroke the horse's nose, but he whickered softly, and she jerked back from him.

"It is all right, love," Tom said. "He'll not hurt you."

She reached out again, and Alethia put his muzzle into her hand, making little snuffling noises that made her giggle.

"His nose is so soft," she said, "but he has whiskers, too. They tickle."

Tom rubbed the horse's ears. "I told you that you need not fear."

"It is easy to be brave when you are with me, Tom."

He squeezed her close once more. Then he picked up the carrot Robin had left behind and handed it to her.

"Now, my lady, I will show you how to make a friend."

Robin gave his mother and Joan tearfully sincere apologies for having worried them and took his promised punishment without protest.

He even seemed somewhat relieved to know he would not be allowed to ride for two weeks now rather than one. Philip expected that in a day or so he would be clamoring again to see the horses, but he felt fairly certain that at least for a time there would be no more willful disobedience.

After they had seen Robin safely to sleep, with Joan herself to watch over him, he and Rosalynde went to their own bed, clinging together for a prayer of fervent thanks that their firstborn had come to no harm and then falling asleep in each other's arms.

In the depths of his dream, he stood again before the burning church, listening to the roar of the flames and the desperate pounding against the barred doors, pounding that always grew louder and louder until he looked away. Unable to break the pattern, he turned his back on the scene, knowing, dreading, already hearing the terrible cries for help that invariably followed. He had usually managed to wake himself at this point, but this time he could not pull free.

"Help us! For the love of God, free us!"

I cannot, he thought. *There is nothing I can do.*

But that was not what came out of his mouth. *"Shan't care."*

He stood there with his arms crossed, his eyes hard, his jaw stubbornly clenched, not turning when the cries turned to screams, not turning when the roof fell in.

There is nothing I can do! he thought again in wordless anguish, choked with the stench of burning flesh, but his dream self only shrugged.

"Shan't care."

He woke with a gasp, and Rosalynde lit the taper that stood at the bedside.

"My lord?"

He lay there for a second, dazed. Then he shook his head with an unsteady laugh. "Forgive me, love, I did not mean to wake you."

She pressed her hand to his cheek, her eyes shadowed with worry. "Something is troubling you, my lord. Can you not tell me of it?"

"What could trouble me here in your little Eden, my sweet?"

He gave her hand a smacking kiss, but she pulled free of him, his flippant tone sparking a flash of impatience in her emerald eyes.

"Perhaps you find the winters here a trifle too warm," she suggested crisply, swiping one finger across his upper lip, showing it wet with his sweat.

He grinned at her and kissed that finger. "Only when you are cross with me, love."

Again she pulled free.

"It is not like you to keep things from me."

"What things?" He stretched and rolled onto his back, draping his arm across his face so she could not look so searchingly into his eyes. "I merely had too much lamb at supper, nothing more."

She shoved his arm down to his side. "Do you think me such a simpleton, my lord, that I should believe the king of all this realm has nothing whatever to worry him?"

"Only trifling things, love, not worth the telling. Bugbears that roar loud in the nighttime but cannot cast a shadow in full sun."

"Well, keep them then," she replied, a queenly touch of pique in her tone. "Make pets of them if you like. I'll say no more."

"You will forgive me," he assured her.

She sniffed. "Can you be so sure?"

"You will." Again he grinned. "Because you love me."

She turned her back on him with no more than a shrug of a delicate shoulder.

"Rose?"

She did not turn around.

"You do love me, Rose?"

There was a little tremor of uncertainty in his voice, and she faced him again, arms outstretched.

"You know I do and would forgive you anything."

He huddled against her. "I am sorry, sweet. You know I would never purposefully hurt you." He pressed closer. "Always love me. Always."

"Always," she soothed, "even when you'll not confide in me."

"It is a trifling thing truly, and foolishness in me to let it shake me so. I'd not have you worried with it."

"Philip, I am your wife. I hold claim to every burden you bear, to share them with you." She held him more tightly and kissed his forehead. "You defraud me, my lord."

"I owe you protection from the ugly things of the world," he murmured.

She kissed him again. "You owe me yourself, my lord, all of yourself and not the tiniest part kept back, as you would have me give all myself to you."

He lifted his eyes to hers, and she could see again the disquiet in them.

"I have these dreams . . ."

Sleep came to him quickly, as if the mere telling had taken the power from his nightmares.

She held him still, watching him. Since their marriage, she had learned so much of him and of herself, realizing how much she needed him and, with some amazement, how much he needed her. For all of his years of leading armies, governing an unruly kingdom, keeping his factious nobles loyal and at accord—despite all these things, he was still young.

He's but twenty-seven, she thought, *and he's been king nearly five years.*

It was a heavy load he carried, insupportable if carried alone. She had come to realize over time the part she played in his reign, in tempering strict justice with mercy, in standing by the iron-willed king who presided day after day over the court and in providing a place of tender refuge for the man, sometimes the boy, who came to her night after night.

She stroked one admiring hand down his side. She knew all of him so well now, his long, sinewed legs, his narrow hips, his flat, hard stomach. She knew every rib in his chest and every muscle in his strong, rounded arms and broad shoulders. Every thick lock of his hair and every curve in his face she knew; yet she never tired of seeing them again and again. Even the fine scar on his cheek and the long deep one down his side were part of his beauty because they were part of him and, so, part of her. Just as much a part of her were those things she could not see—his mind, his heart. How did he think he could keep his worries from her?

"I had thought there was something for some while now," she had said after he had described the fiery terror that had so many nights broken his sleep. "Do you recall when the dreams first began?"

"After Sarto came to court at New Year's. That was part of the reason I did not tell you of this. After what happened to Tom's child, with you still carrying ours, I did not want to have you remember it."

"You know what the dreams mean, do you not, my lord?"

"I am not certain," he had told her, his eyes not quite meeting hers.

"I think you are, love," she had replied, a tender understanding in her voice. "The burning church could only be Reghed with her poor citizens trapped, helpless against the destruction around them, and only you there to hear their cries."

"Perhaps."

"Surely you are meant to free them from Sarto's cruelty. You told me before that you'd think on some way to help them. Will you not?"

"What would you have me to do, Rose? Take my army to Reghed and battle my way to Sarto's stronghold to kill him and hundreds of these same poor citizens in the doing of it? Is that what you think I'm meant to do?"

"I pray not, my lord. Is there no milder way to bring peace there? If Sarto could be made to see there is a better method than brutality to rule his subjects, if someone could perhaps bring him to the gentleness of Christ—"

"Do you think I've not realized that myself?" he had asked. "If I could make him my ally, then perhaps I could show him the peace he could have, the peace he could give his people."

"He wants trade with us, my lord. Does that not give you the opportunity to do just as you have said? Is it not perhaps divinely appointed to be so?"

"I have thought so, too," he had admitted. "But then I remember his lustful eyes on you when he came to court, remember how he butchered that man before your face, remember Tom's child lost because of it, and I know I could never stand face to face with the blackguard and speak to him of the love of Christ." He had looked at her again, angry and ashamed. "And that was why I did not tell you of any of this. I did not want to stand less in your eyes for refusing to receive him. Put a fair name on that sin if you can, my lady."

She had smoothed the troubled lines from his brow.

"It cannot be easy for you, my love, I know, but you cannot leave a whole people in suffering because of his wrongs."

"I know it is not right. I know I should help them, even if it brings war between me and him, but, sweet heavens, Rose, you know how long and hard a fight it's been for me to reach this place of peace we have now. Is it so wrong in me to want to keep it awhile? To play with my children and see my kingdom prosper? To know your love and not fear it may at any moment be swept away from me? Is it so very wrong?"

"But have you peace, my lord? Knowing you leave God's commission undone, have you had true peace all this while?" She had pressed her cheek to his. "I do not condemn you, love. Truly I do know what it's taken to conquer all the hurts you've had in the past, but should that not make you wish to ease the hurts of others all the more? Could you have overcome your own had you not been given a hand of help?"

"Such loving hands," he had murmured, kissing hers. Then he had taken a deep, steadying breath. "When we return to Winton in the spring, love, I will receive Reghed's ambassadors and see if I cannot find a way in time to reach Sarto himself. I pledge it."

It seemed to bring him peace, that pledge, and afterwards he had fallen asleep as easily as one of the children. Even now when she touched her lips to his, he did not stir. Holding him close, she prayed over him with a special tenderness. Then she, too, slept.

PHILIP'S SLEEP WAS SOUND AND MERCIFULLY DREAMLESS AFTER THAT.
Several nights later, it was Rosalynde who woke with a start.
She lifted her head, unsure of what she had heard. For a long while
there was only the roll of the sea and Philip's measured breathing
beside her. Then she heard it again—a scuffle in the sand, a low, muffled cry, and then nothing.

"Philip," she whispered. He slipped his hand under her hair, mas-
saging the back of her neck, gently pushing her head back to his
chest, making no other sign that he had heard.

"Philip, there is something wrong."

He stretched a little and turned toward her, his breathing still
slow and deep. "What?"

"I cannot tell. Go see."

"That is what the sentries are for, love."

"Please," she urged, knowing he could hear the fear in her voice.
"Out on the beach. Go see."

He groaned and then sat up and struggled into his breeches.

"On the beach?" he asked, looking back over his shoulder at her.
She nodded, and with a wicked lift of one eyebrow, he unsheathed
his new broadsword, the one he had leaned against the wall following its arrival earlier that evening, and crept with melodramatic
stealth to the balcony.

"Do not tease me now," she protested, but he shushed her.

Keeping his back to the wall and his sword battle ready, he stepped outside.

Barring the sentries he expected to see, the beach below was empty. He looked to his left. Another soldier patrolled the wall there and to his right yet another. The one on the right saluted, and Philip noticed that he was not the same man who had been there earlier. Doubtless the guard had changed at midnight.

"Give the sign, soldier," Philip said softly.

The man saluted again. "White rose, your majesty."

Philip nodded. "Carry on."

Rosalynde's face paled when he came back into the room, swiftly, urgently.

"Hurry, my lady, we've no time to waste."

"What is it?"

"There is a fire-breathing dragon even now at the walls. The sentries told me he has a particular fondness for tender white flesh."

He pinched her cheek, his grin half angel, half devil, and all Philip.

She pushed his hand away. "You did not look at all."

"I did, love, I promise." He resheathed his sword and, not bothering to undress, crawled back into bed and wrapped her once more in his arms. "There was nothing to see."

"But I was certain—"

"What could harm you so long as you are with me?" he asked, teasing the corner of her mouth with one finger to get her to smile. She laughed softly and laid her head once more on his chest.

"Whatever could I have been thinking?"

A few minutes later, when they were again asleep, two silent shadows, both wearing the golden lions of Westered's livery, emerged from the balcony and came to stand on either side of the bed. At a nod from the other, one of them slipped his hand over Rosalynde's mouth and dragged her from Philip's arms, bedclothes and all. Instantly awake, Philip lunged toward her.

"Rose—"

He dropped insensible across her lap, felled by a blow to the back of his head from the hilt of the other man's dagger. Clawing and kicking, Rosalynde screamed his name, but her cry was muffled by the suffocating press of her captor's hard hand.

"Be still," the other one hissed, holding his dagger to Philip's throat. "Be still or he dies."

With a sob, her struggles ceased.

"Now, girl, hear me well. If you make one sound, if you do not do precisely as I tell you, your precious King Philip will be dead. Understand?"

Her eyes round with terror, she nodded.

"Let her go, Hugh."

"Owen—"

The shadow called Owen smiled and gave Philip's cheek two or three rough pats. "She will keep silent."

With reluctance, the one called Hugh released his hold on her, and she shrank back against the pillows away from him, holding the sheet to her throat with one hand and holding Philip against her with the other. Owen grabbed the shift that lay on the floor at the foot of the bed and tossed it into her lap, partially covering Philip's slack face.

"Put that on."

She gathered it up, her emerald eyes enormous.

"Put it on," Owen repeated, his eyes roaming over her, "or we take you as you are."

He grabbed Philip by one leg and dragged him off her, landing him on the floor with a dull thud. Rosalynde reached toward him with a barely audible cry, and Hugh tried to jerk the bedclothes away from her.

"Now, woman!"

"No, please," she whispered, sinking deeper into the bed, clutching the sheet closer, very aware of Owen's wolfish eyes upon her. "I will."

She pulled the delicate linen and lace over her head quickly before either man could touch it or her again. Then she got out of bed and knelt beside her husband's limp body.

"Philip." She touched his cheek, but he did not stir.

"Get up," Hugh demanded.

She looked up at him, imploring. "Please. My husband, my children—"

"Now!"

He grabbed her arm, and she swiftly pressed her lips to Philip's. "I love you."

Hugh yanked her to her feet, making her gasp.

"Gently, friend Hugh," Owen said, grinning, "lest she raise the guard and I be forced to kill the king."

"No," she begged, daring no more than a whisper. "I will keep silent."

"Go on, Hugh." Owen grinned again. "I will stay behind a moment, my lady." He tested the edge of his dagger with his broad thumb. Then he sliced off a hank of Philip's dark hair, rolled it between his thumb and fingers, and blew it into the air. "To be certain you keep to your part of the bargain."

"Do not hurt him," she pled, looking back over her shoulder as Hugh pulled her toward the balcony. Owen followed them as far as the door.

"I will meet you at the boat when it is done," he told his partner.

"When what is done?" Rosalynde asked, trying to turn to him. "What do you mean to do?"

"I think he means to take his foul hands off you, love, before I split him and his accomplice both into halves."

"Philip!"

Seeing the king standing there, his massive broadsword in both hands and his eyes as cold as its burnished steel, Owen grabbed Rosalynde by the hair and cut the air with his dagger.

"I will kill her!"

With a lightning flash of his blade, Philip sent the dagger flying. "Not if I—"

"Philip!" Rosalynde screamed as he fell to his knees with a groan, clutching his ribs, almost losing hold of his sword.

"Get her out, Owen," Hugh said. Then once more he raised the wrought-iron candlestick he had turned into a weapon. "The guard'll be on us now for sure."

Already there was a clamor down the corridor and the unmistakable clatter of armed men.

"In here!" Philip shouted as he scrambled back to his feet, only to meet a wicked blow from the makeshift bludgeon to the side of his head. The momentum of the impact flung him against the wall.

"Stay down, boy!" Hugh advised as Philip struggled, half-dazed and bloody-nosed, to stand.

"Never."

Hugh swung the heavy iron again, striking him across the face, leaving him sprawled on the floor and still.

Owen threw his shrieking prisoner into his partner's arms and picked up his dagger, a sick gleam of anticipation in his eyes. "Take her, Hugh. I will finish him."

"No time." Hugh caught Rosalynde's flailing hands and pulled her over his shoulder. "They're here."

The royal guard burst into the room, Tom leading them. With one fierce glance at Philip's motionless body, he rushed toward the two intruders.

"Come on!" Owen urged his confederate, and then he dove over the balcony.

"Tom!" Rosalynde cried, fighting harder, breaking free enough to claw at her captor's face. With a curse, Hugh pinned her arms to her sides and leapt with her into the darkness.

"My lady!"

Tom was on the balcony in two strides, in time to see them land in the large square of sailcloth several men were holding to catch them.

"Archers!" Tom shouted. "And some of you men get down there!"

"Do you value your queen, my lord?" Owen called up to him as Hugh dragged Rosalynde toward the beach. "If not, order your archers to shoot, send your soldiers down, come yourself. She'll be fair to look at in a tomb."

"Tom!" she pled.

"Stay where you are, men," Tom ordered tautly. Then he raised his voice. "Is it ransom you want? We can settle it now—whatever you ask."

He heard a faint laugh and the slosh of boots in the water. "We have what we came for."

"This is not the end."

Tom gripped the carved stone railing, his knuckles whitening as the night winds caught his words and flung them back into his face. By the faint moonlight, he saw a small boat put out to sea with a small white-clad figure huddled, weeping, in its stern.

"We must follow after them, my lord!" the captain of the guard insisted, but Tom shook his head, not taking his eyes from the fast-fading sight.

"No. If we make pursuit, they will only kill her and throw her body into the sea. We must go wisely and slowly now. They'll pay dearly though. I swear it to God Himself, and if they've killed my brother, they'll not find all hell wide enough to hide them." With rigid control, he released his hold on the railing. "Get your men back to their posts and tell the duke what has happened."

He went back inside, dreading what he would find. Rafe was at Philip's side, wringing out a cloth in the washbasin. Philip was still lying facedown on the floor, a puddle of blood widening under him. Tom pressed his trembling lips together.

"Is he dead?"

Rafe shook his head. "They've sent for the physician."

Tom knelt down and carefully, fearfully, turned Philip onto his back.

"My dear God!"

Blood matted Philip's hair and gushed from his nose, running in dark streams down the sides of his bruised and swollen face. His breathing was shallow, sometimes ceasing altogether and then coming back with a half-choked gasp. Beyond that, he did not move.

Tom set aside the broadsword that still lay in his limp fingers. Then he took the wet cloth Rafe had prepared and touched it to his brother's cheek. Philip sucked in a ragged breath and fought to sit up, his eyes wild and fierce as he flung his fists at his imagined enemies.

"Easy, easy," Tom soothed as Rafe held him down. "They've gone, Philip, they've gone."

Philip tried to throw both of them off, and then the words finally pierced his vague consciousness.

"Tom?"

He said it indistinctly, barely moving his lips, and Rafe gave Tom a grim look.

"I suspect they've broken his jaw as well, my lord."

"Where's Ros'lyn'?" Philip slurred, struggling again to sit up. "Ros'lyn'?"

"We'd best put him into bed until Livrette comes," the old man advised, and Tom nodded in assent.

"I'm sorry, boy," Rafe said as he lifted Philip in his arms, but Philip only groaned in answer.

Though he tried his best to walk easily, every step Rafe took sent visible pain jolting through Philip's body. By the time the old man laid him down on the bed, he was again on the verge of unconsciousness. Still he would not lie quietly.

"Where's Ros'lyn', Tom? You di'n' let them take her?"

Tom looked up at Rafe, his worried eyes begging help, and then he leaned close to the bed. "I will see to it, Philip. I promise."

He took his brother's hand to seal the pledge, but Philip could not hold back a gasp of pain at that.

"His arm is broken," Rafe said. Then he, too, leaned down, making his words slow and distinct. "Can you hear me, my lord?"

Philip could hardly breathe for the blood and swelling in his mouth and nose. Talking was almost beyond him, but he managed to open his eyes halfway. "Mmm."

"The physician will have to splint that arm, my lord. Likely he'll have to set your jaw and your nose, too. Do you think you've got anything else broken?"

"Mmm. Riss."

"Your ribs?" There was a huge blackening bruise on Philip's right side, hot to Rafe's touch. "I will tell Livrette."

"Rafe, where's m'lady? Di' they take her?" Philip's breathing suddenly grew more rapid, and he began struggling again. "The chil'ren. They di'n' take my chil'ren?"

"No, my lord, the children are safe."

"But Ros'lyn'—"

"Everything is being done that can, my lord."

"Cannot jus' leave her, Rafe. Mus' fin' her."

"You must lie quiet," Rafe said, holding him down again, and Tom tried once more to wash the blood from his face. Philip flinched at every touch, trying with his good arm to push him away.

"Who's gone af'er her, Tom? S'm'one mus' b'fore they take her too far 'way."

"Philip—"

"If you will pardon me, my lord."

Livrette took Tom's place beside the bed, took the cloth from his hand, and with quick proficiency used it to staunch the flow of blood from his patient's nose. Philip jerked at the contact, unable to keep back another groan.

"Hold this," Livrette said, putting Rafe's hand on the cloth in place of his own. Then he turned Philip's head to one side to examine the bruised, bleeding place above his ear. With an ominous shake of his head, the physician rummaged in his satchel and brought out more clean cloths.

"Wet one of these," he told his young assistant, and the boy was quick to obey. Livrette used it to soak the drying blood out of Philip's hair. With knowing caution, he probed the area with his fingers. Philip's whole body went rigid at the touch, and then he went limp. Again Livrette shook his head.

"I fear there is a fracture here, my lord," he told Tom after he made a quick examination of Philip's other injuries. He parted Philip's hair and showed Tom the wound. "The rest of him will mend soon enough, but this wants careful watching."

He folded one cloth into a thick pad, pressed it over the wound, and bound it there with some thinner strips of linen. Then, with Rafe and Tom supporting Philip on either side, Livrette sat him up and wrapped several tight strips around his rib cage.

Philip came back to consciousness with a moan, trying to pull away from the pain.

"Rest easy," Tom urged, and then he turned to Livrette. "Have you nothing to make him sleep through this?"

The physician shook his head. "After such a blow to the head, he likely would never wake again."

He signaled them to lay Philip back against the blood-stained pillows and began to make a more careful examination of his other wounds. After a moment's hesitation, he looked at Tom. "My lord," he said, too low for Philip to hear, "perhaps you would do best to leave now. What I must do will not be pleasant for you to watch."

Philip moaned again. "Tom?"

"I am here." Tom squeezed his good hand and looked steadily at Livrette. "I'll not leave you, Philip."

Philip passed out again when Livrette wrenched the bones in his forearm back into place a harrowing eternity later. The physician looked grim as he began splinting the break.

"He would have done better to do that before I set his nose. And before I put his jaw back into place. We must be thankful it was merely dislocated and not broken."

Tom pressed one hand to his brother's feverish cheek, his own face beaded with tense sweat. "He fought it hard, the going under."

"How he lasted so long is beyond me." Livrette tied off the bandage and tucked it in at Philip's wrist. Then he listened again to his breathing and to his heartbeat. "I daresay he'll not move again till morning, but he must have constant watch." Certain his patient was beyond overhearing, he turned again to Tom. "What of the queen, my lord?"

"No doubt by now her father has sent scouts to follow after her, but across the sea? God have mercy, I cannot see what good they will be."

"Surely whoever has taken her will send his demands soon. Then we will know where best to search."

Tom emptied the bloodied water out of the basin the physician had been using and filled it again from the pitcher. Then he splashed the fresh water on his face.

"I do not think there will be any demands."

Rosalynde's father hobbled into the room, and Tom said no more.

"The devils did their work well," Westered said after he had spent a moment studying his son-in-law's battered face. He pushed back a lock of dark hair from Philip's forehead, and his expression softened. "You fought as fiercely as a lion, boy, I'll credit you that."

"He would never have let them take her without a fight, my lord," Tom said softly. "He would be after them now if he could."

"They found the men assigned to patrol the beach and this part of the wall all murdered," Westered said, taut anger in his expression. "Was he able to tell you anything? I've sent my ablest men out, but I've nothing to go by in telling them where best to begin the search."

Tom shook his head. "We only know they took her out to sea. If we knew why they took her, we might fathom where. They were not after ransom. They made that plain enough."

"What then? Revenge?" Westered glanced again at Philip's still form. "Against him?"

"I suppose every ruler, just or not, makes enemies, but I know of no one who would hate him so deeply as to do this. Killing him outright would have been kinder than taking the queen from him."

Philip came to once during the night. His whole body ached beyond belief, especially his face, his broken nose and jaw. It was still difficult for him to breathe, and when he tried to turn his head, it hurt so badly he could not suppress a cry. Tom was immediately at his side.

"Do not try to move, Philip. You only make it worse."

"Wa'er," he murmured.

Tom brought him a cool dipperful. "I will try not to hurt you."

Philip managed to take down most of it, as he was so thirsty, but he could not for very long bear the pain swallowing caused him.

"You are very hot," Tom said, one hand on Philip's forehead. "Try to drink more."

Philip tried to shake his head, then groaned with the effort.

"I know," Tom said. "I am sorry."

"Tom, di' they fin' her yet? Where's she?"

"We're not yet certain."

"Ros'lyn'?"

He made a sudden attempt to sit up, and Tom just barely caught him as he fell back into unconsciousness.

⁂

There were voices, vague and far away, and Philip strained for a while in the darkness to understand them. One was Tom's, he knew, though he could not make out any of the words. He was not yet certain of the other.

". . . danger of more bleeding, but if we are careful, especially in the next few days . . ."

The voice droned on. Philip lost the words again, but he was certain now that it was Livrette's. After a few more minutes, the words once again came clear.

". . . be well in a few weeks if we can keep him quiet."

"I will see to that, Master Livrette."

That was Rafe's voice, Philip realized. *Of course he would be here, too.*

"He will want to go after the queen," he heard Tom say, "the very moment he can stand."

"You must prevent that, my lord," Livrette urged. Philip opened his eyes enough to see the three of them at his bedside conferring.

"He could hardly expect to ride with his ribs so lamed," Livrette continued. "I doubt he could hold his head up long enough to mount a horse. He must be made to understand the danger."

Philip grabbed the physician's wrist. "You talk t' me."

"Forgive me, your majesty," Livrette said, not losing his professional composure. "As I was telling Lord Tom, your injuries are serious, and you must try to keep still until it can all be put right."

"Do wha'ever you mus', but be quick abou' it. I cannot was'e any more time lying here."

"It will be some while before you can leave your bed, my lord."

"I give you one hour, tha's all."

"My lord!" Livrette and Rafe gasped simultaneously, but there was steely determination in Philip's slurred voice and behind the pain in his eyes.

"One hour. S'm'one mus' go af'r her."

"I will see to it, Philip," Tom said. "I promise."

"You prom'se?" Philip glared at him. "You prom'se? What good 's that? What kin' of prom'se 's tha' when you stan' i'le here?"

"Philip—"

"Who've you sent af'r her, Tom? How m'ny arch'rs? How m'ny cav'liers?" He tried to draw a breath, and a sudden fit of coughing came over him, leaving him spent and gasping, collapsed against the pillows.

"You know you cannot go," Tom said when the worst of it was over and Livrette had spooned one of his potions down his patient's throat. "What good could you do her like this?"

Philip squeezed his eyes shut, and a tear of frustration ran down the side of his face to be lost in his dark hair. "I canno' jus' lie here an' do nothin', Tom. It woul' be jus' like—"

He turned his face to the wall, unable to go on.

"I know." Tom gave his shoulder a gentle squeeze. "But this need not be the same. Lord James has sent his best scouts in search of her. I am going myself this morning. There is hope yet."

Philip looked at him again, the deep purple bruises under his eyes making them seem wider and more desperate. "How can I s'ay here, Tom, when I know wha' mi' be hap'ning to her?"

"We do not know where she is or what she may be facing, but God does. Your best help to her now is to pray, and you can do that where you are."

"Tom—"

"Who can most help her in this? You or He?"

Philip drew a deep, painful breath. "Fin' her, Tom. I do no' know how I'm meant t' live withou' her."

⁂

"What am I to tell the children, my lord?" Joan asked Tom as he came from Philip's chamber. "They've been at me all morning to see their parents, and I've managed to distract them from it, but I cannot do that forever."

She looked worn these days, and he knew it was not merely the strain of looking after the children by day and Philip by night.

"The children. God's mercy, Joan, whatever I tell them, it will frighten them."

"Yes, my lord, I expect it will, but they've got to learn to live in this world sometime or other, and at least they will have the comfort to know that, fair or foul, you'll speak them the truth."

Tom went into the nursery and was immediately commandeered by both boys.

"Take us to the beach, Uncle," Robin demanded.

Tom took him and John into his lap, one on each knee. "I have to go away this morning. I do not know when I will come back."

"Is Papa going with you?" Robin asked.

"I want to go," John insisted, tugging his uncle's sleeve.

"Not this time, John," Tom told him. "And your papa is not going either. Now I do not want you boys to be afraid. Master Bonnechamp and all your grandpapa's soldiers will keep you safe, but some bad men came into the castle last night and hurt your papa very badly and took your mama away."

"Why?" Robin asked.

Tom shook his head. "I do not know, but I am going to find out."

There was a little wrinkle in John's brow. "Where they tooked Mama?"

"I do not know that either, John, but I am going to go after her. Some of the soldiers have gone already."

"Is Papa going to die?" Robin asked, a quiver in his lip.

Tom held him closer. "I do not think so. Master Livrette says he is getting better, but we must pray for him. He may not be well for a long while."

"Is Mama coming back?"

"We must pray very hard she does and that our Lord will watch over her while she is away."

"Does He know where she is?" John asked.

Robin gave him an annoyed, impatient look—one of Philip's looks. "Of course He does," Robin said. "He knows everything."

"Then why do you not ask Him to tell you, Uncle?"

There was such innocent simplicity in John's question. It should be as simple as that, just as straightforward, but Tom had asked, again and again, and heaven was silent. He took a deep breath and held both boys very tightly.

"I will ask again."

⁂

Out on the water, in the cramped, squalid ship's cabin that served as tavern for Rosalynde's abductors, the one-eyed man popped the cork from their fourth bottle of the evening. His partner wiped the sweat from his face and threw back the last of the third.

"The wench maddens me, Hugh. I must have her."

"You know what our master would do to you if you so much as touch her. Death would be a kindness!"

"Curse the madman," Owen growled, helping himself to the most recent offering. "We'll have our pay and be gone and him none the wiser."

"You're the madman! Unless you mean to take her and then kill her and lose us our pay entirely—our lives as well, if he catches up to us."

"Hardly." Owen shoved his chair back and stood up, grinning nastily. "No one misses a swig from a bottle that's already uncorked."

He drained his cup, steadying himself against the table as the ship rocked. Then giving his partner a leering wink, he opened the cabin door and stepped across the threshold.

"Hang the fool," Hugh muttered, slamming the door after him. Then he poured himself another drink.

Owen went down the dim passageway, staggering with the ale and the roll of the ship, recalling again the soft, shapely curves of his captive's body under the fine shift she wore, smelling once more the tantalizing perfume of her hair, relishing the way she had struggled against him.

There had been fear in her eyes, helpless fear that made his breath quicken and his body shake, that sharpened his senses to the keenness of a stalking jackal's. This would be a delicacy unlike any he had before tasted, nothing like the coarse, common women of his experience. Doubtless the girl had always been petted and pampered and shielded from men such as himself.

"Satin sheets and feather beds," he muttered. "Time a little dirt and good honest sweat touched that white skin, my lovely." He grinned his nasty grin. "You might soon have a taste for it once that precious sanctity is gone."

He put the key into the lock, anticipation making his hand unsteady as he opened her door. There would again be fear in those emerald eyes—

"Well, my lady—"

He took a swift step backwards, nearly gagging as the stench of seasickness assaulted him. The girl was huddled beside the bed, her shift and her dark hair wet with sweat, her face buried in her arms on top of the coarse cloth that served as her coverlet.

With a curse, he grabbed her by the shoulders, pulling her up to him, and her head dropped back, showing her blotched, swollen face. The stench intensified, and again he took a swift step backwards, this time landing his foot squarely in her brimming washbasin. Disgusted, he shoved her back onto the bed and stalked out of the room.

Hearing the key once more in the lock, Rosalynde breathed a faint prayer of thanksgiving for such unlikely blessings as seasickness.

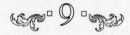
I T WAS SEVERAL DAYS BEFORE THE FEVER LEFT AND PHILIP COULD bear the pain of sitting up. His constant headache had dulled somewhat, and his ribs did not hurt quite so fiercely every time he took a breath, but there was no ease for the agony in his heart and mind. With every day that passed, he became more moody and restless, and Rafe found it more and more difficult to keep him quietly in bed.

"Stop that, my lord," Rafe scolded, seeing him fidgeting with the wrappings around his jaw.

"Itches," Philip said, having nearly learned to talk clearly despite the bandaging. He rubbed his cheek gingerly against one splint, and Rafe pulled his arm away.

"You will hurt yourself."

"Bring my razor, Rafe."

"My lord, I have told you before—"

Philip sighed and lay down again, his cheek resting on his good arm.

Rafe's severe expression softened. "Well, I suppose I might try to shave you if you promise to keep still and not talk."

Making sure Philip knew he was not in favor of the idea, Rafe left the room and came back with a ewer of hot water.

"Now you promised to be still," Rafe reminded him. Philip nodded apathetically.

"And no talking."

"No talking."

Rafe carefully unbound his jaw. "It seems that most of the swelling has gone down, my lord." He began patting Philip's skin with soap and water. "I will be careful."

He shaved the uninjured side of Philip's face first and his chin. Then, steadying himself, he cautiously shaved his upper lip. Philip watched him warily, remembering his broken nose and the pain that was only now waning, but Rafe was gentle, and it was quickly done.

"Now this side, my lord. Tell me if it hurts you."

Philip nodded a little and felt the blade scrape his skin, tug at his jaw. There was some pain. He had expected there would be, but it seemed trivial to him after what he had already been through.

"Bring me a mirror, Rafe," Philip said after he had finished.

"You're not to talk, my lord."

"Then do not make me repeat myself."

"I've shaved you since you were old enough to sprout a beard, my lord. Surely you can trust me to do it properly."

"I want to see, Rafe."

"Livrette says you'll mend. Why not leave it there?"

"Rafe."

With a reluctant frown, Rafe held the mirror where his master could see himself.

Philip started, seeing the face that looked back at him. His nose was bruised and swollen, but it looked as if the physician had at least set it straight. The bruises under his eyes had turned green and purple, half healed but more unsightly, he was certain, than when he was first hurt. Rafe had had trouble coaxing him to eat even those things he could manage with his battered jaw, and now his cheeks were sunken, and his eyes were hollow. Anyone seeing him would be hard pressed to believe he had a drop of Chastelayne blood in him.

He took the mirror from Rafe and studied the right side of his face more closely. There was a decided unevenness in his jaw now and a deep black bruise, a broad, oblique line that ended just below his cheekbone. The mark widened into various shades of purple and blue from under his chin to almost as far back as his ear and all across his cheek.

"I suppose I ought be grateful it is no worse," he said with a strained attempt at a smile. Grimacing, he tossed the mirror face-down on the coverlet by him and lay back against the pillows. "I am almost glad she cannot see me now."

"Rest, my lord," Rafe said gently. "Let me put that away."

"No."

Philip held the mirror where it was and began tracing his fingers over the exquisite silverwork, over the enameled white saint's rose. He hesitated over the ornate R wrought there.

"She would love me still, would she not, Rafe?"

"Of course, my lord. You know she would."

"Even though I've failed her."

"You did what you could, my lord. Even her father says as much."

Philip touched the mirror again, pain in every line of his face. "And I promised him I would defend her with my life."

Rafe busied himself putting away the razor and straightening up the room, wisely saying nothing. After a moment, he picked up the wrappings he had taken from Philip's jaw. "I suppose we'd best have this back on now, my lord."

"You should never have taken it off." Livrette stalked to the bed-side, his face a study in indignation. "I cannot be held responsible for your recovery, my lord, if you refuse to follow instructions."

He glared at Rafe, snatching the bandage from him.

Rafe frowned. "I was merely trying to make my lord more comfortable by—"

"I can see that," Livrette replied as he examined Philip's freshly shaved jaw. "I would have had to order it done anyway, but next time, Master Bonnechamp, I will thank you to consult with me before you interfere with my work."

"It was by my command, Master Livrette," Philip said wearily.

The physician shook his head. "Please, my lord, for all your king-dom's sake, have a care for yourself. You do not appreciate how seri-ously you have been hurt."

He inspected Philip's other injuries, looking reluctantly satisfied with his patient's progress.

"You are mending, my lord," he said after making a close study of the battered place over Philip's ear. "If you will take care, I think you've come far along enough to have visitors."

"Papa! Papa!"

Philip's expression lost some of its listlessness at the eager little voices. Molly came into the room, holding Robin and John each by the hand.

"Quietly now, young gentlemen," Livrette cautioned.

Their faces suddenly subdued, the boys approached the bed. Robin was just barely tall enough to see his father's face, and his eyes got very round. "Did you fall down, Papa?"

Philip gave him a wry smile. "I suppose I did." He reached out his good hand and ruffled his son's hair. "Have you been a good boy?"

Robin was distracted by an impatient tug at his sleeve.

"Can't see, Robin!" John complained.

Philip laughed a little, and Rafe set a stool beside the bed and stood John up on it. "There, my princeling."

John smiled brightly and immediately poked his finger at Philip's jaw. "Pretty colors."

Philip flinched and laughed again. "I do not know if your mama would think so."

His smile vanished and so did John's.

"Where is Mama?" Robin asked, a quiver in his voice.

John's lip trembled. "I want my mama."

"Please, John," Philip said softly, feeling a sudden, choking need to cry. John climbed up into the bed next to him, huddling under his arm, sobbing as if his baby heart would break.

"Now, boys, you were to be brave for your papa," Livrette said gently, his expression anxious as he watched his patient's face. "We would not want Mistress Molly to have to take you back to the nursery."

"No!" John wailed, clinging closer.

Robin got up on the stool and clutched his father's hand. "Please, Papa, let us stay with you." He swallowed hard, and then he put his shoulders back and held his head up. "We will be brave."

"Of course you will, son," Philip said. Drawing a steadying breath, he managed a faint smile. "You come up here with me, and I will tell you about your mama. What I can."

"My lord, I beg you to consider," Livrette urged as Robin crawled over Philip to snuggle up to his other side. "Your ribs—"

"It is all right," Philip said, paling a little from the pain. "What has your uncle told you, Robin, about Mama?"

"That some bad men hurt you and took her away." Robin drew his brows into a hard line and tightened his little mouth in a fierce, cold look Philip knew the child had copied from him. "You should have taken your broadsword, Papa, and struck off their traitor heads!"

Philip felt that same tightness in his own expression. The desire to do just as Robin had said was still too raw and hot inside him. It was an ungodly, vengeful fury that tore at him and left him writhing in helplessness, one he did not want these little ones to see.

John lifted his head, still sniffling. "Why—why they tooked Mama away?"

"I do not know, John," Philip said, pulling him closer. "They did not say why."

"Why you did not stop them?"

"I, uh—" Philip's throat tightened. He had asked this of himself over and over again. "I tried, son."

John nestled against him once more. "I want her to come back now."

"So do I, son," Philip said thickly. "So do I."

"I think 'Lyssa misses Mama, too," Robin said. "She just cries and cries."

Philip shot Livrette a hard look.

"The child's not taken well to the wet nurse we found for her, my lord," the physician explained, "but that is being seen to." His expression turned more anxious. "Please, sir, you should not let all this trouble you now. Let us take the princes back to the nursery. Perhaps it was unwise to—"

John ducked his head against his father's side, sobbing again, and Robin clung to his arm.

"No, Papa!"

"It is all right, Robin. Shh, John, you shall stay." Philip looked again at Livrette, his expression stern. "I want them with me awhile. Just leave us, all of you."

Exchanging a look of concern, Rafe and Livrette did as they were told, taking Molly with them.

When Rafe came back into the room at dusk, both of the children were fast asleep, John with his thumb in his mouth and Robin with his small arms wrapped tightly around his father's sinewy one. Philip lay there between them, absently stroking John's thick hair, something distant, something dark and determined in his expression.

"Shall I take them to the nursery now, my lord?" Rafe asked softly. After a moment, Philip nodded.

"I suppose it is time and past." He stroked the younger boy's hair again. "Come, John."

Catching a quivering breath, John curled up into a tight little ball under Philip's arm and started sucking his thumb again.

"No need to wake them, sir."

Rafe picked John up and then carefully disentangled Robin from the sheets and from Philip's arm.

"Papa," Robin whimpered, his eyes still closed.

Philip stroked his sleep-flushed cheek. "Shh, son. Go to sleep."

Rafe balanced the boy on his hip, and Robin nestled against his shoulder, asleep again, his legs hanging limp at the old man's side.

"Take them, Rafe," Philip said, his expression grim again. "It is time and past."

"You ought to have some sleep yourself, my lord," Rafe suggested, wary of the look in his master's eyes. "For the sake of these little ones."

Philip nodded slowly. "Yes. For their sake."

Rafe met Livrette on the way back from the nursery.

"I was just going to look in on the king, Master Bonnechamp," the physician said. Then he shook his head. "I had thought it would cheer him to see the children. I never suspected it would drive him deeper into melancholy."

"He calmed the little ones enough to get them to sleep, I know, but as for himself—" Rafe frowned. "He is too quiet, Master Livrette. I know that boy too well not to see there is something stirring in that stubborn head."

"I have thought the same," Livrette replied. "You mustn't let him be alone, not for even a moment. He is not out of danger yet by far."

"I will see to it," Rafe assured him. Then he pushed open the door to his master's chamber. Philip was half-dressed, sitting on the bed with his legs stretched out in front of him, struggling, white-faced, to pull on his boots.

"My lord!" Rafe cried, suddenly as pale as his master.

"I must go, Rafe." Philip's voice was low and determined as he pulled the boot straps as tight as his trembling hands could manage.

"You cannot get up, your majesty," Livrette said aghast. "It would be nothing short of suicide. My lord, I beg you, for the sake of your children!"

Philip nodded, his determination now backed with a fierce, warning defiance. "Yes, for their sake. They need their mother." His voice shook. "I need her."

Seizing the cloak draped over the chair beside him, he swung his legs off the bed. Rafe grabbed his arm.

"Please, my lord."

Philip tried to pull away from him, a murderous look in his eyes, but Rafe did not loosen his grip.

"Let me go, Rafe."

"Pardon me, my lord, but I'll not let you kill yourself."

Philip swore. "By your allegiance, man, I command you to release me!"

Rafe only tightened his hold. "By my allegiance I cannot."

"I am your king!"

"I have been your guardian far longer than you have been my king, boy," Rafe said, his expression stern. "I would betray that trust if I did as you command."

"Please, your majesty," Livrette urged. "You mustn't upset yourself. Any violent movement could—"

With a sudden jerk, Philip wrenched away from Rafe and lurched toward the door, but the old man was too quick for him. He grabbed Philip's arm again.

"My lord!"

Philip swung wildly at him with his bandaged arm, but Rafe caught him by the wrist, stopping him mid-blow.

"Let me go!" Philip raged, but Rafe's expression was carefully restrained.

"You know you are not fit yet, my lord."

"Fit enough!"

"Are you?"

Rafe released his wrist. Then before Philip could move, the old man seized him by the hair and yanked his head backwards. Philip groaned and sank to his knees, almost blacking out.

"Have you gone mad, man?" the physician gasped. "What have you done?"

"Made him see reason." Rafe half led, half carried his master back to the bed and settled him in it. "How far do you think you'd get, boy, with someone who meant you harm?"

Ashen-faced, Philip could only lie there, dazed and breathing hard, as Rafe unstrapped his boots, stripped off his shirt, and then sponged the cold sweat off him. Livrette mixed something from a reddish-brown bottle into a cup of water and made Philip drink it down.

"I will . . ." Philip panted. "I will . . . go to her."

"And I will stop you, my lord," Rafe said, as determined as his master. "If I must tie you to that bed, I will stop you."

"It can only be by some miracle, Master Bonnechamp," the physician said after he had reexamined his patient, "but he seems no worse for your 'reason.'" He noticed the growing vagueness in Philip's expression. "You will sleep now, my lord."

"I will . . . go . . ." The last flash of defiance dimmed from Philip's eyes, and despite his attempts, he could not keep them open. "I will
. . ."

"I did not want to have to use that on him," Livrette said once

Philip was still. "There is some danger in it, but it is better than risking him hurting himself as he is like to if this goes on."

"It cannot go on," Rafe replied. "Not long."

In the stifling closeness of her cabin, Rosalynde tried to pray, tried to make a petition that was not distorted by the pitiless rolling of the sea, and hoped desperately that God would understand and rescue her anyway.

"Dear Jesus," she moaned, "take me from this place."

The door swung open, and she looked up. This time it was the one called Hugh who stood there. Without a word he picked her up and threw her onto the bed.

"No, please," she moaned, holding up her hands to ward him off but too weak to really struggle. "Dear Jesus—"

"Keep quiet, woman," Hugh said. He rolled her in the rough blanket, covering even her face, and tossed her over his shoulder.

She heard his steps as he carried her down the corridor, and then she heard the other man's voice. "He is waiting."

"There is something not right about him, Owen. I say we take the money and clear off."

"Not too quickly, man. It never hurts to have a patron highly placed. It could be he will have other employment for us in the future."

Rosalynde felt Hugh shift uneasily. "Still, I do not like it," he said. "I had just as soon you took her to him and collected the money alone. We can meet at the tavern there to portion it out."

"I'll have an extra share then," Owen countered.

"Fair enough," Hugh agreed.

Rosalynde felt herself shifted from his shoulder to his partner's. The rough motion made the sickness rise again in her throat, but she managed to keep it down, begging God as she did to somehow deliver her from whatever fate she had been sold into.

"Go see to it the boat is ready, Hugh," Owen added, and

Rosalynde felt him carry her out of the hold and onto the deck of the ship.

The crash of the surf and the keening of the gulls told her they had come ashore somewhere, but where? She tried to wriggle free of the blanket that still covered her face, hungering to breathe the clean open air and see the sun once more, but Owen merely increased the punishing tightness of his hold on her.

"Hush up, girl," he growled when she whimpered weakly at the pain. "We'll be quit of each other soon enough." He laughed to himself. "And Hugh, too. He'll be a long while at the tavern waiting for his money."

He laughed again and gave Rosalynde's thigh a cruel squeeze.

"It will go some to make up for what I missed with you, my fine lady."

A few minutes later, Hugh returned. Rosalynde felt herself taken down the dock and dumped into the bottom of an open boat and carried away again on the water, but she could feel a difference here. What reached her ears now was not the crashing of the sea, but the rushing of a wide river.

She could not tell how long this part of the journey lasted. Sometimes she fell into an exhausted sleep only to jerk awake after what seemed like hours later, but she never heard more than her abductors' petty bickering and the roar of the water until they docked again.

When Hugh handed her up to his partner, she tried once more to see where she was, but Owen merely tucked the stifling blanket more closely around her face.

"Be still."

He said nothing more to her after that, and she merely lay limply against him, listening to his steps, the hollow sound of the planking of the dock, the uneven scuff of cobblestones, the creak of a wooden stairway, then the smoothness of long, wide corridors.

"Where is the king?" Owen asked when they finally came to a stop, and Rosalynde's heart leapt. Had they sold her back to Philip?

"This way," a low voice said. Again she felt herself carried up steps, winding and narrow. Then at last she was set on her feet.

"She is here, your majesty."

Owen pulled the blanket off her, and she put her hand to her throat, feeling a sudden blackness threaten to overtake her.

"Sarto!"

The King of Reghed stood back from her, his dead eyes glittering as they raked down her body. She lifted her head and pressed her lips together to keep them from trembling.

"Why have you done this, my lord?"

He smiled and walked slowly around her, still caught up in merely looking at her. She pulled her rumpled shift closer to her throat.

"My lord?"

He dropped to one knee.

"You are welcome to Reghed, gracious lady."

He tried to kiss her hand, but she snatched it from him and took a swift step backwards, her eyes darting around the room. There was an eerie oppressiveness about the place. Everything was crimson and ebony, from the sable-curtained bed and the heavy scarlet drape that covered most of one wall, to the long ebony-covered box that lay enshrined beneath it. Red and black. Blood and death.

"Why have you done this?" she asked again.

"You must be weary from your travels, my lady."

He brushed a limp strand of hair out of her face, and once more she pulled back from him.

"Do not imagine, my lord, that my husband will stand by and let you have your way in this."

"I know you must grieve for him, gracious lady. All Reghed mourns your unhappy loss."

"He is not dead!" she cried, blinking hard to keep back the tears. Sarto looked piercingly at Owen.

"He is, my lord," Owen said, dropping his eyes and then his head.

"He is not!" Rosalynde insisted. "The man lies to you, as you will see when my husband brings all his army to Reghed to take me back."

Owen's eyes widened in fear. "He is dead, my lord. I saw him myself lying in his own blood."

"You have proof?" Sarto asked coldly. "You know I can step no further in this until I know for certain."

"My lord, he is. He must be! No man could take such blows and live long."

"So what you are saying is that you think him dead, but you've no proof of it."

"My lord—"

A blow from Sarto's heavy fist sent Owen crashing to the floor. "Please, my lord."

"Hear me well, man. You've failed me twice. The third time will be the last. Bring me proof of his death . . . or of your own."

"You shall have it, your majesty." Owen scrambled to his feet and backed out of the chamber, still cowering. "I swear you shall."

"Why have you done this?" Rosalynde demanded when he was gone.

Sarto grabbed her by the arms, looking deeply into her eyes. "Truly you do not know? Truly?"

"No, my lord," she replied, trying to wriggle out of his tight grasp. "Please, you're hurting."

"I have for some long while heard of your beauty, gracious lady, and even sent one of my men to your court that he might bring me word if such tales were true. Then seeing for myself—the hair, the eyes, the fair, delicate flesh—I knew for certain that you were like— that you *are*—"

"My lord—"

"You cannot have forgotten, my lady. Though it has been an eternity since, we do not forget what we pledged to each other, you and I."

"I made you no pledge, my lord. I am pledged only to my husband."

He looked still more deeply into her eyes, a blazing intensity in his own.

"That is not so. Before you ever saw him, before he was even born, you pledged yourself to me, in flesh and in blood, for all eternity. When you were taken from me, you swore to return. You swore it, and I've waited all this long while. Will you deny me now?"

"My lord, I never—"

"Will you deny this?"

He seized the scarlet drape in both hands and tore it down with one savage motion, revealing a gilt-framed portrait. A portrait of herself.

She breathed out an exclamation of surprise. "Where did you—"

The portrait showed a woman cloaked in ermine, her hair swirling dark and voluminous about her and the painted torch light throwing malevolent shadows into her alabaster face. The fashion of the clothing and style of the hair were from a generation before, but there was an undeniable resemblance.

"Now you will remember." There was a gleam of triumph in Sarto's eyes. "You cannot deny me now."

Rosalynde examined the portrait more closely and realized that the likeness was not so remarkable as she had first thought. The thick, dark hair, the fair skin, the delicacy of feature—truly these were much like her own. But there was the sly, almost disdainful upturn in the blood-red lips and the gemlike hardness in the emerald eyes that slanted slightly under upswept brows. These were not at all the same.

"This is not my image, my lord," Rosalynde said. "I know not who she might be, but you deceive yourself to think she and I have any connection."

He smiled blandly. "As I said, it has been an eternity since you were taken from me, but you will remember in time. You will be glad to come back to my arms once we are married."

"Married?"

"I could not give you that before when my father was king and forced me to wed elsewhere, but this time you shall be queen, and no one may say that the son you give me after is not fit one day to reign."

"My lord, I am married already."

He frowned. "Yes, well, that shall be seen to soon enough. You must forgive me that our joy must be postponed yet again, gracious lady, but not for much longer."

"I am not this woman, whoever she was! Please, my lord, I am sorry for whatever parted you from her. I can see you loved her well, but I am not she!"

He only smiled indulgently and gestured toward the portrait

once again. "You have seen, gracious lady. What more proof could be wanting that you are my Rosamund?"

"That is pure chance," Rosalynde breathed, feeling again as if she might faint, feeling again the oppressive heaviness in the room. His smile was so like the one in the painting. "Please, my lord, let me return to my husband and my children. I am not your Rosamund. I cannot take her place."

"You are weary," he told her. "Come, rest yourself. I have provided everything for your care and comfort, and soon you will recall all that has passed between us. Then I shall make you my queen, as always I pledged I would."

"I cannot be your queen!" she said in sudden, fierce desperation. "I cannot!"

"Rest, gracious lady." He kissed her hand and went to the door. "I will send your ladies-in-waiting to you. They will see to your needs, and then you will have some time alone here. Time to remember."

Alone. Her heart pounded harder. *Alone here.*

"Please, my lord—"

The door swung shut. For a breathless moment she stood there listening to the silence, her eyes darting again about the room. Red and black. Blood and death.

With a low cry, she ran to the door and tugged at the handle, pounding her fist against the unyielding wood. She could not hope to escape by force. There must be another way out. She turned to search for a window, and her stomach tightened when she realized there was none. Surely there was some way.

She flung open the intricately carved door of the wardrobe, hoping to find something that would be of help, but it held nothing but clothes, rich and gorgeous, all from the same period as the portrait and all of them, like the room, crimson and ebony. That left only the draped box that lay beneath the portrait. If there were only something in there.

She pulled away the heavy black cloth and swallowed down a half-strangled scream. Lying there in a crystal coffin, still clad in ermine, still cloaked in a swirl of dark hair, mocking her with an eyeless grin, was an ivory skeleton.

"Rosamund," she breathed, darting a glance at the portrait and then back at the coffin. It was all the same, down to the heavy rings that hung on the fine bones of the hands.

. . . he truly dressed his dead mistress's bones in the royal robes and crown and forced his nobles to swear loyalty to her . . . even to kiss her hand though there was no more flesh left on it . . .

"Guard me, Jesus," she breathed, unconsciously clutching the black drape against her, backing away until she felt a cold hand touch her shoulder, and she knew no more.

CHAPTER

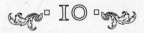

As Philip recovered, Westered spent many hours at his bedside, trying to comfort his grief and forget some of his own. They often played chess to pass the time, but Westered found his opponent preoccupied and easily distracted, and the older man took little pleasure in his effortless victories.

"Your move, my lord," Westered prompted after Philip had spent several silent minutes merely staring at the game.

"I cannot seem to reason it out," Philip murmured, pressing his hand against the bruised side of his head. Then with a sharp breath, he dashed the board to the floor with a violent sweep of his arm. "It makes no sense! Why should anyone take her but for ransom?"

For a moment there was only the ivory rattle of black and white chessmen to break the silence, and then even that settled into stillness.

"They will find her, son," Westered said gently.

Philip dropped his head back down to his pillows. "Forgive me, sir, there was no need of such a display. I know it must be as great a frustration for you to be kept here as it is for me, and, God help me, even that is my fault."

"Let's not begin with that again, my lord. We must merely content ourselves that everything possible is being done, and we will both be more able to lend our help if we first mend. I know you would go to her if you could. You've always loved her so."

"Not always," Philip admitted painfully, "not at first, but she never would have written you that. She always believed me better than I was. Better than I am. All the rest of my life cannot make up what she has due in kindness from me." He took his father-in-law's wrist in a painful grip. "You must believe me, sir, I love her. More than I have words to tell it."

"I know, son. Had I not believed you would come to that, I would never have given her to you, no matter her pleading or the agreement I had with your father."

"It's been five years since he died, and I can see him a little better now for what he was and what he meant to be. I think I've even learned to love him again, despite all the wrong he did, but I can never give him my respect, as a king or as a man, not a tithe of the respect I have for you, sir. I, uh—" Philip looked up at the ceiling, his voice unsteady. "I had begun thinking of you as my father, not only hers, and now I've failed you both. I pray you pardon the presumption, if not the failure."

Westered squeezed his shoulder, his own voice thick with emotion. "I never had a son, my lord, but I look on you with as much love and pride as if you were my own. It grieves me to see you scourge yourself for what you could not have prevented."

"There were things I might have done—"

"She was taken from my own castle, my lord, from the midst of every defense I had raised. Do you think I've not accused myself in all this?"

Philip drew a shaky breath, wiped his eyes, and gave his father-in-law a wry smile. "I know once I've turned maudlin, sir, it is time I was left alone awhile. Perhaps we'd best take up another game tomorrow."

"When you will, son," Westered replied, getting up from his chair with the aid of his crutch. "Rest well and know, wherever she is, God is watching over her."

Philip nodded and closed his eyes as Westered hobbled silently from the room. Before the duke reached the end of the corridor, he met Tom coming the other way.

"Any news, my lord of Brenden?"

Tom untied his travel-stained cloak and draped it over one arm. "It is as if the earth has swallowed her up, my lord. I found no trace of her."

"She is somewhere," Westered said impatiently. "If I were allowed to—"

"You know you mustn't attempt it, my lord," Tom said. "If you're ever to walk alone again, you must let that bone heal. No doubt you're meant to be resting even now."

"Were I but thirty again, I'd not let such trifles stop me. I can but pity your poor brother trapped here in helplessness."

"How is he today?"

"I've just come from him. As you may expect, it is no easy thing for him to lie still through all this."

"It is torture, I know, especially after what happened before."

"Before, my lord?"

"Perhaps you know he had a wife before he married your daughter."

"Indeed?"

"He loved her very truly, but our father had greater plans for him than marriage to a mere serving girl and had her made away with. Philip was wild with grief, so violent they had to tie him down until he came to himself again. I've no doubt this brings it all back to him and worse, because he loves the queen so much more."

"God comfort him—I had no idea."

"Would I had some comfort to bring him now, even the tiniest hint of hope to tell him, but there is merely nothing. Even the proclamations I've sent out offering reward for any information have proved fruitless."

"Pardon me, my lord," Rafe interrupted.

Tom could read the urgency in his face. "Yes?"

"There is someone at the gate, sir, who would speak to you."

Tom sighed wearily. "Tell him I will see him tomorrow, Rafe, if it is nothing you can see to for me tonight."

"She will speak to no one but you, my lord, and says she has news of the queen."

"Thank God," Westered breathed.

Suddenly the weariness left Tom's expression. "Have her taken to the library. I will be there straightaway."

"At once, my lord." Rafe bowed and scurried off again.

"Something at last," Westered said. "We must tell the king."

Tom shook his head. "Not yet, my lord. If this proves to be nothing, it would better that he not know of it at all."

"Of course, of course," Westered agreed, calming. "Shall we go see?"

When he and Westered went into the library, Tom was surprised to be presented with a little street urchin of about twelve with dirty blonde hair and wiry brown limbs that seemed never to be still.

"Do you have food?" she asked, not waiting for introductions. "He said you would have food."

"Who, girl?"

"The one-eyed man."

Tom and Westered exchanged an uneasy glance.

"He said you would have food," the girl continued, "and I needn't tell you anything until I'd had as much as I cared to."

"Wait a moment."

Tom said something quietly to Rafe, and in a few minutes the library table was covered with platters of mutton and fish, with fruit and hot bread, and with sweetmeats of all varieties. The girl's eyes widened in amazement. Then she began stuffing as much as she could manage into her mouth and into her filthy skirt pockets.

"Now what do you know of the queen?" Tom prompted when she first showed signs of slowing.

"Are you Lord Tom?" she asked around a mouthful of cheese. "I'm to tell no one but Lord Tom."

"I am he. Tell me, where is the queen?"

She scooped up an armload of sausages, watching him all the while. "I do not know."

"You do not know?" Westered grabbed her by the shoulders, shaking loose half of the plunder she had just gathered. "Then why have you dared—"

"Please, my lord," Tom interrupted, "we shall gain nothing by this. Let her go."

Westered released her, and she scrambled to retrieve everything she had dropped.

"Forgive me, girl," the duke said. "Pray you, tell us why you've come."

She merely looked at him in haughty disapproval and then turned again to Tom. "The one-eyed man, he said I was to get the reward from you and bring it to him. Then he would tell me what he knows, and I shall come back to tell you. And then I shall have more food."

"We have a bargain then," Tom said at once. "Rafe, bring the reward."

Westered looked at him incredulously. "My lord, you cannot mean merely to give it to her. If this is the same—"

"We shall have what we've bought, my lord," Tom replied calmly, and he handed the girl the heavy bag Rafe brought. "Tell your one-eyed man we shall expect to hear something of him soon."

"All right."

She bolted out of the room, at the last minute snatching up a bright, juicy apple that sat on the far corner of the table.

"I fear we shall never see her nor the reward again, my lord," Westered said. "Do you not recall the one-eyed man who tried to kill you on the road here? Likely the same one the king described who took my daughter. What are the odds but that it should be this very man?"

Tom only smiled grimly. "I am hoping precisely that."

❧

As soon as he had a chance to change into fresh clothes and kiss Elizabeth as she slept, Tom went to see his brother.

"Tom, at last! What have you found? Is she well? Where is she?"

"Calmly now," Tom said. "Even if I knew those answers, I could not tell them all at once."

"But you must have found something in all this while! Sweet heavens, Tom, you cannot mean to say you've not."

"Have courage, Philip. There's been nothing until I returned here tonight, but now we may have just the thing that leads us to your lady."

"What? Tell me."

"There was a little peasant girl who claimed—"

"They've brought the man, my lord," Rafe interrupted, entering the room. "It took five of the duke's soldiers to do it, but they have him in the courtyard."

"So soon?" Tom asked amazed.

Philip looked at him narrowly. "What man?"

"Have him taken to the guardroom, Rafe," Tom ordered. "I will see him at once."

"What man?" Philip asked again.

"As I was saying, this girl claimed she knew a man who would give us news of the queen in exchange for the reward, so I gave it to her. Did she run as we thought, Rafe?"

"She did, my lord. No doubt anyone but that rascal Jerome would have lost her in the streets, but, as you planned, he kept with her until he saw where she went and could bring the soldiers for her one-eyed friend."

Philip sat up, a sudden intensity in his expression. "Bring him here."

"Philip, let me—"

"Do not argue with me about this, Tom. I will see him."

"Bring him, Rafe," Tom said with resignation.

Rafe bowed. "At once, my lord."

A moment later the castle guard brought Hugh, wrists and ankles shackled, into Philip's chamber.

"Here he is, my lord," Rafe announced, and the guard pushed him at once to his knees. He never dared to lift his eyes.

"My lord of Brenden, I—"

"He is one of them!" Philip lunged toward him, but Tom held him back.

Hugh looked up in terror. "The king!"

"What have you done with her?"

Hugh made a frantic, futile attempt to escape, but the guard easily overpowered him and forced him again to his knees.

"Mercy, my lord king, I beg you!"

Philip fought his brother's hold. "Let me up, Tom! Let me up!"

"Philip, be still."

"He is one of those who took Rosalynde!"

"Be still!" Tom thundered. There was a sudden utter silence in the room.

"Be still," he warned Philip again, and then he went to the cowering prisoner. "Are you very bold or merely incredibly foolish thinking you could make away with the king's gold on top of all your other crimes?"

"Mercy, my lord," Hugh begged. "I've only come to right the wrong I did."

"Liar," Philip grated. "Tell me what you've done with my lady."

"She was unharmed when we delivered her, my lord. I swear it upon my soul."

"Delivered her where?"

"To Stonekeep, to the king of Reghed. It was he who commissioned us."

"Sarto!" Philip breathed. "Oh, God, dear God, not that."

"Steady," Tom said softly. "At least we know now."

"Why did I not know it all along?" Philip closed his eyes until he was no longer trembling. "Remove that creature from my sight, or I cannot answer for what I might do."

"I will see he's securely locked away until he can be tried," Tom said. "Come on, men. Rafe, look after his majesty."

Rafe nodded, and Tom led the soldiers down to Westered's dungeon.

After he had gotten every scrap of information about Rosalynde's whereabouts from the cowering Hugh, Tom went back to tell Philip his findings. Rafe was waiting for him outside the chamber door.

"I must warn you, my lord, we've been forced to tie him down."

"Oh, Rafe! Had you to do that?"

"He insists he will go after the queen himself," Rafe explained. "Tonight."

"But to be tied down again, God's pity. Of all things you might have done, surely there was some other way."

"He would not hear reason, my lord. I know it is a terrible thing to him, but there was nothing else to do. Livrette fears yet to give him potions to make him sleep, and anything else we might have done he would have fought until he got free or died in the trying. Even were we to put him into a cell, he would most likely injure himself trying to pry the bars apart." Rafe shook his head. "You know him, my lord. When he sets his will to a thing, God Himself is hard pressed to shift it."

Tom drew a deep breath. "Well, I had best go see him. Pray God I have strength enough to weather his temper."

Philip did not turn his face from the wall when Tom came into the room. He lay on his back, bound to the bedposts, his wrists and ankles wrapped in soft cloth to protect them from the chafing rope.

"Philip?"

Philip looked up in surprise.

"Tom!" Relieved, he began to tug at his bonds. "Thank God you've come back, Tom. They've all gone mad here, daring to bind me like this." He twisted his wrist, shifting the knot to one side to make it more accessible. "Here, Tom, this one first. Did the swine tell you anything more? As soon as you've freed me, I will—"

Tom merely stood there, and Philip jerked the ropes impatiently.

"Tom, you cannot mean to leave me this way."

"Can you be trusted free?"

"I will keep still." Philip tugged at the ropes again. "This is ludicrous, Tom. I will keep still."

"Until Livrette says you are fit?"

"Until I am fit."

"Until Livrette says you are fit, Philip. I'll have your word on it."

"Tom, I am all right, truly."

"Livrette does not think so."

"I feel fine."

"Your head does not ache?"

"No."

Tom looked at him dubiously. "No?"

Philip pressed his lips together. "Yes. Yes, it aches. My ribs ache, my arm aches, my jaw aches, my whole body aches from lying in this wretched bed! What does that matter? Rosalynde is being held at that madman's mercy, and you tell me I should let a few aches keep me from going to her?"

"Livrette has tried again and again to make it clear to you that if you do not keep still, that blow to your head could kill you yet, but you insist on getting up."

"Because no one else seems too concerned about what has happened to my wife or how to rescue her from it."

"That is not fair, Philip. Do you think I left Bess, as frightened as she is, because I am not concerned about your lady? I will do everything that can be done to take her from Stonekeep, I swear it. The duke is prepared to send his whole army if need be."

"Never let him, Tom. Sarto will only kill her before anyone by force could reach her."

"I know, and he knows it as well. We will think of some way to free her."

"Let me up, Tom!" Again Philip struggled with the ropes that bound him, a deep, sick fear in his eyes, as if he had just lost his last hope. "Tom, please, please, I beg you, let me up. Do not let them do this to me, not this time. You of all people should understand."

"I do understand, truly I do. Give me your word you will lie still as Livrette says, and I will free you this very moment."

"I cannot promise that."

"Then I am sorry, but I cannot release you. Not yet."

Philip turned his face again to the wall. "I am tired, Tom."

"I am sorry, Philip," Tom repeated, "but, believe me, this way is best."

"Yes, Father always said so."

Philip's voice was bitter and hopeless, and Tom knew he was again remembering Katherine and their father's claims that her murder was for Philip's own good.

"You cannot compare this to what he did."

For a long while, Philip said nothing. Finally he took an unsteady breath. "What did you learn from the prisoner?"

Tom stretched his tired shoulders. Then he pulled a chair up close to the bedside and began repeating every detail of the story Hugh had told him. Gradually his voice trailed off into incoherence and then silence. Philip was certain he was asleep, but he waited an agonizing quarter of an hour before he tested that.

"Tom?"

Getting no response, Philip lifted his head and made his voice not quite so soft.

"Tom?"

Still Tom did not stir. With a look of grim satisfaction, Philip wriggled toward him, every ache in his body intensifying as he wrenched against the hold of the ropes, straining closer and closer, stretching, reaching, until his trembling fingers closed on the dagger that hung from Tom's belt. Carefully, he worked it free. Then he turned it and slid it under the rope at his wrist, grateful for the cloths that shielded his skin from the well-honed blade.

It took him only a moment to free himself, pull on his boots, and then strip the bandages from his arm and from around his head. He kept the ones that bound his still-tender ribs. They would not show.

Tom did not waken, and Philip knew he would likely sleep until morning, even sitting up as he was. Philip only needed a few minutes head start anyway. On such a moonless night, it would be hard for anyone to follow him.

He slipped the dagger into his belt and picked up his cloak. Then, considering, he put it down and put on Tom's instead, careful to arrange the hood so it concealed the bruised side of his face. Cat-quiet, he opened the door, and then he paused. A long golden chain spilled over the edge of the jewel box that sat on the dressing table, and he picked it up. He pulled off his ring, the king's ring, and strung it on the chain. Then he put the chain around his neck and stuck it inside his shirt. That done, he stepped into the empty corridor.

He made his way rapidly through the castle, passing a handful of Westered's men here and there, men who knew him and Tom only slightly, men who would take no more than a sleepy glance and not think it strange that Lord Tom would be leaving again in search of the queen. He acknowledged their salutes tersely, taking swift, purposeful strides that carried no hint of the pain they cost him.

"My horse," he said to the groom who stood at the door, careful to stay in the shadowed archway.

The boy bowed. "At once, my lord of Brenden."

Philip smiled slightly at the ease of his deception and then froze.

"Tom! Tom!"

He turned and saw Elizabeth coming toward him as quickly as her pregnancy would allow. Her hair tumbled, unbound, down her back, and she wore only her shift and robe. Doubtless the guards had told her they had seen "Lord Tom" leaving the castle.

"Were you meaning to leave again before you had even seen me, my—" Her eyes widened in surprise. "Your maj—"

"Bess!"

He grabbed her and pressed his lips to hers, holding her tightly until her struggling stopped.

"Hear me, my lady," he murmured against her cheek. "One word from you, and they will put me back into bed. Then Tom will feel he must go again to rescue the queen. I think he belongs here with you now, does he not?"

She stood stiffly in his embrace, her eyes filled with fearful uncertainty.

"Your horse, my lord," the groom said, leading Halcyon up to them.

Elizabeth threw her arms around Philip's neck, hiding his face against her. "Must you leave me again so soon, my Tom?" she said aloud. Then she moved her mouth close to his ear, dropping her voice to a whisper. "He will be so angry. What shall I tell him?"

"Tell him your king commanded it."

She looked up at him for a long moment and then touched her lips shyly to his cheek. "May God bless you, my lord."

She stepped back from him, and he mounted the horse, clinging to the saddle through a moment of dizziness before he straightened and smiled at his sister-in-law.

"Good-bye, Tom," she called. "I pray you have good success and bring the queen back safe."

He blew her a grateful kiss and spurred Tom's horse into the night.

"Wake up, my lord."

Not opening his eyes, Tom stretched and groaned at the stiffness in his back. "What is it, Rafe?"

"He is gone."

"Huh?" Tom said through a yawn. He leaned as far backwards as the chair back would allow, stretching his arms and shoulders.

"The king is gone, my lord."

Tom's eyes snapped open, and he leapt to his feet. "Gone? How?"

There was nothing left of Philip in the bed except a few creased strips of linen and the severed ropes that had bound him.

"How could he have—my dagger!" Tom put his hand to his belt and exhaled heavily. "Philip, I swear—"

"According to the guard, he's been nearly four hours gone."

"The guard? And they did not stop him?"

"They all of them swear they thought he was you, my lord. He was wearing your cloak, and seeing him taking leave of Lady Elizabeth and riding your horse, what else might they have believed?"

"My lady saw him?"

"Called him by your name, they say."

Tom's expression tightened. "Get Palmer and Jerome, and the three of you meet me at the stables. Tell Palmer to pack my things for a journey. I am going to speak to my lady."

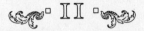
TOM WENT TO ELIZABETH'S DOOR AND KNOCKED SHARPLY. AFTER a moment, Nan answered, her eyes pleading for his understanding. "I am to tell your lordship that my lady is asleep and not to be disturbed."

"I'll not hear that," he said tightly, "not this time."

She made a brief curtsey and stepped back to admit him. Elizabeth was sitting up in the bed, a guilty roundness to her eyes as she watched him come to stand beside her.

"Go, all of you," he told her attendants, and in another moment the two of them were alone. "My lady?"

"He commanded me," she breathed, shrinking back from him. "I could not disobey."

"What is this, Bess? Fear?" He touched her cheek and felt her trembling. "Have I ever given you cause to fear me?"

"I helped him go. I wanted him to go! She is his wife. Why should *he* not go?"

"Bess."

"You promised you would never leave me."

"I said by my choice. I have no choice in this."

"I need you with me! Does that mean nothing to you?"

"Of course it does, but he needs me as well."

"So you choose him over me."

"No, Bess, never. But it may be I can help him. There is nothing I can do to help you."

"You can stay with me. You can be with me when our child comes."

"That's months yet," he soothed. "I will be back to you well before then."

"You are going into Reghed. Everyone says so. You will never come back." There was that same hopeless fatalism in her eyes that had been there when they lost their last child. "I will lose the baby because you will not be here, because you left me alone again."

He sat on the bed and put his arms around her, drawing her head down to his shoulder.

"Bess, Bess, you know that's not so. There was nothing I could have done had they let me stay the last time. Livrette said it was too late already. I told you all this."

"No. It was because you were not with me. God wanted to punish me, and you were not there to turn His anger away."

"Bess," he breathed in astonishment. "You cannot think so. It is Satan who brings destruction, Bess, not God. God gives only life."

She looked at him emptily. "No, it is His punishment. Because I was false to you."

"That was years ago, sweetheart. He's forgiven you."

She shook her head. "He's punished me since. Three children lost, Tom. Not one, nor even two, but three. And He'll take the fourth as well, I know it."

"Bess, have you forgotten the Scripture that says when we ask His forgiveness, He is faithful and just to give it to us? You've confessed before Him. I know you have and many times, too. Do you know what you say when you claim you are yet unforgiven? That He is unfaithful and unjust and, above all that, a liar as well. Do you think so of Him? Truly?"

"No," she sobbed, "but because I know He loves you and I hurt you, I cannot help thinking He is punishing me."

"Bess, no," he murmured, pulling her closer. "Never that. He loves us all every whit the same. He loves you, sweetheart. He does, full as much as He loves me. Even did He not, Bess, do you think He does not know I feel every pain you feel? Would He punish you for hurting me by hurting me, too?"

She started to cry. "I do not know. I do not know."

"Never believe such lies," he murmured, rocking her gently. "He loves you. You must know that."

"Stay," she begged again. "If you leave me now, I will die."

"Look at me, Bess." He took her by the shoulders and forced her to face him. "There is nothing I would not do for you, love. You know that's so, but I am merely a man. I love you, but God loves you more than I could ever hope to. You must rely on Him, not on me. Apart from Him, nothing in this world is promised to us."

"Tom—"

"God will hear my prayers for you, whether I make them here or in Reghed. You know I would not leave you for any light cause, but I must go now."

"Then go!" she cried, trying to shove him away from her, but he did not let her go.

"Let's not part this way," he pled. "Not this way, sweetheart."

"Just go, my lord. I see plain what is dearest to you."

"Please, love. I feel bad enough as it is."

"You should!" she snapped back at him. Then seeing the wounded tears that came to his eyes, she clutched him to her. "Please, do not leave me. Please, please, do not go. I will die if I lose this child, too, and you are not with me. I cannot bear it without you."

"You can, love. We both can."

"How?" she moaned.

He wrapped her in his arms. "Two things, sweetheart. First, trust that God knows best how to lead us and will never lead us wrongly."

"And second?"

He held her more tightly. "Second, know that none of this will be forever, however long it seems."

"Oh, Tom," she whispered, her tears soaking his shirt front.

"And one thing more," he murmured against her hair. He tilted her face up to his. "Always remember I love you."

He pressed his lips to hers in a lingering sweet kiss, and then he put his hand on the gentle roundness in her middle.

"Dear Lord God," he said softly, closing his eyes, "watch over this little one You have given us. Fill it with life and wholeness and in Your time bring it safely into the world. For sweet Jesus' sake, let it be so."

He leaned his cheek against her.

"Take care of your mama, little one. Tell her she must not be afraid while I am away. I will come back the very moment I am able." He touched his lips to her forehead. "I love you both so much."

He left her crying against her pillows.

Rafe, Palmer, and Jerome were waiting in the stable, packed and ready to leave when Tom arrived.

"I must tell you all that I do not know how we are best to proceed in this. We know the king means to go to Reghed. Our best chance is to stop him before he can cross the border, but, failing that, we've no choice but to go in after him. I suppose we must merely go there and, if need be, find a way across ourselves."

"I can show you, my lord."

Tom turned, surprised. "Molly."

"I was born in Reghed, my lord. It's not been five years since my father took us all from there. I can show you how to keep from the patrols at the border and the quickest way to get to the king's palace."

"You could not have been above fourteen when you left there. Are you certain you remember so much?"

"We lived in Stonekeep, my lord, in the shadow of Sarto's court where it was certain death to take a misstep. Trust me, I remember."

He looked at her intently for a moment and then turned to the others.

"Ready my horse, Palmer. I will meet you all in the courtyard in just a moment. Jerome, you had best fetch Livrette to go along with us. The king is likely to need him."

The boy bowed. "At once, my lord."

"And, Rafe, I trust you've already prepared everything else he'll be needing."

"I have, my lord, including a sound thrashing. That, believe me, I will be sure to give him directly when we find him."

There was not a trace of humor in the old man's eyes or in his voice, and Tom knew that if they found Philip in good condition, Rafe would more than likely make good his promise. Having had Philip and Tom in his charge since they had first stepped out of babyhood, Rafe had a singular freedom from the confining idea that kings and princes were to be obeyed without question, especially when such obedience conflicted with his duties as guardian. He had devoted most of his life to those duties, and he obviously did not mean to fall short in them now.

"We will find him, Rafe," Tom assured him.

Rafe nodded. "Yes, my lord. We will."

Tom dismissed the three of them and then turned again to the girl stoically awaiting him. As she had promised, she had kept herself quietly out of sight since they had come from Winton, and he had almost forgotten the awkwardness between them. It came back to him now with a rush.

"Molly, you know that my lady—"

"Neither of you need fear I will say anything more of what I confessed to you in Winton last spring, my lord. I well know my place, and, in any case, this is hardly the time to consider such things. We all must think of the king and queen now."

"It will not be a pleasant journey, and there will be no other women along. Are you certain you are prepared to put yourself into such a position when you could stay safe here in Lynaleigh?"

"My lord, I cannot forget their kindnesses to me any more than I could forget yours. If I can repay them in some little way, I would think myself most fortunate."

"It would hardly be a little way, Molly, were you to go willingly into such danger." He gave her a small, grateful smile. "But it would not be something I would quickly forget either."

There was a sudden spark in her dark eyes, and then she dropped her head. "I thank you, my lord."

"You had best gather your things then, Molly," he said, reproving himself for bringing back that longing look, determined it should not happen again when they were forced together in Reghed. "We're to leave at once."

⁂

Tom was surprised to see Elizabeth waiting for him when he went into the courtyard to meet the others.

"Are you certain you should be out of your bed, sweetheart?"

"I had to see you just this once more, my lord."

She nestled close to him, oblivious to the others there, and he held her tenderly.

"You needn't say it as if I were never to return."

She looked up at him, her face pale, and he caressed her cheek.

"Two things, sweetheart. Remember?"

"God knows how to lead us," she whispered, "and none of this will be forever." She swallowed hard and managed to smile faintly. "And you love me."

"Always," he murmured, touching his lips to hers.

Then Molly came into the courtyard, obviously packed for a journey.

"She is going, too?" Elizabeth asked, her eyes wide.

"She knows Reghed, love. She is our best hope to catch up to Philip and free the queen. Please, sweet, do not—"

She stood away from him and calmly called Molly to her. "I understand you will be going to Reghed with the others."

"His highness has said I might be of some help," Molly replied, curtseying meekly, "so please your ladyship."

"He is dearer to me than my life," Elizabeth told her, looking every inch a princess despite her shift and robe, "something I would not wish to let out of my sight, but that I know I must and that he must. I trust you will do what you are able to see him cared for. I will—" Her cheeks reddened, and Tom knew it was no easy thing for her to humble herself before this slight peasant girl. "I will be truly in your debt, girl, for whatever help you can be to him. Please, if there is any love in you for him, any love that is love, see he comes back safely."

Molly, too, was flushed. "My lady, I pray you believe me, I would never presume—"

"I well know what a difficult thing it is to try not to love him, but I believe you would never presume to act on that either. I know, too, he would never wrong my trust in him. So I must trust him to you now for this little while. After the wrong I've done you, I know I've no right to ask it."

"I will do it gladly, my lady, to see him safely back to your arms. If there is nothing else I've learned in all this while, my lady, I know his happiness lies in you. I need know nothing more."

The girl curtseyed again and went to stand with the others awaiting Tom's command to begin. He kissed his wife once more and then led them away.

Philip rode toward a faint light that flickered from the base of the slate mountains far ahead of him in the mist-shrouded night. His vision blurred from lack of sleep and from the blows he had taken, he thought at first the light came from somewhere in the mountain itself. As he drew nearer, he saw that it came from a small chapel built of the same stone as the mountain. He knew he would soon be in Reghed under Sarto's dark reign. It was not a place he could go into unprepared.

He walked through the chapel's rough arched doorway. The old priest did not turn at his step, did not rise from his knees, did not stumble in the quiet fervency of his prayer.

". . . for those who suffer in darkness and oppression, those who live in desperation wanting Your light, send Your truth, Your hope, Your salvation. Most especially I pray Your mercy upon the people of Reghed. You know their sorrows and how long they have awaited Your deliverance. Please send it to them." He crossed himself. "In the name of the Father and of the Son and of the Holy Spirit. Amen."

He was silent for a moment. When he spoke again, he still did not turn. "A cold night to come so far alone, my son."

"Forgive my intrusion, good father, but I have need of your holy offices before I continue my quest."

"Ah, a quest." The priest looked up, a gentle smile on his lips and in his age-blinded eyes. Philip realized that the candles were lit for devotion and not illumination. "A knight then truly. And how may I serve you, sir knight?"

Philip knelt on the cold stone beside him. "I need your prayers, good father. Before I go into Reghed, I need God's blessing."

"Yes," the old man considered, "any man going into that unhappy land assuredly needs God's presence with him." Again he smiled. "But surely if He has sent you there, you need not doubt He will go with you." He felt for Philip's hand and patted it between both of his own. "God has at last heard my prayers and sent someone to Reghed."

Philip glanced above the altar at the images painted there, saints gone on before. He could hardly see them in the uncertain candle-light, yet still he knew their eyes were upon him, weighing his service to God against their own.

"So shall we pray here together? Will you tell me your name, sir knight?"

Philip moistened his lips. "Philip. My name is Philip."

"Well, Sir Philip, if you will help these old bones to stand, I shall fetch the bread and the wine."

"Bread and wine, father?"

The old man got to his feet, steadying himself against Philip's shoulder, a touch of mirth in his mild face. "I can hardly serve you the Blessed Sacrament without it."

"Father, I merely wished—"

The priest's expression turned serious, and he seemed almost to see through the opaqueness of his eyes. "Have you some reason, my son, that you may not partake?"

Philip looked down at the floor, away from all the eyes upon him. "No, father."

"Perhaps I have misjudged, and it is not God's errand that takes you to Reghed. You ask His blessing, but have you first asked His will?"

Philip lifted his head, a flash of anger in his eyes, but he kept his voice tautly even. "I have known some while that He meant me to go there. Do I do wrong in going now?"

"That would depend upon whether you go to do His will or your own."

"I go to right a wrong. That's enough."

"Examine yourself, my son. As you shall answer unto God who knows all hearts, consider what it is you do. For if you shall eat this bread and drink this wine unworthily, you shall be held guilty of the very blood and body of our Lord. In His name I charge you, lay down the sins you have brought here to His altar. Hatred and strife and malice of all kinds you may not harbor in your heart lest in eating and drinking unworthily, you eat and drink damnation unto yourself."

Philip did not move, did not speak. He knew the Scripture as well as the old man. If he dared touch Holy Communion while holding this hatred inside him, feeding on it, nurturing it, reveling in it, he would reap nothing but damnation.

"There are some things I need no eyes to see, my son," the priest said softly, laying one thin hand on Philip's head. "Ask God to cleanse your heart. Vengeance belongs to Him alone; He will repay. Ask His guidance in this quest you have set yourself. Only the foolish man sets his course and then asks God's blessing on it. Better far to ask the way He would have you to go and walk in that, knowing your blessing is assured. Search your heart for the truth, ask His pardon, seek His way, trust in His loving care."

Still Philip did not speak, and after a moment the old man patted his shoulder. "I shall bring the bread and wine, my son, and when you are ready, we shall partake of it together."

When he returned, the chapel was empty.

It was only when the woman brought her breakfast that Rosalynde knew another morning had come. This was the same silent peasant

woman who had been sent to her the first night she had been con-
fined here, the one who had brought her out of her swoon and made
wordless apology for frightening her with her unexpected presence.
She had served Rosalynde every day since, but this was the first time
she had come alone.

"Please," Rosalynde begged. "Help me. My husband is the king
of Lynaleigh. He will give you anything you ask if you will help me
now."

The woman set out the food in grim silence, not looking up from
her task.

"Send to him then," Rosalynde urged, clinging to her arm. "For
Christian charity, I beg you, merely see he has word of where I am.
Please."

The woman glanced behind her, then shook her head, a trace of
pity on her face.

"I have two little boys and a baby girl not yet a year old,"
Rosalynde told her. "I need to be with them. Perhaps you have children. You must know."

Again the woman shook her head, tears mixing with the pity in
her dull brown eyes. She pointed at Rosalynde and indicated a
height of about three feet and then another slightly lower. Then she
cradled her arms in front of her and made a gentle rocking motion.

"Yes," Rosalynde said. "Two boys and a little girl."

Nodding, the woman pointed to herself and made the rocking
motion again.

"You have a baby!" Rosalynde cried. "Then you know what it is
to be separated for even a moment. Please!"

Shaking her head once more, the woman drew her arms closer
to herself, as if she were holding her baby more tightly, as if she were
cuddling it against her cheek. Then she reached out pleadingly with
her empty hands.

"It was taken from you?" Rosalynde asked. "But why? Who?"

Again the woman glanced toward the door. Then she put her
finger to her thin lips, and Rosalynde knew. The child was being held
to ensure the woman's silence and loyalty until Sarto's plan was
complete.

"Send to my husband," Rosalynde pressed. "When he comes for me, he will see that you get your child back."

The woman shook her head frantically, clutching her hands.

"He will," Rosalynde insisted. "Sarto will never—"

"Never what, gracious lady?"

Both girls turned at Sarto's rumbling voice, and the waiting woman cringed away from him, overturning the tray in her haste, spilling food everywhere. Terrified, she fell to her knees, her face flat to the ground. Sarto tumbled her onto her side with a kick.

"Get up! Dare you to soil this place and spoil my lady's breakfast?"

The woman scrambled to clean up the mess, but he yanked her up and gave her a ringing slap that split her lip. Then he flung her out into the corridor and slammed the door. He turned again to Rosalynde.

"Your pardon, gracious lady, that I have set such a fumbling fool to tend you. You'll not see her again."

She stood there wide-eyed, backed against the table.

"Please, my lord, it was a fault unintended, more mine than hers, not worthy of such a blow. Please, my lord, in all honor—"

"She is mine, gracious lady, as all Reghed is mine to do with as I will. Will you say I may not?"

"All Reghed is yours, my lord, as you are her king, but I do not belong to Reghed. I am the queen of Lynaleigh, and it is her king, not Reghed's, who has right to me."

"I had first right to you," he said. "I had thought some time in this place would recall it to you, but I see I was mistaken in that. Perhaps a few more days here—"

"No, I beg you, if nothing more, let me out of this room. As you have so often asked, I will attend your court, I will answer to what name you choose; so long as you do not ask me to break my vows to my husband, I will be your Rosamund." She clasped her hands in supplication, her eyes wide with pleading fear. "I beg you, my lord, let me out of here."

He smiled faintly. "You need only ask, gracious lady. As for your vows to your husband, you need not fear the breaking of them on my account. Until you are free of them, you have my pledge on it, they shall remain inviolate."

"You are a man of honor," she said, calming. "Surely that honor would not allow the taking of another man's wife. Please, my lord."

He grabbed her by the arms, and she shrank back from the rage that blackened his face.

"Please!"

"It was he, your fine, honorable husband, who took what was not his! But perhaps you've not had time enough here, gracious lady, to recall the vows you made first to me."

"No, no, my lord, I beg you, I will say no more."

"You need only ask," he said, releasing her, a possessive, triumphant gleam in his serpent eyes. "I would be most pleased, gracious lady, to present you to my court this evening at supper."

He studied the rumpled shift she yet wore. Seizing her arm once more, he pulled her to the carved wardrobe. He flung open the doors and began rummaging through its contents.

"But you must be properly dressed for such an event. Of all your gowns, the one you most favored . . ."

He glanced at the portrait and then at the ebony-draped box below it. Rosalynde felt a sudden revulsion. He meant to take the musty velvet off of that ghastly thing in the coffin and—

"No!"

She could not suppress the cry, and temper flared again in his eyes.

Steadying herself, she managed a pale smile. "What I mean to say, my lord, is that I had far rather keep that for some great occasion when I've a right to wear it." She looked up at him, her eyes full of meaning. "As your queen."

That pleased him, she could tell it.

"Yes," he murmured. "Yes, of course."

He kissed her hand, and she did not draw back. That also pleased him.

"I will leave you to choose then, gracious lady."

"But I will need someone to dress me, someone who might see to my hair." She looked steadily into his eyes as if she had no need to fear him. "I would prefer the girl who brought my breakfast today."

"The other women shall see to you. So clumsy a creature is unfit to tend to any lady. I have said you shall not see her again."

"Please, my lord." She touched his arm in entreaty. "If I am to be presented to your court, I should like it to be a joyous occasion not marred with the sorrow I would feel if anything happened to her on my account."

For a moment he stared at her hand, and she thought she could feel him tremble at the light touch.

"I will send her and her child back to their home," he said at last. "They shall not be harmed."

"I thank you, my lord."

"And I shall number my every breath until this evening."

"Until this evening," she said, making a deep curtsey.

With the courtliest of bows, he left her.

She was prepared for his return that night, spending far more time in the interim gathering her courage than preening for the feast. The instant he came into the room, he took her hand. There was no smile on his lips, but his cold eyes held a fierce gleam of pleasure as they roamed over her.

The black velvet bodice of the gown she wore, the most modest in the wardrobe, was cut very tight and low, and though it was laced in front, beneath the laces in a narrow V that finally closed at her waist was only her white flesh. He reached toward her but merely touched one finger to the collar of blood rubies at her throat. She did not allow herself to draw back or tremble.

Without a word he took her arm, and for a breathless moment he stood with her there before the murky glass, his eyes fixed on her reflection, on theirs together. Then he led her down to the great hall.

CHAPTER

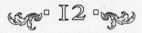 12

THE MULTIPLIED HUM OF CONVERSATION DIED INTO SILENCE AS Sarto led Rosalynde through his courtiers to seat her at the lavish table. She did not know if the image of Sarto's mistress was well known by all his people still, but she could tell by the incredulous expressions on the faces of some of the older ones, those who must have known her all those years ago, that they too saw the resemblance.

"Rosamund," she heard breathed from every side, but at an expectant look from Sarto, even that was smothered into stillness.

"Twenty-five long years," he told them, a sepulchral hush in his voice, "but had it been twenty-five thousand, I would have waited. But see, my lords and ladies, my Rosamund has returned as she pledged me she would do." He brought her hand to his lips, that consuming possessiveness again in his eyes and in his touch. "And soon, very soon, I shall make her my bride. She shall be my queen and yours, and you shall again pledge her your loyalty."

The announcement was met with low murmurs. Two of the younger noblemen exchanged a few low heated words, and one of them stood.

"Surely, your majesty cannot believe this girl could be—"

"Sit down, you fool," his companion hissed.

Sarto stared at the first man, a look of cold amusement in his eyes. "You wish to speak?"

The man glanced at the rest of the company, saw he was the only one standing, and abruptly sat again, leaving only an uneasy silence in the great hall.

Sarto smiled once more, looking expectantly at the rest of the company. One of his barons got slowly to his feet.

"Long live the queen," he said, lifting his goblet uneasily, as if he were half convinced she was some phantasm Sarto had summoned out of the abyss. One by one all the court rose, echoing his halting toast. Rosalynde could not help wondering if they had themselves been conjured up from the past. All of them, young and old, had on clothing from the same period as the gown she was wearing, like all the dresses in Rosamund's wardrobe from a quarter of a century before. The clothes themselves did not seem old, merely the fashion of them, as if anything more recent was forbidden.

"This is as it should have always been," Sarto told her as they all sat again. "As it will forever be."

There was a moment of silence. Then the last of the nobility, a fair-haired, slender young man perhaps her own age, perhaps slightly older, got to his feet and raised his goblet. "May the queen live forever," he said, staring at her intently, as he had since she had come into the room. She judged from his position at one of the lower tables that he was of little importance in the kingdom, and it surprised her to see the black, baleful look Sarto gave him. Without another sound, the young man sank back into his chair.

"At last, my people," the king said, "our queen is with us, and we shall have nothing but pleasure and merriment to take the place of our sorrow. Here before you all I make royal decree that there shall be no more a Day of Mourning. That day and every day shall instead be a celebration of my lady's return, and there shall be as great a penalty set for those who do not celebrate as there was for those who did not mourn before. Are my lords agreed?"

"So say we all," they replied in dutiful chorus.

Looking pleased, Sarto continued, "Now, my lords and ladies, in keeping with this new fashion of merrymaking, we shall have—"

"Hail the queen!"

With all the court, Rosalynde looked toward the back of the

great hall. Standing in the doorway was a woman of perhaps thirty-eight wearing a man's shirt, vest, and breeches, with her black hair in two thick plaits over her shoulders. She was possessed of the height and brawny strength of an amazon. The only dainty thing about her was the pouncet box, a filigreed silver orb that hung around her neck.

Still with her quiver strapped to her back, still with her bow in her hand, she strode to Sarto's table. Taking no note of the glare he gave her, she made a mocking curtsey with a flourishing swirl of her imagined skirts.

"You must pardon my coming so tardily, my queen, but I was not told you would be among us this evening. The king is always forgetting to tell me such things. Why just last week, we were lying abed together, and he said—"

"Brenna!" Sarto growled.

She smiled fiercely, enhancing her strong, martial beauty, a beauty as opposite Rosalynde's delicate femininity as autumn is to spring. "I do beg your pardon, my lady," she said, undaunted. "I merely wished to see if I had any need for jealousy now." She laughed. "You'll not hold his interest long, girl, no more than the other pretty alabaster dolls he's broken and tossed aside."

Sarto stood, a dangerous anger in his eyes. "Lady Brenna, you are dismissed."

"As you say, my liege," she replied, still smiling. "But when you have done playing with your toys, you know where I am."

With another taunting curtsey, she swept out of the court, and Rosalynde looked up at the king, wondering what punishment he would decree for the woman's insolence. He merely smiled.

"As I was saying, my lords and ladies," he said, "in celebration of the return of the queen, tonight Stonekeep shall have music and dancing and revelry we've not seen for five-and-twenty years."

The lords and ladies of Sarto's court threw themselves into the commanded festivities with an uncertain, giddy desperation. The musicians stumbled through the lilting tunes. The dancers faltered in the sprightly steps with unaccustomed feet, the older courtiers demonstrating the once-forbidden measures to the younger. As the celebration progressed, Sarto led his prospective bride among the murmuring clusters of onlookers, making introductions here and there, seemingly oblivious to the conversations that were squelched at his approach, to the furtive looks that sometimes blazed with hatred when his back was turned. She was fairly certain that hatred did not extend to herself, but neither was she aware of anything in the eyes upon her that approached concern or kindness or even pity for her plight.

When the festivities finally ended, Rosalynde was surprised to find herself escorted to a room with large glassed windows and a bed draped in cream-colored linens. She had not thought such light delicateness could exist here in Stonekeep.

"Will this chamber perhaps suit you better, gracious lady, until we can at last be together?" Sarto asked.

Relief flooding through her, she gave him a faint smile. "I thank you, my lord. It pleases me well."

She knew this was a dangerous game she was playing, and she had been afraid that in that other place, surrounded with Rosamund's things, with Rosamund herself, she might not be able to keep firm hold on her reality, that she might slip irretrievably into his. Here perhaps she could keep up the pretense until deliverance came.

"You must pardon the clumsiness of my nobles tonight, lady," Sarto said, "and the ill-preparedness of my musicians. I shall command them to dance and play better tomorrow."

"It has been a very long while since they last had dancing, my lord," she replied. "You must have patience with them."

"If that pleases you, they shall have my patience. But the court, gracious lady, does that please you as well?"

"My lord?"

"It is all the same, my lady, all the same. I've not let them change anything, for I wanted you to know it when you returned to me. But there was one thing I could not keep for you, though I tried."

"What is that, my lord?"

"Do you not know? Is there nothing you miss?"

"My lord, I do not—"

"Cordell—he is dead."

She looked at him, puzzled, startled to see there were tears in his eyes. "He is dead?"

Who was this Cordell, and what was he to Rosamund?

"You would have been proud of him," Sarto said with a pitiful attempt at a smile. "He was hardly more than a baby when you last saw him, but he grew into such a man. It was comfort to me knowing I had that much of you still, and then he, too, was taken. It's been not quite a year, and all this while I've wondered what I was to tell you when you returned to me and found he was gone."

"What happened to him, my lord?" she asked gently.

He responded with a vague shake of his head, as if he were far from her, far from the present. "Gone," he murmured, "gone, gone, gone. Oh, Rosamund, forgive me, he is gone."

To her astonishment, he sank to his knees and wrapped his arms around her waist, huddling there. She dared not struggle away from him.

"I could not keep him safe for you, Rosamund," he murmured, "and now you can never forgive me."

She felt a genuine pity for him, for his loss, for his madness. As if she were quieting a child, she held him tenderly against her.

"Shh," she soothed.

He began to sob. "Once we had married, Rosamund, he would have been counted legitimate, true heir to my throne. I wanted our son to rule next in Reghed. *Our* son! Oh, forgive me, Rosamund, forgive me."

He said more, all of it rambling, babbling unintelligibility, and she merely stood still and silent, not knowing what would calm him and what might push him deeper into his dementia.

"Rosamund, Rosamund," he moaned, holding her more tightly, pressing his face against her. "Rosamund."

He stroked his hands up her sides, and she gasped at the feel of his lips on the bare flesh her laces left exposed. Panicked, she shoved him backwards, twisting out of his grasp.

"My lord!"

He scrambled to his feet and grabbed her by the shoulders, his fingers sinking deeply into her white flesh, a frenzied gleam in his eyes. "What is to prevent me from taking you right now, marriage or no?"

She drew a deep breath and then looked up at him, her green eyes as serene as the sea after a storm.

"You are a man of honor, my lord. Should you give me a child, you would want it to carry your legitimate blood, the royal blood of Reghed. You did not give Cordell such blood."

He stood for a long moment staring, the fierceness in his expression turning into uncertainty as he searched her eyes. Then he smiled slightly and shook his head.

"When he was born, she wanted so much—" He closed his eyes and once more shook his head, the determined lines returning to his expression. "You. *You* wanted so much for him to be king one day." He tightened his hold on her, and the fierceness came again into his eyes. "You."

"My lord—"

His passion died as suddenly as it had come.

"You speak true, gracious lady." He released her shoulders and then caught her hand, touching her fingers with a courtly kiss. "The child you give me shall have no stain upon it. I bid you good night."

She did not move until she heard the turn of the key in the lock. Then she hugged her arms around herself, trembling with helpless fear. "Oh, God, take me from this place!"

There was hardly a moment of silence. Then to her amazement, a narrow passageway opened in the wall behind her, and the man who had raised the final toast that night at supper stepped into the room. "Good evening," he said with a slight bow. "Mother."

"What do you mean, sir?" She moved warily away from him. "Who are you, and why have you come?"

"I hear you are to marry my father," he replied. "That will make you my mother, will it not?"

She was too startled to answer that, and there was more than a touch of irony in his thin smile.

"He did not tell you he still has a son. Never mind. He rarely remembers it himself."

She studied him for a moment, searching for some resemblance to Sarto's dark heaviness in the reedy blond who stood before her. Perhaps it was there in the blunt nose, in the broad line of the brow, but that was all.

"You are going to marry him, are you not?"

"Surely he would not make such an announcement if that were not his intent," she replied cautiously.

He smiled again. "You are like her, you know, but I cannot quite tell where the resemblance falls down. The hair, the fair skin and delicate frame, the eyes—hmmm. They are alike in color truly, but yours haven't the same look to them. Hers had the color of emeralds—and the hard lifelessness of them. I do not remember her, not truly, but I've seen the portrait, all my life heard the tales, and until last winter faced more tangible proof of her perdurable hold on my father."

"You mean your brother Cordell."

"Hardly my brother. We had civil words perhaps a dozen times in all our lives. He was like her, too, though. To see him, you would have sworn he was an angel from heaven, but knowing him better, you'd far sooner say he was one of those fallen ones. He was my father's pet, you may readily guess, and until he died, I suppose my father was more or less content with his memories and the satisfaction of knowing that Rosamund's child would one day rule Reghed."

"But he was—"

"A bastard? In every sense of the word, but my father thought he could find a way around that somehow." He studied her for a moment. "Perhaps through someone like you."

"What happened to him, my lord? Your father would not say."

"If he did, he would only say that some envious sorcery took his life. The truth is much less glamorous. Cordell set himself to drink an entire cask of Father's best wine simply because Father had forbidden him to drink any. The physicians said he strangled on his own vomit."

"Oh, my lord!"

"My father had them hanged because they could not save him, no matter that they were not called until he'd been some hours dead." There was a touch of bitter cynicism in his faint smile. "It paints a pretty picture, does it not?"

"I take it then that Rosamund was not your mother."

"Oh, no," he said with an offhanded gesture. "I am only Sarto's firstborn, his lawful heir by his legitimate wife, but in Reghed, at least for now, that means little."

"Your mother is—"

"Dead. Yes, quite dead. She died giving me life and pleased my father greatly in doing so. He thought that would make his way clear at last for him to make Rosamund his wife and eventually his queen. Grandfather thought otherwise and had her poisoned." He shrugged. "For some odd reason, he did not think a harlot and sorceress fit to sit on the throne he'd served all his life."

"My lord, you are well aware I am not Rosamund. I cannot be what your father wants. Help me get away from here, and you shall have whatever reward you ask."

Again he smiled his bitter smile. "And can your ladyship give me back my life after my father has me flayed alive for such betrayal?"

"Why have you come here if you have no help to offer?"

"I wanted to know who you really are. A lady born, without doubt, but of what breed? Nothing less than a princess, I'd say."

"I am the queen of Lynaleigh. Please, there must be something you can do."

"Know this now, my lady, queen or jade, no one here can help you. There is no escape from my father, no way to fight him, no way to deceive him, even the attempt would be rewarded with torturous death. Only a fool would consider it."

"My lord, I pray you—"

"Save your prayers, madam, or, if you must, pray that his madness does not turn and leave him with no need of you."

With a bow, he walked back into the open passageway, and it shut seamlessly behind him. Nothing she attempted could make it open again.

Philip did not know how long it had been since he had left the little chapel at the border. A blur of days and nights marked his progress toward Sarto's stronghold but brought little variation to the wet cold that shrouded this land of his enemy. As long as he could remember, he had taken pleasure in keen, fresh winter, but this Reghed did not have the brisk, exhilarating crispness he had always loved in Lynaleigh. This was a dismal, unfriendly cold that seeped into his still-healing bones and made them ache with his mount's every jarring step. Only the thought of Rosalynde gave him the strength to keep going.

He was reluctant to stop for even a moment's rest for fear that that moment would become hours, even an entire night, but sometimes exhaustion and the merciless throbbing in his head would drive him to huddle under a tree or beneath a makeshift shelter of sodden brush, to sink into oblivion until he could stagger up again and press on.

The towns he passed through were as bleak as the weather, the people grim and silent, grudgingly giving him the information he asked for, offering nothing without payment and much urging. When he had stopped last, only a few hours earlier, he had learned that it was a long road yet to Stonekeep. Now, his body swaying limp-jointed with the motion of his horse, he wondered vaguely if he would ever reach there, if he would ever see Rosalynde again.

"Please," he murmured, lifting his head, but the dawn sky was as heavy and gray as lead, looking proof against his meager prayer. He pressed his face against his mount's warm golden neck. "God, please."

A fox darted out of the forest with a scrawny winter rabbit in her mouth. Startled, Halcyon shied away from her. His hands numb and clumsy with cold, Philip lost hold of the reins. Before he could recover them, the horse reared up with a whinny of protest. Philip grabbed at the saddle, trying to hang on, but he tumbled backwards, clutching nothing but air. Then his head struck the ground, and there was only darkness.

It was midmorning before anything stirred along the forest road. Then the faint sound of singing, joyful multi-part harmony, threaded through the trees. Soon a brightly painted wagon creaked over the hill, followed by another and then another. The driver of the first wagon was built small and light, his boyishly eager face belying his close to forty years. The woman sitting beside him had the same weight and build as he, the same swarthy complexion, and sang low harmony to his piping tenor lead. It was she who first noticed the man sprawled in the brown grass alongside the road.

"Look there, Credotti," she said, and the man reined in the horses, forcing the rest of the wagons to stop as well.

"Poor place for a nap," he observed. She snatched the reins from him. "Now, Anna-Maria, my treasure—"

"See if he is dead," she insisted. He jumped down from the wagon and walked toward the trees.

"Have a care that this is not a ruse to rob us!" she called after him as he stopped cautiously at Philip's side.

"Here now, fellow." Credotti prodded him not too roughly with the toe of his boot and then turned him onto his back. "This is no place for sleeping, man."

"Credotti, you jackanapes, can you not see that the poor man is hurt?" Anna-Maria took a wine skin from under the seat and scrambled down. "Give him some of this."

Credotti took the skin from her and poured a little of the contents into Philip's mouth. Philip coughed and turned away from it, and Credotti tried again to wake him. "Come now, man."

Philip only moaned a little and was still.

"It cannot be a good thing for him to be out here alone and hurt so," Anna-Maria said after a quick glance around. "I think he'd best come along with us. Reynaldi! Arnaldo!"

The two lanky young men driving the next wagon leapt down and lifted Philip up.

"Well, put him inside," Anna-Maria scolded when they did not move quickly enough to suit her. "Must I tell you everything?"

They carried Philip to the first wagon and laid him on a straw pallet surrounded by precariously balanced chests and bundles. The mat was a good foot too short for his long frame.

"Now, Arnaldo, go back to your wagon," Anna-Maria directed. "Reynaldi, you drive this one. Credotti, come help me."

In another moment, the wagons were again winding their way through the forest.

※

"It must have been thieves," Credotti said after he had gone through Philip's clothes. "He has nothing left but this fine ring and the little scarred one on his hand. And it must have been days ago. These wounds have been healing for some time now."

Anna-Maria studied Philip's face for a moment. Then she turned his head and saw the bruised place over his ear.

"This is bad, Credotti. He is healing of it, as you say, but he should be keeping still, not lying in the wood in the cold and damp like that. Do you think he comes from one of the villages nearby? Let me see the ring."

She held the royal ruby by its chain, still around Philip's neck, and examined it closely. "This is some nobleman's, or I miss my guess. Look, Credotti. Stolen, too, no doubt."

"Or he wears it in such a fashion to conceal his identity," her husband offered. "Look at these clothes, at the man himself. He's no peasant thief."

Anna-Maria wet a cloth in the water barrel. She touched it to Philip's face, and his eyes snapped open. "Where am I?"

Credotti smiled and made a sweeping gesture with both arms. "Traveling with the Great Credotti!"

Philip studied him for a moment, puzzled. "Acrobats?"

"Acrobats? For all the world, fellow! And jugglers, magicians, players—the finest players in all Reghed! And for music—"

"Be still, Credotti," Anna-Maria told him. Then she turned to her guest. "How did you come to be hurt?"

"I was set upon by thieves," Philip said after a brief hesitation.

Credotti looked triumphant. "Ah, you see, my treasure, I was right."

"Be still," Anna-Maria told him again. Then she turned back to Philip, her eyes narrowing. "Thieves, eh? You must have lost something precious to have fought for it so fiercely."

"I did." There was a sudden tautness in Philip's face. "And I mean to have it back."

"My husband claims you are more than a peasant."

"At least no worse," he allowed. "I am in your debt, mistress, for your kindness, but I'll not impose upon you further."

He sat up, and a rough jolt of the wagon made him grimace and clutch his ribs.

"Well, we will put you back on the road then," Anna-Maria said tartly. "My husband keeps a stout cudgel under our wagon seat. If you like, I will have him strike you with it several times before you go. It will be quicker and no less certain to start you bleeding again."

"I am grateful to you truly," Philip protested, "to you both, but I cannot spare the time—"

"Where is it you must get to in such haste, man?" Credotti asked. "Wherever it is, if it is on the way to Stonekeep, you might as well come along with us. We will be there as soon as you could be walking, and it may be that by then you will be rested enough to do whatever it is you've set yourself to do."

"You are going to Stonekeep? Truly?"

"By royal command!" There was pride in the diminutive acrobat's eyes. "We are summoned to perform in celebration of the wedding of the king himself."

"Sarto!" Philip's eyes widened. "Whom is he to marry?"

"What does it matter, man? We are to play before the royal court of Reghed! Our fortune is made!"

Philip grabbed his arms. "You must know something of her. Anything."

Credotti shrugged. "They say she was his mistress many years ago. Rosaline? Uh, no, Rosabelle? No."

"Rosalynde," Philip breathed.

Credotti slowly shook his head. "No, it was—"

"Credotti, you fool," the woman scolded, "it was Rosamund."

The acrobat snapped his fingers. "That was the name. Just a bit of a girl, if that much of the tale is true, though how she could be if she was his mistress so long before, I cannot tell."

Philip sat there silent, fear and fury fighting for control of his emotions. Cold determination won out. "I will go along with you, Master Credotti," he said after a moment. "If the offer still stands."

"Come and welcome," Credotti said heartily. "We will be in Stonekeep well before the wedding, and then you shall see the lady yourself. I'm told the heavens themselves envy her beauty."

"No doubt, no doubt," Philip agreed, a grim tautness in his mouth. "I must see her then. Do you not think so?"

"If you're to come along with us, boy, I'll not be tending you the whole way," Anna-Maria put in. "You'll lie quiet and let yourself mend. When we reach Stonekeep, you'll work."

With a nod of assent, Philip eased himself back down onto the thin straw pallet that barely cushioned him from the jouncing wagon bed and closed his eyes. It was hours before his whirling thoughts were lulled into sleep.

Well past noon the next day the wagon came to a rough halt and jolted Philip awake again.

"If you are highwaymen, you'll take nothing here!" he heard Credotti warn from the wagon seat.

"You mistake us, man. We are merely seeking someone and thought you might tell us if you've seen him."

Tom's voice! Philip lay still, his half-dazed mind scrambling for a plan.

"We see many in our travels," Anna-Maria said offhandedly. "Who is this one you seek?"

"My elder brother," Tom told her. "We look much alike, but he is bruised here across the jaw and on the side of the head. Across the ribs, too. Have you seen him?"

"Your elder brother, you say? Does he fear you, boy, that he'd go so far to escape you?"

"Not at all. But he's set himself to go to Stonekeep, no matter the risk to himself. We merely mean to see him safe."

"Why Stonekeep?" Credotti asked.

"He's had something taken from him, and he'll not rest until he's gone to reclaim it, hurt or no."

"Something taken from him?" Anna-Maria sounded suspicious. "His inheritance perhaps, younger brother? Say nothing, Credotti," she advised her husband. "The world is full of young upstarts eager to take what's not rightly theirs."

Under other circumstances, Philip would have laughed at her assumptions and at the frustrated impatience in Tom's reply.

"No, upon my honor, woman, that is not so! I swear to you, I intend only his good. You've seen him. You've admitted as much already. Tell me at the least if he was well."

"We ought to search these wagons," Philip heard Palmer suggest. Then he heard the scrape of a cudgel as Credotti took it from under the wagon seat.

"You might consider that twice, my friends," the little acrobat warned. "There are many more of us than your poor few."

"Philip," Tom called out, "I know you hear me. Will you let this come to a battle between us?"

His temper flaring, Philip threw open the little door in the back of the wagon and climbed out. Rafe and Jerome and Livrette were with Tom and Palmer. Philip was surprised to see Molly there, too.

"Well?" Philip demanded.

"You have refuge with us still, boy, if you wish it," Credotti said. Philip noticed that the rest of the troupe were standing in the road, armed with clubs and a couple of rather wicked-looking blades. Livrette swept indignantly past them and began to examine the battered side of his patient's head.

"I see you've not yet killed yourself," Tom observed, looking Philip over. "I suppose I owe thanks to your friends here."

"How is it you found me, Tom?"

"We came across Halcyon wandering some way back, found where you must have fallen and the traces of several wagons. It was nothing to track you here."

"I am glad you have him again. Now ride him home."

"Philip—"

"What is it you want, Tom?"

"What is it I want? By all the saints, Philip, did you think I would merely stand by and let you walk into that madman's lair alone? He's twice attempted at your life, and bless me if you are not trying as best you can to help him take it."

"I hardly think—"

"Well, I would have to agree with you upon that point."

"Tom—"

"I will take you back," Tom warned, "if I must strap you across your saddle to do it."

"Do not make me fight you over this, Tom. Turn loose of me, man!" Philip snapped, shoving Livrette away from him. "I am weary of your meddling."

"Please, my lord," the physician said, "if you are to heal properly, you must—"

"I must be let alone! Tom, you might just as well take yourself and all the rest back to Westered. I told you I will go to her. I will, and neither you nor all of you together will turn me from that."

"We've had this discussion before, my lord," Rafe said. "When you are fit enough."

"I'll not go back, Rafe." Philip jabbed his finger repeatedly into the old man's chest. "It is time you remembered who is king here and who—"

Without warning, Rafe took a thick handful of Philip's hair and jerked him backwards. An instant later, the old man was flat on the ground, blinking in astonishment. Philip stood over him, breathless and rubbing his fist.

"I'll not go back."

Rafe sat up and moved his jaw gingerly from side to side. Then he dusted off his hands. "As I said, my lord, now that you are fit enough . . ."

Tom shook his head and hauled the old man to his feet. "I suppose that's settled then."

Philip narrowed his eyes. "Rafe?"

"Yes, my lord, it is settled."

Philip nodded. "And, Rafe?"

"My lord?"

"Never do that again."

"You see, my treasure," Credotti said to his wife, "I told you we had stumbled onto more than a thieving peasant here. He is a king!"

Anna-Maria looked at Philip dubiously. "Oh, king, eh? Very nice and very easily said. King of what?"

"I am Philip of Lynaleigh, though I'd not have that told outside of yourselves. No doubt Sarto thinks me dead, and I should like to have him think it still."

"And this precious thing he's taken from you?"

"Rosalynde. My wife."

"Sarto's bride!" Credotti exclaimed. "Then I take it she did not go to him willing."

Anna-Maria scowled at him, then gestured toward Philip. "Would she go of choice from him to a mad old tyrant? We come from the hill country far west of here, boy," she told Philip. "We know little of the king's court, but we have seen all along the way the bloody cruelties of his reign."

"You must call him 'my lord' now, my treasure," Credotti said, looking uncertainly at Philip. "You cannot say 'boy' to the king of Lynaleigh."

"You may call me what you will, Madam Credotti," Philip told her, "so you let me come along with you to Stonekeep."

"We will be going with you," Tom said.

Philip shook his head. "I can see to this alone."

"We will be going with you," Tom repeated. "Do not forget, brother, I have the same stubborn Chastelayne blood as you."

"Come then," Philip agreed finally, "but see you do not stand in my way."

CHAPTER

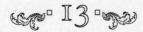

13

AFTER THE TROUPE STOPPED EACH EVENING AND BETWEEN SETTING up camp and preparing supper, they practiced their feats, readying themselves for the royal performance. Tom had made quick friends with the two lanky clowns, Arnaldo and Reynaldi. Seeing his natural aptitude, they taught him several of their tricks and even picked up a few from him.

"Well done, my lord," Arnaldo said, seeing Tom's perfect execution of the backwards handspring he had just learned. "Should you care to give up your princely duties, you have a sure living as a performer, I can see it."

Tom grinned and blotted the sweat from his face with his sleeve, glad to have something to turn his thoughts even temporarily from the grim purpose of this journey.

"I have two young nephews who insist upon such trifles from me, and you both have taught me enough to keep them amused for a good while. Now I suppose I've got to pay for my schooling by helping fetch the water we were sent for."

With a nod, Reynaldi picked up two of the buckets they had brought along with them, and Tom followed him down to the stream that ran alongside the road.

"You are a silent fellow," he observed, and the acrobat merely shrugged.

"Our king means his decrees to be obeyed," Arnaldo said, coming after them. "Most especially the Day of Mourning."

"What is this Day of Mourning we've heard so much of?" Tom asked. With a flash of his eyes, Reynaldi plunged a bucket down into the water.

As usual Arnaldo answered for him. "It was set to mark the death of the king's mistress a long while back . . . before any of us was born. There is to be no singing, no laughter, no light talk on that day. No one is to leave his home unless he goes clothed head to foot in black. Two years ago Reynaldi was in a tavern late, making merry with his fellows. Afterwards he and one of his mates wandered toward their beds, drunk and not knowing the time, not remembering that it was the eve of the Day. The other man was singing a bawdy song at the top of his lungs, and shortly after midnight Sarto's soldiers arrested them. The two were brought at once before the king, but he was in a generous mood that day. The man who did the singing was pulled apart on the rack, but Reynaldi, since he had not himself desecrated the Day of Mourning, only had his tongue torn out."

"Generous," Tom agreed grimly. Reynaldi stood, jerking the two full buckets up with a slosh, watching Tom's expression as if he expected sudden loathing or, even worse, contemptible pity.

Tom merely clasped his shoulder. "It shall be a pleasant change for once to have a friend who does more listening than talking."

Reynaldi smiled wryly, and, gesturing for Tom to bring more water, he went back toward camp.

"Truly it was a pity," Arnaldo said once he had gone. "He could sing to make the angels weep for envy."

"I noticed him when your people were practicing the music," Tom replied. "There was such a longing in his eyes, but I thought it was the song that had made him melancholy."

"But you won a smile of him, my lord, not an easy thing for any stranger. You've not seen us in full costume yet, have you? We dress alike, Reynaldi and I, in every respect save one. Where my face is painted to be weeping, his is set forever in a smile. I think that just now was the only smile I've seen from him this month that was not drawn on."

"How is it the people do not rise against the king here?" Tom asked. "Why do they stand like sheep to his slaughter?"

"They've had the fight burned and beaten and tortured out of them. The few rebels there have been were fueled with nothing but hate, and it took Sarto nothing to snuff them out. Until we have someone willing to lead us for the sake of right rather than vengeance, we shall continue to sink under his rule until we can never be set free." He looked warily around him, then lowered his voice. "There is someone we might follow, were he ever to show himself strong against the king."

"Truly? Who?"

"No one knows his name, only that he is sworn enemy to Sarto, but he shows it strangely. Just a fortnight ago, we heard that he and a handful of his men had stopped a shipment of the king's favorite wine and then after a time sent it on to Stonekeep. Of course, the king suspected it was poisoned and had it tasted."

"And?"

"The rebels had merely salted it. Barrels and barrels of the finest claret to be had, and they salted it all."

"No more than that?" Tom asked, surprised,.

Arnaldo nodded. "There have been occasions, incidents here and there, that have sparked hope in us, but it always seems that just as this rebel might strike hard against the king, he pulls back and lets the opportunity slip by. It's been almost a year since he began to make himself known, and I've heard there were many who risked everything to follow him then, but now most of them have given up, certain there is nothing any of us can do to win our freedom."

"I fear we in Lynaleigh must carry some of that blame. We have known some while of Sarto's cruelty. I meant to do something myself to help, but I've let my own cares distract me from it. Truly, before she was taken, our queen had won a promise from my brother to receive your king's ambassadors and work toward a friendship between our two lands in the hope that Sarto might be influenced to rule with a gentler hand. Now I fear there is little chance of that."

"Poor lady," Arnaldo said, "to have her kindness rewarded so. And your brother must be half-mad with grief for her."

"He bears it as well as can be hoped. There is a rare love between the two of them, one that did not come easily for him, one I fear he might die now for losing."

"If there is any way we might be of help, my lord, I know I can speak for my master to say that you need only ask."

"Once we reach Stonekeep," Tom assured him, "we may take that offer."

They brought the water back to the wagons. As they transferred it from the buckets into the barrel, Tom noticed Molly sitting on a fallen log at the edge of the camp, plucking the partridges some of the men had caught for supper, making a studied attempt not to watch him. All this while she had done precisely as she had promised. There had been nothing in either word or expression to betray her feelings, but he was still aware of it sometimes, times as now, when the way she did not look at him spoke more plainly than anything she had said before.

The two acrobats went back to the river for more water, and Tom turned to follow them.

"My lord."

He turned again at Molly's hesitant voice. Then he went reluctantly to her. "Yes?"

"Forgive me presuming to summon you to me, my lord, but I thought I might not have another moment away from the others to speak to you."

"I thought we had agreed there was no need for private talk between us."

"I know, my lord, but I must tell you this one thing."

"Molly, you know nothing you might say will ever change the truth."

"Please, my lord, I must tell it. I know you remember that night back in Winton when Lady Elizabeth sent me to you in her place."

He looked at her warily. "I remember."

"I let you apologize to me afterward as if you'd done the wrong, but I've carried a great sin from then till now, God pardon me. Please, my lord, you must pardon me as well."

"My lady should never have commanded you to do such a thing, Molly. It was no sin of yours. Surely you no longer think—"

"But I wanted it. I knew you would have been shamed to discover you'd been made to be false to her, to all you hold sacred, but I agreed to the deceit all the same. I wanted, if only once, to know that gentle tenderness you have for her and to taste the sweet fire as well. I knew many men in my trade, my lord, but there was never one of them I desired, never one who sparked anything in me but loathing, never one but you, and you never would—"

"Molly?"

"So you see, my lord, it was I who used you selfishly." Her smile was bittersweet. "I suppose I shall always be a harlot after all."

"No, Molly, that is not true."

"But I wronged you, my lord, even loving you as I did. As I do."

She looked very young as she said it, and he felt as he had back then what a pity it was for her to waste such a loving heart in a hopeless cause.

"Molly, you've just told me how you meant to wrong me to please yourself. That is not love. Can you not understand?"

"Yes, my lord, and that is why I wished to ask your forgiveness. Grant me that, and I will speak of this no more."

"I do, Molly. I have already, but will you not believe me that there must be someone who would give you the love you crave if you would only look about you? And if you'll believe it of none of the others, I pray you know yet that there is One who loves you and wants all of your love."

"I know it, my lord," she replied, lowering her eyes. "You have shown Him to me again and again."

"Seek after Him, Molly, not after me, and you shall find what you desire and much more than I could ever give you."

"Will you leave us with all the work, my lord?" Arnaldo chided amiably as he and his partner came back into the camp, sloshing water with every step.

"Think on it," Tom told the girl quietly, and then he went back to the others.

Molly watched him disappear into the trees.

"I do love you," she whispered. "Someday you will know it."

At dusk two days later they reached Sarto's stronghold. It had been decided that Molly would go in at once in the guise of a servant to find out where the queen was being kept. Then they would better be able to know what to do next.

Philip did not sleep that night, did nothing all that next day but stand watching Stonekeep as it huddled covetously over the barren countryside. When evening came again, the setting of the scarlet sun behind the castle blackened its dun-colored stones, sharpened its spires into preying talons, left its gates grim eyes in the gathering shadows. Below it the river added its menacing roar, giving the beast a voice.

"You shall not have her," he swore in steely certainty. Then he dropped to his knees, closing his eyes in a wordless plea to heaven. When he stood again, Molly had returned.

"She is there, my lord," she informed him. "As you feared, he means to make her his queen."

Philip's face was flint, his eyes ice. "You saw her?"

"I did, my lord, in the great hall. I've been given a place in the kitchen."

"So easily?" Tom asked.

"But you saw her," Philip repeated.

The girl nodded. "When I went in to gather up the things from the feast they had. She seemed well enough, but I was never very near to her, to know for certain. She did not see me."

"Where is she kept?"

"In the north tower, my lord." Molly pointed toward the castle. "There, the chamber with the great glassed windows. At the very top."

"Where we can never hope to reach her without an army."

"A touch of cunning often prevails against an opponent you cannot hope to best with force, your majesty," Credotti observed. "It was a lesson I learned early."

Looking at the little acrobat, Philip smiled grimly. "I expect you did. So what is this cunning you have in mind?"

⁂

"Could it be done?" Philip asked once Credotti had explained his plan. "I can shoot the distance sure enough, but could we be certain the bolt went in deep enough to hold your weight? If it did not, or if the shaft should break—"

Credotti grinned. "Then I merely keep my hold and swing back to where I was."

"But the heaviest line we could expect to travel so far—"

"Is heavy enough, my lord, for the Great Credotti."

"But not for me, and you could not possibly do everything alone."

"No, my lord, but it is merely a matter of tying a heavier rope about my waist and securing it to the north tower once I am across. Then you come after."

"And if we are seen in the crossing?"

Again Credotti grinned. "Our Arnaldo will see we are not. True?"

The weeping clown nodded. "If I cannot keep their eyes on me, master, may I be condemned to serve out the rest of my days as turnspit in Sarto's court."

"Very well," Philip said. "We will do it."

"Not you, Philip." Tom shook his head. "Not this time. You know you could not."

"Of course I could. You are not the only one who can aim an arrow."

Tom frowned. "Do you think I've not seen it these past few days? The dizziness? The blurred sight? It's been only God's grace and your vast stubbornness that's kept you on your feet all this while."

"Tom, she is my wife. When I think of her with him—"

"Do not let pride and vengeance rob you of your wits, Philip. You owe her the best opportunity you can make to get her free. I am better at this than you—you know I am."

"I know no such thing."

"Very well," Tom said calmly. "Prove me wrong."

He picked up a bow and arrow and pointed out a tree stump a good distance away.

"Do you see the knothole on the left side of that stump?"

Philip squinted at the target and then nodded.

"If I cannot hit it closer than you," Tom said, "I will make no more objections to your going."

Again Philip nodded, and Tom took a swift shot that hit the mark dead center. Then he handed the bow to his brother.

"Philip?"

His mouth in an obstinate line, Philip drew back his arm until the bowstring was almost to his ear, and then he squinted again, straining, struggling to see. Finally he relaxed his hold and lowered the bow, dropping his head in frustrated defeat. "I cannot even make it out."

Tom took the bow and arrow from him. "I thought as much."

"That will pass in time, your majesty," Livrette assured him.

Philip grimaced suddenly and pressed both hands to the side of his head. "When?" he demanded through clenched teeth.

The physician took his arm. "Soon, my lord, truly, but you prolong that day's coming with each day you do not properly rest yourself. What benefit is that to the queen?"

Philip said nothing for a moment. Then he took off his ring, the battered ring he had gotten from Westered, and handed it to his brother.

"Bring her back to me, Tom."

❧

Back in Westered Elizabeth woke from her restless sleep, no longer able to ignore the growing pain inside her. It was not too great yet, but she recognized this pain, the same kind of pain that had ripped through her each time she had lost a child. She forced herself to breathe slowly, wishing Tom were there to comfort her with his gentle words and strong arms.

"Send him back to me," she whispered into the darkness, rubbing her hand again and again over the wrist that still felt bare without his bracelet. "Send him back to me. Send him back to me."

It had been her constant prayer since Tom had gone to Reghed, but she realized now that it was not because she wanted him with her, no matter how desperately she missed him. More than that, she wanted him to intercede for her with his God. His God, she realized, Tom's God, not her own. Oh, she claimed Him, she prayed to Him, but she did not truly believe He would answer her for her own sake.

Tom had promised her his prayers while he was away, and she knew, for all his soldier's reputation, he was a greater warrior on his knees than on any field of battle. God heard his prayers, she knew He did, even the ones He answered with a no. And she had trusted those answers, even the hard ones, because Tom was with her. Now Tom was gone, and she was left alone with her doubts and fears, left to stand bare-souled before his God, only daring to ask that He send Tom back to her.

Without warning, the pain intensified. She sucked in a hard breath and drew her knees up, trying to ride out the agonizing pangs.

"Oh, Tom," she gasped. But Tom was not there to intercede for her, to breach that gap between her and God Himself. Perhaps he never would again. She had no choice but to go before Him on her own, and He had not heard her. Or had He heard her and, as Tom claimed He sometimes did, simply answered her with a no?

"Oh, God," she cried, and she felt the warm wetness seeping into her shift, the bleeding that went with the well-remembered pain.

"Oh, God," she sobbed again. "For his sake, if You cannot hear a prayer for myself, for his sake do not let me lose this child."

Shall I do nothing for your own sake, my beloved?

She was more startled by the words than that she should hear them with such nearly audible clarity.

Beloved? She His beloved? It was Tom's sweetest endearment, the one that made her most certain of his unquenchable love. Did his God use that tender term for her, too?

The pain jolted through her, and she cried out once more, "Oh, my God, You have shown me mercy before. I know I have nothing to give in return, but do not let me lose this child."

Trust in me, beloved, and you shall have your desire.

She drew her knees up tighter and clenched her teeth, refusing anymore to give voice to the pain.

"I trust in You, my Lord," she panted. "I trust my child to You."

She listened to the night, hoping to hear again that still, steady assurance that calmed her fears, but there was nothing.

"Please, Lord," she breathed, "do not leave me now. What more must I do?"

As if in answer, Nan came into the room, holding a candle to light her way. "What is it, my lady? We heard you cry out."

"Send for your grandmother, Nan," Elizabeth said, a little tremor of relief in her voice. "I think I need her now."

"The child?"

Elizabeth nodded. "But it will be all right." She bit her lip, fighting the pain again. "I am certain of it."

Joan arrived only a short while later, bringing lights and warmed blankets and a steaming herbal drink that eased Elizabeth's cramps and made her comfortably sleepy.

"You needn't fear, my lady," she said once she had sponged Elizabeth clean and changed her shift. "Just a little scare—nothing more, thank God."

"Thank God," Elizabeth murmured drowsily.

Westered's physician, a solemn-countenanced man of forty, came into the chamber and conferred for a moment with Joan.

". . . lose the child of course," she overheard him whisper, and her eyes flew open.

"No!" she wailed.

Nan and Joan both were immediately beside her, trying to keep her from sitting up. "Now keep still, my lady," Joan soothed. "You must keep still for the child's sake."

"But my baby!"

"Nonsense! Why, by the time this so-called physician was born,

I had already brought more little ones into this world than he ever will, even were he to stay in practice another fifty years."

The physician cleared his throat gravely. "My lady, you must realize—"

"I've seen those in just her case, sir, who've given birth to healthy babies," Joan said combatively. "Unless they were first frightened into losing them."

"I do not doubt your experience, mistress. I know our unfortunate Lady Rosalynde speaks most highly of you. The princess must merely choose whom she most trusts to care for her."

Elizabeth was silent for a moment, remembering. Then she closed her eyes. "Thank you, sir, but I have no need of you. I am very well seen to."

Somehow she knew she was.

The performers' wagons were admitted into Stonekeep the next morning. When night fell, the great hall was alive with light and music, a quarter century's desolation uneasily displaced with a king's command. Rosalynde sat beside Sarto's throne watching a cadaverous man put a pair of small dogs through their paces. They leapt through hoops of fire, walked on two legs, danced on large, brightly colored balls, did still more that amazed the court, but she could not help noticing their cringing fear each time their master came near them. It made her want to weep for all things trapped and helpless.

"You do not care for such frivolity, gracious lady?" Sarto asked, seeing her expression.

"I cannot but pity the poor creatures, my lord," she admitted.

With a clap of kingly hands, the dogs and their bewildered owner were hurried from the chamber.

"Our mountains are famed for the performers they breed," Sarto told her, "the best in all Reghed, the best in all the world. I warrant you, they shall bring a smile to those fair lips."

Again he clapped his hands, and a lively, whooping company of acrobats, their faces colored as brightly as their costumes, tumbled and somersaulted and turned back flips into the great hall. Two tall clowns, one's painted face smiling, the other's weeping, lifted their bantam leader to their shoulders, and he raised his hands for silence.

"My gracious liege lord and king, my lords, ladies, and gentlemen, the Great Credotti now presents to you feats of strength, feats of daring, feats of wonder, all in honor of our fair and beloved Lady Rosamund, soon to be our queen. For the space of an hour, gentles all, we bend time and motion to our will, to dazzle your eyes and astonish your imaginations and to boldly prove that all things are not precisely as they seem. Behold!"

He removed his billowing golden cloak and showed it front and back to his audience. Then with a dramatic flourish, he tossed it over his head, letting it completely cover him. The smiling and weeping clowns each seized one side of the cloak and with a sharp snap shook it out before the court. The audience gasped as a flock of doves fluttered into the rafters with a rushing beat of wings. The small clown had vanished.

With a wave of his hand, the weeping clown produced a single rose. Bowing to Rosalynde, he laid the rose on the cloth of gold and rolled it into a bundle. He tossed the bundle to the smiling clown, who swiftly unfurled it at the king's feet. The Great Credotti tumbled to his knees out of it and presented Rosalynde the sheaf of roses he held.

"As I said, pretty lady, all things are not precisely as they seem."

She took the flowers, smiling in spite of herself, and Sarto pounded the table in approval. "More! More!"

There was more. For the next hour, as the Great Credotti had promised, there were all manner of feats to delight and amaze, and between times the delicate a cappella harmonies they had brought from their mountains. Over and over again Rosalynde found herself looking at the tall clown with the painted smile. He did not sing with the others, and he never spoke, but there was something familiar in the strong, lissome motions of his body, something that reminded her painfully of Philip. She sighed.

With a glance toward her, Sarto pounded the table once more.

"Enough of that caterwauling!" he commanded. "We will have more of your acrobats."

Credotti leapt to his feet, once more with a smile and a bow. "At once, great king! Come, lads, to it again."

There was an instant flurry of boundless energy as the acrobats tumbled and leapt with impossible precision. Rosalynde watched them make an inverted pyramid, the husky strong man at the bottom with another acrobat on each of his shoulders and three more balanced above those. The silent smiling clown was in the middle of the top row, and the instant the pyramid was steadily in place, he began to juggle a trio of striped and spotted balls. He went slowly at first, then faster and faster, expanding and narrowing the whirling circle as he did. The memory of Tom juggling eggs to make Robin and John giggle came back to her with sudden clarity.

It is Tom! she thought with a catch in her breath, and she closed her eyes and forced herself to think calmly. It could not possibly be he. Though she was certain he would be one of those searching for her for Philip's sake, he would have no way to know where she was, no way to get to her if he did.

She opened her eyes and once again studied the tall clown with the painted smile. Under the makeup and fantastic costume, it was impossible to tell what the man looked like. Surely if this was Tom, he would have given her some sign, some hope, but this man never turned his attention toward her, never acknowledged her with so much as a glance.

I merely see what I wish to see, she told herself, and, determined to keep a firm hold on reality, however grim, she refused to look at the smiling clown anymore.

"My lady is melancholy this evening," Sarto observed as he returned her to her chamber when the performance was over. "The entertainments did not please you?"

"They were very good, my lord. I thank you."

"Tell me what grieves you, lady."

She pressed her lips together, forcing herself not to beg him to release her, knowing he had convinced himself that she was willingly at his side.

"Forgive me, my lord, it is nothing."

"Come, say what it is, and all heaven and earth shall be moved to right it."

She dared not confess her longing for her husband. That would only bring his rage, but perhaps something else would speak to his heart and soften it toward her.

"I have been a long while away from my little ones, my lord. I cannot help missing them." She clutched his arm in pleading. "You have lost a child, my lord. You must know something of my yearning for them. If only I might—"

"It cannot be done, gracious lady. Your sons are heirs to the throne of Lynaleigh. I could not in good conscience deny their father the dying knowledge that one of them will continue the royal line after him. It is only right they stay where they are."

"No, my lord, I only meant—"

"But you need not let that trouble you, my lady. You shall have another child soon enough to soothe that longing."

She breathed out a hopeless sigh.

He lifted her chin. "Your youngest, lady, the one you carried yet when I was at your court before—how old is he now?"

"She will be a year old upon St. Valentine's Day."

"It was a girl then."

"Yes, my lord," she replied guardedly.

"Then I see no reason why I cannot have her brought here if that would please you, my lady."

"Oh, no, my lord, I beg you!" She clutched his arm again. "I beseech you, my lord, if you mean to please me, do not do such a thing!"

"But I would not have you unhappy, gracious lady."

"No, please, my lord, it is a mere trifle I'll not speak of again." She forced her trembling lips into a smile. "With such pleasures as your court affords, how can I long be sad?"

"Just so," he replied. "And when at last we are wed, you shall find no time for thoughts of the weary past—only of our future together."

With that word of encouragement, he kissed her hand and left her in her chamber.

"God, keep my little ones safe," she breathed into the silence. "Keep them from this place."

The faint sound of laughter drew her to the window, and she looked into the courtyard. As late as it was, one of the tall acrobats, she could not tell which, was doing tricks for the soldiers. They were gathered around him spellbound.

Trying not to think of the smiling clown anymore, she gazed up into the night sky. From the way the sun came through this window during the day, she knew that she was facing Westered, but it seemed so far away now, along with the rest of her life. Children, husband, home—all of that had been taken from her that brutal night there by the sea.

She had to turn away from the window, had to turn her thoughts away from the ever-present memory of Philip lying beaten and bloodied at her feet, telling herself with stubborn certainty that he was still alive. She made herself remember instead another time she had seen him lying still and vulnerable, asleep on the nursery floor in a patch of cool, bright sunlight particular to late fall, with Alyssa sprawled across his chest, her plump, rosy cheek mashed against his, her little turned-up nose pushed sideways. That put a throbbing ache in her heart, and she had to bite her lip to keep the tears from her eyes.

"Longing for home, my lady?"

She spun to face the window once more. Hanging upside down from the edge of roof, grinning down on her, was a swarthy, bright-faced monkey of a man.

"Who—" She laughed faintly. "The little acrobat?"

"Aldo Credotti, my lady, at your service," he replied. He swiftly secured a rope to the iron torch holder set into the stone near the window, and then he dropped lightly to the chamber floor.

"What are you going to do?" she asked with a furtive glance toward the door. "Why have you come?"

Again the little acrobat smiled and handed her the scarred ring. "I was sent, my lady."

"Philip! My husband sent you. Oh, tell me he is well."

"He is mending, my lady."

She looked up at the window again, recognizing the voice. "Tom! It *was* you!"

Tom shinnied down the rope he had lowered, and she ran to him and clutched both of his hands. "Oh, my lord, tell me."

"Mending, as I said, my lady. He is here in Reghed."

"Here? And he did not come?"

"He is not yet well enough for that, though it was no mean feat to convince him of it. He is waiting for us."

"And the children?"

"They are well, my lady, safe at your father's."

She smiled, batting away the new tears that sprang to her eyes. "My poor little boys, my little Alyssa."

"You've not lost them, my lady," he said softly, and she squeezed his hands again.

"And you have had to leave your lady to come for me. I am sorry. She is well?"

He nodded. "Pray for her. She fears for our child."

"I do pray for her, for us all, and for God's deliverance from this place. How are we to escape? The door is locked and always guarded."

"We have a plan, my lady." He took some clothes from the pouch he had slung over his shoulder and handed them to her. "You must wear this and do just as I tell you."

"Sarto has taken great pains to keep me here," she said, looking them over. "I do not think he will be easily deceived."

"Ah, but he has never set himself against the Great Credotti, pretty lady," the acrobat replied with a flourishing bow.

Rosalynde could not help but smile. "Then we shall surely outwit him."

THE NEXT MORNING CAME IN COLD AND BLUSTERY, AND THE guards at the castle gates were reluctant to leave the comparative warmth of their fires to search the performers' wagons.

"They search them coming into the city and at the castle," one of them grumbled as he rummaged through the same chests he had inspected two days before. "They search them going out of the castle, and now we must search yet again. They're all thieves, no doubt, but if they'd taken anything here, the castle guard would have found it."

"Better to search them all fifty times each way than to have something slip past us and the king know of it," his companion offered, and the first man crossed himself hastily.

"Check that barrel again."

The captain of the guard, the only one on duty who could read, was checking over the list of those counted in the party coming in, comparing it to the assembly of brightly dressed clowns standing before him.

"Credotti, leader of the troupe."

The small clown made a sweeping, jingling bow.

"Arnaldo and Reynaldi, acrobats."

The weeping and smiling clowns also bowed, their painted faces stark against the soft snow. The captain blew on his hands to warm them and then read over the rest of the list. Clowns, jugglers, acrobats—everything seemed in order.

"Anything?" he called to his men as they climbed down from the wagons.

"Nothing, sir."

He looked over the multicolored faces once more. Then he stuffed his list into the small clown's hand. "Pass."

Again the troupe bowed, and the weeping clown produced a trio of apples seemingly out of the air and began to juggle them.

"You have our thanks."

He tossed the apples to the grinning soldiers as the rest of the party piled back into the wagons. As soon as he had boosted the small clown into the lead wagon, he leapt up and took the reins.

"May you have kindnesses in the measure you give them!" he called. Then he whipped up the horses, and soon the wagons had rumbled out of sight.

Satisfied, the captain of the guard left his men on duty at the gate and strode through the courtyard back into the castle. His boots made purposeful thuds down the corridor until he reached the great hall and went inside to make his report to the king.

For a moment the corridor was still. Then there was a furtive movement in the heavy folds of crimson silk draped to frame the archway. A sparkle of excitement in his eyes, Credotti popped his head up, and, certain he was unobserved, he did a neat back flip out of his hiding place to land solidly on the stone floor below. He smoothed the dragon emblazoned on his doublet and walked swiftly away.

Hoping he was heading toward the kitchens, he made his way through the hallways, boldly ignoring the guards he passed, giving the impression he was on an errand for one of the lords or ladies of the castle and not to be detained. It went smoothly until he turned a corner and collided with a portly nobleman whose temper was not improved by the effects of last night's overindulgence in wine.

"Mind where you plod, knave," the nobleman grumbled. Then he looked at the supposed servant more closely. "You are that acrobat!"

"You mistake, my lord," Credotti said, smiling as he backed away, but the captain of the guard, coming from the court, had already spotted him.

"Stop there!"

Credotti broke into a desperate run that ended against a solid wall of soldiers at the other end of the corridor. His eyes darted to the left, then the right, and then he turned to the captain and made a broad bow.

"I would not have dreamed that his majesty's guard would be such ardent admirers of a mere traveling performer."

"How did you get back in here?" the captain demanded. "You were seen leaving."

Credotti made an airy gesture with his hands. "Every magician has his secrets."

The captain grabbed him by the doublet and jerked him upwards, forcing him to balance on his toes to keep standing.

"Why are you still here?"

Credotti smiled. "I could not go without Lucette."

"Lucette?"

Credotti rummaged in his shirt and brought out a squirming baby rabbit. "Lucette. She has rarely seen such splendor as you have here in the palace, and she was reluctant to leave it."

"How did you get back in here?" the captain demanded again, shaking him. "And how dare you wear the king's livery!"

"As I said—"

"What is this man doing here?" a rumbling voice demanded, and all the soldiers jerked to attention.

"It is the magician, your majesty," the captain said. "He claims he came back for—"

"And he merely passed by your guard," Sarto accused, "while your men sat there on their loathsome, spotty behinds and saw nothing."

The captain paled. "My—my lord, I—"

"Well?"

"My lord king!" Another of the palace guards came running down the corridor, panicked. "She is gone! The lady is gone!"

Sarto turned in fury. "Gone?"

The guard fell to his knees. "Your mercy, I beg you. I do not know how it could be so, but when I looked in on her just now, she was gone."

"You fell asleep and let her walk right by you?"

"No! No, my lord! I swear it!"

"Then you were paid to let her by!"

"Mercy, my lord, not so! She was taken through the window. There is a rope stretched still from the east tower."

"Impossible!"

"See for yourself, my lord."

"That might explain her escape from the chamber, but to leave the castle—" Sarto looked at Credotti, and his eyes blackened with fury. "Stop the wagons!"

"My lord?" the captain asked.

"The performers' wagons. Stop them. Now!"

"At once, my lord!"

A short time later a throng of horsemen thundered after Credotti's troupe.

"Hold there!" the captain of the guard commanded, and the riders swarmed around the lumbering wagons, forcing them to a stop.

"What is it, my captain?" the weeping clown asked, his voice innocently cheerful.

"Where is he?"

"Where is who?" He grinned at his fellow travelers. "They've misplaced someone."

The captain grabbed the other clown's arm. "Where is your master? Credotti."

The smiling clown merely shrugged and shook his head.

"Master Credotti is like the air and the bird song," the weeping clown answered for him. "Sometimes here, sometimes there—who can say?"

The smiling clown produced a flower from nowhere and offered it to the captain, who instantly slapped it out of his hand.

"Credotti is asleep in the back," the weeping clown amended

quickly. "Why do you come for him? He's done nothing. Reynaldi's done nothing. I've done nothing."

Just then one of the soldiers spotted a flit of red, yellow, and green among the trees.

"Look there, captain!"

Five of them spurred into the forest. It was the captain himself who finally seized the fugitive.

"Stop there, my lady!"

The small clown fought against him, the struggle knocking off the multicolored hat, releasing the cascade of thick dark hair hidden under it.

"You've been found out, my lady. It is no use to make further protest."

"Take your filthy hands off me, pig!"

From there, the prisoner spat out the most scathing shrill expletives the captain, even in all his years of soldiering, had ever heard.

The weeping clown grinned once more. "Our Anna-Maria has been called many things, my captain, but, alas, 'lady' has rarely been one of them."

"It is useless to continue this masquerade, madam," the captain said. "You cannot so easily deceive the king."

"It was that scape-grace I must own for a husband!" the still-struggling prisoner scolded. "'Yes, Anna-Maria,' he tells me, 'you hide among the props until we are safely in the castle. Then when the wagons go out, you are Credotti, and I stay behind to liberate some of the finery the lords and ladies use to ornament themselves.' Ha! Now we will both hang and for what?"

The captain grabbed a cloth from one of the wagons and scrubbed the paint off her face. It was a very plain face indeed.

"It is not the lady." He looked around him in frustration and then seized the silent smiling clown. "Where is she? Speak, man, or I'll have your tongue."

"Too late, my captain," the weeping clown said, his smile now sharp and caustic. "Our good king has had it out already."

With a wave of his hand, the smiling clown produced a piece of wide red ribbon and let it unroll to its whole length. With an exaggerated grimace of pain and a sudden lurch, he dropped it to the ground.

The captain looked into his glittering eyes, chilled to see that for once his smile was not just painted on.

"Tear the wagons apart."

Tom perched outside Rosalynde's chamber window, concealed behind the heavy iron-braced shutter, listening to the stark silence left in the wake of the soldiers' frantic, hurried searching. After a seemingly endless wait, hearing nothing still, he edged out of his hiding place and peered into the room. Grateful to see that the door to the chamber was closed, he dropped lightly from the window sill to the floor and then crossed to the bed.

"My lady?"

He rolled back the top mattress and then the second, and Rosalynde sat up, wide-eyed and breathless. "Oh, my lord, I was so afraid. What if they had searched more thoroughly?"

"They saw no need," he said with a smile. "They were certain their dove had already flown. Now while they are riding after the wagons, we merely walk free."

He helped her to her feet and pushed the feathers back into the center of the bottom mattress, erasing the deep furrow he had made to conceal her. Once the first two mattresses were back in place, he arranged the bedding just as the soldiers had left it.

"Now, my lady, a bit of this."

He grimed her face with some soot from the hearth and put a little on his own. Then he looked her over. She was dressed as one of Sarto's lower servants, a scullery maid or ash girl, but still there was a queenly delicacy about her that would not serve. Her hair was already in a rumpled braid down her back, but it was thick and luxurious and bound to catch the eye of some groom or cupbearer, so he

tucked most of it under her kerchief, allowing just a meager handful
to hang limply down her back, dulled with a little more soot.

"One thing more," he said after he had looked her over again.
He handed her some cloths from the chest that sat in the corner of
the room. In another moment, her graceful figure was padded into
unremarkable shapelessness.

"Now, my lady, if we are asked?"

"My husband is with the army in Allston. He is hurt and they've
sent you to bring me to him."

"Good." He took one last look at his own disguise, the uniform
of one of Sarto's soldiers, and then he squeezed her hand. "Have
courage."

She nodded and took a deep breath. He pushed open the door.

"Surely you were not thinking of leaving us, gracious lady."

Rosalynde muffled a cry and shrank back against Tom. Sarto was
standing there waiting for them, a gleam of triumph in his reptilian
eyes.

"Allow me to welcome you to Reghed, my lord of Brenden," he
said, smiling as he stroked the small white rabbit he held.

"Where is Credotti?" Tom demanded.

"Ah, it is he we have to thank for this merry meeting—once he
could be persuaded to reveal your plan. Pity your stay with us will not
be a long one."

"No, my lord, not long," Tom replied. "Merely the time it takes
for me to return her majesty to Lynaleigh, to her husband."

"But I hear the lady has no husband in Lynaleigh. Surely she
would have no wish to return there." Sarto turned to his guard.
"There will be three of you here at all times to see to my lady's safety.
And see to it that window is sealed."

He gestured towards the room, and, feeling an opportunity to
wriggle free, the rabbit began to squirm. Sarto tightened his hold
until she no longer struggled, until only her wide-eyed stare and frantically twitching nose showed sign of life. Again he gestured towards
the room.

"Gracious lady, if you will."

"No." Rosalynde glanced at the helpless rabbit and then looked up at Sarto, her small fists clenched and her head held defiantly high. "I will never do as you wish. I belong to Philip, and you can never change that. I beg you, let me go to him."

Sarto smiled as if she had just thanked him for the use of so pleasant a room, and then he signaled his soldiers. Deaf to her protests, three of them escorted Rosalynde inside.

"And now, my lord?" Tom asked.

The rabbit flinched as Sarto began stroking her trembling ears. He was still smiling.

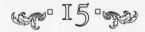
WE'VE FAILED, MY LORD," ARNALDO TOLD PHILIP, FALLING TO HIS knees in exhaustion when he reached the rendezvous clearing in the forest. "Your brother, my master—they never left the castle. The soldiers came after the rest of us, and everyone has been taken back to Sarto's prison. I escaped by a miracle."

Philip smashed his fist into his palm. "Failed!"

"The word has been given out already," the acrobat panted. "Excepting the lady, of course, all of the prisoners will be released in exchange for you."

Philip snapped the chain around his neck and put the royal ruby back on his finger. Then deaf to Livrette's warning pleas, to Rafe's insistent demands, he merely walked out of the forest and up to the castle's main gate.

"I am Philip of Lynaleigh. Tell your king I am prepared to make trade with him."

He stood unresisting as the guards searched him. Finding him unarmed, they escorted him into the castle, hardly able to keep pace with his long, swift strides.

"I have come as you asked," Philip said when he was finally face to face with Reghed's king, iron determination in his cold expression. "Release my brother and those who were taken with him as you pledged you would do."

"You will kneel before the high majesty of Reghed," the captain of Sarto's guard barked, forcing the prisoner down with a blow of his pikestaff to the back of his knees.

"Release them," Philip insisted, his crystal eyes growing even colder.

"Captain, take some of your men and bring the prisoners here," Sarto instructed. Then he smiled. "There, you see, my lord, between men of honor it need be no more difficult than that."

"I demand you return my lady as well," Philip said as Sarto's soldiers hurried to do as they were bidden. "You had no right, nor nothing like to right, in taking her from me."

"I give those words back to you, my lord," Sarto replied. "She was mine long before ever you saw her, and it is you who had no right to her."

"She is my wife!"

"You could not have known she belonged to me, my lord, and for that I do pity you. The men I sent to bring her were meant to kill you, to spare you the pain you've no doubt suffered in losing her."

"Your mercy is extraordinary."

"But things must be as they will. The lady belongs to me now and for all time, and you and I have no more to say."

"I have more I would say to you, my lord." Philip looked at him steadily, fighting his fierce hatred of this man. "Perhaps had I said it when you were in Winton before, I would not be here now."

"And what is it you would say?"

"I come to offer you a different sort of mercy than that which you have so graciously offered me."

Sarto looked amused. "Tell me then, my lord. With you kneeling here at my feet, what would I want with your mercy?"

"You mistake me, sir. The only mercy I have for you is the quick thrust of a dagger between your ribs, but I must ask God's pardon for that, for He wishes me to tell you of His mercy and not my own."

"Ah, yes, your merciful God. I have heard of Him, you know. My long-departed wife, she was among those who claimed Him. She pled with me countless weary times to repent of my ways and turn to Him." Sarto chuckled. "What she meant was for me to give up my mistress and live with her in canting pale piety. We have all seen what has come of that. She is dead, and despite your God I finally have what I have long awaited. What benefit could His mercy bring me now?"

"My lord, for the sake of your people then—"

"The prisoners, my liege," the captain of Sarto's guard announced, and Tom and Credotti and the rest of his troupe were led into the great hall.

"It would have been our finest performance, my lord," Credotti said ruefully, the words coming with difficulty from his bruised and swollen lips. "I could have withstood them for my own sake, but when they began on my wife—"

"A brave attempt," Philip assured him, feeling his anger intensify when he saw the raw marks on the woman's wrists and the jagged cut along her cheek. Then he looked coldly at Sarto. "I see your valor is as extraordinary as your mercy."

"Pig," Anna-Maria muttered, glaring at her captor and then spitting at his feet. Sarto did not even spare her a glance.

"As promised, my lord," he told Philip. "They are released unharmed."

"You should never have come," Tom said, going to his brother. "There is nothing now to keep him from doing as he has planned."

"He has not won his way yet, Tom," Philip said steadily, still on his knees before Sarto's throne, "and things are far from over between us." He dropped his voice. "Have you seen her, Tom? She's not been—she's not been harmed?"

"She is whole and well but for missing you."

"Thank God."

"The bargain is made, my lord," Sarto announced. "Your brother and his companions may go now."

Credotti glanced at the king of Reghed and then at Philip. "The bargain was for all my company, was it not, my lord?"

"It was," Philip replied. "Are they not all here?"

"My rabbit, my lord," the little acrobat urged, and then he glanced once more at Sarto. "Surely even to the mighty king of Reghed so helpless a creature can be of no importance."

At a nod from the king, one of the guards took the little rabbit from a cage and returned her to Credotti, who quickly thrust her back into the warm safety of his shirt.

"Now take them as far as the forest," Sarto instructed his guard.

"You cannot think I will merely leave now and let you have your pleasure in this, your majesty," Tom told him.

Philip stood, stern command in his expression. "You will do as we have agreed, my lord of Brenden. By your allegiance, you will."

"Philip—"

"My lord of Brenden."

Tom set his mouth in a tight line. "As you say, my liege."

Philip held out his hand, and Tom took it, pulling him into a solid embrace.

"Philip, consider—"

"Do we not still have a God?" Philip asked quietly.

Tom nodded, releasing him. "Still."

At a signal from Sarto, Tom and those with him were led out of the great hall.

"What now?" Philip asked.

Sarto looked at him almost benevolently. "Why what else, my lord? You have come to my kingdom to take something rightly mine. What would follow, once you've been captured, but immediate execution?"

"And what else to precede an execution but a trial, Father?"

Sarto turned, surprised, and Philip looked guardedly at the fair-haired young man idling next to the throne.

"You've a great reputation as a just and honorable monarch, King Philip," Alaric continued. "Do you imagine your Lynaleigh is the only place can boast such a ruler?"

Philip returned him a sardonic smile. "Why, no, my lord prince. How foolish of me to think otherwise, but your father's decree—"

"There shall be a trial," Sarto announced as if the very idea of proceeding without one was an offense to his good name. "We're no barbarians here, my lord."

"I expect you would best know that," Philip replied. "And when is this trial to be held?"

"Tomorrow morning," Sarto decreed. "What say my lords?"

"So say we all," his nobles answered.

"Then for the sake of your honor, my lord," Philip said, "as one gentleman to another, I ask that you grant me a moment to take leave of my lady. We hadn't time for such when last we parted."

The king of Reghed considered that, his face unreadable. Then he nodded.

"Of course, my lord. Captain, take your men and escort his majesty to my lady's chamber." Sarto gave the soldier an intense warning look that said plainly his life would answer for the loss of this prisoner. "See to it."

"At once, my liege," the captain replied, and he led Philip out of the court, down a long corridor and up a circular stairway. At the top he unlocked a door, let his prisoner inside, and locked it again after him.

Rosalynde turned when the door opened, and Philip merely stood there, his eyes full of longing as he gazed upon her. "I did not think you could be more beautiful, my lady, than the dreams I've had of you."

With a cry she ran to his arms, unable to speak for the tears that would not stop. "I've not wept once since I have been here," she sobbed after a while, "not till just now."

She twined her arms around him, and he held her head against his chest.

"I've not said it often enough or well enough, but Rosalynde—" His voice broke with sudden emotion. "I love you, Rose. I love you so very much."

In rapid succession he kissed her temple, her cheek, her jaw. Then he kissed her mouth, and she clasped him more tightly.

"Hold me," she breathed. "Never let me go."

"You must forgive him, gracious lady, if he cannot pledge you that."

They both looked up, still huddled together, an almost guilty furtiveness in the gesture.

Sarto smiled. "Pardon the intrusion, my lord, but it is time you were put somewhere a trifle more secure for the night."

"We did strike a bargain, my lord," Philip reminded him.

"So we did, and I have fulfilled it. You've had your moment."

"It is not enough!" Philip protested. "This much and no more is cruelty, not kindness."

"My lord, as we agreed."

Philip clenched his jaw, his expression tightening as if he would go in proud silence, and then there was an abrupt pleading on his face. "For mercy, my lord, a moment more."

"More time will but ask more time," Sarto replied coldly.

"Please, my lord," Philip said, holding Rosalynde closer, "from a man who does not beg, I do beg you now. Have you never been parted from someone and wished forever after that you had been given a moment of farewell?"

There was a flicker of emotion in Sarto's serpentine eyes. Then he looked out toward the fast-falling night. "You have until the sun goes behind the mountain there and no more."

He stepped into the corridor and locked the door again.

"Thank God you've come for me, my lord," Rosalynde whispered. "What it is you've planned?"

"Nothing," he said with an unsteady laugh. "He would have killed Tom and all of Credotti's troupe had I not come to him, and now I know no way to get us free of here."

He looked up. There was only a thin slice of sun still visible over the mountaintop. "He's given us hardly any time. Forgive me for letting you be drawn into such a coil."

"You protected me as best you could, love," she said, caressing the fading bruise on his jaw.

"Had I done what I knew I was meant to, Reghed would now be an ally, not an enemy, and we would both be safe at home. I deserve this punishment, but not you, poor innocent Rose."

"Please, love, do not believe God would mete out such punishment to one of His own."

"No, but I might have prevented Sarto's plan had I done as He wished me to. I could have stopped so much suffering had I looked beyond my own comfort and desires. Last summer you told the boys I was not a heathen, but one of the Lord's bravest and best. Yet here I have let a whole people suffer for my hatred and unforgiveness and put you into terrible peril with me. It seems only just that I should be left to face the consequences of my disobedience."

"I know you remember when Robin disobeyed you and went into the stable alone. By your reasoning here, you should have left him to be trampled that day."

"Of course not, but—"

"Do you think you are a better father than God Himself?"

"Oh, Rose," he breathed.

She kissed his cheek and traced the fine scar there. Then she took the little ring he had sent her by Tom and put it back on his hand.

"God will see us through this yet, love. There is nothing we give into His care that He does not turn to our good. Not always to our pleasure but always to our good."

"I know, Rose, I know," he said, rubbing the battered gold ring. "I did not walk into Sarto's stronghold with no plan for escape without first putting myself into God's hands, and I can see He's held you safe there, too, all this while." He glanced once more at the setting sun, barely a bright halo now for the rugged mountain. "We've no more time, sweet."

They kissed again, locked desperately together, and then froze in breathless silence when the door swung open.

"The sun is set, your majesty," Sarto said.

Philip felt the unshakable grasp of soldiers' hands as they pulled him out of Rosalynde's arms. For her sake, he did not resist them.

"You have been most generous, my lord," he told the king of Reghed.

"A point of honor, my lord," Sarto replied. "Now if you will be so good as to go with my men, they will escort you to your quarters. They will not be such fine accommodations as those to which you are no doubt accustomed, I regret to say, but it will be only for the night. Then tomorrow—"

"Send me with him, my lord, I beseech you," Rosalynde sobbed, clinging to her husband once more. "If you must take his life, take mine as well. I cannot live without him."

"Gracious lady, surely—"

"You are the queen of Lynaleigh, madam," Philip reminded her sternly, freeing himself from her embrace. "Behave so."

"Oh, Philip—"

"As I told you just a moment ago, my lady, our fate rests in hands other than our own now, and we must never forget that."

He looked with pleading love into her eyes, hoping she understood, and she drew a deep, calming breath.

"Forgive me, my lord," she said, lifting her head with queenly dignity. "I will not forget."

He kissed her hand, feeling her fingers tighten on his as he did, and then he walked through the door without a backward glance.

The soldiers bound his wrists and escorted him down the stairs he had just come up. Down and down they went, until they reached the long, dank corridor that led to Sarto's dungeon. A tall black-haired woman stood waiting for them, looking at Philip with a half-amused smirk. "So I see our little triangle has a fourth side."

"I beg your pardon, Lady Brenna," the captain of the guard said, "but the king has commanded that he be secured immediately. Should he escape my custody, it would mean my head."

"He will be no nearer escape for the sake of a few moments' delay, captain. Stand off awhile."

"My lady?"

"Stand off, I say. I merely wish to see what sort of man would walk willingly into death for such a prim chit as our dear queen-to-be."

The guards obeyed her, and she came closer to the prisoner, sweeping her eyes appraisingly over him. "What you or Sarto either see to prize so in the whey-faced little mouse I am certain I cannot tell."

"You have the advantage of me, my lady," Philip said guardedly. "It seems you know who I am, but I do not—"

"I am Brenna of Redwen, Sarto's mistress."

"Allow me to congratulate you."

"His harlot you would say, no doubt, or worse," she added, taking insolent pleasure in his disdain. Then she looked him over again. "I see what they say of you is true."

"And what do they say?"

"That you are as beautiful as Lucifer—and as proud." She stroked his cheek, and there was a mocking light of laughter in her eyes when he pulled away from her. "You needn't tell me of your honor and your vows to your queen, my lord. I've no desire to put them to the test. After nearly twenty-five years with Sarto, I've no taste for anything so tamely well-mannered as you. No doubt I'd choke with five minutes of your puling love talk." She smiled slyly. "Still it might be worth it in sport for what came after. You'd make a trifling pretty plaything, but tomorrow you will be dead, and we shall never know."

"My lady and I have as little wish to be here as you have wish for us to be." He glanced back at the guard, certain they were out of hearing. "Help us escape, and Sarto will be yours alone once more."

"True," she agreed, "until you brought your vengeful army back again to take his life and his throne. Do you think I hunger to call you king, boy?"

"I've no desire to rule this cursed place."

"Better you than that sop Alaric."

"I want only to see my lady safe away from here. What benefit does my death bring you?"

"None," she admitted, "but it does not greatly inconvenience me either. You are to die tomorrow, and as for the girl, he will grow weary of her soon enough, especially once she has given him an heir. Your lives are no concern of mine."

"I've seen his eyes upon her. This is no mere fancy that will die with time."

"Neither is mine. I have been his mistress since I was but fourteen, my lord. I used to disguise myself so I could go out on the royal hunts as one of the boys who kept the hounds."

He looked her over. "I well believe you did."

"Sarto liked my doughtiness and took me with him more and more. Then late one day we were separated from the others amidst a storm and forced to take shelter in an empty cottage. He quickly found my secret." She smiled her sly smile. "After that I was allowed to hunt with his courtiers, and they were made to call me "Lady" Brenna, and I had no more to hang my head before their proud nobility. More than that, he and I are well matched as lovers and as companions, far better than any delicate swooning wench. I'll not lose that, my lord, not for you nor her nor all your holy kingdom."

"It looks as if you *have* lost it," Philip told her. "He's taken another, and this one's to be his queen, something he'll never grant to you."

"There are many ways one might rid oneself of a rival, my lord," she said, nonchalantly swinging the silver orb she wore back and forth on its chain. "One will suit as well as another."

She summoned the guard with a crisp snap of her fingers and then sauntered away from him, still swinging her necklace.

Philip paced his windowless cell, fighting the desolate helplessness he felt, fighting the choking memories of other times he had been locked away.

"God forgive me," he murmured. "For my willfulness, my anger, for my refusal to do Your will, forgive me. I would not hear Reghed's cry for help, and now in my need I am answered so as well. Please, sweet Lord, do not also turn away from my cries."

No, God would never turn away, not from one of His own come to Him in humble repentance. Philip had always found it so, all the many times he had cried out and been swiftly answered, and something from the Scriptures came back to him, a small, steady reminder of unchanging truth. "*I am sorely tried, but I will hope in the Lord. He will not fail me. . . .*"

"I will hope in You, my Lord," he whispered, rubbing the scarred ring again. "I will trust in You, and You will not fail me."

He stopped, listening, and then he crept toward the metallic scraping sound he had heard from near the door.

"Who is there?" he asked, his voice still at a whisper, but there was nothing more.

He moved a cautious step closer and heard the sound again, something metal scooting along the stone floor, this time something he had by chance pushed out of the way with his own foot. On hands and knees he groped in the darkness, finding nothing at first, and then at last touching cool metal. It was four or five inches long, ringed at one end, notched at the other.

"A key!" he breathed. "Oh, God, thank You—a key."

He listened for a long while. Then certain there was no guard, he stood and felt for the keyhole. After a moment's futile search, his heart began to pound. There was nothing; there would be nothing. Even a madman would not build cells that could be opened from within.

"You mock mercy!" he raged, pounding the door with the key still in his fist. Unresisting, it swung open.

He stood there astonished for an moment. If the door was unlocked, why had someone passed him this key? A key to what?

"Rosalynde!"

He stepped out into the corridor's flickering torchlight, expecting at any second to find himself face to face with one of the soldiers, but there was only deserted silence. All the way up the winding stairway, it was the same, all the way to the room where Rosalynde was being held.

He will not fail me, he reminded himself as he put the key into the lock. *He will not fail me.*

For a harrowing moment, it stuck there, refusing to turn. Then it moved, and the door opened. He stepped noiselessly into the room. Rosalynde was on her knees beside the bed, the candlelight catching the tear that rested on her pale cheek.

"Oh, Lord, if I might only see him again," she whispered.

He touched her wet face. "Sometimes He is quick to answer us, love."

"Oh, Philip!"

She clung to him, and he quieted her with a swift kiss.

"We've no time, sweetheart. Come this way."

They crept down the empty corridor. Whoever had left his door unlocked and provided the key to hers had also seen to it that the guards were occupied elsewhere.

The fugitives made their way in perfect silence back down the spiral stair, stopping a dozen times along the way to hide in the shadows, to wait until the sound of footsteps or of voices passed by them. Rosalynde breathed a little easier to see they had reached the bottom unnoticed and returned her husband's encouraging smile. She huddled against him as he listened at the door to hear if the way was safe.

Hearing nothing, he put his hand to the latch, and then he drew back and grabbed her arm. He shook his head, warning her again to silence, and took her back up the way they had come, faster, more desperately. A door below them opened, and there was the sound of soldiers' boots, the bark of orders. Philip increased their speed, taking the steps sometimes two at once, pulling her with him until they reached the top of the tower and stepped out into a driving rainstorm.

Her face was white when they began to run along the top of the castle's grim walls, and she feared she might faint. Again and again she stumbled until he was almost dragging her behind him. He was dripping with cold rain and sweat, the effort straining him in his still-weak condition. She tried to keep going, to keep from pulling him down, but she fell once more.

"I—I cannot—"

He put his arm around her waist, half carrying her. "Stay with me, love. I cannot make it without you."

She stumbled on, leaving one velvet shoe behind her.

"There, men!"

The soldiers swarmed out of the tower, Sarto himself leading them.

"You'll not take her from me, boy!"

Philip glanced back at him and quickened his pace. "Come on, love."

Rosalynde clung to him, following blindly, and fell against him when he came to an abrupt stop. They both looked down into the rain-swollen river that rushed alongside the castle wall. She looked up at him, her eyes wide.

"Philip?"

With a glance back at the soldiers running at them, he shoved her up on the edge of the wall and scrambled up after her. Then he pulled her into his arms. "Trust me?"

She clung to him, her arms tightly around his neck. "Always."

"Stop there, boy!" Sarto demanded.

Philip's hold tightened. "Whatever happens, love, do not let go."

She felt his muscles tense, and then they were falling toward the churning, roaring water. She hid her face against his chest, her body tightening in anticipation of the impact.

She caught her breath just as they hit the icy river. Every natural impulse made her want to release her hold and fight her way to the surface, but, remembering his words, she did not. She felt him struggling upwards, felt his legs driving them upwards, his arms and shoulders straining to pull them upwards. Her lungs screamed for air; she could feel the painful pounding of her heart and his in her ear. She could feel her heavy skirts dragging through the water, dragging them downward with every stroke he made upward. She was certain she would never see light again.

Oh, Jesus—

They broke the surface, and she drew the blessed air deep into her lungs, heard his gasp loud in her ear as he, too, drew breath. Then the roaring water crashed into them again, plunging them into its murky, cold depths. Still she clung to him, still she prayed, and he fought upwards once more, letting the river sweep them away from Sarto's castle, around the sharp bend that marked the edge of the forest.

The next thing she knew, Philip had taken tenuous hold of an overhanging tree limb, letting it drag them toward the river bank as the current drove them downstream. Each movement slow and painful, he pulled closer to land. Seeing his strain, feeling from the shift in his body that his feet were touching ground at last, she released her hold on him and struggled on under her own power.

He let her go, stumbling behind her, pulling himself up the bank after her and then falling exhausted on his face among the muddy river grasses. The water sucked her skirts up against her legs, and she had to fight free of it to get to him.

Trembling and crying with fear and relief, she dropped down beside him and pulled his head into her lap.

"Philip."

She patted the water from his face with her wet hands, and he smiled faintly, his breath still coming hard.

"Rose." His right arm lay limp at his side, but he reached up with his left and cupped her face in his hand. "All right, love?"

"Yes." She pushed the hair out of his eyes. "It is all right."

He took a deep satisfied breath and passed out.

She looked around them, frantic to find a place of shelter where Sarto's men could not find them. Just the smallest niche would be better than lying out here all night, but there was nothing but solid rock behind the brush at the foot of the mountain and only sheer cliff above.

"Oh, God," she sobbed, "is there no refuge for us?"

She held Philip closer, pressing a hard kiss against his wet forehead, and then she settled him on the ground and stood up. Hunching her shoulders against the storm, she walked alongside the cliff face, searching until he was almost out of sight and she knew she would have to turn back, and then she felt a sudden warmth coming from a crevice in the rock. She moved closer to it and found, disguised by the shadows in the cliff and covered by brush, a low, narrow opening just big enough to crawl into. She followed it a little way and then went back to the riverbank.

"Philip," she urged, shaking him.

With a groan, he struggled to his knees. "We must leave here now, my lady," he panted, looking as if he might go under again. "If we do not find shelter—"

"I've found someplace."

"Far?"

She put his arm around her shoulders and helped him to stand. "No, and warm as well."

"Warm?"

He shook his head as if he did not trust his ears, and she pulled him toward the niche she had discovered.

"I do not know how," she told him breathlessly, "but it is. I almost missed it for the brush and all. They'll not likely find it either."

She led him to the place and pulled him behind her into it. They passed the point where she had turned back earlier, and she began to wonder as she groped in the darkness why she found no evidence of other inhabitants. Every moment she expected to confront some wild hibernating beast or be suddenly shrouded in spider web, but she found nothing.

"Perhaps this way is not so untraveled as I first thought."

He mumbled something indistinct in answer, and she noticed she could no longer feel the rock walls on each side of her. Reaching up, she felt nothing above her either.

"I think we can stand now," she said. From the way her words echoed back to her, she realized they had reached a cavern of considerable size. It was warmer here, too, and the sound of water told her there must be hot springs nearby. "Stay there, my lord, so I do not lose my way back to you."

"Rose—"

"I'll not go far."

She stood and, keeping her hand on the wall beside her, took a cautious step into the darkness. She had not gone ten paces when she felt something iron, a ring, set into the stone.

"I've found a torch holder," she called back to him, grateful she did not find it empty. "Have you your flint and steel yet, my lord?"

She heard him fumbling in his pouch as he worked his way to her side. "Where?"

She put his hand on the ring. Twice he tried to strike a light, and then he exhaled heavily. "I cannot hold it aright, love," he told her. "My arm—"

There was a sudden faintness in his voice, and she slipped her arm around him.

"My lord?"

"Forgive me, sweet."

He sank against her, and she eased him down to the ground. In the darkness she found the flint and steel he had dropped. After a few awkward tries, she managed to strike a spark and set the torch ablaze. By its light she saw he was huddled against the wall unconscious.

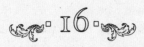

PHILIP WOKE TO THE BOOM AND SLAP OF THUNDER AND LIGHTNING
and a deafening torrent of rain. His wet clothes were gone, and
only the pile of blankets over and under him kept him from the cold.
Rosalynde was standing at the narrow mouth of the cave, and he
smiled faintly to see that she, too, had shed her rain-and-river-
drenched clothes and was wearing a man's shirt as an impromptu
shift. The garment was so large on her, it came almost to her knees
and had fallen off one shoulder.

"Had I known how fetching you would look in them, my lady, I
would have shared my shirts with you, too. Though I must confess
some jealousy toward the owner of that one."

She turned from watching the storm and came to his side, a glad
light in her eyes. "You frightened me, my lord, nearly sleeping the
clock around."

He reached up for her hand. "I am all right, love, truly. Perhaps
I haven't all my strength back yet, but I am all right." He noticed his
roughly splinted arm and winced as he flexed his hand. "I suppose I
might have had a bit more time in mending."

"You should have stayed at my father's until you were well," she
said, looking searchingly into his eyes. Then she pressed her hand to
his side against his ribs. He did not flinch.

"I am all right, sweetheart."

He put his hand over hers, holding it against him, and she put her other hand to his face.

"You should have stayed," she repeated, stroking his cheek, "but I am so very glad you did not. I've missed you so."

"Where is this place?" he asked. "We were not here last night."

"We were here, my lord, or at least just back through there a ways." She pointed to a dark opening at her right. "There is another cave in there and then the passage back to the river below Sarto's castle. This one opens into the forest, and it looks well hidden by brush as well. I think someone has been using these caverns as a hoarding place for the plunder he's taken. There are all manner of things secreted here."

"And it's rained so all this while?"

She nodded, and he smiled again.

"I doubt there is any sign left for them now. Thank God for the rain."

"And for leading us to this place where we can be warm and dry and have all we need of food and clothing. And where you will have somewhere to rest." She pressed his side once more. "Are you certain that does not pain you, love?"

"Certain."

She moved her hand from his cheek to the side of his head. "And your head does not ache?"

"Some," he admitted, and then he leaned into her caress with a bewildered sigh. "Oh, Rose, how am I to get us out of this now? Whoever belongs to this place is sure to return, and we must not be found here."

"Shh," she whispered. "There will be time to think on that tomorrow."

She bent over him, rubbing his temples. He closed his eyes and let the breath drift out of him, savoring her touch and the easing of the hammering inside his skull. She leaned closer, and a deep contentment washed through him like the strong, gentle flowing of the Westered sea.

"I've missed you so," she said again, wriggling under the blanket, too. He pulled her to him, close and tight to his side, and they fell asleep to the sound of the storm.

It was gray morning when they awoke, and it was raining again. Or still.

"You asked me once long ago if ever I felt I belonged to a place," she murmured, "as if I'd not be whole outside it." She laughed softly. "I doubt you'd remember now."

He smiled. "I remember. It was in Treghatours. When I was fool enough to think I could live and not love you."

The thunder crashed, and she nestled closer to him in the warm protection of his arm, nuzzling his shoulder. "Wherever we are, this is my place."

He pressed her hand fervently to his lips and then to his cheek. "I shall never forgive myself for letting them take you from there."

"Shh," she murmured. "God has brought us back together again and protected us both all this while. They might have killed you or hurt you so badly you'd never have recovered, but now—" She stroked his cheek. "Now you have but a few bruises that will fade with time." She touched her lips to his hair softly and gently, just over his right ear. "If you are careful."

She stroked her hand down his side again and the other across his chest. His drowsiness suddenly gone, he put his arm around her waist and pulled her closer. She caressed his cheek and pressed the tenderest of kisses against his bruised jaw.

"It does not hurt you anymore, my love?" she whispered.

He smiled slightly. "No."

She traced one delicate finger down the straight, aristocratic line of his nose. "You are so beautiful."

"You think so still?"

Lightning illuminated them both for an instant, lighting her secretive little smile. Once more in the dimness, she kissed his forehead, his nose, the corner of his mouth. "I know so."

Pressing nearer, she kissed him again slowly and sweetly, and his arm tightened around her. Without breaking the kiss, he tried to turn to his side, but she held him where he was, and he lay back again, having no desire to waste what strength he had struggling against her. Her hands stroked through his hair and down to his shoulders, and he closed his eyes at the whisper-fine touch of her lips on his.

"I feared I would never see you again," she murmured, "never touch you, never—"

She broke off, pressing kisses, light and lingering, all over his face. He held her even tighter, and her kisses grew more intense.

"You are certain you are feeling better?"

He answered her with a kiss, surrendering to the passion that swept over him like the rushing of the river and the raging of the wind.

On the other side of the forest, Tom was sitting in the shelter of one of Credotti's wagons studying the diagrams he had drawn of Sarto's castle, trying to devise some strategy for rescuing the supposed captives. A burst of activity outside drew him to the doorway.

"What is it, Credotti?"

"They've escaped, my lord. Your brother and the pretty lady both—they are gone. Arnaldo here had it of one of the tavern wenches that they leapt from the castle wall into the river two days ago and have not been seen since."

"Could they have survived it, Arnaldo?" Tom pressed.

The weeping clown smiled. "Sarto thinks they did, my lord. He has soldiers searching everywhere for them. We must simply find them first."

"You fear your brother might not have made it?" Credotti asked, seeing Tom's apprehensiveness.

Tom shook his head. "He would have survived a leap into hell if it meant keeping her safe. But Arnaldo is right; we must find them before Sarto does." He looked up at the leaden sky, still hurling down rain. "At least his men will have no better weather for it than we."

For a long while the storm roared around them, howling and moaning through the trees, frightening in its all-encompassing fury. Then it died away as quickly as it had come, leaving the rain only a gentle patter on the leaves, the thunder no more than a muffled rumble in the distance. Philip lay in the cave with Rosalynde draped, sleeping, across his chest, with her face pressed against the side of his neck and her arms around him still. He wriggled one of her hands free and held her soft palm against his cheek.

"This is my place," he whispered. "With you, my Rose."

She woke at that and laughed a little to realize she had fallen asleep again. He kissed her forehead.

"I forget to be afraid now," she told him, sitting up. "Now that I am with you again."

He kissed her ear.

"If only we had the children," she added wistfully, "I would ask nothing more than this."

He kissed her chin and then looked around them. "Truly this is quite a cave of wonders you've found for us, my lady," he observed. "Blankets, clothing, bandages—"

"And food and wine," she added.

"Truly a cave of wonders, this thieves' den." He looked around again and rubbed his chin. "You've not come across a razor in there anywhere, have you, love? I may be forced to live awhile as a beast, but hang me if I'll be furred like one."

She found a reasonably well-honed blade among the bandages, and while their breakfast porridge bubbled on the fire, he shaved himself. She knelt beside him, holding up the elaborate gilt-framed mirror she had found with the other supplies.

"Whoever he is," she observed, "this prince of thieves is not a poor man."

He thrust out his chin and turned his face to one side, making certain he had not missed a spot. "I wonder if they are thieves. Perhaps 'rebels' would be a better term."

"Who would dare run a rebellion here under Sarto's very nose?"

"Who would dare a rebellion at all against the madman? One of his own nobles, I daresay. Such a lunatic as he would never suspect a man who stood in his own court cowering before him." He set down the razor and rinsed his face. "But that is Reghed's worry. Let them cut one another's throats if it please them. We are leaving here today."

"Surely, love, another day's rest would—"

"Would be a waste of time. If you will, my lady, find us both something to wear."

"Very well, my lord," she agreed, looking unconvinced.

She stood, and he noticed a deep purple bruise high up on her white thigh. He knit his brow and examined the back of her leg. There were four more bruises there—four fingers to match the thumb. A mixture of fear and fury filled his eyes.

"Rosalynde, did Sarto do that—"

She laughed. "You put those marks there yourself, love. When you tossed me up on the wall before we jumped."

"I did?"

She took his hand and put it on her leg. It matched perfectly, the thumb and four fingers.

"Forgive me, sweet," he said sheepishly, "but I could not help fearing—"

"No." She smiled and cuddled close to him again. "It is a miracle in itself, but he never touched me."

"God forgive me if he ever had."

There was something in the quiet gravity of his words that made them more forbidding than the bloodiest oath of vengeance.

"You must forgive him for what he's done, my love," she said softly. "I'd not have him come between us."

He looked at her puzzled.

"You know it would be so, my lord. Were you to hold so great a hate in your heart, you would perforce have to let go some of its love. That love is mine by right, and I mean to have every bit of it."

"I could never love you less," he murmured.

"Then if just for my sake, because I would have you free of such a burden, forgive him."

There was a sudden hardness in his eyes. "Always, always, always I'm to forgive! No matter how vile, how monstrous the wrong, I'm to forgive! Rose, how many times until it is past forgiving?"

"How oft are we forgiven, love?"

He looked for a long moment into the gentle pleading in her emerald eyes, his expression calming as he did. "I know. I know it all too well and bless God for it, but what Sarto did—sweet heavens, Rose, willful and unpardonable, all of it."

"Did you ever wonder, my lord, why it was he took me?"

He laughed cynically. "I think that was plain from the very first."

"Perhaps not so plain, love. He took me not for myself but because I was like someone he'd lost."

"Someone he'd lost?"

"You remember the tale of his mistress Rosamund who died before he became king? It was she he took me for."

"Many men lose their wives and mistresses," he said sternly. "That does not give them license to take other men's."

"Hear me out, love. I do not say what he did was right, God forbid it. Only you might understand him, better than anyone else would, were you to hear his tale."

"Why me more than any other?"

She took his hand. "Because of Katherine Fletcher."

"What has she to do with this?"

"Because Sarto's father did not think this Rosamund fit to be queen, he—"

"You needn't finish it, my lady," he said, looking away. "It is an old tale."

"He had her poisoned."

"Rose—"

"This Rosamund Sarto loved more than his life, she died in his arms, vowing to return to him. All this while he's waited for her."

For a moment he said nothing. Then he turned back to her, a determined coolness in his expression. "I've heard of her since I've come to Reghed, this Rosamund," he said, taking his hand from hers. "She was a harlot, a sorceress. You cannot compare that to what I had with Kate."

She caressed his cheek, all tenderness. "I know there was nothing but honor in the love you had for her, my lord, and little enough in his for Rosamund, but his pain was the same, his loss as dear to him as yours to you. You've told me before how close to madness your grief brought you and what kept you from it."

"God's grace," he said thickly, "and the love He gave me in you."

"Sarto knew no God, love, but he had that same grief and no one to comfort him in it. You might see; you might pity . . ." She took his hand again. "You might forgive."

He let his breath out slowly, and then he looked at her once more, tears standing in his eyes. "Let me take you safe home again, Rose, and I will see if there is not some godly way of settling this between him and me. God helping me, I will forgive him."

She held him for a long, tender moment. "Do not wait to do it, love," she told him. "It only grows more difficult over time."

"I know," he murmured, the words almost lost in a sudden clap of thunder. "I know."

The storm returned more fiercely than before and would not relent, forcing them to keep their borrowed shelter another day. He had planned to leave that morning, to take himself and Rosalynde out of Sarto's realm and out of danger, but now he had no distracting journey to occupy his mind and quiet the persistent voice in his spirit. *Forgive.* It ran through his thoughts all that day and into the stormy night as he tried once more to sleep. *Forgive. Forgive.* Why was it a lesson never learned?

He lay there listening to the night wind howling and moaning through the barren forest, listening to the deafening thunder that seemed to shake the very rock that sheltered them. What must it be like outside in the heart of the tempest?

How well he knew the burden of unforgiveness, the pressing weight of hatred and vengeance. How well he knew the feel of it raging inside him, howling and moaning like the storm. He had felt it there when Katherine had been taken from him, felt it there growing and growing, becoming part of him—no longer just what he was feeling but who he was. How long he had clung to it then, telling himself it was his right, that justice and honor demanded it of him.

How mercifully free he had felt when he had finally released it, this "right," this "justice." Why was he struggling with this same thing again now? Would it never come easily to him, this forgiveness?

He knew already what unforgiveness brought. He knew the Scriptures that said God would not hear a prayer from a heart that held unforgiveness inside it, that He would not forgive until the one seeking forgiveness also forgave.

I was the one wronged, he told himself, but he knew that changed nothing. His unforgiveness, his willfulness, his lack of faith—these too were sin. If he had done no wrong, if his motives were so pure, why had he left the chapel at the border of Reghed without the blessing he had sought? Without the sanction of God? Fearing to touch what was holy?

Still, I could never have done such things as Sarto has done. I would never—

It came back to him in sudden, searing clarity—the pain, the blinding rage, the fierce need to make someone, anyone, hurt, too. When he had been told that Kate was dead, he had been filled with a madness he had feared would consume him. Sarto had been young once. He had loved, too, and had his love torn away from him.

"*. . . you might understand him, better than anyone else would . . .*"

He remembered striking his fists, his head, against the cold stone walls of his prison cell, relishing the physical pain that had at least in some small measure dulled the raw, howling grief that had ripped through him back then. He remembered the cruelties he had committed, cruelties to those who had never done him wrong. But in all those black days, even when he could not comprehend it, there had been those who stood by him, those who loved him despite his cruelties, despite his madness. Tom. Rosalynde. God Himself. Without that, might he not have become—

"*Sarto knew no God. . . . his pain was the same, his loss as dear to him as yours to you . . . he had that same grief and no one to comfort him in it.*"

What might it have been like if he, too, had gone through that hell all alone? What might that madness have grown to?

"*You might see, you might pity . . . you might forgive.*"

All his life he had been shown mercy in his own failings, and he knew how undeserved that mercy had been. But when it came to extending such mercy to another, to one who had done him such profound wrong—

"I am not You, God!"

His fierce whisper was a sibilant echo in the cavern, and Rosalynde stirred against him. "Mmmm?"

"Shh," he murmured, kissing her forehead. "Go back to sleep, sweet."

She said nothing more, but he knew she was not asleep. He knew she was praying for him, the silent, fervent, ever-present prayers that had carried him through so much. But this was not something she could do for him; only he could make the decision to forgive. But he had tried all that day, all that endless night, and still the dry, hot tightness that marked his hatred lived and thrived inside him.

"How can I ever do it?" he asked her finally, knowing she would understand the question without explanation. She was so long in answering, he thought perhaps she had fallen asleep again after all. "Rose?"

"Do you think you are the only one with anything to forgive Sarto, my lord?"

Her voice was soft, gentle as always, and it occurred to him that he had never before considered that she had had to battle the same hatred, the same fury, the same unforgiveness. For no wrong she had done, she had been torn from her husband's arms, had seen him beaten into unconsciousness, had been separated from her children, dragged into another land and held captive there. Yet she had forgiven the one who had caused all this. He knew she had.

"No," he admitted finally. "I merely do not know how you were able to do it."

"I simply chose it, love. As I chose to receive our Lord's salvation." She squeezed his hand in the darkness. "As I chose to love you . . . despite the doubts that sometimes came, despite the pain, despite anything but the simple choice and the trust that God would make up the lack in me to do it." He could hear the smile in her voice. "There were times when you were not so easy to love."

"I know. But, Rose, what Sarto has done to us both—"

"What he has done to us both is now past. You are alive. I am alive. We are together and shall soon be safe home. Rather than dwelling on the evil that was done us, consider instead our deliverance from it. Thank God for it, love, and forgive Sarto. He is as wretched and bound in darkness as the poor souls they keep in the madhouses. Do not let his wrongs make you like him."

He was silent a long while, considering her words. "I merely choose it?"

She sighed and nestled closer to him, and he knew this time she really was asleep.

He awoke the next morning and smiled to see her sitting beside him, her legs tucked under her as she watched his face.

"Hello, love," he said, his voice husky with sleep.

She smiled, too, and leaned down to touch her lips to his. "Good morning, my lord. I have breakfast ready."

He stretched and sat up. "You've been about early."

"Not so, love. The sun has been hours up, but I hadn't the heart to wake you. You had such a look of peace, I could not help but wonder . . ."

He slipped his hand into hers. "I could never conceal anything from you, could I, my queen? I thought a long while on what we spoke of last night. As you said, we are both well, we are together, and we are going home. What could I do but rejoice? I, uh—I thought on Sarto as well." He took a deep breath and then gave her a crooked smile. "And, God making up my lack, what could I do but forgive?"

She threw her arms around him. "Oh, love, I am so very glad."

He cuddled her close for a moment, and then he flashed her a bright smile. "It sounds as if we finally have a break in the storm. If you will fetch me my clothes, sweet, if I still have clothes, we shall see about finding Tom and the others and going home."

"Yours are well dried by now, my lord, but I fear mine were hopeless." She fingered the rumpled shirt she wore. "I wonder if our thief has robbed any dressmakers of late."

"We must take a better look through our storehouse here," he said with a wink, and she smiled.

"I did find something you might favor, my lord."

She disappeared into the cavern, and then he heard a metallic scraping along the rock floor. A moment later she reappeared, dragging a sturdy broadsword with her.

"I came across this yesterday while you were asleep."

He took it from her, testing the feel of it in his hands before he laid it down beside him.

"It may be of use to you," she said.

"It just may be," he agreed, giving it an appreciative pat.

She held the gilt-framed mirror for him once more while he shaved, and then she got his clothes. Once she had helped him dress, she brought him a bowl of steaming porridge and some not-too-stale bread she had found.

"Are you certain you feel well enough to go, my lord? It is a long way back, and I fear you are not yet strong enough—"

"Of course I am," he claimed, snatching the spoon from her, but she as quickly snatched it back.

"If you are going to insist upon leaving here today, you must let me have my way at least until you have had your breakfast."

"Oh, Rose, no," he protested, realizing what she intended. "You cannot truly expect—"

She stifled his objections with a heaping spoonful of porridge. "Behave yourself and I might agree to go today."

"You might agree?"

"Eat," she commanded, shoveling in another mouthful.

"Rose—"

"Eat."

He started to laugh and almost choked. "I will, I will, but not quite so much at once." He grabbed her wrist and tried to catch his breath. "I must make a fine sight at table if you think I down my food so quickly."

She giggled and attempted to stuff a chunk of bread into his mouth with her other hand. He struggled briefly and then growled in mock ferociousness and made her squeal by trying to nip at her fingers as he gobbled it up.

"Bad," she scolded, swatting his hand. He set the bowl aside and pulled her into his arms.

"I see you've yet to be shown who is master here."

"Brave words from a trespasser!"

They both started at the gruff voice. Philip grabbed for the sword that lay beside him, but the intruder merely pinned it to the ground with his foot, brandishing his own blade. "Best leave that lie for now."

"Who are you?" Philip demanded.

Under his unkempt reddish mustache, the other man curled his lip in disdain. "I think I've more right to ask that than you, boy." He looked at the borrowed things that surrounded them, blankets and clothes and dishes still half full. "You and your hussy here seem to have made very free with what is not yours."

Philip's temper flashed into his eyes, and Rosalynde clutched his arm, her expression fearful. "I told you we must not stay, Jerome," she said in a perfect imitation of one of the kitchen girls from home. "We're caught now sure."

For an instant Philip looked startled, and then he quickly picked it up. "It seems we are, Joan." He ducked his head sullenly. "We meant no harm, master, only we were cold and hungry."

The stranger lowered his blade, looking annoyed.

"I'll see you paid, master, truly, for all we've taken," Philip said in sudden earnestness. "We meant no harm, but we had to shelter some place we'd not be found."

"Someone is seeking you then," the stranger surmised.

With a glance at Rosalynde, Philip nodded. "It shames me to tell it, but she has a husband."

"A husband, you say!" The stranger laughed. "You might have chosen warmer weather for wife-stealing, boy." He looked at Rosalynde, still kneeling there in the shirt she had borrowed, and grinned. "Then again, perhaps you've heat enough as it is."

"He is a beast, her husband," Philip told him, spitting on the ground with all the contempt of one of his stable boys. "I've seen myself his cruelty written in her flesh, sweet delicate thing that she is, and him not fit to carry her slippers."

"I could not bear to stay where I was, master," she said. "But for modesty, I could show you the marks he's left on me."

"You are not from Reghed," the stranger observed. "Your speech smacks of something further south."

"We come from east of here," Philip told him.

The stranger nodded. "You come from Halden then."

"I thought at first her husband would never make it so far. It is not an easy place to get to, your Reghed, nor an easy one to live in."

The stranger merely shrugged. "Reghed has her troubles, that's sure, but you can never say what lengths a man might go, having his woman taken from him."

There was a sudden hardness in Philip's expression, but he managed still the submissive deference of a peasant. "There is talk of rebellion here, master," he said. "Is it so?"

"I've heard it said," the stranger replied with another shrug.

Philip looked around them. "All these provisions, they might serve a rebellion well, might they not?"

"Perhaps."

"Is it just, then, this cause against your king?"

"You are full of questions, boy. A trifle too many for a Halden man come here by chance, but perhaps enough for one of the king's spies." The stranger lifted his blade again and began tracing delicate arcs in front of Philip's face. "Surely you know you cannot leave this place now you've found it. We cannot have anyone, even wife-stealers, betraying us to all the world."

Philip threw back his shoulders and clenched his jaw, daring the man by the regal lift of his chin to do his worst.

"Mercy, master," Rosalynde pled, pulling him back from the stranger, and Philip quickly ducked his head again.

"Please, master, we've no interest in your king or your rebellion. We mean only to make our way into Lynaleigh where there is peace and plenty. Have some of your company deliver us there if you doubt me."

"We haven't followers enough for such foolishness," the stranger said. Then he grinned and teased Rosalynde's borrowed sleeve with his broadsword's point. "Better to have you hanged for a thief, boy, and throw the wench to the men."

Philip sprang on him, knocking him down, grabbing his sword arm and pinning him on his back with the blade resting against his throat.

"Perhaps it would be better to have you separated from your head," he panted, his eyes crystal flame. "I've no doubt we can find our way to Lynaleigh on our own."

"You're no peasant," the stranger gasped. "Who are you?"

"You choose a fine time to ask, Griffith," someone drawled.

Rosalynde's eyes widened. "Prince Alaric!"

"Come no farther," Philip said, pulling the man called Griffith in front of him as Sarto's son sauntered out of the cave's dark recesses. "I know not what deceit you have in hand here, but we'll not be taken back."

"Not by me at any rate, my lord," Alaric said, "and not by him. You look twenty kinds of fool, Griffith. Close your mouth."

"What is this, my lord?" Philip asked, shoving his captive into a heap at Alaric's feet, still holding the broadsword ready. "I thought we had stumbled upon the rebels' lair. What could you want with all this?"

"Why, what any loyal son would want, my lord." He smiled. "Any loyal son of Reghed."

"You are the rebel leader!" Rosalynde breathed.

Alaric graced her with a deep bow. "So I am, royal lady."

"Royal?" Griffith looked in amazement from his former prisoner to his master. "Who are they, my lord?"

"You might not know it to see them now, man, but you stand, or rather sprawl, before the high majesty of Lynaleigh—King Philip and his queen."

"What sort of just cause is it you lead, my lord?" Philip demanded. "Hanging helpless refugees, abusing women—"

"Who of my cause has done this?"

"This man," Philip replied, nodding toward Griffith. "By threat at least."

"No, no, my lord prince," Griffith assured his master. "I merely meant to frighten them away, to keep this place secret still." He got up on his knees, still wary of the blade Philip held. "Hardly helpless."

"We want no more than to return to Lynaleigh, my lord," Philip told the prince. "I see no reason for you to hinder us from that."

"You told me you came from Halden," Griffith protested.

Philip shook his head. "*You* told me we came from Halden. I told you we came from east of here. Winton is a good way east of here—once you've gone a good way further south."

"And I have every intention for you to return there, your majesty," Alaric said. "Did I not, you would be locked up in my father's dungeon still."

"Then it was you who freed us," Philip said guardedly. "I must thank you for it."

"I think I am due a better payment than that," Alaric replied, "in all equity."

"Name it."

"Your aid in our cause."

Philip studied him for a moment, then nodded. "Whatever you ask. The moment I reach Lynaleigh, I will see to it."

Alaric laughed cynically. "The moment you reach Lynaleigh, you will forget it rather."

"You doubt my word, my lord?" Philip asked him icily. "Have I such a name as oath-breaker here in Reghed?"

"No, in truth, your majesty, but Reghed holds no claim on you. You've no cause to help us once you've reached the safety of your own kingdom."

"No cause save my honor. There's cause enough. And if it were not, there is a stronger bond that holds me to my word. My God requires it of me."

Alaric hesitated for a moment. "All those things you speak of would be most welcome, my lord, but that is not what I most seek from you."

"What then?"

"Kill my father." Alaric's eyes held equal parts fear and recklessness as he whispered the words. Then he looked behind him as if he were afraid Sarto would hear him even now. "There's no one in all Reghed bold enough for that, no one from outside with cause enough save you. Do it, and all our kingdom shall be free. Surely that is what your God has sent you for."

As hungry as he had been to plunge a blade into Sarto's conscienceless heart, Philip knew that that was not why he'd been sent here, not why he had felt the urging again and again to bring succor to this place. He knew too well the ways of God, infinitely more merciful than his own. Murder would never be His design.

He looked at Reghed's prince with regal disdain. "I play hired assassin for no man. I marvel you've not yet done it yourself."

Alaric shook his head with a faint laugh. "I could not."

"He *is* your father," Philip said, relenting a little.

"No. That has no bearing on this. I merely cannot. He would know of it. Somehow he would know of it beforehand, and what he would do then—" Alaric paled and clenched his fists to keep his hands from trembling. "I cannot."

"I *will* not," Philip returned. "I will send you any aid I can—men, money, weapons—you need only ask, but expect nothing beyond that."

"My lord, you have your freedom, your life I daresay, and your lady as well. I would think you owe a great debt to the one who made that possible. Would you deny me now? Perhaps it would profit me more to have you both taken back to my father."

"No, please, my lord—" Rosalynde began.

Philip stilled her. "Do not plead with him, my lady. Any man who would consent to such a thing is not a man I could help to power even in Reghed." He looked coldly at Alaric. "Clearly, we are at your mercy here, but I tell you now and truly you have no hope of any aid from Lynaleigh unless it is through friendship and not coercion."

"You fear him," Alaric said with a derisive laugh. "For all your brave words, you fear him as much as I."

"Not so," Philip replied. "Let him do what he will to me, he cannot stand before the name of my Lord, that I know. But I'll not stay here to keep my lady in danger of his madness for your cause or anyone's. I have made you my offer. The choice is yours."

"Merely think on it," Alaric urged. "Grant me just the space of one night before you make your final decision. Consider what we face here and the aid you claim your God means you to bring us. If by morning you still cannot find occasion to stay, I'll provide you food and clothing for your return and ask no more of you."

"Very well then," Philip agreed. "But do not expect that one night will alter my view of this."

That night the rain turned to snow, and Philip's nightmare returned without warning. This time the images were even stronger, more vivid. This time the smoke was stifling, the heat almost unbearable. Hearing the piteous cries from inside the burning church, he tried to move the heavy iron that barred the doors, tried despite the blackened metal that seared into his flesh, but he could not budge it. This time it was chained there, and he had no way to open the lock.

"The key is inside!" he shouted to those shrieking for his help. "The key is inside!"

He grabbed the chain with both hands, fearing he might black out from the fierce pain, and to his horror the links snaked around his wrists and began dragging him toward the flames.

"Use the key!" he cried. "The key is inside! Inside!"

Rosalynde had to shake him awake.

"Oh, God, help me," he gasped, huddling against her. "What is it I'm to do here?"

"It is inside, my lord," she said when he had told her the dream. "The key, the way to help these people—it must come from inside, from within Reghed. You are not meant to free them, only to make them understand that they have the means."

"Who, Rosalynde? Who is it that I must tell before I am pulled into their destruction?"

"There is only one, love. Their own prince. Alaric."

CHAPTER

WE HAVE VERY FEW BOLD ENOUGH TO NUMBER THEMSELVES WITH us even in secret," Alaric said when he and Philip spoke the next day, "mostly those who have nothing more to lose by it, and even those are losing heart. We must show them something to give them hope, or they will merely give up. We must have you to lead us."

"I think there are more, many more, who would stand with you if you faced Sarto man to man. From what I've seen, the people, the nobility, the army—all would come to you if they knew you would stand for them."

"If you believe that, my lord, perhaps you are not so clever a man as the tales speak. They'll never follow the likes of me. I know."

"I cannot stay here, man, and leave my lady in such peril. I cannot even think to give you my aid until she is returned home."

"I will have some of my men see her back safe to Westered then. You need not go."

Philip laughed grimly. "You think I would trust her to them? After all this? I think not."

"It will take far too long if you insist upon seeing her there yourself," Alaric protested. "Something must be done now."

"I will compromise with you then, my lord," Philip countered. "Let me find my brother and his men. Give them some of your men as guard, and I will send my lady back with them. Tom can lead my soldiers back here himself."

Rosalynde's hold on his arm tightened, and he read in her eyes her pleading not to be sent away without him. She looked so helpless somehow, wearing the simple dress one of Alaric's men had found for her and with her hair only loosely bound.

"Are we agreed, my lord?" he asked Alaric, forcing himself to hold firm against her silent entreaty.

Alaric glanced uneasily at his lieutenant. "I fear that will not be possible, your majesty."

Philip's eyes narrowed. "Why not? What has happened?"

"I have had word that your brother has been taken by my father's men, he and those with him."

Philip glared at him. "And just when were you meaning to tell me of this?"

"I was brought the news only a moment ago," Alaric protested.

"I told him myself, my lord," Griffith confirmed.

"It seems you must now change your plans," Alaric added. "I doubt truly that my father will wait the time it would take for you to go to Lynaleigh and back before he has your brother put to death."

"A most convenient turn of events for you, my lord prince of Reghed," Philip replied, his voice steeped in sarcasm. "You could have found no better argument to keep me here."

"It is a sad passage, my lord, truly," Alaric said, "but it could be turned to our advantage."

"You mean it could be turned to *your* advantage!" Philip shot back. "Do you think I do not see what you've done? I know your rebellion has ears and eyes everywhere. No doubt they came upon my brother and the others and told you where they were. You've betrayed him to force my hand, to leave me no choice but challenge Sarto."

"My—my lord!"

Philip took fierce hold of his shirt front. "Coward! Miserable coward! You grovel before your father and now before me! You've betrayed my brother! At least be a man and own up to it."

"Please, my lord," Rosalynde urged gently, but Philip shook free of her.

"Coward," he spat again. "However do you expect to rule this kingdom if you cannot even rule your fears? By my faith, at this moment I'd as soon leave that madman on the throne as put such a milksop in his place."

"I am afraid," Alaric admitted, his voice trembling. "I am terrified of my father. I have been all my life. He thinks me a weakling or an idiot or worse, and he knows I would never dare stand against him. How can I? He knows everything, sees everything, hears everything . . . punishes everything." He swallowed painfully, his breathing harsh and uneven. "He will kill me if I give him the slightest cause. I think he would have before, but he thought I was no threat to him. Now I am his heir by default, but he would still kill me if he even suspected I had betrayed him."

Philip shoved him away in disgust. "Here I stand offering you my army and all the power of my kingdom, and you betray me? You betray my brother who has never done you wrong, who has no stake in this, to force my hand because you fear to lift your own! Coward!"

"I am no coward!" Alaric cried. "Stand you here in my place, live all your life in fear of your own father, and tell me you would be any more brave."

"I would never use the innocent as means to my end."

"Can you not see, my lord?" Alaric pled. "It is the only way. For the sake of the God you have said sent you here to deliver us all, I beg you."

"He sent me to help you, my lord. I see that now. He could have sent me with all my army to slash through Reghed and rip your father from his place and leave your people thinking you too weak to rule them, but that is not His way. He had rather you take the throne yourself, show yourself strong to your people, and lead them in His way, as your father has never done. Trust in Him, and Sarto cannot stand against you."

"Have you no fear of him?"

"What is he but a madman? A reckless tyrant? Who of his followers would stand with him were it not for fear? He's held you all with that all this while, little more than fear. Before God, man, you are a whole army, a whole people, and you grovel before one madman? Let me no longer call myself a man when I stoop so low. He may overpower me, he may even kill me, but he'll not frighten me into doing nothing while he takes my wife, and he'll not see me stand by while my brother lies in his dungeon."

"How is it you do not fear him?" Alaric asked again, his breath coming harder. "Rosamund was a sorceress, and he calls still on her powers. With them, he is stronger than any of us in the army or in the whole kingdom. It is real, my lord—never doubt that."

"That I can believe, and do, but he and a whole hell full of demons together cannot stand against my God. I'll not fear him on that account."

Alaric looked at him for a moment, considering. "He was my mother's God, this God you speak of, and they say she followed Him faithfully in all things. If He is truly stronger than Rosamund's black arts, then why did He let my mother die so young? Before I could even know her?"

"I do not know the answer to that," Philip said, "but there is a passage in the Scripture that speaks of the righteous being taken away to be spared from the evil of this world, that they find peace and rest in death. Perhaps your mother was one such. It could not have been easy for her to live with your father, knowing he valued his mistress over her, knowing the child she carried would likely be kept from the throne even though he had the right."

"That may be so. They say she was a good woman, even if her only beauty was in her gentle heart. And she believed. She believed in your God. She meant for me to know Him, too. She wrote letters to me before I was born, as if she knew she would not live to tell me herself. Perhaps God was preparing her even then." He drew a deep melancholy breath. "But why did He spare her this life and not me?"

"I cannot answer that," Philip said, "but He knows His plans for us, and doubtless He had a purpose for you even then. Perhaps a kingdom for you to rule in time."

"I took Him once for mine when I was a fool of fifteen, but I could not stand in that belief all this while alone against Rosamund's devils." His voice trembled. "Why, if He is stronger, has He never come to me? Why has He never done anything to stop my father's madness?"

"You may be an even greater fool than I first thought," Philip told him. "Why do you think He sent me? I have asked Him all this while why He has let us suffer through this. My brother, my lady— they are more truly His than anyone I know, and He has not kept them safely at home, and it is because He counts you worth everything He has. He sends us in His service to bring you to Him because more than you or I or anyone, He would have your people free. He sent us here for you."

"For me?" Alaric bowed his head, and his tears left dark splotches on his brown doublet. "Oh, my lord, how do I take that strength? That fearlessness?"

"You merely take Him."

There was a long expectant silence.

"My lord?" Rosalynde urged gently.

Alaric did not look up. "I—I could not," he stammered weakly. "He would know. My father would know, and he would murder me for it."

"You must trust in the Lord to look after you!" she cried, but Philip stilled her.

"I will see to it myself then," Philip spat as he stripped the splints off his arm and tossed them at Alaric's feet. "Stay here with your fear. Salt Sarto's wine and play at soldiering while he robs and murders your people till you've none left to save. I am going to take back my brother and all those with him and leave you to your pantomime rebellion."

"My lord!" Alaric called after him, but he and Rosalynde were gone.

"We must find Credotti, my lady," Philip explained as they strode through the forest. "They managed to get in before. No doubt we can think of some way to do it again."

"But Sarto's men will be watching for such a trick now," Rosalynde panted. "Surely they will."

"Molly is yet undiscovered in the kitchens. She might somehow get us in. It might be that Rafe and Palmer and Livrette were not all captured. If not, we might together come to something. No doubt before he was taken, Tom had them all searching for us."

"But will not the soldiers be searching for us as well? What if they—"

"Shh," Philip warned, pulling her into the trees.

From somewhere ahead of them they heard the faint sound of someone barking orders to his men. "Come this way."

He led her deeper into the forest, away from the voice they had heard, but, looking back, they saw that they had left clear prints in the snow.

"This is no use," he said, coming to a full stop. Then he pulled her forward again until they reached an evergreen with dense overgrown branches. "Remember Tom's adventure in the forest on our way to Westered?"

She nodded, baffled, and he swung her up into his arms.

"The soldiers will think by the tracks that I've put you up in this tree. Perhaps it will slow them down enough for us to escape."

They trudged on, but he could not keep up so swift a pace carrying her. It was not long before they heard the soldiers again, nearer this time.

"Put me down, my lord," she insisted. "We can both run."

"No. You'll never make it far afoot. There must be some hiding place we can find."

"The tracks lead this way!" one of the soldiers called behind them.

Philip looked around frantically. Choosing randomly, he turned sharply to his left and came upon a fairly well-traveled road. The tracks there were smeared with much trampling, and it would be impossible for anyone to distinguish one or two from all the rest.

"Thank God," Rosalynde whispered as he set her on her feet. Hand in hand, they hurried on.

"They've taken to the road!" a soldier's voice cried, and Philip knew they were losing ground. Still he searched for a place to hide.

"There," he said, pointing to their right. Along the side of the road was a stout-looking oak tree, apparently solid from three sides, but from the fourth he could see it was rotten almost through.

"There is just enough room for you inside, love. We'll pull some branches over you, and I'll come back for you when I can."

"Oh, Philip, no."

"Whatever happens, you must not make a sound."

"Philip—"

"Please, my lady, do this for me."

She crawled into the hollowed out space, glad it was winter and not lively spring, and he made a perfect blind for her.

"I love you," he whispered, taking a quick kiss. Then he put the last branch in place and darted away.

He had not gone a hundred yards when he heard the soldiers once more. He saw two of them. An instant later, they saw him.

"There he is!"

He forced his legs to go faster, but a glance backwards told him they were closing on him. He tried to break for the trees, tried for one last frantic burst of speed, but already they were on either side of him, seizing him by the arms, dragging him off his feet, wrenching his body one way and then another at their horses' jolting pace. Approaching a stream, they dug their spurs into their horses' flanks, and he felt his heart lurch as they jumped the rushing water. He tried to tear himself free when they touched ground again, but the two soldiers had grasps of iron, and he was carried helplessly along. Finally they came to an abrupt stop in their makeshift camp and tossed him down at the feet of Sarto himself.

"Where is she, boy? You cannot hide her forever."

"She is safe," Philip panted, rubbing the strained, screaming muscles in his shoulder. "You shall never find her now."

"She will come to me," Sarto said confidently, scanning the trees that surrounded them. "And beg to come."

He nodded to his men, and they jerked Philip to his feet. In another moment he was standing with his back against the thick trunk of an oak tree with his wrists bound. The soldiers had laid a fire a few feet away.

"Do you hear, my lady?" Sarto called out, his voice ringing through the clear, cold air. "I have your Philip. Show yourself, and he shall have mercy, I pledge it."

"She knows your mercy, Sarto!" Philip spat. "He will kill me just the same, Rose. You must not—"

"I will kill him, gracious lady. You know it must be so, but there are ways not so gentle as others." Sarto took an iron from the fire, long and pointed, heated white. "My men have been heating these irons for some while now in the event I was compelled to—" He smiled slightly and then raised his voice. "To coax your abductor into revealing your whereabouts. Imagine, my lady, how many hours, how many days, it might take for charitable death to finally come. And, pity, what would be left of this regal flesh for you to hold in your memory save the cruel echoes of his cries begging after it is too late for you to come to me?"

"Rosalynde, you will not hear him," Philip called, his voice distinct and commanding. "As I am your husband, and as I am your king, by every tie of love and allegiance that is between us, I charge you, stay where you are."

Sarto put the iron back into the fire, blowing on it to heat it more. "Perhaps you never saw such in Lynaleigh, gracious lady, but I know you have seen here in Reghed what one of these can do, and slowly, oh, so slowly."

Philip gasped, jerking his head to one side as Sarto drove the hissing iron into the tree not a quarter of an inch from his ear, tainting the air with the smell of burnt hair.

"Rosalynde, you will not—"

Philip jerked back the other way, flinching from the heat of another sizzling iron plunged into the tree just as close to his other ear. Sarto took a third iron from the fire and brought it close to Philip's face, knowing he could not move his head to either side now without burning himself on the first two.

"Eyes are such delicate things, gracious lady," Sarto shouted toward the trees, bringing the glowing metal even closer. "You would no doubt think it a pity to have this laid against such handsome ones."

Philip's breath quickened as the heat stung his eyes, making him shrink back in spite of himself. Sarto took him by the hair, holding him helpless.

"Gracious lady?"

"No! No!" Rosalynde scrambled out of the forest, almost tumbling down the steep embankment to Sarto's left. "I beg you, my lord."

Sarto smiled and handed the iron to one of his men. "Whatever pleases you, gracious lady. You need only say."

She ran to Philip's side. "I could not let him, love," she said, reaching up to caress his cheek. "Forgive me."

"Shh," he whispered, touching his lips to her wrist.

Sarto pulled her back from him. "There must be an end to that."

Philip struggled against the ropes that held him, the hatred and fury and unforgiveness he had thought he put behind him just the day before pumping once more through his blood.

"I challenge you for her, Sarto! If you are a gentleman, if there is any honor left in you, let us meet in battle to see who is most worthy of her."

Sarto merely laughed and pulled Rosalynde tightly against him. "Why should I fight you for her, boy? I have her already."

"You'll never have her," Philip shot back. "You may kill me and force her into some mockery of a marriage, you may force her to bear you a dozen children, but she will never be yours."

Sarto squeezed her more tightly, making her cry out. Then he tossed her up into his saddle and swung up behind her.

"Bring him," he told his soldiers. Then he spurred away, calling back to them, "And this time no mistakes."

"Philip!" Rosalynde cried as the forest swallowed them.

He strained toward her once more. "Courage, love! We are not done yet!"

One of the grim-faced soldiers knelt down and swiftly bound his ankles as a second pulled the still-warm irons out of the tree trunk and tossed them on the ground.

"Let me go," Philip said softly as the first man reached up to cut the ropes at his wrists. "I can see it in your face—you hate and fear him. Let me go, and you and all your countrymen shall be free of him."

"Sarto is my king, my lord," the man said clearly. "I am loyal only to him." He glanced back at his companions and dropped his voice. "Forgive me, sir, but I cannot, I must not. I would risk my own life and gladly to free us all, but Sarto would not stop there—my wife, my children, my whole village would not satisfy him were I ever to betray him."

"But surely you are not alone in this. If all the army together rose against him—"

"We dare not!" He dropped his voice again and busied himself with retying Philip's wrists behind his back. "I know there are others," he said rapidly. "There must be, but I do not know which I can rely upon, which will stand fast with us and which will buckle at the king's threats. And there are always Sarto's spies, urging this man and that to speak his mind, to plot against the king, and then denouncing him for the reward. We none of us know who is to be trusted."

"Listen to me, man. If you were to—"

"Help me, Dardo," the soldier called to one of the others, and the two of them tossed Philip into the wagon. Soon they were making their way back toward Stonekeep.

"We are not done yet," Philip said through clenched teeth.

It began to sleet.

Eventually the wagon creaked to a stop, and the soldier called Dardo trudged around to the back and dragged Philip to the edge of the wagon bed. He cut the ropes at Philip's ankles and then pulled him to his feet. The hard-packed path was slick with ice, and Philip fell against him, helpless, with his wrists still bound, to catch himself. The first man, called Petri, steadied him.

"Were there any hope . . ." Petri murmured when their eyes met.

He said no more, but Philip knew his meaning. Were there any hope of success, any sign he was not alone, he would gladly give Philip his aid, gladly rise against the tyranny of his own king. How many were there like him in Sarto's army, ready, waiting—*Were there any hope . . . ?*

Philip was familiar with the walk from the courtyard up the steps to Sarto's court, knew Sarto himself would be sitting spiderlike in his worn throne. He found it all as he expected, except Alaric was leaning carelessly against the wall at his father's left, and the throne at Sarto's right was empty.

"Where is my lady?" Philip demanded, as if he were king here and not captive.

The guard shoved him to his knees, but Philip held his head high, and there was nothing of submission in the stubborn tightness in his jaw. "Where is she?"

"You'll not see her again, my lord—know that," Sarto answered him. "I've been far too lenient in all this matter. If I had not, you would be long dead, and she would already carry my heir."

Philip's eyes blazed with fury.

Sarto smiled slightly. "But that shall be quickly seen to. Philip Chastelayne, lord of all Lynaleigh, for your unprovoked acts of aggression against the kingdom of Reghed and the person of her king—"

"Unprovoked?"

"—for the fomenting of rebellion and the misleading of her loyal subjects—"

"Loyal to what? Fear?"

"—for the abduction of our beloved queen-to-be—"

"Before God, you are insufferable!"

"—you are sentenced to be beheaded here before me at this very moment. My lords?"

The noblemen glanced first at Alaric and then at one another and then dropped their heads. "So say we all."

Alaric had doggedly avoided Philip's eyes since he had first been brought in. Now Philip glared at him. "And what say you, my lord prince? What, nothing still? Shall I say it for you?"

"My lord—"

Philip looked fiercely at Sarto. "Think you, my lord king of Reghed, that you kill your rebellion in killing me? Shall your people be loyal when even your own son is not?"

Alaric paled as his father's cold eyes swept over him.

"Spineless perhaps," Sarto said, "but loyal still. Come, man, no such fantasy can save you now. Make peace with your God. For the lady's sake, I'll not deny you that, and then you must—"

"Prince Alaric is the leader of your rebellion."

Sarto burst into a low, rumbling laugh. "Alaric? The leader of the rebellion? A fine jest, is it not, my lords?"

The nobility did not laugh, and Philip's expression was cool, controlled. "Ask him."

"Are you the rebel leader?" Sarto asked, a curl of contempt in his heavy lip.

All of Reghed's nobility stared at their prince—dukes, earls, barons—all with their eyes, their hopes, fixed on him. Philip knelt there still, feeling the sleet melt into his hair and clothes, wondering if Alaric would see that pleading in their eyes, the furtive, almost nonexistent hope on their faces.

Dear God, let him see it!

"Well?" Sarto demanded once more.

With a quick glance at the prisoner, Alaric pushed himself away from the wall, straightening his shoulders as he turned to face his father, the great formidable tyrant of Reghed. "Yes. Yes, I am."

For a moment, Sarto was speechless. "You do not amuse me, boy," he said slowly. "Perhaps you had best answer me again."

"I have led the rebellion since the very beginning, my lord." Alaric took a deep, slow breath. "A long while now, but it shall go on no longer."

"No," Sarto said coldly, "not a day longer."

Like the strike of a snake, his hands were at his son's throat, squeezing his life from him as the court stood by in stunned horror. Then Alaric grabbed his father's wrists and slowly, determinedly pulled his hands away, looking surprised at the ease of it. There was a sudden strength in the prince's face as he shoved the bewildered tyrant back into his throne.

"No longer, my lord. In the name of God and of the Christ I now call upon, no longer."

"You die today, boy, prince or no!" Sarto gasped. "We shall have another beheading. What say you, my lords?"

The nobles looked again at each other, and then came one by one to stand at their prince's side. "No, sire," one of them said quietly. "This court shall see no more tyranny."

"Traitors! Traitors all! Dare you defy your king?"

Sarto scrambled up from his throne, clutching the carved arms, working his way around until he was almost concealed by the high back.

"It is over, Sarto," Philip said, standing as Alaric cut his bonds. "They fear you no longer, and it seems your son has embraced a greater Power than all your Rosamund's devils." He looked at the former tyrant, feeling a sudden pity for the bewildered fear he saw in Sarto's sunken face, and he remembered the choice he had made to forgive this man. His voice became more gentle. "I pray you, sir, surrender your crown in peace. I have no doubt your son will show you only mercy, and I will join my own voice with his on your behalf before your people. There need be no more death here."

Alaric moved toward the throne, his hands outstretched. "Please, Father."

Sarto looked wide-eyed around him, slowly stepping back until he was against the wall. "It seems you will have this kingdom after all, Alaric," he said. "You have the legitimate blood; perhaps you should have the crown by right. But I shall have my Rosamund still."

In quick succession he pressed two places in the wall, and a passage opened behind him. With a mad laugh of triumph, he stepped into it, and it vanished as if it had never been.

"Where's he gone?" Philip cried, shoving the throne aside, pounding the wall with his fists. Sarto's wild laughter echoed back to him, and he threw his shoulder against the panel. "How does this open?"

Alaric pressed the same places his father had, but nothing happened. "He's closed it off behind him."

"Where's he gone?" Philip demanded again. "Does this lead to where he has my lady?"

"There are passages throughout the castle, my lord. I will go to one of the others and see if I cannot find him before he reaches her.

You'd best go by the stairs. I've no doubt he has her in Rosamund's chamber where she was before, in the west tower."

Philip knew the way.

⁂

When Sarto and Rosalynde had returned from the forest, Sarto had brought her at once to Rosamund's windowless chamber, unwilling to take any risk of losing her again.

"Soon now, my love," he had promised her, thrusting her inside so roughly she almost stumbled. "I go now to remove the final hindrance to our joy, and when I have at last made you mine again, you shall remember your pledge to me and no other."

"Please, my lord, I am not—"

He had slammed the door, again leaving her shut up with the lifeless remains of his morbid fantasy. She knew too well what that final hindrance was, knew that only an instant with a rope or a blade would make her a widow, make her free in this madman's eyes to become his bride.

"Oh, God, deliver us," she had prayed and prayed still. "For Christ's sweet sake, send your angels to shelter us, to defend us in this stronghold of the enemy. Dear Lord, do not let my love be taken from me, not for such a cause as this."

Clasping her hands together to steady them, she forced herself to think of all the times in the past when she had thought Philip was lost to her, only to have God send him back into her arms. Surely in the face of such faithfulness, she could trust Him now.

Hearing the door open, she turned and was surprised to see Brenna standing there holding a crystal chalice. "Quickly, girl, the army has betrayed the king in favor of his son."

"Where is my husband?"

"Sarto is coming for you to take you with him into hiding. I heard it from the corridor. I will get you away before he does."

Rosalynde stepped back from her. "Why should you help me?"

"If you were not such a fool, you would know why. Do you think he would leave me behind if you were not here? I do not mean yet to lose him. Hurry, girl, get your cloak." Brenna grabbed her arm and pressed the chalice into her hands. "No, do not swoon now. Take this. I feared that such a milk-fed mouse might have to drink her courage."

"I do not feel faint," Rosalynde protested. "Tell me where my—"

"Drink," Brenna insisted. "He will be here in another moment."

"But my husband—"

"You will be together soon," Brenna said with a glittering smile. "I pledge it. Now quickly, drink."

Rosalynde tried to pull away from her. "No."

Brenna's smile turned colder, and her strong fingers pressed more deeply into the soft flesh of Rosalynde's arm as she forced the sparkling chalice toward her lips.

⁕

Down in Sarto's dungeon, Tom heard a soft voice call to him from the empty corridor. "It is Molly, my lord," she whispered urgently. "I have the key."

There was a slight scrape of metal against metal as she fitted the key into the lock, and then he heard a half-strangled cry from out in the corridor.

"Molly?" Tom rattled the door, but it would not budge. "Molly?"

"Two-faced little strumpet!" a rough, deep voice railed. "Did you think I'd let you betray me in exchange for a tumble or two?"

Oh, God, Tom thought, *that was how she got into the castle so easily. Not so easily. Dear Lord, and for my sake.*

"I will break your cheap harlot neck!" the man roared, and Tom heard a solid thump and Molly's gasp as she was hurled against the door.

"Molly!" he shouted once more, throwing his shoulder against the stout wood, hoping to somehow force the door open. He heard a brief struggle, Molly cried out again, and then there was sudden stillness.

"Come no closer now, Jack," Molly warned. "I will use this."

"Give me back my dagger, girl," the one called Jack coaxed, his voice much gentler now. "Come, Molly, my kitten."

"Stay back!"

Tom heard the turn of the key.

"Come out, my lord," Molly called to him. "I will—"

Again Tom heard the sounds of a struggle, of Molly's faint cries, and twice the man's deep groan. Once more Tom threw his shoulder against the door. This time it gave.

"Let her—"

Tom stopped midstride. The man was crumpled on the floor, his empty eyes wide with surprise, his lifeless hands covering the still-welling wounds in his chest. Molly was standing over him holding the bloody dagger.

Tom touched her shoulder. "Molly?"

She turned to him, her dark eyes enormous in her chalk-white face. "I had to get you free, my lord, but I never meant to kill him. Never. I thought he was drunk enough—I had to get you—"

Pain twisted her face, and clutching her stomach, she fell against him. "Forgive me, my lord," she murmured.

He eased her to the floor. Then he knelt beside her, gently pulling her hands from the gaping gash in her belly.

"Oh, Molly, what have you done?"

"They've brought your brother in, my lord. I saw them and went at once to steal the key. Neither of you will be spared long if you stay here. I had to get you free."

He wadded up her apron and pressed it against the wound, dyeing it vivid red. "Where is he, Molly? Do you know?"

She shook her head, stifling a whimper of pain. "But there is another danger, my lord. Their king, Sarto—I heard him give the order the moment he returned from the forest. He's sent someone to take the baby, to bring her here."

"The baby? You mean Alyssa? Any reason why?"

Again she shook her head. "The one they call Owen—he left here no more than two hours ago. Please, my lord, you must stop him."

She cried out, and he held her against him, cradling her head on his shoulder.

"Shh, shh, I will. You mustn't fret yourself about that."

"But there is something more, my lord."

"It can wait," he soothed.

"Please, my lord, I must. I beg you, forgive me all the wrong I've done you. Let this now make it right. Let it prove how truly I have loved you."

"I know, in your way, Molly, like all else you've done, it was meant to be love, and I shall remember it so."

She reached up to caress his cheek, a sudden gladness in her eyes that outshone the pain. "You must hurry, my lord, before the soldiers come." She pressed her lips together. "Please," she sobbed, "do not waste your chance."

"I must ask you, Molly—"

"I remember what you told me, my lord, that there would always be One who loved me and wanted all my love. I am ready to go to Him."

He nodded, not knowing if he could speak,

She clutched at him. "Please, my lord, you must go."

"You know I cannot leave you."

She bit her lip and managed to smile, too. "You were ever kind to me, my lord. Will you grant me one last kindness?"

He put his hand over hers, squeezing her fingers. "Anything."

"One kiss," she breathed. "Just one."

"Molly—"

Tears filled her eyes. "Just one."

He touched his lips to her forehead and knew at once that she was dead.

"Give her mercy, Lord," he murmured, gently pressing her eyes closed. Hearing the running beat of footsteps down the corridor, he picked up the dagger.

"My lord prince!"

He slipped the blade into his belt. "Here, Jerome."

The boy sprinted around the corner and came to a sudden stop. "Oh, my lord, it is Molly!"

"She is dead," Tom told him. "God pardon me, but I haven't the time to give her sacrifice the dignity it merits. We must leave her for now. Where is the king?"

"Prince Alaric's taken the kingdom, my lord. Sarto's fled somewhere inside the castle, and the king's gone after him. He fears for the queen."

"Where is she? Have you seen her?"

"No, my lord. I heard she was kept in the west tower, but I cannot say that's so. All's in a coil in the great hall and through the castle. Prince Alaric and all his soldiers are searching. Shall we go, too?"

"I will," Tom told him. "I have another task for you. Sarto's sent that brigand Owen to Westered to take Princess Alyssa and bring her here. I do not know why he's to do it, but you must stop him. Take this key, release Palmer and the others, and then go after Owen. I will see if I can find the queen."

"At once, my lord."

Jerome disappeared down the corridor and, with a last glance at Molly's peaceful face, Tom sprinted toward the west tower.

P HILIP REACHED THE TOP OF THE STAIRS, HIS HEART POUNDING from running, with fear, and there stood Sarto with the chamber door behind him pulled almost shut.

Philip raised the blade he had gotten from one of Sarto's own guards. "Do not force me to this now, man. You've lost, and I see no profit in taking your life. For what you have done to me and mine, I freely pardon you, but let it end here. Give my lady back to me, and I ask no more than that."

Sarto looked at him speculatively. Then with a sardonic grin, he flung open the door. "There, boy. There is your beloved just where I found mine a lifetime ago and just as dead."

Rosalynde lay where she had fallen, under the baleful gaze of her painted image, with one hand at her white throat and the other clutching in desperation the sable bed curtains—still, so still. There was a crystal chalice on the floor at her feet.

With a low, hoarse cry, Philip dropped his broadsword and stumbled to his knees beside her. "Dear God, Lord God, no," he sobbed as he took her into his arms and buried his face in her flowing hair. "Rose, Rose, my Rose. Oh, Jesus, no."

"You should not have left this behind you, boy," Sarto said, the words accompanied by the unmistakable clang of Philip's sword.

Philip did not even lift his head. "Kill me then and have done."

A look of death in his face, Sarto wound his left hand into

Philip's hair and jerked his head backwards, baring his throat to the blade. Philip made no struggle. He only pulled Rosalynde closer and closed his eyes.

"It would be mercy," he murmured. "The only mercy left." His chest heaving with the pain of his loss, he waited, but no blow fell.

"Do it then!" he cried, frustrated rage boiling up in him, flaming from his crystal eyes. "Do it!"

"Do and I kill you where you stand."

They both turned at Tom's steel-edged voice. "I swear I speak true."

Sarto brandished the blade he held and then tossed it aside with an evil laugh. "What do I care for your killing, boy? I am dead already. But he is right—it would be mercy, a mercy I'll not grant." He loosed his hold, and Philip's head dropped back against Rosalynde's limp body. "Live, boy. Live to draw pain with every breath and remorse with every memory. Live as I have done, the whole length of your life again, remembering her. I'll not spare you that."

"Keep still," Tom warned, taking up Philip's sword.

"I will be still soon enough," Sarto said with a grimace. He shoved the chalice to one side with his foot and then looked up at the portrait, the flush on his face turning to dead white. "I suppose it takes longer in all this flesh than in such a delicate flower. It was so before. She was gone like a fresh-bloomed rose."

Tom took in Rosalynde's still form and the chalice, and then realization flashed into his eyes. "You drank, too."

"That ebony-haired witch there thought she could separate me from my Rosamund," Sarto said, "but she was wrong, and I've paid her for her treachery."

Following his gaze, Tom saw Brenna's body sprawled backwards over a footstool in the half-curtained alcove near the hearth, the little silver pouncet box on her necklace dangling over her shoulder. The angle of her neck and the deep bruises on her throat left little doubt how that payment had been made.

Sarto's lips tightened, and he bared his teeth in a death's-head grin. "My Rosamund is gone again, but this time I go with her. I gladly leave you the mourning, boy," he flung back at Philip. "Grow old with it."

He lurched to Philip's side, and Tom moved warily toward them, but the older man merely ruffled Philip's hair, an almost fond gesture. "I know the pain, boy. I do not envy you."

He reached down, fumbling until he caught Rosalynde's lifeless hand. "Such a delicate hand my Rosamund had," he said, pressing it against his numb lips, "and I kissed it cold like this."

He dropped her hand and then staggered toward Rosamund's coffin and pulled the black drape from it. Then he looked again at the portrait.

"Rosamund," he wheezed, reaching toward her as she looked mockingly down upon him. "Rosamund, how can it be so dark where you are?"

He drew a rattling breath and toppled forward, tearing the portrait from the wall, its weight and his shattering the crystal coffin with a terrific crash, scattering glass and crushed fragments of old bone across the floor. For a moment afterwards, there was only stark silence. Then Tom moved cautiously toward the wreckage and looked into the tyrant's wide, staring eyes.

"He is dead."

Tom lay down his sword and knelt at his brother's side.

"He is dead, Philip. Philip?"

"Why, Tom?" Philip's voice was muffled with tears and grief and Rosalynde's lush hair. With sudden, fierce accusation, he lifted his head. "Why did you stop him? Why would you want me to live the rest of my life in torment without her?" He kissed her, and a desolate cry rose from deep inside him. "Warm. Oh, God, holy God, her lips are yet warm." He clutched her close again, rocking her against him.

Tom put his fingers on her wrist. "Her heart beats still. She is not dead."

"Oh, God, God," Philip moaned, not hearing. "Oh, Jesus."

"Philip, she is not dead." Tom forced Philip to look up at him. "She is not dead. Feel that."

He took Philip's hand and pressed it over her heart.

"The beat is faint, but it is there."

"Rose?" Breathing harder, Philip patted her wrist, her cheek.

Frantically he chaffed her hands, and then he sat her up, shaking her. "Rose?"

There was no response, and the hope died in his eyes as she fell limply against his shoulder. "It is no use, Tom. You heard what Sarto said. It would require far less poison to take so delicate a thing as she, and he is gone already."

"She lives yet," Tom insisted.

Philip shook his head wearily, hopelessly. "It is no use."

Again Tom forced him to look up. "Do we not still have a God?"

Philip squeezed his eyes tight shut and drew a shaky, steadying breath. "Still."

Tom clasped his shoulder. "And if you were lying there and she in your place now, what do you think she would do?"

Philip caught his breath again.

"She would pray." He wiped his sleeve across his wet face, calming a little. "She would pray and trust God for me, just as she has always done . . . even when I seemed most lost."

"She would."

"She would believe. I believe." Philip touched his fingers to her ashen cheek, and the sobs tore through him again. "Oh, God, help my unbelief."

Tom helped him put her on the bed, and a few moments later the physician was standing over her, little hope on his solemn face. "She's been poisoned, true enough, my lord," he pronounced grimly. "By something I've not seen before."

"But you can save her," Philip said, his lips trembling and his eyes too bright.

"Doubtful, my lord."

Philip looked at his brother. "Tom, surely—"

"Have you nothing to even try, Master Livrette?" Tom asked.

"I told you, my lord, it is something I've never seen. If I give her the wrong antidote, it could be worse than giving her nothing at all."

"No," Philip insisted, "there must be something." He closed his eyes. "Please, God."

Tom picked up the crystal goblet that still held a few drops of the tainted wine. "Surely if this Brenna planned to use such a poison, she would have the cure for it, too."

"Have everyone look, Tom," Philip urged. "See if Alaric will lend his men to search, tear the castle apart if need be. Find it. Dear God, show us where."

Tom went to the alcove and looked at Brenna's body. Then he knelt down and lifted up the silver orb hanging around her neck.

"It could not be there," Philip said. "It is punched through with holes and could never hold something liquid."

"But it could hold something that could."

Tom picked it up, and Philip snatched it from him. "Please, God, please."

He snapped the chain and wrenched the bauble into two halves, scattering dried leaves and fragrant petals across the red satin bodice of Brenna's dress. A tiny stoppered bottle fell among them.

"There!" Philip grabbed it and rushed to Rosalynde's side, forcing it open as he went.

Tom grabbed his wrist before he could pour the liquid into her mouth. "Philip, wait!"

"It could save her!" Philip insisted.

"It could kill her!"

Philip froze where he was.

Livrette quietly took the bottle from him. "Please, your majesty." Careful to keep it out of Philip's reach, the physician touched a drop of the contents to his tongue. Immediately he spat it out. "The poison, my lords, or I miss my guess."

"What might I have done?" Philip whispered, turning whiter than before. "What might I have done?"

"We must have patience," Tom told him, laying his hand on his sister-in-law's clammy forehead. "We must have faith and do nothing rash. Do you remember in the Scriptures where it says that if anyone who believes should drink any deadly thing, it shall not hurt him? We know she believes. We must believe, too."

Philip took Rosalynde's hand and pressed his lips to her still fingers. "Believe, sweetheart," he murmured. "You will soon be well. God did not give you to me just to take you from me again."

"I will have your men search for the antidote if there is one, your majesty," the physician said, "but first let us take her from this place." He looked uneasily at the destruction surrounding them. "Surely another chamber—"

They carried Rosalynde to the airy room she had occupied before, into the winter sunlight that came, brief and bright, through the large windows.

A day passed . . . two days, more, and there was no change. Alaric and some of the other Reghed nobility, too, had come to express their sympathy, promising to add their fresh prayers to the others being lifted on Rosalynde's behalf. Even Credotti and some of his troupe came with words of encouragement and hope that "the pretty lady" would soon be well. It seemed a perfect time for God to display His might and majesty, but He seemed not to hear.

Still Philip stood at Rosalynde's side, waiting, praying, speaking words of comfort, words of love. She was white and motionless, barely breathing. He was much the same.

"It's been days, Philip," Tom said. "Let me sit with her awhile, and you have some sleep."

Tom had been with him almost constantly, and now he looked tired, but at least he had taken time to eat and sleep. His urging for Philip to do the same proved as futile as had Livrette's search for an antidote to Brenna's poison.

"You sleep, Tom," Philip said, his cheeks sunken under his scraggly, half-grown beard. "Come back in the morning. Tell the others, too."

Tom reluctantly agreed, knowing there was little any of them in their own strength could do. "I still will pray for her," he said, hugging Philip tightly. "Sleep if you can."

Philip prayed again once he was alone, clinging to the promise the Scripture had made to those who believe.

"Make her well, Lord," he pled. "Your own Word promises that. And what better way to show these who have just now come to know You what comes of trusting in Your name?"

In frustration he rose from his knees and began to pace.

"I have done what You asked of me, Lord. Reghed is free, Alaric is king. I was prepared to stay here when I might have left, risking everything I hold dear, because I thought it was what You wanted of me. Have I not earned this one thing of You?"

Even as he said it, doubts goaded him. Had he truly done what God had asked? Everything? Every day, every night, he struggled with his feelings of hatred for Sarto and for Brenna, too, despite the many times he had forgiven them both. How much easier it had been to forgive when he and Rosalynde had been back in Alaric's cave and he had thought they would soon be safely home. How much easier than now when he must stand helpless and watch her lying there sinking further and further away from him. Still, even here, even now, he had made the choice to forgive. But was that choice enough, as Rosalynde had said? Or was his failure to conquer his feelings the cause of his prayers for her going unanswered now?

"Lord," he pled, "I forgave them the best I was able. God, the best I *am* able I forgive them both! Please, God, do not turn from my lady because of some lack in me."

Yet was it not because of so much lack in him—his lack of faith, his lack of patience—that she was here now? Because of his stubborn insistence on doing things his own way, in his own strength? Another lesson he seemed never to learn. He shuddered to remember that he had almost poured more of Brenna's poison into her mouth. Still, surely God understood his fears, his desperation in such terrible circumstances. Surely He had not forgotten His creature's frame, that he was no more than dust.

"God, I know my faults. I have confessed them and repented of them again and again. I know nothing more to do!"

His stride quickened, and his voice grew more desperate.

"If that is not enough, Lord, take my kingdom, my lands, my wealth. I will give it all to the poor; I will work among them, telling them of You. I will spend the rest of my life in praise and thanksgiving and never raise my sword against a man again. I will—I will—"

It was a pitiful bargain to offer the God of all the universe. He knew it before the words left his mouth. He could never do enough to earn God's mercy. He stopped where he was and turned his face upwards, letting his arms hang limp at his sides.

"What is it You want from me, God?"

Everything.

It was not a word spoken, nothing he could hear, but something he knew deep inside. God would be God of all of him or of none of him. There was no middle ground. But Rosalynde—

"Not her," he whispered. Then the pleading whisper grew to a moan and then to a defiant cry: "Not her!"

He glanced at her, lying still and silent.

"Anything else, Lord, anything! I swear I will give You anything else with all my heart, but not her."

He went to the bed and pulled her close to him, huddling over her as if he would shield her from anything that would try to separate them.

"You cannot take her from me," he cried. "You gave her to me! Please, God, my Father, in Your mercy spare her, and I will spend all the rest of my life in Your service and in Your praise."

And if I do not?

If He did not?

Philip clung to Rosalynde's sweat-dampened body, feeling the pain knife through him, wondering if this was how it felt to die. What if He did not? If He did not restore her—did not give her back to him? What if He did not?

Again Philip felt that deep knowing inside himself, knowing he had to make answer, knowing he had but one. If he lost Rosalynde, if he lost the children, Tom, the kingdom, his life—he knew there was but one way for him, one pervasive truth from which he could not turn.

"Oh, God," he whispered finally, "You know I have nothing that is not Yours, she more than all else."

He lay limp against the pain, his head sinking deeper against Rosalynde's soft breast, his words almost lost in the tight constriction of his throat.

"Do Your will, Lord God. I am Yours still."

IN WESTERED ON THAT SAME NIGHT, NAN RUSHED INTO HER MISTRESS'S chamber. "Wake up, my lady!"

Elizabeth sat up in bed, the urgency in Nan's voice and the commotion she heard from outside bringing her fully awake.

"There is a fire in the stables, my lady. The duke thinks it best that you and the children leave the castle until it is doused."

"Has it reached here as well?" Elizabeth asked, smelling the faint, acrid smoke that had drifted into her chamber. She put one hand on her swollen stomach. "Are we in danger?"

"No, my lady, but for the smoke and because there is a chance the flames might spread, he thinks it best."

Elizabeth got out of bed and was glad for the cloak Nan draped around her shoulders. "It is freezing. Are you certain the children will be warm enough?"

"My grandam will see to that, my lady," the girl told her as she slipped her shoes on her feet, "and, please God, we will not have to be out long."

Soon Elizabeth was standing on the hillside near the forest below the castle, watching the orange flames that shot up into the night sky. Nan had the boys each by one hand, and Joan was holding the sleeping baby. Westered had sent one of his men to watch over them, a boy of no more than eighteen who looked far more eager to play soldier than nursemaid.

"They'll need every man we have to quench that blaze," he said, looking impatiently toward the fire, "even with the women to haul the water. I think they've brought all the horses out safe already, though they lost one of the stable boys to smoke. God help the man who's done this if his lordship ever finds him."

"Was it set then?" Elizabeth asked.

The soldier shrugged. "So it seems, my lady. Even straw is unlikely to catch of itself in three or four separate places at once."

Just then one of the pages ran up to them, his face and clothes blackened with the fire. "I pray you, Mistress Joan, come to the courtyard. Another of the men is hurt, and they have no one to tend him."

"Go, Gran," Nan urged as she took Alyssa from her. "I will look after the children."

Joan looked uncertainly at Elizabeth. "My lady?"

"Yes, Joan, go! I can see to things here."

Joan bobbed a swift curtsey and scurried up the hill.

"I want to go, too," John insisted, bouncing up and down and tugging Elizabeth's hand.

"Stop, John," she scolded, jerking her hand free, and both boys watched her speculatively.

"She is always cross when our uncle is away," Robin observed coolly, looking very like his father in the flickering light.

John cocked his head to one side. "Does that make you cross, Aunt 'Liz'beth?"

She gave him a small relenting smile. "I suppose it does."

"Why?"

She smiled a little more. "I suppose because I have no one to play acrobat for me. Do you know anyone who can do that, John?"

"I can! I can!"

In another instant he was tumbling head over heels down the hillside, squealing with laughter, and Robin was tromping after him.

"Not too far, boys," Elizabeth called to them. "Stay clear of the trees." Seeing them running into the wood, she took an awkward step toward them and then looked helplessly at the soldier. "Would you bring them back, captain?"

"At once, my lady," he said, smiling at his sudden promotion. "Come back, my young lords."

He went into the shadowy wood after them, and then Nan handed the baby to her mistress.

"He'll never ferret them out in the darkness there, but I know their tricks. See to the angel, and I will be back in no more than a moment."

Nan, too, disappeared into the night, and Elizabeth balanced Alyssa against her hip, listening. After a moment, she did not hear Nan or the soldier anymore, only the distant clamor from the fire.

"Come back, John," she called. "Robin, you are eldest. Bring John back here and—"

"Have you misplaced these, my lady?"

Owen came out of the forest, holding a struggling John over his shoulder and dragging Robin by one arm.

"Let us go, traitor!" Robin cried, landing a sturdy blow to Owen's midsection.

"Be still, brat," Owen growled, shaking him.

John seized two fists full of Owen's shaggy hair. "You better put me down! My papa will come back and lock you in his dungeon!"

"You!" Elizabeth breathed, remembering him from before, from when he had held Tom prisoner. "What is it you want?"

"The little one. Just lay her there on the ground, and there need be no more bloodshed."

Elizabeth held the baby closer. "What do you mean to do with her?"

"She'll come to no harm, I swear it."

"As if I could trust the oath of an abductor and murderer. What did you do with my maid? You set that fire, did you not?"

"It served my need," he told her impassively.

Robin punched him again, harder this time. "'Lyssa shan't go with you! You hurt our soldier!"

"Quiet!" Owen thundered, holding him by both wrists and reaching up with his other hand to snatch John by the hair, to dislodge the little teeth sunk into his shoulder. John swung at him, and

Owen shoved him under his arm, wedging him so tightly to his side he could not wriggle free.

"Now, madam," Owen panted, "if you would still have heirs to your king's throne, give me the child, and I will give these two little hellions back to you. If not, I can as easily kill you all and take her still." He looked pointedly at the roundness in her middle. "You should consider your own child now, lady. Will you risk it for another man's?"

She clutched her stomach, feeling the suffocating terror rise up inside her. Then there was something else. A promise remembered.

Do not fear, beloved. Trust in Me, and you shall have your desire.

She looked uncertainly at the child she held, still lying in perfect peace in her arms, and knew what she must do.

Oh, God, she pled, *let this be right. Give me a sign I cannot mistake.*

"Choose, woman!" Owen demanded. Still keeping John pinned to his side, he managed to reach into his pouch.

"Think on your husband, lady, and the grief your loss, your child's loss, would bring him." He pulled out her bracelet and tossed it at her feet. "You are greatly beloved of him, judging from the value he's set on just that bauble."

Greatly beloved. She was greatly beloved.

She picked up the bracelet and fastened it around her wrist, drawing courage from its heavy solidity, Tom's courage, the courage to trust.

Lord, let me have chosen right.

"Let the children go, and you have my pledge that I will lay the baby down."

Owen smiled. "The pledge of a princess and a wise one at that. I could not ask more."

He released his captives, and they rushed to her and clung to her cloak. She laid Alyssa on the ground.

"As I pledged," she said, and then she spun the boys toward the castle. "Run! Tell the soldiers to come! Hurry!"

They raced up the hill, Robin dragging his little brother by the hand, but Owen made no attempt to stop them.

"I expected as much, princess, but I shall be long away before anyone can return. Now for my errand."

He leaned down to take Alyssa, but before he could touch her, Elizabeth jerked her knee up as high and hard as she could manage, catching him under the chin, landing him sprawled on his back. Before he could scramble to his feet, she snatched up the baby and tried to run. He caught up with her and flung himself against her, throwing her forward, hurling her to the ground with a sickening thud.

A sudden gush of blood and water soaked her shift below the waist, and a familiar pain tore through her. "Oh, God," she sobbed, clinging to the wailing child. "Oh, God."

"You seem to have chosen wrong, my lady," Owen panted, driving his knee into the small of her back to hold her there. From the corner of her eye, she saw his dagger flash as he raised it.

"Oh, God, Your promise!"

With a roar, something, someone, rushed out of the darkness and wrestled Owen off of her, but she saw no more than that. The pain was worsening now, coming in wrenching contractions that made her unable to do more than lie there in gasping helplessness, only vaguely aware of the struggle going on beside her.

How long it lasted she did not know. Finally there was an abrupt stillness, and she heard the rustle of boots in the dead grass in front of her. She opened her eyes and saw someone reaching for the baby.

"No," she moaned, clutching at the child being taken from her. Then she heard a soothing voice, one she recognized.

"Shh, my lady, she is safe with me."

"Jerome," she whispered, managing to lift her head enough to see his face. It was bloody, and already his left eye was turning black. She stretched out her hand to him. "Jerome, help me."

At the first hint of Reghed's dawn, Tom came back into Rosalynde's chamber with Rafe and Livrette anxiously behind him.

Philip was standing turned toward the wall, his face pressed against one arm, the other dangling beside him. His legs were braced apart as if he had come a long way and had just stopped for a moment to gather his strength. He did not move when they came into the room, and Tom thought he might have fallen asleep where he stood.

"Philip?"

Philip lifted his head, blinking as if the dawn light were a surprise to him. There was more color in his shirt than in his face.

"I thought you might take some breakfast, my lord," Rafe said, setting down a tray, but Philip took no notice of him. He was intent on Livrette's examination of the frail figure on the bed.

"She is no better, is she?"

It was not really a question, and Livrette looked into his king's empty eyes.

"Have you slept, my lord?" he asked, taking Philip's wrist to feel for his pulse. It was slow and steady, beating methodically, disinterestedly, because it was meant to.

"She is no better," Philip said again.

Livrette could only look at him in pity. "If there were something more I could do, my lord—"

"She is in God's keeping now."

Philip took his wife's pale hand, fondling it absently, his eyes fixed on her face as if there were no one in the room but the two of them alone.

"My lord, will you have something to eat?" Rafe asked.

Livrette picked up the goblet from the tray. "At least a cup of wine, my lord, if nothing else. I must insist."

Philip shook his head, the gesture so remote it was almost imperceptible, and Tom went to him.

"Drink it, Philip. Think of the children. If it comes that they must lose their mother, do not take their father from them as well."

"Please, my lord," the physician urged.

With a weary sigh, Philip took the cup from him and drank deeply of it. Immediately he spat the whole mouthful onto the floor and with an oath hurled the cup at Livrette. "Curse you and your potions, man! Did you think I'd not know the taste?"

"Forgive me, my lord, but I—"

"Philip," Tom said softly, a restraining hand on his brother's arm, "you will be ill yourself if you do not take some rest. Livrette only—"

"No!" Philip jerked away from him. "No."

He backed toward the bed, holding up both hands in front of him.

"No," he said once more. Trembling, he wiped the back of one hand across his face. "I cannot—cannot sleep knowing when I awake, she might be . . ."

He turned to the bed, then fell to his knees beside it.

"Everything, Lord," he sobbed, and he buried his face in his arms, his shoulders shaking with silent weeping. After a while he was aware of a soft hand, feather light, stroking his hair.

"Let me alone," he pled. "I beg you, for pity."

"Do not cry."

His sobbing stopped. For a moment he did not breathe, and then he lifted his head. Rosalynde was smiling at him, more with her eyes than with her mouth, too weak to do more than stroke his hair again.

"You mustn't cry, love."

"Rosalynde?" he managed.

She moved her hand shakily to his unshaven cheek. "Has Master Bonnechamp misplaced your razor again, my lord?"

He clasped his hand over hers, laughing faintly as the tears coursed down his face. "No, Rose, I—I—oh, Rose."

He pressed his face against her, against the steady beating of her heart.

"Oh, sweet God of mercy."

Tom began the ride back to Westered that same morning taking only Palmer with him. Though he had sent Jerome to intercept Owen and knew that Alyssa was already well guarded, he felt an urgent need, now that Philip and Rosalynde were safe, to make certain the children were in no danger either. He had not told Philip of Owen's mission. It would have been a needless worry to him and to Rosalynde, but he wanted to see for himself that everything in Westered was as it should be. And, though his own child was not due for some time yet, he wanted to see that Elizabeth, too, was safe and well.

They had just crossed the border into Lynaleigh, back into Westered's dukedom, when Palmer slowed his mount, listening. "There is someone coming, my lord."

Tom, too, heard the approaching hoofbeats and then a voice he knew.

"My lord! My lord!"

Jerome galloped into the clearing, and Tom spurred his horse to meet him.

"I am glad I've found you, my lord."

"What of Owen, Jerome? Is the baby safe?"

"She is, my lord, and Owen is now a threat to no one." The boy's face took on the grim lines of a soldier. "I caught up to him just outside Westered's walls."

Tom saw from the marks the boy carried that the ruffian had not been easily dispatched.

"The king himself will have a reward for you, Jerome, I've no doubt."

"He is safe, my lord? And her majesty?"

"They are now, by God's grace. I must tell you of it."

"My lord of Westered is preparing his army to bring them out of Reghed. He will be pleased to know that is not necessary now, but I have more news, my lord. Your lady was brought to bed with her child Monday a week ago. They sent me ahead to bring you as quickly as you can come."

"It is too soon yet," Tom gasped, feeling a rapid hammering in his heart. "How could it come now?"

"It was Owen, my lord. He tried to take the little princess, and Lady Elizabeth would not let him. He did not use her gently, I fear, and they say that's what brought on her child so early."

Tom closed his eyes, battling the sick dread he felt, trying not to think what it would do to Elizabeth if anything happened to their baby now.

"Dear Lord God, for Your own goodness, for Your own grace, let this child come to us alive and whole." With another deep breath, he looked up. "Go back to Reghed, Jerome. See if you can be of use to the king. Palmer, come with me."

It was several days more before Tom and Palmer reached the courtyard in Westered. Praying for courage, begging for faith, Tom leapt out of his saddle, tossed the reins to Palmer, and took the steps two at time, stretching his legs to their long length.

"My lord of Brenden!" Westered cried when he came into the great hall. He stood up from his chair as soon as Robin and John had scrambled out of his lap.

"Did you bring Mama back?" Robin asked, tugging his uncle's hand, and John threw his arms around Tom's legs.

"Where's Papa?"

"They are coming," Tom said, untangling himself, and then he looked urgently at Westered. "Where is my lady?"

"In her chamber, boy, but—"

Hearing no more, Tom sprinted from the room, his boots thudding on the stairs, ringing down the corridor. Just as he reached Elizabeth's door, it swung open, and Joan bustled out of the room, her arms full of rumpled sheeting. Seeing him, she put one finger to her lips.

"Come in, my lord, but quietly."

There were myriad questions in his eyes, but he merely went inside, and Joan was wise enough to let him go alone.

"Oh, Bess," he murmured, and his eyes filled with tears.

Elizabeth lay asleep, her dark auburn hair spread out on the white pillows. Sleeping there against her breast was a tiny new baby. Tom knelt down beside them, scarcely daring to breathe.

"Oh, my God, my sweet Jesus," he whispered in thanksgiving, and the baby's eyes opened.

"Who is this?" Tom asked, smiling tremulously, and Elizabeth awoke, too.

"Tom."

He took her hand and pressed it to his lips.

"Bess, my love."

"She has your sweet mouth, Tom."

"She?" He touched one finger to the baby's soft cheek in wonder. "A little girl."

"Do you want to hold her, my lord?"

With another unsteady smile, he cradled his daughter in his hands. She hardly filled them.

"She is so very tiny, Bess."

"She should not have come for another month at the least, Joan says, but she is strong and healthy and notices everything."

He cuddled the child against him, marveling at the miniature completeness of her, at the way she was a mixture of both of them and yet so entirely herself.

"Oh, Bess," he murmured again, the tears once more in his eyes. "I have no words now, love, for what I would say to you, for what I feel. I wish only that I could have been with you when she came."

"I wanted you, Tom, so much."

She reached up to him, and he took her hand, using it to cradle the baby still.

"I am sorry, sweetheart."

"No, love," she said, drawing him and the baby closer. "As much as I wanted you with me, I was not alone. And I knew I need not fear."

She reached out her other hand, and he saw the bracelet on her wrist.

"You have it back!"

"A promise," she told him, "from One who cannot lie."

He pulled her close to him, and with both of them holding the baby, she told him of that night at the edge of the forest and how in a moment of reckless abandon, she had trusted herself to God's protection and found Him well worth the trusting.

"I was terrified that night, and yet I knew He would not leave me." For a moment, she said no more. Then she looked at Tom uncertainly. "Does He, uh, does He ever speak to you, my lord?"

"Sometimes. Sometimes so clearly I think I've heard it with my ears, sometimes with just a knowing that is beyond myself. Did He speak to you, love?"

"He called me His beloved," she said with a catch in her voice, and she pressed her face to his shoulder. "Oh, Tom, why should He love me so?"

"Because He cannot be false to Himself, Bess, any more than He can be false to us, and it is all His nature to love." He squeezed her tighter. "I do not know why, only that it is a wondrous thing to be certain of."

"I am so glad you are with me now. You must send Molly to me so I can thank her for watching after you so very well."

"She'll not be coming back again," he said, and as gently as he could, he told her why.

"Poor girl," Elizabeth said. "I wronged her, and yet she saved you for me. I pray God will give her His mercy."

"I believe He has."

She looked up at him again. "After the soldier disappeared into the forest and Nan after him, I did not know what to do, and I was so frightened."

"But they are unharmed?"

"Both of them had headaches a day or two afterward, but no more than that." Elizabeth laughed a little. "There was such a turmoil that night with the baby coming and all, Nan forgot to be angry at Owen's treachery until it was all over with. Then she told me that had he not hit her from behind, she was fairly certain she could have taken him."

Tom laughed, too, remembering the brawny redhead's considerable strength. "I would never doubt it."

Just then Nan herself came into the room, only the egg-sized knot on the back of her head to mark her brush with danger.

"I heard you had returned, my lord," she said with a quick bobbing curtsey. She came to look at the baby. "You should be nearly bursting with pride to be able to lay claim to that one, sure. Not that any of us expected the tiniest bit less. My lady would not choose without you, but have you thought what you might call her?"

"Why something after her brave mother, of course," he replied, pressing a nuzzling kiss to his wife's forehead.

"Something to bring to mind that her father is a Chastelayne prince," Elizabeth urged, "and that she has no less than a king for her uncle." For a moment she watched the baby, who had fallen asleep again in their arms, and then she added, "And something to dedicate her to the One who gave her to us."

Tom smiled.

"All of that," he assured her. "Somehow."

CHAPTER

A FEW DAYS LATER, THE DAY BEFORE CHRISTMAS, PHILIP AND
Rosalynde returned to Westered, greeted first by the cheering people who lined the streets, then by the complete retinue of the
castle servants assembled in the courtyard, and finally by their own
family. The moment the carriage slowed to a stop before them, Robin
and John rushed down the steps.

"Mama! Papa!"

Philip leapt from the carriage and scooped them both up, crushing them against him, giving and receiving several dozen kisses.

"Where is Mama?" John demanded finally.

"She is here, but you boys must be gentle with her. She has been
very ill."

"Now you mustn't frighten them, my lord," she said lightly as she
climbed out of the carriage. "You are the only one who thinks I must
yet be coddled."

"Rose, love—"

He broke off, smiling to see that even the slight pallor she had
brought with her from Reghed was gone at the sight of the children.

"Oh, my babies, you've grown so," she cried, kneeling to take
them into her arms. "And where is my Alyssa?"

Westered carried the baby down to them. A short way from
them, he set her down to take a few toddling steps.

"She can walk now, Papa," John announced, "like we do."

"So she can," Philip declared, reaching toward his daughter. She only looked at him uncertainly and then lurched to an unsteady halt where she was. "She does not know me," he said, his smile fading into disappointment.

"Come, Alyssa," Rosalynde coaxed, but still the baby did not move.

Philip took a step toward her, meaning to merely pick her up, and then he knelt down and stretched out his arms again. "Little 'Lyssa baby," he called softly.

With a gurgling coo, she teetered toward him again, grabbing both of his hands to stop herself.

"Sweet baby," he said, laughing at the way she scrunched up her whole face for a kiss, and then he handed her to Rosalynde. "Here, my love. No one could look into that angel face and doubt she belongs to you."

"But she has your eyes, my lord, and I've no doubt she will keep them that color by this time, as blue as the sky and sea together."

Rosalynde held the baby close, filling her ears with soft baby talk, and Alyssa answered her with a flood of expressive, indecipherable prattle.

"You were just so at that age, sweetheart," Westered said, hugging his daughter and granddaughter both at once.

"And is still," Philip added. Suddenly serious, he glanced toward the castle again. "I had thought my brother would be here to meet us. Jerome told us what happened to Lady Elizabeth. I fear almost to ask it, but is she—"

"How could she be but well?" Tom asked as he came from the castle, padding swiftly down the steps holding a blanket-wrapped bundle. "In so fine and wondrous a world, how but well?"

He laid the bundle in his brother's arms, watching his reaction as he uncovered the baby's delicate face.

"A wondrous world," Philip agreed, relieved to know that no tragedy would mar this sweet homecoming, "and, by the grace of God, a fair wondrous child."

"It's only just another girl," Robin grumbled.

Tom laughed and ruffled his hair. "Never be unthankful for

God's gifts, Robin. They are always the most perfectly suited to every need. Besides," he added with a wink, "in time you will find there is no such thing as 'only just another girl.'"

Robin made a face, and Rosalynde gave Alyssa to Westered and took Tom's child. "Oh, my lord, what a precious thing she is. Our Alyssa seems hardly a baby anymore compared to her. I know your lady is pleased."

"More than you know, Lady Rosalynde," Tom replied. "It means more than just a child to her. It is a new beginning and an assurance that all the old is wiped away."

Rosalynde smiled. "I must go see her. Father, will you bring the children?"

"So I trust we shall have trade with Reghed after all," Tom said as he and Philip followed the others back into the castle.

"I told Alaric I would sign the agreements with him come spring. It was the strangest thing coming home just now—Reghed feels so different from before, as if a great cloud had been dispelled."

"Truly, it has."

"He will make them a good king, Tom, now that he's found true strength and hope rather than fear. I mean to give him my hand of help until he feels able to stand on his own." He felt something rubbing against his ankles and looked down to see that even the cat had come to welcome him. He picked her up and scratched under her chin, and she cuddled purring against him. "Reghed will be a strong ally to Lynaleigh one day."

"I expect Credotti's troupe shall have more work than they can tend to now," Tom said with a grin. "Celebrations are bound to be in much demand throughout the kingdom."

"I did not tell you, did I? They're to stay in Stonekeep now, part of the royal court. I told Alaric it shall be written into our agreement that he shall send them along with his ambassadors when they come in the spring. They are just some of the considerable few I am indebted to for our safe returning, and I mean to see them paid."

"I trust Jerome shall be one of those you speak of. Now that he's come back, I mean to give him some reward of my own for what he did for my lady and our child."

"Let me see to it, Tom. I think you'll not be disappointed."

A week later Philip followed his wife up the stairs to their chamber, feeling the comfortable weariness that came after another long, satisfying day. Tomorrow would bring another new year, another day for hearing the petitions of the people and granting those he was able. It seemed very far away, that New Year's Day when Sarto had come to court and turned his world upside down, when his faith had been tried and strengthened, when he had learned that there was truly nothing that could separate him from the love of Christ or pull him from His hands.

This Christmas had been only a time of thanksgiving for the gift of God's Son and for the continual salvation He brought. There had been little opportunity to prepare anything else in the few days since their homecoming, but he did not want to miss the season entirely.

"What would you have for Christmas, my queen," he asked, stopping her a step or two above him, his hands on her waist.

"Christmas is past, my lord," she said with her lilting laugh.

"I am the king," he replied, "and will you dictate times and seasons to me? Tell me what you would have."

She turned to him, smiling. "From you, my lord?"

"From me."

"Anything?"

He pulled her down to him. "Anything at all."

For a moment she simply looked at him, and he was unable to resist kissing her.

"Tell me," he murmured, nuzzling her neck.

She held him to her. "Nothing but that you love me."

"You have that already, always. What would you have now?"

"Anything?" she asked again. "Even if it is something you've denied me before?"

"What? Is there anything you could ask that I would deny you?"

"Give Paxton back to Lady Marian."

"I did deny you that, true, but I thought you understood why, love. Jerome would never be bold enough to ask her for her hand if she were mistress of such holdings, and after he has saved our child along with Tom's and Lady Elizabeth as well, I feel I owe him better than that."

"Might it rather not give him cause to ask her, knowing now she need not live her whole life beneath her birth because he cannot provide such things for her?"

He considered for a long moment. "I will see to it, love."

She smiled and twined her arms around his neck. "Grant me one last thing tonight."

Reading the wish in her eyes, he swung her into his arms and carried her up the stairs.

❧

The next morning after they had had their breakfast together in bed, Philip had escorted Rosalynde to her chamber so her ladies could prepare her for the grand audience that day. An hour later he returned for her.

"Dismiss your ladies, madam. I would speak to you alone."

"Of course, my lord, but they've not finished putting on my jewels. It will take but a moment more."

"Julia," he ordered, "if you and the others would be so kind as to leave us."

"At once, my lord."

The girl made a giggling curtsey and led the rest of the women out of the room.

"My lord is peremptory this morning," Rosalynde observed when he went to her open jewel box and began rummaging through it.

"Wear these," he said, handing her a pair of sapphire and diamond earrings. She slipped them on, almost as puzzled as she was amused by his sudden interest in her jewelry. The earrings were followed by a matching bracelet and a pair of rings, all worked so daintily that despite their richness they did not overpower the fair flesh that carried them.

"Anything else, my lord?" she asked.

"Close your eyes."

She laughed. "My lord?"

"Close your eyes."

She obeyed, and he scooped her hair up and put her hand on top of her head to hold it.

"Now wait," he told her. She felt something heavy at her throat. Her eyes flew open, and she was breathless at the magnificence of what she saw. He had given her a delicate collar of gold and sapphire laced with diamonds, a perfect compliment to the deep sapphire of her ermine-trimmed gown. The morning sunlight danced over the thousands of brilliant facets in the necklace, and the multiplied reflection lit the mirror just as pleasure lit her face.

"Oh, Philip," she sighed.

His image smiled at her, almost shyly, from the looking glass. "It seems you have a particular fondness for sapphires, my lady."

She turned and threw her arms around him. "It is exquisite."

"It was created for you, you know," he said. "I told the goldsmiths to make something that would equal you in beauty, but I see now that they could not help but fall short."

His voice took on that particular soft sweetness she found so hard to resist, and she was drawn inescapably by the look in his eyes, his undeniable sapphire eyes. She clasped him closer, and he kissed her in that slow, intense way he knew she loved.

She was warm and breathless when he pulled back from her. "They will be waiting for us, Rose," he murmured. "One kiss more— then we must go down."

He took his one kiss, then compulsively three more. Then they gathered their children and went into the great hall.

"My lords, ladies and gentlemen, our liege lord, King Philip, fifth of that name, and our sovereign lady, her beloved majesty, Queen Rosalynde," the herald announced.

Rosalynde smiled at her husband as he led her to her seat, knowing he must have requested that tender little addition to her title.

She noticed, too, the look Tom and Elizabeth exchanged at hearing that word *beloved* and knew the special meaning it held for them as they stood there with their baby.

"As is his custom," the herald continued, "and in keeping with the grand tradition of our kingdom, his majesty is now pleased to give ear to the petitions of his people."

"Before we begin," Philip announced, "I should like very much here before you all to express my thanks to my dear father-in-law, Lord James of Westered, for his help and hospitality."

"It has been my great pleasure, son," Westered replied, and he cuddled Alyssa closer in his arms. "I could have asked no better gift than this time we've had all together, even as difficult as it has been."

Rosalynde gave her father and daughter a loving glance.

Then Tom cleared his throat. "Your indulgence, my liege," he said, bowing formally as Elizabeth made curtsey beside him, "but I would like to be the first on this first day of this new year to ask a boon of your majesty."

Philip bowed in return. "My lord of Brenden."

With an eager smile, Tom took the baby from his wife and held her up for the court to see. "May I present to your majesties and to all here the newest and most incontestable proof of a gracious God, our daughter, Lady Philippa Elise Chastelayne of Brenden. Philippa for her royal uncle, of course," he said, grinning at the mingled surprise, pride, and pleasure on his brother's face. "And Elise is from Elizabeth, which is to say 'consecrated to God.'"

His expression turning tender, he touched his lips to Elizabeth's cheek and then looked down at his daughter once more. "It seems rather an overwhelming name for such a tiny thing, I know, but we call her merely Elise when we are not at a formal audience with the king."

The people smiled and applauded, but the newest addition to the royal family merely slept through it all, safe in her father's arms.

"And is there nothing more I might grant my chief courtier and most trusted counselor, my lord?" Philip asked.

Tom smiled again. "No, my liege, unless it be that you arrange for this year to be a trifle more peaceful than the last."

"I say amen to that," Philip said, smiling, too, "and the next forty along with it."

With that Philip turned his attention to the petitioners awaiting him. Standing uncertainly at the first of the line was Lady Marian. She looked as if she might swoon when she realized it was time for her to move forward, and only Rosalynde's silent encouragement kept her from running away.

"Your majesty." Marian curtseyed deeply, her pale face turning even paler at Philip's suddenly aloof expression. "Your majesty—My lord—" She glanced at Jerome and then helplessly at Rosalynde. "My lady, I cannot—"

"Ask," Rosalynde urged with a touch of a confident smile. "Go on."

Drawing a little courage from her, Marian curtseyed again. "My lord king, all the court well knows the kindnesses you've granted me despite my father's treason. Because I know them, too, I have not wanted to presume upon them."

Faltering, she glanced again at Rosalynde and then at Philip.

His eyes narrowed slightly. "Well?"

"My lord—" Marian's voice trembled. "My lord, out of your bounty, I ask that you grant my father's lands back to me."

Philip nodded his head. "I have long expected you would ask such a thing, Lady Marian, and I know there are many here who would think it just, too." He looked at Rosalynde and then back at the girl who stood pale before him. "In good conscience though, my lady, I must deny you."

"Philip!" Rosalynde cried over the murmuring of the court.

Marian dropped her head. "Forgive me, your majesty," she said, her eyes brimming with mortified tears. "I should not have presumed—"

"Oh, my lord, surely—" Rosalynde began, but he motioned her to be silent.

"No, my lady. I have determined to make a gift of those lands to someone whose steadfastness has earned them a thousand times over and whose loyalty has been tested again and again and has come up true every time."

She suppressed a smile at the little glint in his eye that anyone else would have missed.

"Now there are other matters I must attend," he said, getting up. "Jerome, stand forward here."

Jerome moved to Marian's side before the throne and made a half-grudging bow. "Pardon my boldness, my lord, but the Lady Marian has always been loyal to you. Whatever her father might have done, she has never wronged you. Those lands are hers by right, and I would be less than a man did I not speak out on her behalf, even before my king."

"Are you loyal to me, Jerome?" Philip asked with a cool lift of one eyebrow.

"Need your majesty ask?" Jerome held his head proudly, his gray eyes flashing. "At the risk of bragging, I think your majesty has not found me slack in defense of either your person or of what you hold dear."

"Even so. Then as I said, should I not reward such loyalty?" Much to Jerome's amazement, Philip smiled. "Do you not think the lands and holdings of Paxton reward enough?"

"Paxton?" Jerome's face was suddenly as pale as Marian's. "My lord, you mean to give Paxton to me?"

"Are you not long past due a recompense equal to your service? Kneel down, Jerome."

"My lord?"

"Now, boy."

Philip motioned to one of the pages, who was quick to bring him his new broadsword.

"Jerome of Hartslynne, I hereby create you Baron of Paxton and bestow upon you and your heirs into perpetuity all the rights and duties concerning such title." He touched the blade to the boy's right shoulder and then to his left. "Rise Jerome, Baron of Paxton."

"My—My lord, I cannot. By right, Lady Marian—"

"Stand up, Jerome," Philip said. "Paxton is yours. If you wish Lady Marian to have it, that now rests with you."

"My lord, you know only a king can make such a grant. My lady knows—" Jerome turned very, very red. "Lady Marian knows I would deny her nothing in my power to give, but—"

Still kneeling, he glanced at Marian, but she was looking up at the king, her eyes shining with a sudden gladness Jerome did not comprehend.

Philip grinned at his puzzlement. "Could you not share Paxton with her?"

"Share, my lord?"

Philip laughed. "Come, Jerome, you are not usually wont to be so backward. Must I command you to marry the girl, too?"

"Marry—" Jerome managed somehow to turn even redder, but then he looked up into Marian's sweet face. "My lady—Lady Marian, I, uh . . ."

"Well, love," Philip told Rosalynde just loud enough for all the court to hear, "you cannot say I've not done my part. Perhaps he's reconsidered . . ."

Again Jerome's gray eyes flashed. Then with a sheepish grin, he took Marian's hand. "I would be most honored, Lady Marian, if you would become my wife."

Her eyes were filled with tears, but there was only joy in them. "Yes . . . my Lord of Paxton."

She made a deep, sweeping curtsey, and he stood up and took her into his arms.

Philip felt a soft hand take his and turned to see Rosalynde looking at him with the same eyes of love Marian had for Jerome.

"Have I pleased you now, my lady?" he asked softly.

She nodded. "And I would ask but one thing more of my lord."

"Yes?"

She stood, and two of her ladies-in-waiting brought out a large roll of fabric—the tapestry they had been working for so long.

"As you well know, my lord, my ladies and I have labored a great while on this, and I meant it merely for a testament to what I have long believed. But in just the last few months, we have all of us been delivered by divine grace from certain death, and I should like to hang this on the wall behind our thrones in Winton, if it please my lord, as an unceasing reminder of what we have been shown so clearly."

The two women unrolled the tapestry on the great hall's wide marble floor, and soft murmurs of wonder rose from the onlookers at the splendor of it. Philip stared in amazement and then pressed Rosalynde's hand fervently to his lips.

"It pleases me, and it shall be just as you have asked—true testament indeed."

There in perfect detail, bordered with the sovereign saint's rose, was all the royal family: Tom with Elizabeth next to him, a baby in her arms; Philip's own children, Rosalynde, and Philip himself, even to the fine scar on his cheek. And all around them, everywhere he looked, there were angels.

The author may be contacted at
missswrite@aol.com